D0435892

ROGUE WARRIOR

TASK FORCE BL

ROGUE WARRIOR

TASK FORCE BLUE

Richard Marcinko
and
John Weisman

POCKET BOOKS
New York London Toronto Sydney Tokyo Singapore

This book is a work of fiction. Names, characters, places, and incidents are products of the authors' imaginations, or are used fictitiously. Operational details have been altered so as not to betray current SpecWar techniques.

Many of the Rogue Warrior's weapons courtesy of Heckler & Koch, Inc., International Training Division, Sterling, Virginia

POCKET BOOKS, a division of Simon & Schuster Inc.
1230 Avenue of the Americas, New York, NY 10020

ISBN 0-671-79958-4

Printed in the U.S.A.

Once again, to the shooters—
fewer and fewer in number . . .
and to
Admiral James "Ace" Lyons, U.S. Navy (Ret.)
A Warrior's Warrior

—Richard Marcinko
—John Weisman

The Rogue Warrior series by Richard Marcinko and John Weisman

Rogue Warrior
Rogue Warrior: Red Cell
Rogue Warrior: Green Team
Rogue Warrior: Task Force Blue

Also by John Weisman

Fiction

Blood Cries
Watchdogs
Evidence

Nonfiction

Shadow Warrior (with Felix Rodriguez)

Politics are a lousy way to get things done.

—P. J. O'Rourke

THE ROGUE WARRIOR'S TEN COMMANDMENTS OF SPECWAR

- I am the War Lord and the wrathful God of Combat and I will always lead you from the front, not the rear.

- I will treat you all alike—just like shit.

- Thou shalt do nothing I will not do first, and thus will you be created Warriors in My deadly image.

- I shall punish thy bodies because the more thou sweatest in training, the less thou bleedest in combat.

- Indeed, if thou hurteth in thy efforts and thou suffer painful dings, then thou art Doing It Right.

- Thou hast not to like it—thou hast just to do it.

- Thou shalt Keep It Simple, Stupid.

- Thou shalt never assume.

- Verily, thou art not paid for thy methods, but for thy results, by which meaneth thou shalt kill thine enemy by any means available before he killeth you.

- Thou shalt, in thy Warrior's Mind and Soul, always remember My ultimate and final Commandment: There Are No Rules—Thou Shalt Win at All Cost.

Contents

Part One

BOHICA

Chapter 1

IT HAS BEEN SAID THAT GETTING THERE IS HALF THE FUN. IF SO, IT MUST have been time to Get There already, because I was in *real* bad need of some fun. To help things along, I finished my quarter-mile, early-morning slog and emerged from the slimy-bottomed salt pond into the cool March Florida rain, looking, feeling, and (more significantly) smelling very much like your unfriendly Creature from the Black Lagoon.

I drained sour, brackish water from my ballistic goggles. I shook sediment from the HK USP .45-caliber pistol strapped to my right thigh in a nylon tactical holster. I squeezed as much moisture as I could from my French braid, retied the black cotton "Do" rag around my hair, slipped the rubber radio earpiece into my ear, and wrestled with the wire lip mike that ran from the earpiece around my face under my mustache (it wanted to take up residence inside my right nostril, not above my lip where it belonged). I pulled a soggy, fleece-lined Nomex balaclava over my head, and then adjusted the forty pounds of Class IIIA Plus Point Blank load-bearing body armor that had slowed me like a sea anchor while fording the pond, making me feel as if I'd been up to my seventeen-and-a-half-inch neck in deep you-know-what.

The armor itself comes in at less than ten pounds—even when

it's wet. The real weight was from the dozen or so modular, custom-made pouches filled with everything from my ever-present Emerson CQC6 titanium-framed combat folding knife, my waterproof tactical radio, miniature 100-lumen Sure Fire flashlight, and four DEF-TEC No. 25 flashbang distraction devices, to the two dozen Flexi-cuffs, the half-dozen door wedges, the roll of surgical tape, the fifty feet of climbing rope, the eight magazines filled with eighty rounds of MagSafe Plus-P frangible SWAT loads, the Mad Dog DSU-2 serrated-blade knife in its molded Kydex sheath, the lightweight surgical steel pry bar, the twenty feet of shaped ribbon charge and three electronic detonators, the—well, you get the idea. I was loaded like a fucking pack-SEAL.

Anyway, I got the goddamn thing shifted around to where it should have been, reattached the Velcro flap as quietly as was possible (old-fashioned canvas web gear with all those buckles and laces does have a certain tactical advantage—in a word: silence), then began to crab forward, moving slowly, steadily, across the wet tarmac a few inches at a time, thinking all the while what an incredible batch of fucking fun I was having Getting There.

There was 150 yards away, at the very end of the taxiway where, almost invisible through the sheets of wind-whipped, driving rain that stung my face, a 727 containing eighty-three passengers and crew of seven that had been hijacked out of San Juan and landed here in Key West sat, an immobile shadow in the darkness. Its tires had been shot out by a Key West Police sniper, after the pilot had been ordered to take off for parts unknown and actually taxied the aircraft this far before anybody reacted. About an hour ago, the aft stairway had been lowered, and a lone terrorist armed with what we'd determined through our eighty-power night-vision spotting scopes from our position 1,500 yards away was a new model Colt 633HB 9mm submachine gun, was standing wet and miserable sentry duty under the tail.

It was my nasty assignment (shades of *Mission Impossible*) to sneak up without being seen or heard, wrest control of the aircraft from the bad guys, rescue the passengers, pat the stews—excuse me, the flight attendants—on their lovely, firm behinds, then climb back on my stallion, the fearless white charger Cockbreath, and ride out of town while everybody'd look at one another and inquire, "Who the hell was that nasty-looking Slovak masked man with the ponytail and the bunch of renegade sidekicks, anyway?"

Yeah, I know, I know—you're asking what the F-word is Demo

Dickie Marcinko, Shark Man of the Delta, the old Rogue Warrior, radio handle Silver Bullet, doing here, up to his bad ass in slime and tangos (which is radio talk for terrorists for those of you who haven't read our last three books), when he could be back at Rogue Manor, enjoying his two-hundred-plus acres, sitting in the outside Jacuzzi with a yard-wide smile and a yard-long hard-on, holding a huge tumbler of Dr. Bombay's best Sapphire on the rocks, bookended by a couple of big-bazoomed hostesses from Hooters doing the bare-bottomed, wet-T-shirt thing in my ozone-filtered, 100-degree water.

Well, friends, the simple answer is that one of those eighty-three passengers on, well, let's call it Pan World Airways Flight 1252, originating in Bogotá, Colombia, and continuing through San Juan, Puerto Rico, Atlanta, Georgia, Charlotte, North Carolina, and terminating in Washington, D.C., was the Honorable S. Lynn Crawford, a thirty-five-year-old registered Democrat and professional fund-raiser, and—as of twelve weeks ago—our most recently appointed secretary of the navy.

Among the other hostages was a pair (actually, currently he was operating solo, but more about that later) of what the descriptive memo writers might call highly qualified, well-trained Naval Investigative Service security agent personnel. In other words, a pair of pus-nutted shit-for-brained pencil-dicked no-load NIS assholes who go to the range twice a year, spend all their time writing memos, and tend to panic at the first sign of crisis.

Why had the Hon. S. Lynn gone to Bogotá in the first place? Who knew. More accurately, who cared. Such policy decisions are determined way beyond my pay grade—which is 0-6, or captain. The only fact that mattered to me was that SECNAV was now at the mercy of somewhere between six and who-knew-how-many nasties, armed to the teeth with bad-boy weapons and functional explosive devices, and that as the OIC—that's officer in charge—of the U.S. Naval Special Warfare Development Group subsidiary known as Unconventional Taskings/Risks, United States, acronymed UT/RUS (and pronounced, with obvious SEAL political correctness, as *uterus*), it was my unenviable job to extract her exalted, sub-cabinet-level butt out of there—preferably in one piece.

It might also occur to you to ask what the hell the SECNAV was doing flying tourist class on a cut-rate airline, when the Navy has all those perfectly good (not to mention reasonably secure) aircraft at its disposal. The answer—I guess I have time right now to explain, even though you've probably surmised the answer already because it's so obvious—is politics.

See, back some months in this particular administration, some of the more self-important, unelected White House and Pentagon panjandrums took it upon themselves to requisition military aircraft for occasional golf outings, speechifying jaunts to such hardship posts as Florida, Europe, and Hawaii, pussy-chasing boondoggles to Barbados, and other sundry nonofficial voyages. First, the notorious journalist & junk-yard dog, Samuel Andrew Donaldson of ABC News, blew the whistle on his *Prime Time Live* show—a tough, sardonic piece he called "Four-Star Airlines." Within twenty-four hours, the rest of the national press, the tabloid TV shows, and the weekly news magazines followed along, gang-banging the subject with weeks of derogatory, disparaging, carping, supercritical coverage. For its part, the White House responded by doing what it does best: it overreacted.

And so, a polysyllabic dictum was depth-charged from on high. It caromed around the West Wing, through the Old Executive Office Building, and finally detonated right in the middle of the Pentagon, creating the kind of ego devastation not seen in Washington since Jimmy Carter was president.

When the decree had finally been ground down into the sort of one-and-two-syllable gist I understand, I took note. Let me give you said gist in translation: "No More Fucking Riding on Fucking MILCRAFT that's MILitary airCRAFT in Pentagonspeak, unless, that is, the fucking travel orders have been fucking signed by the fucking supreme commander in fucking chief and leader of the Free fucking World himself."

This new and immutable guideline has left the service secretaries, their deputies, their deputies' deputies, their military assistants, and other assorted bureaucrats—not to mention scores of two-, three-, and four-starred brass—to the untender mercies of commercial air travel. There are no more choppers idling on the Pentagon landing pad for the seven-minute flight to Andrews Air Force Base, where they land one-hundred yards from an Air Farce JetStar or Navy C-9 for a quick, efficient, nonstop flight to said panjandrum's destination. Nope. That kind of efficiency is gone forever.

Today, everyone from the chief of naval operations to the head of military intelligence hails a Farsi-speaking cabby driving a farce of a cab at the Pentagon's Mall entrance, or descends into the crowded Washington Metro to ride the three stops to National along with the panhandlers and buskers. That trip is followed by interminable waiting and the high probability of a canceled flight.

Now, I'm not a big believer in perks, especially for political appointees. But if you were to ask me, rank—certainly someone who has been appointed SECNAV—should have a bit of privilege every now and then. Especially when security is concerned—and flights into and out of Colombia, where Coke Is It, certainly seem to fit that category.

But then, nobody ever asks my opinion. I'd never even seen a picture of the goddamn SECNAV before they handed me a faxed publicity photo five, maybe six hours ago, and I wouldn't know a panjandrum if I bumped into one. The only time my phone rings and my cage door gets opened is when clusterfucks like this happen, and they need someone to quickee-quickee makee-makee all better.

Which is why I was currently dressed in my workaday party-time outfit of basic black sans pearls: the always popular ensemble of Nomex balaclava, rip-stop BDUs, and body armor, not to mention the ever-fashionable high-top, currently squishy, black Reebok aerobic shoes. It also is why I was in my normal condition: cold, wet, uncomfortable, and dinging various extremities on rough macadam.

I stopped to listen for anything untoward. Nothing. I resumed my crawl. So far, the mission was going perfectly. Of course, we'd been at it for less than a minute since we'd emerged from the salt pond.

The rain drummed steadily, whipped into stinging ball bearings by the twenty-mile-per-hour winds. That was good news and bad news. The good news: it meant that the fifty or so TV cameras atop their microwave trucks just outside the airport perimeter fence would have a hard time catching any of this early-morning action. The rain also would help stifle any ambient sound we made as we approached the plane.

The bad news was that it would make our assault highly goatfuck prone because everything we carried, touched, or assaulted was going to be as wet and slippery as a horny eighteen-year-old cheerleader's pussy on homecoming weekend. From the wings we'd have to traverse, to the ladders we'd be climbing, to the emergency handles we'd have to ease open without alerting the tangos inside, this was one big clusterfuck waiting to happen.

Two yards behind me, Machinist Mate First Class Stevie Wonder's lean, mean body inched forward as armed and dangerous he wormed his way across the black taxiway. Ever the fashionable dirtbag, he was dressed to kill. Literally. I turned to make sure he was keeping up. When he threw me a one-fingered salute I knew everything was okeydoke. Hot on Wonder's tail (and joined by the ladder they carried between them), Doc Tremblay, master chief hospitalman and sniper, slithered steadily in the darkness, his long handlebar mustache moving like antennae as he crawled on padded knees and elbows, a suppressed HK slung over his back.

Behind Doc and Wonder, seven more shooters completed my lethal contingent. Senior Chief Nasty Nicky Grundle was rear security, protecting our six with his omnipresent Heckler & Koch MP5-PDW suppressed submachine gun. In front of him crawled Duck Foot Dewey, Cherry Enders, Half Pint Harris, Piccolo Mead, Gator Shepard, and the Rodent. Each pair of my UT/RUS swim buddies was responsible for carrying one of our four padded assault ladders.

I would have liked another seven men for the assault, but like the thin gent sings, ya cain't always git whatcha wont, and I didn't have another seven men. So we'd simply do the job with the shooters on scene. We'd had enough time to rehearse on a 727—albeit a 727-200, not the older 727-100 sitting out here in the rain—that was stowed inside a hangar we'd commandeered as our HQ. That way we'd been able to refresh our beer-sodden, pussy-whipped memories about how to open the exit windows and doors, ease onto the wings without shaking the fuselage, and get inside the cabin without tripping over all the assorted ratshits, batshits, catshits, widgets, midgets, and other miscellaneous paraphernalia that's normally stuffed, tied, gorged, screwed, crammed, bolted, wedged, and taped inside airplane cabins.

The one question that nagged me most since I'd arrived was precisely how many tangos we'd encounter. There had been no intelligence about that most crucial element of hostage rescue since the plane had landed on Key West International's single runway just over fifteen hours ago.

Okay, then, what *did* I know? Well, I knew very little more than what the rest of the world knew: PWA 1252 had left Bogotá at 0710, arrived in San Juan two and a half hours later, departed for Atlanta at 1100 hours, and was hijacked nineteen minutes later, just north of the Dominican Republic.

I'd listened to a tape of the pilot's initial transmission. It had been brief and to the point: "San Juan center, this is PWA 1252 November. We have half a dozen or so fellas here who want me to divert to Key West. Since they've got guns and bombs, we're gonna do exactly what they want us to do."

Since PWA 1252 had touched down here, there had been only half a dozen conversations with the plane. None had lasted longer than a minute. Each had been initiated by the pilot. None contained any further information—even oblique references—about the number of hostage takers, or their weapons. And those pieces of intel are absolutely critical for a successful aircraft takedown, believe me.

Let me digress here just long enough—I am cold and wet, after all, and in the middle of work—to give you a short course in aircraft hostage rescue philosophy and tactics, and a primer on the physical characteristics of the Boeing 727-100 aircraft, so you'll understand what I was up against.

The philosophy and tactics are simple enough: the key to success in any aircraft hostage rescue is surprise. Surprise. Remember that word—you will see the material again. The entry team must be totally dynamic—that is, they have to swarm the aircraft in less than six seconds, or they will probably lose hostages. If they fail to hit at the same instant, or they take too much time, or if Mr. Murphy of Murphy's Law fame is along for the ride, innocent people will die. It's as simple as that.

So what's so hard, you ask? Go storm the fucking plane.

Well, friends, it's like this. Take our current situation. (*Pul-eeze* take it. It's yours for the asking.) We were ten men out on the wet macadam. The 727-100 aircraft has nine possible entry points. You do the arithmetic.

Ideally, it takes seventeen shooters to storm a 727. (If the plane's a wide-fuselage model like a 767, an A340 Airbus, or a big old 747, you might need upwards of two dozen in the initial assault team, with another two dozen in the second wave to control passengers, sort the good guys from the bad guys, and generally make sense of the situation.)

Now, to be honest, there were other shooters available tonight. While the FBI's Quantico-based, national HRT—the Hostage Rescue Team—was stretched past the limit (it was dealing with a prison riot going full blast at Leavenworth, a white supremacist and six hostages barricaded behind barbed wire in Oregon, and a disgruntled commuter who with the help of a hand grenade had commandeered a puddle jumper somewhere in California), the Bureau had, nonetheless, managed to scramble a twelve-agent SWAT team out of Miami. It had arrived here three hours after me and mine, and set up its own perimeter. But that was all it had done so far.

Why? Slight problem: three weeks ago, the attorney general's office put out a Department of Justice Executive Directive. It said that forthwith and immediately, all local FBI offices and the units attached thereto, "Shall make every possible effort to reflect the cultural, ethnic, sociological, and gender diversity common to the location of the office."

You people think we're making this stuff up, don't you? Well guess what, folks—this crapola is real. I've even seen a copy of the goddamn thing, because it was faxed to my office anonymously by somebody at the Hard Glock Cafe—that's shooter slang for the FBI's Quantico HRT headquarters—who wanted to make me spit my coffee through a nostril.

Anyway, the twelve-person SWAT unit that showed up included seven females (one of whom had bigger pecs than Nasty, and he presses four-hundred pounds), six Hispanics, three African-Americans, two conspicuous representatives of what might be called in Bureauspeak, single-sex relationships, one Asian, one Native American, and one lonely, white WASP male. They sure were diverse. The only problem was that they hadn't ever trained together. They'd probably all been too busy going to EEO—that's Equal Employment Opportunity—classes to bother with unimportant details like learning how to shoot, loot, and function as a team. Well, I have my own form of EEO, too—I treat everybody alike: just like shit.

But enough about me. Let me tell you about them. *They* were led by the Special Agent in Charge of the Miami FBI field office, a red-haired, five-foot-two, eyes of black pedigreed bitch Latina—Cuban, to be precise—named Esmeralda Lopez-Reyes. I immediately dubbed her La Muchacha. Incredibly, she'd appeared on scene as if she'd come straight from a dinner party, clad in a dress that probably cost more than a chief makes in a month, shoes that were equally expensive, and a Chanel clutch purse. Where she stowed her regulation, FBI-issue firearm I hadn't the foggiest. Actually, I had an inkling—and: (1) she must have been real uncomfortable, and: (2) her quick draw must be a sight truly to behold.

Her attitude—if you could call it that—was infuriating. Obviously, she hadn't been told that my team and I were coming—and when she arrived to find us already in place, she treated us like *campesinos*.

To make matters more interesting, about an hour after we'd arrived, five deputies from the Marathon Key Po-lice arrived. *They* were led by a potbellied, Pancho Villa–mustached, snaggle-toothed, paint-by-the-numbers, order-barking sergeant named Bob. *They* were all decked out in matching starched camouflage fatigues, hobnail-soled Cochran jump boots squeaky fresh from the mail order catalog, and they carried enough brand-new automatic weaponry to wage a six-month guerrilla war. *They* traveled in a big white Ford step van with MARATHON KEY SWAT TEAM magnet-signed in foot-high letters on the side. Sergeant Bob tapped the sy-reen twice, climbed out (leaving the lights flashing), twirled his mustache, chawed, spat into a handy Styrofoam cup, and volunteered to lead us all to victory.

Thanks but no thanks, fellas. See, the problem, folks, is this: dynamic entry—read surprise—demands not only good intelligence, but also great teamwork. Your shooters must not only have some idea where the bad guys are (that way they won't shoot the passengers), they must also function as one. Timing is everything. Indeed, so far as I'm concerned, the absolute essence of hostage rescue—the core, the basis, the nucleus of every other element—is unit integrity.

And what is that? To me, it has always translated as a bunch of assholes who care enough about each other to eat, sleep, work, and party—all of it together, as a group. A bunch of men who know how each of the others thinks; a unit that can read one another's minds; men who react to one another without having to stop and think about it.

Bottom line? You simply cannot assemble a patchwork quilt of shooters, no matter how talented they may be individually, and expect them to function as a team without having worked together. They won't function as a team—and hostages will get killed.

I expressed this point of view in my usual shall we say blunt style. Marathon Bob chewed on his mustache, spat tobacco juice into his empty coffee cup—and finally, grudgingly, agreed with me. But, if it was okay, he added, he'd sure like to stick around and help out. That was all right with me. I had a gut feeling that ol' Bob and his boys would turn out to be just fine under pressure. And besides, they, at least, had trained together as a unit, which was more than could be said for the FBI's personnel.

But similar persuasion didn't work with La Muchacha. She had twelve shooters to my ten, which, she insisted, gave her tactical superiority. The airport—a civilian site, she stated somewhat pedantically—came under her, not my, jurisdiction. Thus, it would be her team, not mine, on the line.

Okay—if the only way to sort this chain-of-command crap out was to give her people a chance, then I was willing to give her people a chance. After all, what was at stake here was the lives of the hostages—and if that didn't bother La Muchacha, who was I to worry? We all repaired to a nearby hangar where I'd had a 727 towed so that we could practice our assault sequence. I handed La Muchacha my stopwatch, let her borrow my assault ladders, then stood back and let her people demonstrate how well they could do.

It took them four minutes and forty-five seconds to get inside the damn plane—and they didn't open all the hatches. That, friends, is just over four minutes too long. You know as well as I do that by the time they got inside, the hostages would all be DOA.

Well, she said, that was the first time—so it doesn't count. Let us try again.

Oh, I'd heard that song before—and the music was just as unacceptable now as then. Back when I was CO of SEAL Team Six, I'd run a joint training exercise with the 1st Special Forces Operational Detachment—Delta, otherwise known as Delta Force. Delta's CO back then was an asshole spit-and-polish colonel named Elwood Dawkins—known as Dawg to the troops. Well, Dawg's mutts charlie-foxtrotted up their portion of the exercise, and he demanded that we do it all over again, too.

I told the SAC what I'd told Dawg. "No fucking way. You get one shot at a hostage rescue—and if you screw up, it's all over."

Then it was our turn. I put my boys on the line. We took twenty-six seconds from the "go" signal to get our ladders in place, and break into the plane. Marathon Bob spat chaw juice into his cup and gave me a big, snaggle-toothed grin. "Sweet Jesus," he said, "it was like watching poetry in damn motion. Can we come north and go to school with you boys?"

La Muchacha was not as impressed as Bob. In fact, when I asked her to join him as the backup force, she refused. FBI agents, she said, did not play support roles. Then she threw a handful of bureaucratic chaff in my direction. The Federal Aviation Administration, she announced, had not a week ago issued a new batch of hard and specific rules of engagement that had to be followed to the letter when storming an aircraft at a domestic location, and until I had read those ROEs and signed a copy, she insisted that it would be impossible for me to take any action.

Now I knew that she was either shitting me, or ignorant of the

Dangerous Fucking Location—and usually, I put my cannon-fodder troops there—by that I mean the newest and most inexperienced men. Not that I like losing anybody—I don't. But I'd rather lose a greenhorn than someone who's had a decade's worth of training. Tonight, the point was moot: I didn't have any cannon fodder available anyway.

Next, there are two overwing windows that can be sprung from the outside. They are adjacent to seats 11F and 14F. Goatfuck potential? Medium to high.

On the positive side, we'd had a lot of practice sneaking onto aircraft wings—it was something we did as part of our normal hostage-rescue training regimen. Duck Foot Dewey, Cherry Enders, Rodent, and Gator Shepard were as stealthy as ninjas. They could move from their ladders onto the wing, creep up and release the windows without the slightest bit of noise or vibration, even when the wings were as wet as they'd be tonight.

On the negative side, the overwing windows are small, and all that equipment you're carrying—submachine guns, bulletproof vests, flashbang devices and other sundries—tends to get hung up as you move through 'em. Well, getting hung up wastes time. And time, as I've said above, is absofuckinglutely crucial to success. The solution is for my over-the-wing guys to carry less equipment. That, however, means they can become vulnerable.

Moving astern, we come to the aft stairs. These are hydraulically controlled, and can be lowered from either inside or outside the plane. The goatfuck factor is medium to high.

To accentuate the positive, the stairs stabilize the plane. So if they are lowered, it becomes harder for tangos to sense the assault force climbing onto the wings, placing ladders against the fuselage, and so on. The stairway is also wide enough so that your equipment doesn't get hung up. On the negative side, you can get only one man at a time up the stairs, and each has to go through a doorway at the top—a door that can easily be secured from the inside, which leaves you standing at the top of the stairs primed, pumped, and ready to go, holding your limp *lagarto* in your hand.

Tonight, the problem was compounded because the tangos had posted a sentry on the ground. If he saw us before we got close enough to eliminate him, we'd be screwed. Under normal circumstances (in other words, during our full-mission-profile rehearsals for situations like this one), I'd have positioned a sniper to take him out. But this was Key West—single runway, single tower, no tall buildings, and the plane was positioned so that it was five-

facts. See, friends, the FAA's authority in hijack situati
when the plane's door opens. Once that happens, all respo
shifts to the ground force commander. And in this case, I
ered myself the GFC.

La Muchacha, however, held the opposite opinion. She i
that she, not I, was in charge. Moreover, she added, it w
understanding that, since I commanded a military unit an
no sworn police powers, I could not legally act until I re
direct authority from the National Command Authority—
translates as either the president, or the secretary of de
Period. Full stop. End of story.

Friends, I'm not an unreasonable man. So we agreed to disa
until everyone checked with his/her/its superiors in Washingt

I punched the secretary of defense's command center num
into my secure Motorola cellular. Would you believe I got a b
signal? What the hell were they doing, ordering pizza?

And now, having brought you more or less up to speed, let
return to the model 727-100 aircraft and its nine entrances. We
begin at the starboard bow (I know the 727's a plane and I'm usin
nautical terminology here, but geez, folks, I'm a sailor). Okay, th
copilot's window can be released by pulling on a gizmo that sits
just below the window itself. Goatfuck factor? In this particular
case, it was high.

Why? Because you need at least two men to use this entry: one to climb the ladder and release the window, the other to steady the ladder, then pop up and wax any tangos inside the cockpit. I didn't have two men to spare.

Working toward the stern, there is a galley access door just fore of the wings. Goatfuck factor? Tonight it was also very high.

Why? Let me explain. We had a ladder that was approximately the right height, which would allow one man to go up, and ever so gently swing the handle that releases and opens the door. But the galley door is extremely heavy and it swings very wide—all the better to allow big food-delivery trucks to back right up to the plane and offload all those delicious gourmet in-flight meals you get served. So man Number 1 generally gets to ride the door as it swings open, while men Numbers 2 and 3 swarm the aircraft. First of all, I didn't have three men for the galley door tonight. I'd have to make do with two. Second, tangos like to hang out in the galley and sip coffee, tea, coke, or anything else with caffeine so they can stay awake. That makes the galley door a PDFL—that's Pretty hundred yards from any decent sniper position. Besides, it was blowing like a banshee, raining like a son of a bitch, and wind and water have the bad habit of deflecting bullets at long range. Nope—it would be easier and more efficient to take him out at close range. In fact, given my current mood and my desire for . . . fun, dispatching said tango in a slow and painful manner was an assignment I'd have liked to perform personally.

Okay—now we move back up the port side of the aircraft toward the bow. There are two overwing windows at seats 11A and 14A, and the main cabin entrance just aft of the cockpit door. Goatfuck factor for the port windows is the same as starboard. And the main hatch has its own problems. The tangos had not allowed a mobile stairway to be rolled up against the plane. Good for them, bad for me. Why? Bad because that stairway is a wide one, and I could get four men up it in less than a second and a half to blow the hatch open. Now, I was going to have to use a ladder, ease the door open, then send two men in. One would have to clear the cockpit, the other would chock the bathroom door so no one inside could get out, then quickly move aft into the first-class cabin.

Finally—and this is really a last resort—you can get inside a 727 by opening the baggage compartment and coming through the cabin decking. It is noisy, inefficient, and can lead to disaster, so I tend not to use it, except sometimes when I want to insert a fiber-optic cable and fish-eye video camera into the cabin floor, using a silent drill. That way I can see where the tangos are.

Such ops, however, can only be accomplished if there's people flow around the aircraft—mechanics, fuel-tanker jockeys, food handlers, and other miscellaneous types—to cause a diversion. Here, the aircraft sat in an isolated location because its tires had been shot out as it taxied prior to takeoff. After that incident, the tangos had allowed no one on board: no food deliveries, no water, not even an APU—that's an auxiliary power unit—attachment, which would allow the plane such creature comforts as air-conditioning, toilet flushing, and the like. Eight hours ago, one passenger who suffered a heart attack—it proved fatal—had been released. They'd allowed an ambulance to approach, but two tangos carrying submachine guns and goddamn LAWs antitank rockets had watched the medics closely, so there'd been no chance for any hanky-panky by the authorities.

And, as I told you before, no one had even spoken directly with the tangos. There'd been no real negotiating. All communication had been over the pilot's radio. So we hadn't been able to use voice stress analyzers or any of the other tools commonly available to provide us with a psychological profile of the bad guys.

Here, in a nutshell, is everything we knew:

- The tangos called themselves the ADAM Group, ADAM standing for Alpha Detachment, American Militia. They did not say where they were from, or what cause they were promoting.
- The ADAMs had boarded the plane in San Juan, knowing that SECNAV was on board.
- The pilot said that the ADAM gunmen had told him they had evidence SECNAV had concluded a secret agreement with the Colombian military—an agreement that the U.S. Navy would turn a blind eye to the thousands of tons of cocaine being exported to the United States. They had taken her hostage to protest her action. Their original goal—now stymied—had been to fly back to Colombia to make her renounce the treaty.
- Since the plane had been prevented from leaving, the ADAMs now shifted their demands. They demanded to speak to LC Strawhouse, a California billionaire who has been making noises about running for president on every media outlet from *Larry King* and the Home Shopping Network to Rush Limbaugh, and G. Gordon Liddy's radio call-in shows.
- When I asked, nicely, thrice, about the situation, La Muchacha grudgingly told me that FBI Washington had made contact with Strawhouse's people, but the Californian was unavailable.
- When the hijackers were informed that LC Strawhouse couldn't talk to them, they went batshit. Fifty-five minutes after they'd been told about LC Strawhouse, they killed one of the NIS agents and tossed his body onto the tarmac. They promised to kill the other one just after it got light—all the better for the TV cameras, we surmised—followed by one civilian per hour, until LC himself came and met with them.

The airport manager, who was handling the negotiations until a professional arrived, raised the plane from the tower radio and asked if they'd be willing to talk to a high administration official—the secretary of defense, perhaps, or the attorney general. The answer was an unequivocal no. What about the vice president? The tangos said it was LC Strawhouse, or no one. If he didn't show, the executions would start in three hours.

Those were the facts. Additional information? There was very little. Had anyone ever heard of the ADAM group? Sergeant Bob chewed, chawed, and shook his head nope. According to La Muchacha, the FBI had washed the name through its computer and come up dry. They had the Michigan Militia (who didn't?) and half a dozen other groups from the region, but no word on ADAM. It wasn't on any of my lists, either.

Still, the fact that they'd targeted SECNAV so accurately told me ADAM had obtained good tactical intelligence—better tac intel, in fact, than we had been given right now. SECNAV Crawford's trip hadn't been prominently covered in the press—and her schedule hadn't been made public at all. Yet they'd managed to secure it, get aboard the right flight during its San Juan stopover, and commandeer the plane.

How had they gotten their weapons on board? The answer to that, friends, is depressingly simple. They got them on board because the goddamn airlines normally pay more to their baggage handlers than they do to their security guards. The folks who toss your suitcases around have union contracts, health plans, and pensions. The folks who check bags going through the X-ray machines generally make minimum wage. They're not even airline employees, but temps, hired sans benefits, from a body broker.

Now, at what motivation level do *you* think they operate? If you answered "slim to none," pour yourself a Bombay and let me get back to work. Frankly, it's wet and cold out here and I'd like to get this fucking thing over with so I can change clothes, then find some cold beer and hot pussy. This *is* Margaritaville, after all, ain't it?

Now, the best scenario in cases like this one is to wait the bad guys out. It may be uncomfortable for the passengers that way, but the more time these things take, the more chance they'll end peacefully. That best-case scenario went out the window thirty minutes ago when the NIS agent was murdered and the killing-of-one-hostage-per-hour threat was made. So, I called the secretary of defense's command post—I actually got through this time—told the four-striper on duty what had happened, and explained that in my not-so-humble opinion, the FBI's team was a nonstarter.

She called SECDEF's aide, who called the boss at home. Fifteen seconds later his voice came on-line and told me he was going to put me on hold while he called the White House. Two minutes later, SECDEF reported that the president had given a verbal "go," and that written confirmation would follow.

That was good enough for me. I gathered my men and told them we were taking the goddamn aircraft down—now.

Well, "now" was relative. When I told La Muchacha I'd been given the go-ahead, and asked her for a little *ayuda*—that's help in Espanol—said SAC forbade me from taking any—her words—

"pro-active action" until she, too, had received a "green light positive confirmation" from the attorney general's office back in Washington that I had indeed received permission to act.

Wait a minute. Full stop. Aren't these chain-of-command problems supposed to be worked out at cabinet level? Or subcabinet level? Or sub-subcabinet level? All I know is that they're way above my fucking pay grade. Frankly, I thought things were reasonably clear—SECDEF had said "green light."

But I was willing to be diplomatic. Okay, I said, here's my cellular—phone the AG. She did. And guess what? She was told by the AG's duty officer that no one from DOD had called the Department of Justice to let it know that the National Command Authority had unleashed the SEALs of war. That being the case, said the SAC, there was no way she was going to allow me to assault the aircraft, or, for that matter, assault the aircraft with her team.

Allow? *She?* I had been given authority to kick ass and take names by the fucking president of the United States and the goddamn secretary of defense. I was getting impatient with the bureaucracy. I punched up the SECDEF's command center again, explained my predicament, and handed the phone to La Muchacha.

She may have heard but didn't listen. So far as she was concerned, unless the orders came from Justice, they didn't exist. Obviously, the FBI didn't recognize the Department of Defense as a duly constituted branch of government.

Now, gentle reader, if you were to postulate that my reaction to this sorry situation was to use the dreaded F-word in a few combinations La Muchacha had never, in her sheltered Latina life, ever heard before, you would be right on target. I told her I'd ream her a new bleeping orifice into which she could insert her bleeper-blanking ROEs, and that we were going to take preemptive bleeping action before another bleeper-blanking hostage lost his life—no matter what the DOJ, the FAA, or any other blankety-blanking alphabet-soup agency might say.

La Muchacha put a manicured forefinger in my face. She said my conduct was out of control, my language was inexcusable, and that since she had explained the ground rules once, she would not communicate with me anymore except through a Department of Justice attorney. She extracted a hundred-dollar pen from her clutch purse, wrote my name down in a Gucci notebook, and told me she would file a formal harassment protest as soon as she returned to Miami. In the meanwhile, her team would monitor what I did and report any infractions.

So much for interagency cooperation. Well, okay—her attitude meant I'd fucking finally be fucking able to go and do my fucking job. (Are you appreciating this ironic repetitive use of the F-word? Yes? Good.) Anyway, with harmony down the tubes I pulled my men into the hangar we'd appropriated so we could make final plans for the assault.

Alone, we ran all the possible combinations. We factored in Mr. Murphy at every twist and turn. And we still knew that despite all the planning, all of our training, and all of our competence, what we were about to do was so fraught with difficulty that somewhere along the line somebody would screw up—and someone would die.

I gave hand signals. Stevie Wonder came abreast of me and took point, while I relieved him and took the front end of his ladder. Since he was the ex-Recon Marine (and he liked this kind of stuff anyway), it would be his job to eliminate the tango at the bottom of the aft stairway. Normally, he'd accomplish the task by putting said bad boy out of his misery permanently. But since we wanted at least one bad boy alive—the better to ask him questions—Wonder carried a leather sap filled with lead shot that would serve the purpose as efficiently but not as terminally as the seven-inch Ka-Bar he habitually carried inverted on his assault vest.

We waited until Boy Wonder disappeared into the darkness, then began moving again. We hadn't gone twenty feet when Mr. Murphy showed up.

"Shit." Wonder's voice in my earpiece.

"What's up?" I whispered back.

"Hold up—he's gone topside—raised the stairs."

Had he seen us? Had we been compromised? I asked Wonder for a sit-rep.

There was no answer. I tried again. Nothing. The fucking radio was dead—or Wonder was.

What the hell do you do at times like this? The answer—so far as I'm concerned—is simple. You keep going.

Moving on hands and knees, we pressed forward, keeping ourselves in the blind spot directly just to the starboard side of the plane's tail. It wasn't until we got within thirty yards that I could make out details on the fuselage—that's how bad the rain was.

The aircraft was now almost totally dark—the interior overhead lights had been turned off. That was unhappy news, too. Either the tangos had seen us coming, or they were being very careful—looking out for potential threats. I don't like careful tangos because they're SUCs—smart, unpredictable, and cunning suckers. I'd much rather they'd had the lights on full—interior lights would have prevented them from being able to see us coming.

We scrambled the last ten yards as fast as we could without making any noise and moved to relative safety under the belly of the plane, where we hunkered for a head shed. The stairway had indeed been raised—it was in a half-up position.

Under it, I discovered Wonder, trying to strangle his radio.

"Goddamn thing's broken," he stage-whispered. "Probably wet."

SEAL radios are supposed to be waterproof. And they used to be. But these days, instead of the top-grade Motorolas I'd always specified for my units, the Navy buys bottom-bid Japanese or Taiwanese goods. *Sayonara,* good communications. Herro, crusterfuck.

I pointed my thumb at the stairs and mouthed, "Sit-rep?"

Wonder shrugged. "He sauntered up like the goddamn mayor of New York, closed the door, and raised the stairs," he whispered, his lips barely moving. "I don't think he saw me or anything—maybe just went to drain the lizard. But we can't be sure. . . ."

As if on cue, I heard the whine of hydraulics, and the stairway dropped. It thumped as it touched the taxiway. My squad dropped flat—almost invisible under the plane. Their weapons and the ladders were ready to go. If we were caught, at least we'd be able to give it a good shot.

God bless Wonder—his radio was already on the ground, his sap was in his hand. I snapped the thumb break on my holster and drew the USP.

There was a four- or five-second pause. Then I heard a door open somewhere above me—a faint puddle of ambient light from the stairwell exit light cut through the darkness, and I closed one eye to save my night vision.

Now I heard careful footfalls on the rough, antiskid stairwell treads.

I watched the stairs buckle ever so slightly from the weight on them. The hair on the back of my neck stood up just the way it had ever since my first combat op with Bravo Squad, Second Platoon, SEAL Team Two, when I was a wet-behind-the-balls ensign.

I went starboard. Wonder went port. No one even breathed.

He came down carefully—moving heel-toe, heel-toe, the way good point men move so as not to disturb anything or make unnecessary noise. Four feet or so above the bottom of the stairway, he stopped. I could sense him there. He was like an animal on the prowl—allowing his intuition, his instincts, to take over and protect him in this hostile environment.

He waited. I counted thirty seconds. Then he moved again, descending another three steps—just enough to allow us to draw a silent breath.

I was sure the son of a bitch heard my heart beat, because that sucker was pumping at least 140. I could hear the pounding in my ears; feel it throbbing and pulsing through my neck and wrists like a Peterbuilt semi going eighty-five through a mile-long tunnel.

The goddamn wait was interminable. I wished that he'd do *something*—anything.

But he didn't. The mother just stood there—out of our sight—quietly taking it all in.

The stairway creaked. The T moved. He started around Wonder's side. But not fast—first he planted his feet on terra firma. Then he turned. I could make out the muzzle of his SMG. It was in what we call the low ready position. This guy was good—he'd been trained.

Now he started his patrol. He began to "cut the pie"—move so as to shave the corner of the stairway, circling in a wide arc so as to gain every advantage if anyone had moved behind the stairway.

Wonder had dropped back into the shadows. He was well hidden. I slid counterclockwise, moving around the stairway to flank the tango.

I tried to move only when the bad guy did—I'd lift a foot, pause, wait, listen, and then drop my foot as I heard him do the same. The two of us were performing a deadly pas de deux.

The T stepped to the side of the stairway and stopped cold—catching me with a foot in the air. I could hear his intake of breath. He'd seen something—of course he had: Wonder's radio.

Shit. We'd had it. Surprise was lost. Then, like a fucking moray coming out of its hole, Wonder struck before the tango could react. I heard the sap's thwock on bone. I came around quick and caught the T as he slid onto the ground—he was so big it was like catching a damn maple tree. Wonder had hold of the SMG, so it wouldn't make any noise. And as if that weren't enough, the guy had a damn LAW—a Light Anti-tank Weapon—looped across his chest like a goddamn quiver. No time to waste—I cut through the strap with my CQC6 and handed the rocket pod to Nasty, who laid it carefully on the ground. We'd come back to visit that little chunk of ordnance later. Oh yeah—I wanted to know where the hell tangos were coming up with these weapons.

But I wasn't about to ask the question now. Wonder's eyes questioned, and I nodded. He tapped the tango again—just to be safe. I slid surgical tape out of my vest. We gagged the T, rolled him over and bound his hands, feet, and eyes. He was one bad guy who wasn't going to go anywhere tonight.

I ran a quick pat-down. Mr. Bad-Ass was carrying two regulation U.S. Army fragmentation grenades and two extra magazines in his safari jacket for the SMG. His wallet contained seven condoms—the guy was an obvious optimist—as well as $200 in small bills, a Michigan driver's license in the name of Thomas Daniel Capel and bearing an Inkster, Michigan, address, a Visa credit card, a registration for a 1991 Toyota 4-Runner, a photocopy of an ad from a La Quinta, California, company called Pajar, soliciting a few good men to go into the personal protection business that had an 800 number on it, and most significantly, a military ID that told me said Capel the maple was an E-6—that's a staff sergeant—in a military police National Guard unit based in Romulus, Michigan.

No wonder he knew how to move. No wonder he'd had access to frag grenades and automatic weapons. If the other tangos up there were similarly trained and equipped, we were in for a challenging morning, to say the very least.

0414. Time to move. I whispered into my lip mike and the team began its prelim.

Doc Tremblay and I would, appropriately enough, enter through the back door: up the aft stairway. Wonder and Grundle would take the forward hatch. They'd be responsible for securing SECNAV, because, according to the seating plan we'd gotten from the airline, SECNAV had been upgraded into first class. She had seat 2A. One of her NIS companions—the one who'd been shot—had been in 2C. The other was riding steerage—15C.

Half Pint and Pick had drawn the big galley door. And my lean, mean quickfooted shooters, Duck Foot and Cherry, and Gator and Rodent, would make their way onto the wings and through the windows.

I went first. Slowly, slowly (so as not to jar the plane at all) I crept up the aft stairway. When I reached the halfway point, still well below the top sight line, I rested my knees on the stair tread, eased a flashbang out of its pouch, and straightened the cotter pin that held the spoon in place. Yeah, I know. In the movies you always see Sly, or Jean-Claude, or Steven, or whomever pulling the pin with his teeth. Well, bub, try it sometime if you want to send your dentist's kid to Yale—because the only thing you're gonna get if you pull a goddamn grenade pin with your teeth, is broken teeth.

I chanced a peek—and was delighted to see that the rear door was still cracked open. That was great—it meant I could toss my flashbang inside without having to go up to the doorway itself—a potentially hazardous move if there was a tango on duty right behind it.

By now, my swim-buddy pairs were positioning themselves. They'd sneak up and lay the padded tops of the side rails on the fuselage next to the doors, or up along the inside, forward edge of the wings. Then ever so slowly, ever so carefully, they'd move into position.

The wing men would creep inch by inch, staying low and out of sight, below their assigned windows. On my signal, they'd pop the windows, toss flashbangs, then swarm.

The door men would ease their ladders alongside the hatches, positioning themselves so that the first man could slide the release handle and open the door catch. On my signal, the first man would open the door, the second man would toss his flashbang, then hit the cabin.

We'd rehearsed the sequence in the hangar, so we knew one another's fields of fire. Doc and I had the longest range—running from row 16 up to row 23. Duck Foot and Rodent had the rear-window fire field—rows 14, 15, 16, and 17. Gator and Cherry took the forward windows. They'd take down rows 9 through 14.

Half Pint and Pick had the rough entry: starboard galley hatch. If they were lucky, they'd clear it and both be alive to sweep rows 8, 7, 6, and 5. That left Wonder and Grundle. They'd come through the front door. Wonder would clear the flight deck then follow Grundle into first class. It was Grundle's mission to secure SECNAV while Wonder dealt with any tangos.

The double tsk-tsks coming through my earpiece told me everyone was in position. Just to be double sure, I whispered "Ready? Count off" into my lip mike. I got eight tsk-tsks—and since Boy Wonder's radio lay on the ground below I knew we were set to go.

Did you ever want to know what's going through a team leader's mind at this instant? Yes? Well, let me tell you. It's not good stuff. Instead, you're thinking of all the things that can go wrong; all the stuff that can get your guys killed. Here is a quick selection from the scores of goatfuck possibilities that were running through my mind as I crouched at the base of the steps, in position and ready to go:

- The tangos had tied off the interior door handles. If they had, we'd have to blow the doors using ribbon charges, by which time all the hostages would be dog meat.
- The Ts had booby-trapped some of the hostages. That possibility made me shiver. You can lose both your shooter, and the hostage, if things go sour—and things often go sour.
- More to the point, had they booby-trapped any of the doors or windows? If they had, I'd lose some shooters as we made our entrance because we'd take more time, giving the tangos an opportunity to wax our asses.
- One of the TV trucks had night-vision equipment and was broadcasting a live picture of us, which a tango was watching on his battery-operated TV set.

I could have sat there all night pondering the unpleasant possibilities. But it was time to move.

"On three," I said, and pulled the pin from the flashbang.

"One." I held the spoon down with my thumb.

"Two." I swung my arm back so the twenty-eight-ounce, gun steel cylinder would get some lift when I tossed it through the doorway.

"Three." I brought my arm forward, pitching the flashbang device softball slow pitch style, in a gentle arc. I watched in horror as it flew three inches to the right of where I'd aimed, bounced off the edge of the door frame, and came back at Doc and me.

The DEF-TEC No. 25 flashbang distraction device has a one-and-one-half-second fuse. When that 1.5 seconds runs out and the explosive takes over, you get a flash that measures 2.42 million candlepower, and a bang that's rated at 174.5 decibels at five feet.

Let me translate that into English for you. It's bright enough and loud enough to scare the living shit out of just about anybody—which is exactly what the fucking thing did to me when it caromed off the stairs, bounced once, and went off precisely six inches due south of my crotch.

The concussion lifted me and my jewels a foot in the air, and I came down in a heap—my legs going out from under me. I hit bad and wrenched my ankle—I felt my talus and proximal phalanx bones (didn't know I knew that, did you?) go pop-pop-pop. I *felt* these things because I couldn't see or hear anything—I was temporarily blind and deaf, thanks to the efficiency of the flashbang.

Instinct took over. I rolled to my left, promptly dinging my knee on the unforgiving steel tread, and smashing my nose against the railing. Oh, that hurt.

So much for surprise. Well, fuck surprise—we'd do this by sheer aggressive force and violence of action.

I pulled another flashbang from my pouch, pulled the pin, and threw it like a Phil Niekro fastball through the narrow opening. This one actually slid through and went off inside, and I charged up the stairs and through the door, Doc hot on my hobbling tail.

There is almost no way to describe the inside of a plane during a hostage rescue, except to say that it is complete pandemonium—and that's an understatement.

There was no light—except the faint glow of exit signs, the lights we carried on our weapons, and the residue from the blinding explosions of the flashbangs. There was a lot of smoke. We were all screaming, *"Abajo, abajo*—down, down—" so the passengers wouldn't jump up and get shot by mistake. Even so, a couple of heads raised themselves. I whacked at 'em as I charged down the aisle, screaming obscenities.

My halogen USP light was on, sweeping the cabin as I moved steadily down the aisle. Three rows forward I saw something—caught sight of a muzzle coming up in my direction. I shouted "Gun—left" at Doc, brought my pistol up, got sight picture through the Trijicons, and squeezed off four pairs of rapid double-taps.

I shot past the asshole five times and hit him three—groin, belly, and chest. The .45-caliber SWAT loads lifted the son of a bitch off his feet and slammed him back against the seats. He fell between two rows of screaming, ducking passengers and I pursued him, oblivious of the bodies I was stepping on.

Damn—he was obviously wearing body armor because even though the .45 had knocked him down, he was still shooting—his 633HB stitching a ragged line in the ceiling as the hostages scrambled to get out of the way. Okay—I'd shoot the son of a bitch again. Except I didn't have a shot—he was between the seats, and there might have been hostages between him and me. I launched myself over the headrests, drawing the DSU-2 as I went. I mashed my face against a tray table, stretched out my arm as far as I could to squeeze between the seats, and stuck the thick, black serrated blade right through his body armor in the center of his chest, and cut upward until I'd eviscerated the cocksucker. Now there was no way he'd get up. I wrested the weapon from his hands and tossed it in Doc's direction. I sure as hell didn't want it sitting unattended.

I sheathed the knife, changed magazines, wiped blood from my nose, and looked forward, where I saw the light beams from Duck Foot's and Rodent's weapons through the rising smoke. They had a tango facedown and were Flexi-cuffing him. Beyond them, in the front of the cabin, there was smoke and shooting—shit that's where SECNAV was supposed to be.

I heard something behind us and turned. Doc was ready—his MP5 caught a shadow coming out of the rear starboard head and stitched a neat three-round burst in the tango's face. "Shit—" Doc screamed, and charged. He scooped something off the floor, flung it down the stairway, then hit the door and the deck simultaneously.

I heard the explosion and then Doc screamed, "Aw, fuck me—"

I would have checked on Doc but I was occupied by another tango. This one popped up between the starboard seats just aft of the galley like a fucking shooting gallery target. He had a submachine gun pointed vaguely in my direction. Now a second asshole popped up on the port side. What was this, a fucking convention?

I double-tapped the starboard T—he was the most immediate threat—in the chest, shoulders, and head. He dropped.

Now, my peripheral vision caught the glint of a weapon in the second man's hand, and I swung to my left, bringing the USP around.

"Yo—scum bag—drop the fucking gun, get down, arms out, palms up and don't fucking move!" It was Gator. Except, instead of shooting the bad guy like he was supposed to do, he was shouting orders. Well, Gator's an ex-cop and he still likes to whisper those sweet cop nothings, like, "Freeze, motherfucker, or name your beneficiary."

This was no time to be polite. No time to lose, no warnings, no Mr. Nice Guy. Nothing but three double-taps. I caught tango two in the chest and neck with two bullets. A third shattered his jaw and he went down, too.

I moved forward, coming right up on the galley when there was a slight pause in the action—we'd been at it for about fifteen seconds now—and then I heard three wonderful words. "Bow section clear." Wonder's New Yawk accent punched through my headset.

A half second later, I heard "Midships clear." That was Rodent's welcome chirp.

"Doc—"

"Aft clear, Skipper." Doc picked himself up off the deck. He'd caught a piece of shrapnel on his cheek, and he looked like he'd been sliced by a straight razor—a ten-stitch repair job at least. I saw in my flashlight beam that he was already slapping a piece of tape on it.

Damn, we'd done good. No—we'd done *great*—ten men had done the job of seventeen, and I was very proud of 'em all. "Okay—let's get SECNAV and secure. And get some fucking lights on—now!"

"Aye-aye, sir." Nasty's voice was followed shortly by the overheads. I winced—my eyes had become accustomed to the darkness.

Incredibly, the minute the lights came on, the passengers started to move, as if they were about to disembark. A couple of 'em even started for the overhead bins.

Well, the authorities were on their way, there were corpses blocking the aisle, and the proprieties had to be observed, so I stopped them real fast by applying a liberal dose of shock therapy. "Nobody fucking move—sit the fuck down and shut the fuck up. Put your hands on the goddamn seat in front of you where we can see 'em."

They complied meekly. Good—that meant we could get to work *sans* interruptions.

"Sit-reps," I barked into my lip mike. "SECNAV? Body count?" No one answered. "Nasty?"

"Clear. Wonder and me got two Ts down up here, no civilians injured—and no SECNAV."

Shit. "Let's find her." That was important—but so was making sure we'd put all the bad guys down. Let's see—I'd killed three, Doc waxed one, and we'd left one alive on the tarmac. That made seven tangos so far—and not a single hostage injured. "Cherry?"

"Clear—nobody down."

"Duck Foot?"

"Clear. Clear. One DOA—he's hog-tied, Skipper."

That was eight. "Pick—"

"Clear, Skipper. One bad guy DOA."

Nine. "Half Pint?"

I got no answer. I called again. What the hell had happened to the fucking squidge? I edged my way forward, slaloming my way up the detritus-filled aisle. "Pick—where the hell's your swim buddy?"

Pick was on his hands and knees in the aisle just forward of row 12, Flexi-cuffing his DOA. He looked up at me and wagged his head. "Beats me, Skipper—last I saw he was hanging on the galley door."

I stepped over him and pushed my way fore of the starboard galley bulkhead, shone my light down, and picked up the inert form of Half Pint Harris, sprawled arms akimbo on the tarmac, lying faceup in the rain.

Well, shit may happen during these ops, but I'm never happy about it. I clambered down the wet, slippery ladder and checked Half Pint's neck. His pulse was strong and there was no blood. Okay—when he came around, we'd find out what the hell had happened.

Meanwhile, it was back to work. And by the time I'd worked my way up the ladder and back inside the cabin, the plane had been surrounded by police cars from half a dozen jurisdictions. Dozens of Federal law enforcement vehicles, cop cars in twenty-one flavors, ambulances, fire trucks, and airport security jeeps were skidding on the wet runway. It was like a goddamn traffic jam of Keystone Kops.

At least Bob and his Marathoners were there. Like an old UDT platoon chief, he simply assumed command of the situation, signaling, barking orders, assigning his men to the entryways so that no unauthorizeds made their way into the cabin. That was good—we SEALs don't pay much attention to the preservation of evidence. With Bob on the job, that detail would be taken care of.

The yang to Bob's yin was La Muchacha, who arrived at the nose of the plane, a bright yellow sou'wester rain suit (and attitude to match) over her street clothes. She went right to work—on me.

Frankly, I had no time for her. There was work to be done—for example, the no small matter of SECNAV. The Honorable S. Lynn Crawford had to be extracted from the plane, debriefed in private, cleaned up, driven the three and a half miles to the Naval Air Station at Boca Chica (where our own C-141 sat), and sent on her way with a minimum of fuss—this time on a hijack-proof, regulation, by-the-numbers U.S. Navy aircraft.

The question, of course, was where the fuck said Ms. SECNAV was, since she hadn't been sitting in first class. I made my way aft, comparing faces with the photo I'd been faxed a few hours ago.

I hadn't gone a third of the way through the cabin, when Doc Tremblay discovered her just behind the galley bulkhead, and summoned me with an urgent whistle and wave. The Honorable S.

Lynn Crawford, secretary of the navy, was sitting on the deck at row 15, staring down at the body of a dead tango. She was in tears —completely unable to speak.

Unbelievable. Talk about classic Stockholm syndrome. (Stockholm syndrome, for those of you who may not know, is the hostage's transference of loyalty from the authorities, to the terrorists. It happens because of emotional stress. Since the hostages are at the complete mercy of their captors, they often begin to identify with them out of a subconscious desire to survive.) Okay, well, this was as perfect a case of it as I'd ever seen.

But despite her Stockholm syndrome—or whatever else she may have had—my orders were to get her off the plane. "Goddammit, Madam Secretary, we have to move—now."

It was like talking to a wall. She didn't react to me at all. I waved Doc over. His bedside manner is a hell of a lot more diplomatic than mine is. He kneeled and faced Madam Secretary, smiled that wonderful New Englander's smile, took her hands in his, and spoke softly.

It worked. She responded to him in a matter of seconds, nodding through her tears. She gulped, hiccoughed, and gulped again, as if she'd taken some coffee down the wrong pipe. With Doc's help, she rose into a kneeling position. Then she shook free of his hands. She inclined her head as if in prayer, pressed her palms to her face, dry-heaved a couple more times, caught her breath, and wiped her nose with the back of her hand.

Then she looked up, catching me, I must in all truth admit, in the radiant, self-satisfied afterglow of a job well done.

Except, her face was contorted in an agonized expression that blended fear, loathing, contempt, and shock. "You moronic ignoramus," she said. "You feeble-minded, Neanderthal knuckle dragger. You contemptible murderer. You killed my bodyguard."

Chapter 2

SHOOTING THE NIS AGENT MAY HAVE BEEN UNFORTUNATE, BUT IT WAS righteous. There was absofuckinglutely no question about that. You don't wave a gun aboard a hijacked plane during a rescue attempt and not expect to get shot. NIS conceded on paper—no doubt in quintuplicate, although I only got to see the mauve copy—that what had taken place was (in their own Navyspeak words) "a deplorable act, which resulted because of an unfortunate, and ill-fated departure (!?!) from appropriate Naval Investigative Service Command security procedure."

The FBI's SAC of shit from Miami, who had no love for me or my methods, wrote in her report that what had happened was inevitable, given the fact that I had acted before I'd received proper clearances. Right. Sure. Her report went on to say that, despite the fact that we'd saved all the hostages, rescued SECNAV, and hadn't destroyed the plane, she was considering filing a sexual harassment grievance against me, for using offensive language and behavior.

I took the SAC's memo as a compliment. In her own bureaucratic way, she was saying that I might be a hell of a brain surgeon, but my bedside manner sucks. Well, doom on her—it does suck, and I'm proud of it.

But neither backhanded FBI compliments nor NIS Navyspeak

did much to assuage SECNAV. The networks couldn't discover anything about the ADAM Group, so they decided that the hijack story was really about me. My face—conveniently plucked from book jacket covers—was all over the network news, along with a lot of inaccurate reporting on my controversial history as a renegade in the United States Navy's Special Warfare commands. CNN used its file footage of me making face pudding out of the Royal Marine Special Boat Squadron CO, Major Geoff Lyondale, after the Portsmouth, England, fiasco you read about in *Green Team.*

It wasn't hard to find a dozen former SEAL officers (whose behinds had at one time or another borne my size eleven double-E boondocker prints) who didn't mind giving ABC, CBS, NBC, CNN, and anyone else who asked, their version of my controversial history as a SEAL. By the time Sunday night rolled around, I'd been described as a stone killer, a sociopathic misfit, and a delusional psychopath—and those were some of my better alleged qualities.

Yeah—the networks called to see if I wanted to respond, but in no-win cases like this one, I've learned to keep my mouth shut. I'd been judged—and the judgment wasn't kind.

Then there was SECNAV. She'd been hijacked on Thursday and rescued early Friday morning. By 1355 the following Monday—that's five before 2 P.M. on your civilian ticktocks—a special assistant to the deputy executive assistant to the executive confidential assistant to the chief of staff to the secretary of the navy had hand-delivered an eyes-only memorandum to the special assistant to the deputy executive assistant to the executive director of the office of the executive confidential assistant to the Acting Chief of Naval Operations, demanding that I promptly be guillotined, drawn, quartered, and (more to the point) dismissed from the Navy with removal of pension and all benefits.

I heard the first rumblings within minutes after SECNAV's mash note was delivered. The news came from a guy I'll call Paul Mahon. I'm going to give you a bit of history about Paul and me here. In the literary world, it's known as backstory. But don't skip it, because as the old chiefs at Organized Chicken Shit (which is how I referred to Officer Candidate School) used to say, "You will see this material again."

Okay, here goes. Paul and I first met as a couple of O-4s (those are lieutenant commanders) during a tour in the Pentagon when I worked for Rear Admiral Ace Lyons as one of Secretary of the Navy John Lehman's briefing officers, and Paul, a former Annapolis linebacker (not to mention promising young submariner) from a prominent New Orleans family, ran interference for a two-star named Black Jack Morrison. You remember Black Jack—he's the pilot who went on to become CNO and as such asked me to devise, create, equip, train, and command SEAL Team Six.

In any case, Paul and I were once assigned by our respective bosses to steal the U.S. Army mascot from the grand foyer of the Pentagon's Mall entrance the week before the annual Army-Navy football game. We succeeded—even though we were chased all over the effing building by a whole platoon of MPs. We finally huffed and puffed our way to the fourth-floor E-ring, where we managed to stash ourselves and our booty safely behind the shiny, mahogany double doors of the Vice CNO's office suite—doors which, as you know, are always protected by a couple of hulkster-size Marine guards.

Since our snatch-and-grab days, we've stayed in touch in a peripatetic way. Paul's now a one-star, with a prime assignment in the intelligence liaison office that should guar-on-tee him enough stars for a subfleet command before too long. But first, he has to spend another year here, followed by a two-year assignment in Moscow as the defense attaché. The Navy is extremely interested in Russian submarine capabilities, especially since, because of stolen Western technology, today's Russkie subs are as quiet—or even quieter—than ours. More to the point, the Navy doesn't trust CIA military estimates and has insisted on having its own man in Moscow.

But that's another story for another book. Back to the story at hand: Paul currently resides in a small but impressive office on fourth-floor E-ring, the same general location where the SECNAV and chief of naval operations' office suites are both located. That made us virtual neighbors.

How did we become neighbors? Well, shortly after I got back from London, orders were depth-charged from the stratosphere (rumor had it they came from the White House, but I was never able to confirm that part of it). All I know is that I received paperwork on CNO letterhead, cutting my Green Team from three platoons to ten men, and temporarily detailing we happy few, we band of brothers, to the acting CNO's office as a new Naval Special Warfare Development Group unit, UT/RUS, which stood for

Unconventional Taskings/Risks: United States. The idea behind UT/RUS, I was given to understand, was to put an operational naval counterterrorism unit in the Pentagon itself. I read it as the Navy's belated reaction to Oklahoma City.

Reaction or not, frankly, I'd been ecstatic about the prospect. A Pentagon-based operational unit was something that hadn't been attempted since Red Cell's heyday. I immediately jumped at the opportunity, even though it meant losing most of Green Team. My reasoning was simple. Operating out of the Pentagon gives you flexibility and mobility because you become system-wide instead of being attached or detailed to a specific command or theater. Moreover, it was a small, clandestine unit—two elements that I deem critical for success. *Small* means no middle management—UT/RUS was me and nine enlisted men. And clandestine meant that my chain of command was simplified: there was the acting CNO, and there was me, and there weren't fifteen administrative four-stripers, as well as the entire Naval Special Warfare hierarchy coming between us.

The setup was almost perfect, so far as I was concerned. UT/RUS's responsibilities were to be twofold. First, we would become the Pentagon's reaction team for hostage rescue and counterterrorism activities concerning all high-ranking Navy personnel, anywhere in the United States. That gave me both the counterterrorism portfolio, and the hostage-rescue portfolio. Both were subjects of concern these days, which would ensure that we would remain busy little boys.

Second, whenever we weren't chasing bad guys, we would implement security assessments that would allow local base commanders to prevent the loss of weapons and ordnance—a growing problem that had been addressed by the Department of Defense's IG—inspector general—in a number of classified reports. That assignment was similar to the old Red Cell mission. Except that here, our role paralleled the new growth of "jointness" in the armed forces. Let me explain that word in plain English. *We* may have been Navy—but our assignment cut through all the service branches. Now, because there was the possibility of offending the Army, the Air Force, and the Marine Corps during our role playing, we'd been ordered not to actually penetrate the bases playing the role of terrorists. We would, it had been told to me, simply conduct administrative inspections and give the base commanders a written eval.

Yeah, right—sure we would. I knew it would be impossible to restrain my irrepressible, playful leprechauns once a target of opportunity presented itself—but I crossed my fingers behind my back, said, "Yes, sir" (spelling it *c-u-r*), and went away ebullient.

When I think about it now, the whole thing sounded almost too good to be true. Even at the time, I had some trifling, picayune doubts—they were stuck back by my skeptical meter, which is located in the right rearmost quadrant of my nasty Slovak brain, just behind the pussy radar. After all, when something is too good to be true, it probably is too good to be true.

I can say that now. The day the paperwork came down, all I thought was, Fuckin' A. After all, I was being handed a great assignment, I commanded the nine best shooters in the Navy, and the goddamn chain of command was going to leave me alone.

If I'd taken more time to reflect, I'd probably have been more suspicious. Why, for example, would the acting CNO, a man known for his caution, sanction a unit so proactive, especially with me running the show?

But, since I've never tended to *regarde la bride de cheval donne* —that's looking too closely at zee mouth of zee geeft 'orse—my nine shooters and I moved happily into the new UT/RUS command post, five floors below Paul's river view. That proximity meant he and I could now grab an occasional burger and beer together at the Union Street Tavern, Bullfeathers, or any of the others in the long list of Old Town hash-and-brew houses, to catch up on gossip and talk trash.

Okay, now that you're up to speed, let's pick up where we left off.

I drove down to the Pentagon at 0500 Monday, dodged the camera stakeouts, opened the office, caught up on paperwork, and waited to get my copies of the after action reports, which had been completed by the FBI on Sunday. There were no tango survivors—the one we'd stashed had been tagged by the frag Doc Tremblay tossed out the rear door and bled to death.

But there had to be other information about these guys from the FBI's huge counterintelligence database—a series of files that take up six floors of the goddamn J. Edgar Hoover Building in downtown Washington, D.C. No matter what La Muchacha had told me, I knew that the FBI plays things very close. And I wanted to know a lot more about these ADAM assholes than I currently did. They'd had good intel about SECNAV's schedule. Where had it come from? Who was slipping it to them? They'd had good weapons. How had they gotten 'em? Who'd been responsible?

And there was more. I wanted to know who they were, what their organization was all about, where they came from, when they'd first formed up, and why they'd wanted so damn much to talk to LC Strawhouse, the California billionaire. I also wanted to learn about Pajar of La Quinta, California—the company whose ad our deceased tango had clipped.

My motivation was KISS-simple.

- *Item.* These tangos had run a good op.
- *Item.* It was UT/RUS's mission to stop groups like ADAM.

When no paper arrived by ten hundred, I called the FBI liaison office, was told there was a delay, and that as soon as they had something, they'd call, so please stay by the phone. At 1400, I was still twiddling my scarred thumbs. At 1405, the phone on my desk finally rang.

I picked up on the first ring. "Marcinko."

The familiar voice said, "Do you know who this is—don't use names."

Of course I knew, and I told him so. "Yeah—you're the other shit-for-brains asshole who's stupid enough to steal U.S. government equipment from the Mall foyer."

Paul gave me an urgent, whispered, watch-your-butt heads up. He ran down SECNAV's behind-the-scenes action. He added that the MIQ (that's the memo in question) had been shredded by ACNO's confidential assistant so as not to leave any nasty evidence behind. But Paul had somehow managed to get a glimpse. The note had been handwritten by SECNAV herself. Its message was simple, precise, and unequivocal: get rid of Marcinko. Now. Permanently.

He rang off, leaving me to wonder how they'd try to dispose of me this time. My unhappy conclusion was that it wouldn't be very hard to do. I was currently without a four-star protector. My man o' warsman sea-daddy, Chief of Naval Operations Arleigh Secrest, had been assassinated not four months ago, and the acting CNO, a ship driver named Wendell Whitehead, was the sort of prudent bureaucrat who stayed away from rogues like me.

Windy, as he was known, was a caretaker less than six months from retirement, who would run the Navy until a long-term CNO could be found. He was a good choice, in that he was politically and socially correct (he's a Naval Academy graduate, who has worked at the National Security Council for three presidents. As a young lieutenant commander, he was once assigned as the White House military aide in charge of making small talk with unattached women at state dinners, so he knows what fork to use, and seldom if ever uses the dreaded F-word). But congeniality wasn't why he was appointed.

Windy was chosen because he was a nonthreatening, administrative-oriented officer (his doctorate from the University of Maryland was in systems management) whose very personna—from the round, rimless glasses to the slight build and tonsure of sandy hair—gave him a benign, professorial countenance. He was the ideal organization man, whose inoffensive demeanor allowed him to interface easily with the nonmilitary and antimilitary types who peopled the current administration.

He was actually an inspired choice. Indeed, Windy Whitehead was the perfect officer to smooth over the recent scandals—outrages that ran the gamut from spies like Johnny Walker and Jonathan Pollard, to the Tailhook fiasco, to all those EEO suits filed by malcontents and whiners—that had plagued the Navy over the past decade. They loved him on Capitol Hill, tolerated him at the White House, and ignored him on E-ring.

Acting CNO Whitehead was, therefore, not about to make, or take, any unnecessary waves. And I was the tsunami that could swamp his barge.

If there was no support coming out of ACNO's cabin, there was even less from next door, where his chief of staff, a four-eyed, balding, dip-dunk one-star named Don Layton, worked. First, Rear Admiral (Lower Half) Layton, who had spent his entire career as a nuclear submariner, openly despised all Naval Special Warfare. He probably considers us manual laborers because we tend to work with our hands. That alone would have been enough. But there was a second element as well that caused the little red light to start blinking in my brain: Don Layton was an Annapolis classmate of my perpetual, persistent, and relentless nemesis, Pinky Prescott.

Pinky has been the bane of my existence since I commanded SEAL Team Six, and he was the grand panjandrum of NAVSPECWARGRU TWO—that's the commodore of Naval Special Warfare Group Two to the uninitiated among you. A paint-by-the-numbers officer whose forte lies in memo writing, Pinky has tried everything in his power to get me court-martialed.

So far, he's failed. So far. But it's not for lack of effort. The Doom on Dickie bottom line, which means I was fucked in Vietnamese (and any other language you care to think of), was there'd be no support for me anywhere. Not from ACNO's office, or anywhere else on fourth-floor E-ring.

Worse, Pinky had returned to Washington to be appointed the acting Assistant Deputy Chief of Naval Operations for Plans, Policy and Operations—the number two position in OP-06. Yes—I know the job slot is for a two-star, and the last time we all saw Pinky he'd been frocked to vice admiral. But guess what? Shit happens, and in this case, it happened to Pinky. No third star. Not this go-round, anyway. So he sulked. And he plotted. And he blamed it all on me. So, I knew Pinky would quietly pull every string he could to make sure that my ass was properly bawled, mauled, and keelhauled—without leaving any telltale fingerprints, of course. He's that kind of guy.

Anyway, I have never been accused of being *un timide.* So at 1500 hours I walked up seven flights of stairs, marched halfway around the building, and presented myself in front of the Grade One Executive Secretarial desk of the executive secretary to the Honorable S. Lynn Crawford.

"Captain Marcinko to see the Secretary."

She blanched. Have you ever seen someone blanch? All the color drains from their face. Anyway, it took her a few seconds to regain her composure. When she did, she said, "The Secretary is not available for you."

I hate taking "no" for an answer. But I wasn't about to argue. I said, "Thank you," and took a hike. She was already picking up the phone to tell SECNAV what had happened before the hydraulic door closer had hissed the thick wood suite door shut.

Lest you think that I was giving up, I wasn't. But since I am an unconventional warrior, I chose to make an unconventional entrance—through SECNAV's back door. I walked fifteen paces down the hall until I came to an unmarked door that was guarded by a push-button cipher lock. It is the door to SECNAV's hideaway office. I know this because when I was John Lehman's briefer, it was the door I used to come and go by, so I didn't have to be logged in by his secretary.

There's something you should know about cipher locks at the

Pentagon: they tend not to change the combinations with every new administration. That way, the career civil servants who really run the place don't have to memorize a whole set of new numeric combinations every four or so years.

When SECNAV Lehman occupied this suite during the eighties, the cipher combination was 3-4-3-5-1. Guess what happened when I punched those numbers in. Yup—the door lock clicked open.

Most cabinet and subcabinet officers have huge, ceremonial offices with great views and lots of antique furniture, where they greet official visitors, hold their photo opportunities, and meet the press.

But they don't work there. No—they tend to work in small—even cramped—comfortable cubbyholes where they don't have to walk half a mile to retrieve a file or a memo from the safe.

SECNAV's hideaway is like that. It is wood paneled and cozy, with one small window that looks out on the Potomac, a small fireplace with gas logs, and a lot of built-in bookshelves. There's a small desk made from the planks of *Endurance,* a British man o' war run aground off Spanish Wells during the War of 1812, a leather-covered wing chair, matching ottoman, and reading lamp that look as if they all came from a London club, and a small sofa with a butler's table sitting on a remarkable antique Persian carpet.

SECNAV looked up as I came through the door. She was sitting in the wing chair, her feet in soft terry-cloth slippers, an afghan on her lap, a pair of half-glasses perched two-thirds of the way down her nose, reading a thick report. She didn't look too surprised, either.

"I've read your file—I had an inkling you'd show up uninvited sooner or later, Captain."

"Madam Secretary, I think we have to talk."

She took her feet from the ottoman, laid the report on her lap, stuck the glasses in her thick red hair, and pursed her lips. "I'm not sure there's very much to say, Captain Marcinko."

"Look, Madam Secretary—"

"No, you look—and for once, please try to listen." She stood up. "This is not personal. It has nothing to do with you and me. It is simply that you are a political liability, Captain Marcinko, and this administration cannot be saddled with political liabilities."

I had to smile. It was the old story. More of the same. I said as much.

Even in her stocking feet she was almost as tall as I. She walked to the desk and put the file down, kicked off the slippers, slid her feet into her shoes, and took her rightful place. "You wear my accusation as if it were a badge of honor. But let me tell you the truth, Captain: it is nothing to be proud of. The Navy has had its share of problems of late. It has had to face downsizing—learning to live with a reduced capability. Then there were the embarrassments. Tailhook. The avalanche of sexual harassment and EEO cases. The stolen Tomahawks. The assassination of CNO Secrest—" She saw me standing opposite her, my arms crossed. She pointed toward the chair she'd just vacated. "Take a seat."

"Thank you, but I'll stand."

"Have it your way." She paused, then rose, so that she looked me in the eye.

I sighed. Fucking power politics.

She continued. "I was put in this job to make things right. My orders are to put the Navy back on course." She picked up a pen and tapped it on the desktop while she chose her words. "Captain, you are preventing me from doing my job. You are a dangerous man."

"That's why they hired me."

SECNAV shook her head. "No—they 'hired' you, Captain Marcinko, because you are a *lethal* man; because you are a *deadly* man—or at least one with deadly talents. But I happen to believe that you are also a dangerous man. You're a loose cannon—a rogue."

I started to say something but she cut me off. "I have seen you in action, twice, Captain, and I do not like what I see. Admiral Prescott sent me a CNN videotape of your assault on a British officer just a few months ago. Just last week I was an eyewitness to your wanton violence. Acts like those are the reason I am seeking to have you discharged."

Pinky again. He's such a help in times of need. I thought of several ways in which to make his body hurt. "I did what I had to do to get the job done, Madam Secretary."

She nodded and tapped the file on her desk with her pen. "I knew you'd argue that the ends justify the means, Captain. That is how you habitually operate—UNODIR. I am told it stands for UNless Otherwise DIRected, and that you use it as a way to evade the chain of command. Well, once again, you succeeded—in your fashion. That is to say, the terrorists are dead. The hostages—myself included—are free. But your work was not flawless: one of my staff is dead, the result of your wanton brutality. According to the debrief, and my own recollection, your man"—she opened the file and turned its pages until she came to a sheet of paper that had several of its typed lines highlighted in bright yellow marker—"Petty Officer Shepard, called out a warning for Special Agent Flynn to drop his pistol. But you didn't give Special Agent Flynn a chance to react—you killed him in cold blood."

It was time to give her a dose of the real world. "Calling on Flynn to surrender was a mistake on Petty Officer Shepard's part."

She looked at me, incredulous. *"What?"*

"Gator acted in error, and I've chewed his ass out for it. Let me be blunt, Madam Secretary—giving warnings isn't my job. Killing terrorists is."

"That's brutal."

I nodded. "Maybe it is—but, like you just said, that's why I was hired. I'm no cop—I don't have to tell suspects, 'You have the right to remain silent'—or anything else. When SECDEF says 'Go' I go. Because when SECDEF gives me the green light, it means I'm sanctioned. It means I don't have to worry about taking prisoners."

"I don't agree with that way of doing business, Captain."

"You don't have to," I said. "You're not an element in my chain of command."

"Perhaps not," she said. "But as secretary of the navy you are an element within mine—and I can deal with you."

She was right about that—she couldn't order me on a mission, but she could end my career. "I'll fight your decision to remove me."

"I assumed you might. But it's gone above both our heads now," SECNAV said. "The Chairman of the Joint Chiefs has asked to see all the paperwork on this incident. It will be his call, now."

She tapped the report with her pen again. "And when he makes his ruling, I think you'll be history, Captain Marcinko—and I believe that the Navy will be the better for it."

I went to SECNAV's cabin Monday afternoon. The boondocker in the ass came on Tuesday morning at 0600, when I was denied entry to the UT/RUS operations center, a small cluster of rooms buried behind bug-proof walls in the Pentagon basement, and dispatched forthwith, at once, and *toute de suite,* to a windowless, six-by-six-foot office in a huge, mazelike, dusty warehouse that backed up against the rear perimeter fence of the Washington Navy Yard. I was put on restricted duty and told to S^2. (That's shut the fuck up and sit the fuck down and make no fucking waves whatsoever.)

What was going on—déjà vu all over again? The last time I was sent in disgrace from the Pentagon to the Navy Yard, the Navy spent more than $60 million trying to prove that I acted improperly. Despite all the expense, and six hundred *man years* of effort, the investigators from NIS failed to find even one iota of evidence against me back then.

Now they were about to try and haul me out of town on the proverbial keel one more once, even though I knew I'd acted within my mission parameters. Incredible.

My cell—that's how I thought of it—came with a dented gray steel desk, a metal chair with uneven legs, and an empty file cabinet. There was no phone. There was no lock on the door. Obviously, there was no Bigelow on the floor either.

Now, at my current stage of life, I won't accept treatment like this. First of all, I don't need the money the Navy pays me. I do the work because I believe in it—and in my men. Financially, I'm secure. I made a dump truck of cash on my autobiography, *Rogue Warrior,* and its two fictional sequels, *Red Cell* and *Green Team.* Besides, I've got Rogue Manor, 6,500 square feet of house and 200 acres of heaven, which backs up pretty close to Quantico, about an hour southwest of Washington. With that kind of real estate at my disposal, who needs a six-by-six at the Navy Yard and two hours of commuting?

So I drove back to the Manor, and went to work.

Work? You out there all look dubious. You're saying, "Dickie's just been shitcanned, and yet he's keepin' on keepin' on. What goes?"

The answer, friends, is that there were too many wheels spinning, and too many targets in the air, and when there are too many targets in the air, my only question is which one do I shoot at first.

See, I knew I had acted according to correct procedure. I'd received verbal permission to act from the National Command Authority. The problem I faced was that nothing was on paper Well, that was nothing new. The president had ordered me and Green Team to snatch a fundamentalist tango from Cairo *sans* benefit of written orders. And somewhere in the Pentagon, someone recorded all the calls in and out of SECDEF's command center so I knew that sooner or later, I'd come up with the right evidence and be vindicated. It was only a matter of time—and effort.

Still, there was no doubt that SECNAV wanted to remove me from the scene—fast. That made sense: it was the politically expedient thing for her to do.

But SECNAV and I had different priorities. Her job is political—keeping the lid on. Mine is tactical—blowing the lid off. And I consider my mission more important than hers. After all, there were bad guys out there who had been given access to Navy secrets, and I was determined to find them and bring them to justice.

Chapter 3

So I didn't just sit around and watch the soaps. There were things to do. Like check up on Alpha Detachment/Armed Militia. Like check up on LC Strawhouse. My efforts would be aided by one facet of my personality that I probably haven't talked much about before: my predilection toward pack-ratness. Simply put, I almost never throw anything away. My ex-wife, COMWRINKLANT, used to call me the last Collier brother.

The godfather of all SEALs, Roy Boehm, was the one who first encouraged me to keep every scrap of U.S. Navy paper that ever crossed my bow. "Never throw a fucking thing away," Roy growled at me when I was but a tadpole and he was a grizzled old frog. "Because someday, the paper warrior sons of bitches are going to come after you, and you'll have to defend yourself. Because you're a fucking man o' warsman, they'll think you're a knuckle dragger who don't keep good records. Well, fuck the fucking fuckers. You keep every fucking scrap of paper ever crosses your desk. You keep meticulous fucking records of who the fuck, what the fuck, where the fuck, when the fuck, why the fuck, and how the fuck." (Yes, friends, Roy Henry Boehm, Lieutenant Commander, U.S. Navy, Retired, actually does talk like this. You have to remember that he, like me, is a mustang—an enlisted puke-turned-officer—who's never forgotten that he was once a boatswain's mate, and a fuckin' good one, too.)

Okay, back to Roy's advice about saving paper. Quoth he, "Save everything. That way, when they come after you, you'll blow 'em out of the fucking water by sheer weight of evidence."

Ever since, I have followed—and even augmented—Roy's shall we say piquantly phrased but solid-as-gold advice. So I went to the files. Sure, I get all the trade publications—ten gun magazines, half a dozen SWAT guides, police catalogs, security-organization bulletins, and military magazines. But there's also a decade of *Time* and *Newsweek, US Snooze, Forbes,* and *Money* in my basement, as well as bulging files of *The Economist. Rolling Stone.* The *Mid-East Report.* Not to mention *American Survival Guide* and *The Liddy Letter*—yeah, I get 'em all. And I keep 'em all, too. While there was no information about ADAM, within six hours I'd assembled a pile of magazine articles and news clips on LC—for Lyman Clyde—Strawhouse.

He had quite a history. According to a hugely favorable profile in *Forbes,* he was the eldest of thirteen children born during the Great Depression to Odessa and Vernon Strawhouse—"redneck sharecroppers from the northeast corner of Texas, Bonnie and Clyde country, close up to where the Oklahoma and Arkansas state lines meet," is how the *Washington Post* Style section had folksily described them back in the mideighties. The article went on to say LC's folks had lost their $125 Sears & Roebuck kit house because they couldn't pay the $8 monthly mortgage. (It also mentioned that his Washington lawyers included one Grant Griffith. That made me put a small black mark next to LC's name. Griffith was the influence-peddling former secretary of defense I'd shot when I discovered he'd been behind the smuggling of nuclear Tomahawk missiles to a Japanese ultranationalist group.)

Well, black mark or no, LC, as Lyman Clyde preferred to be known, was that authentic American original, a self-made man. The David Burnett portraits I found in *Forbes* showed him to be an elongated—six-foot-plus—coyote-faced, knock-kneed, jug-eared, sinewy country boy whose Desi Arnaz pompadour haircut was pure fifties. He dressed well but not flamboyantly in London suits, and favored cowboy boots to lace-up shoes.

He came by the country-boy angle honestly: he'd picked cotton and rice as a six-year-old, worked in a slaughterhouse as a teenager, and carried hundred-pound blocks of ice for twenty-five cents a day instead of going to high school. At eighteen he was drafted—and volunteered for Airborne training. Three years later, as a sergeant, he won the Congressional Medal of Honor when he saved his Eighth Army Ranger Company platoon from decimation by the Chinese Communists on Ipsac Hill, North Korea. They'd been overrun when the Chicoms crossed the Yalu River to intervene on behalf of their North Korean allies. Still on crutches six months later, he was decorated by Truman at a White House ceremony.

After the Army he'd drifted back to Texas and found himself a job in the oil fields. According to a six-month-old profile in *Time,* "he was happiest when he worked with his hands and sweat till he stunk."

He was also, it turned out, enterprising. According to *Business Week,* by the late fifties he was a small-time wildcatter. By the time Kennedy was elected, he'd made his first five million and moved lock, stock options, and fifty-gallon barrel to California. The day Nixon took the oath of office, he was worth half a billion. And if I believed what I read in the newspaper clips I was holding—and I had no reason not to—LC Strawhouse, now in his midsixties and the chairman and CEO of LCI, International, was worth somewhere between twenty and twenty-five billion dollars.

Let me put that in perspective for you folks out there. It is more than the GNP—gross national product—of Peru, Chile, or Syria. It is twice the GNP of Malaysia. Let me use a financially technical description: LC Strawhouse was one rich son of a bitch.

But it wasn't his money that made him famous these days. It was his politics. It seemed that whenever you turned on the TV these days, there was LC Strawhouse, telling us how ineffectual, bloated, and useless "gummint," as he called it, had become. "If the gummint was in bidness," he told Larry, and Phil, and Oprah, and Geraldo, and whoever else would have him on their shows, "it would have gone belly-up long ago." LC's solution was for the American people to put him in charge and let him fix things—singlehandedly. He had been registered as an independent presidential candidate in all fifty states—and his organization was bringing in millions of dollars in contributions—not that he needed a penny of it.

Now, I'm not a political animal. I have spent most of my life in the military, working for a series of politically motivated commanders in chief and Congresses who hadn't the foggiest idea how to use me and my deadly talents. But they were my commanders in chief and my Congresses—that's what the Constitution's all about, and I took an oath to defend that very same Constitution.

Anyway, it seemed apparent (even to me) that old LC Strawhouse wanted to make major changes in the Constitutional area. News clips chronicled his appearances and presentations at such venues as *Soldier of Fortune* conventions, weapons trade shows, and political gatherings over the past year and a half. Let me put his political philosophy succinctly for you.

LC believed we needed a chief of state who was less the poll-driven, touchie-feelie-I-will-never-lie-to-y'all politician, and more like one of those Latin American *caudillos*—paternalistic, tough dictators like Trujillo or Batista. There was a part of me that agreed with him. I want a head of state who is decisive—a man who leads from the front. LC certainly did that—he *ran* his businesses. He didn't leave 'em to others to run. And in many areas, our philosophies were similar. He argued that we didn't need a Department of Defense that ran rescue missions in the Third World instead of staying ready for war. I thought so, too. He thought we should lead, not follow, in world affairs. No argument there, either. He was tough on crime, and believed in education. Right on.

Where I got uneasy with LC was in the constitutional area. He never came out and said it in so many words, but it was kind of like he hinted that we didn't really need the Constitution. I found that downright scary.

But guess what? Current polls showed that many Americans agreed with him—felt that we needed a strong man running the gummint, and to hell with the Constitution. One poll—from a *USA Today* not three weeks old—showed that 22 percent of Americans would be willing to give up some or all of the Bill of Rights if that meant cutting down on crime, drugs, and welfare fraud. That fact alone should tell you something about the mood of the Nation these days. Frankly, it made me very nervous.

It made me even more nervous to know that a group of well-armed, well-informed tangos had wanted to talk to him more than they wanted to talk to the vice president of the United States.

At 0530 Wednesday morning, knowing he'd be awake, I called Stevie Wonder. "Busy these days?" I asked.

"Sure." He chortled. I hate him when he chortles. "Since I don't have an office to go to, I've been sitting at home playing with myself. What about you?"

I told him about my meeting with SECNAV, and my suspicions. I could just see his head swiveling left-right-left, right-left-right. "Sounds righteous to me."

"Has anybody seen anything from the FBI?"

"Nah." Wonder paused. I heard him slurp his ever present 7-Eleven coffee. "Once they shut us down, nobody bothered to pass any poop."

"Well, I'd like to see it—"

"Me, too." He laughed. "Let's call La Muchacha and see if she'll fax it out to the Manor."

"Fat fucking chance of that." I paused. "How do you feel about a little breaking and entering on Federal property?"

"Any property in particular?"

"I was kind of thinking about the J. Edgar Hoover Building."

"Gee," said Wonder, "it's been about five, maybe six years since we've done that. Probably about time."

It was raining when Wonder drove my car into an underground garage on Tenth Street just north of E Street, less than a hundred yards from the two-and-a-half-million-square-foot J. Edgar Hoover building. We parked and watched as hundreds of FBI employees streamed into the headquarters building at the start of the morning shift. Neither Wonder nor I had been inside this huge, ugly concrete fortress in a while, and my preliminary evaluation as I watched and noted was not especially promising.

Some background here. The Hoover Building covers the square block between Ninth and Tenth streets, and Pennsylvania Avenue and E Street, directly across Penn from the Department of Justice. There are seven stories on the Pennsylvania Avenue side, and ten on the E Street side. More than seven thousand FBI employees work there. They are divided into three shifts that cover twenty-four hours.

The place was designed in the heyday of the disturbances—read antiwar demonstrations and civil rights riots—of the sixties, and built in the late sixties and early seventies. Hence, its castlelike architecture—incorporating such elements as a huge dry moat, a small number of chokepoint entrances, and a mazelike interior—didn't encourage the sort of B and E I was used to performing at loosely guarded military installations.

Worse, from my point of view, was the fact that the FBI had obviously buttoned things up considerably since the Oklahoma City bombing.

Used to be you could just park your car next to the building, stick a quarter in the meter, and wander in simply by waving a generic Federal ID in the general direction of a bored rent-a-cop. That's how I'd gained entrance when I commanded SEAL Team Six. These days, you couldn't park within a block and a half of the building itself. And I realized after half an hour of standing in the rain that all FBI employees now wore photo identification cards that had magnetic identifier strips. They showed their cards to a guard—a hard-working guard wearing an FBI badge—who actually compared the picture on the card with their faces. Then they inserted their cards in a reader, which in turn allowed them to go through a security turnstile. The fact that they'd punched in was also recorded on a computer somewhere.

It took me another hour to comprehend a further refinement: the cards were entry-specific. I discovered that because I saw repeated instances of people sauntering up the street together, but walking into different entrances. At, say, the State Department or the Pentagon, it doesn't matter what office you work in—you can go into any entrance and get there. Not, I discovered, at FBI Headquarters.

If, for example, you're a researcher in the forensics lab on the third floor, you can enter the building on the Tenth Street side, but not through the Pennsylvania Avenue door. Why? Because the Pennsylvania Avenue door does not lead to the forensics lab. I saw only males in good suits and females dressed for success wandering through that particular door. Assessment: the Pennsylvania entrance was probably one of the "executive" doors, which led to the elevator bank specifically assigned to the Bureau's top-level offices on the sixth and seventh floors.

Even the garage was partitioned. It would be possible, I realized, to gain entrance by concealing myself in the back of someone's car. But once inside, I'd still have to use a photo ID—and I'd still be admitted only to a specific portion of the building.

After two hours of walking and watching, I met Wonder in a coffee shop on F Street, where we dried off and compared notes over breakfast. His findings were as depressing as mine. He'd checked out the janitorial side of things—one of the best ways to break and enter is as a janitor, because clean-up crews are generally

given access to an entire site. He discovered that the FBI's jan
were all dedicated FBI employees—and that they cleaned spec
sections of the building.

We drank bad coffee and went over our B and E possibility list.
Sewer entry? All the manhole covers within two blocks of the building were spot-welded. Sneak undetected? There was a subterranean tunnel from the Department of Justice across the street, but Wonder's recon indicated that the tunnel led to an elevator that ran directly to the director's office suite—a dead end, so far as we were concerned. Steal an ID and brazen my way in? That works only if the guards don't look at the pictures. At the FBI, the guards did their jobs—and I was screwed.

Pose as a phone repairman? The FBI did its own phone repair to keep the opposition from installing listening devices. Take a tour and drop off? No way. Unlike tours at State, the Pentagon, or even the White House, the FBI tour was conducted by and in a self-contained unit. Tours left at half-hour intervals and were led through a secure series of corridors that had no access to any of the Hoover Building's working areas.

Well, I have never surrendered. There is nothing that is impossible—you just have to be flexible. So there had to be some way to break in undetected and secure the information we needed.

Wonder munched on a pumpernickel bagel piled high with cream cheese and sipped his coffee. "Arferskopic," he said, his mouth full.

"What?"

Wonder chewed and swallowed. "Arthroscopic," he said.

"Yes?" I was willing to humor the boy.

"Don't you see?"

I told him that I didn't see, and what the fuck?

He shook his head at me more in sorrow than pity. "You are an *old* asshole," he explained. "You come from the Leo Gorcy school of life—by which I mean that *you* think the only way to get anywhere is to break inside *avec le crow bar and la sledge hammer*."

I love it when Wonder speaks French. "So?"

"So, Dickhead, *sir,* there are other, more sub-tile ways of doing business these days. Like, we break in electronically." He wiped a bit of cream cheese from the starboard corner of his mouth. "Look—you don't even know where the goddamn records you want are being stored—and there are, what—six, seven floors of fucking s and records over there. So let's find what we need fast by using computer. Besides—that way they won't ever know we've come nd gone."

He had a point. I tend to look at things in an old-fashioned way. That is because I was schooled by a bunch of old-fashioned chiefs whose idea of having fun was blowing things up. But they also taught me to be flexible.

So I listened to Wonder. Sure, he's a youngster. But he's computer literate. Besides, he's a natural-born thief. There's not a whole lot he can't break into—including, I was willing to bet, the United States' most top secret computer network, Intelink.

Well, that's its name now, but since I've told it to you they're probably going to change it.

If you're one of the 99.9 percent of the population who hasn't heard about it, Intelink is a classified computer system that *link*s the *inte*lligence agencies, DOD, the Department of Justice, the White House, and the State Department. It was built about five years ago and is run on a series of huge, 32-bit supercomputers, similar to the immense Cray servers CIA, DIA, and No Such Agency are currently using.

I'd used information from Intelink's databases, but I hadn't ever sat down at a terminal and played with it myself, because so far as I am concerned, all computers are programmed in gibberish. Still, the basic concept is simple enough: all users must have a Secret clearance to access the system and receive the most basic information from the databases, the most basic classification being "Confidential." To get the real pearls—all the information rated above confidential (the two classifications are Secret, and Top Secret) you have to undergo an EBI or an SBI—which stand for Extended (civilian) or Special (military) Background Investigation—clearance process. SBI is a fine-tooth-comb affair—one of four do not make it through the process successfully.

Once you have been cleared, which can take more than two months, then you are initiated into the rites that permit you access to the holy of holies—a series of special passwords. Those passwords are chosen at random, and then encrypted so that they remain secure.

Once you reach the top tier, the system allows you to call up a plethora of highly sensitive goodies. At the basic level, if you punch up Islamic Terrorism, for example, you will be able to see Department of State cables and some of the CIA and DIA analyses. At the Top Secret stage, the system will toss in NSA intercepts, and DIA TECHINT. When you get to the code-word stuff, there are real-time NRO (that's the National Reconnaissance Office, home of big bird and friends) satellite pictures, and DIA HUMINT materials, including the kinds of names and faces you need to see if you're running SEAL Team Six or Delta missions.

But to get access to Intelink, you have to be operating a classified computer work station, you have to know the current passwords, and you have to be able to program your requests in a complicated computer language created exclusively for Intelink. Moreover, the system has built-in security measures. All users are logged by date, time, access code, and password. Terminals are kept under lock and key—they don't simply sit out on desks where visiting crackers—standing for CRiminal hACKERS—can get at them.

There had, for example, been a terminal at the UT/RUS offices in the Pentagon. But it had been removed within minutes of SECNAV's nasty memo. Go to the Pentagon and find another? A possibility. But weak tactics. Okay, we could break into the Navy Yard—if you read *Red Cell* you know I've done that before—and use one of NIS's terminals. But that, too, was a nonstarter.

Wonder explained that, unlike Irish sex, these things take time. It might take him a few days to get what we needed—and there was no way we could set up in someone's office, whether it was the Pentagon or the Navy Yard, and use their secure terminal.

So far as I was concerned, we were screwed. But none of the above considerations seemed to bother Wonder. "Come on, Cochise," he said. "Let's get back to the reservation and play with the tom-toms."

Ninety minutes later we were sitting at the 100-plus-megahertz Pentium workstation that I've got in my office at Rogue Manor. Wonder opened himself a Coors light and fired up the computer.

He connected the modem, and dialed the number for the Navy Yard's computer network—an unclassified system.

******* WASHINGTON NAVAL DISTRICT ********
********* DEFENSE DATA NETWORK ***********

LOG IN:

Wonder typed *system.*

The computer answered

PASSWORD:

Wonder typed *operator.*
The screen, went blank, then:

***** WELCOME TO NDW COMPUTER NETWORK *****

It had taken Wonder less than fifteen seconds to break into the Navy Yard's secure computer network.

He grinned at me. "Easy, huh?"

"How the fuck—"

I could tell you"—Wonder grinned—"but then I'd have to kill you."

"*Won*der—"

"Okay, okay. Remember when I went to Iraq a couple of years ago?"

"Yeah." He'd been sent over masquerading as a U.N. nuclear weapons inspector.

"Well, the Iraqis bought a bunch of old Digital VAX computers, and I had to break into them and retrieve information about their missile sites.

"So before I left for Baghdad I went to visit the people at Digital. And guess what? It turns out that all DEC VAXes come with built-in passwords—the *same* built-in passwords. Workstations all come with log-in prompts that show the word *user,* and require the password *user.* The mainframes all come with a system log-in, which uses the words *system,* and require the password *operator."*

"Yeah, but—"

He was too pumped up to let me get a word in edgewise, or sideways. "And guess what, Dickhead—most people, and that includes the Iraqis, and the asshole panjandrums at the Pentagon —are too lazy to change the goddamn passwords, which means that it's easier than you'd realize to shimmy the door open."

I was impressed. But this wasn't Intelink. It was a nonclassified computer network—and I mentioned as much to Wonder.

He looked at me with his goofy smile, and swiveled his head left-right-left, right-left-right, just like the other Stevie Wonder, and said, "Right on, Mr. Dickhead, sir."

He is such a polite boy. He worked at the keyboard with the flowing shoulder action and rapt concentration of a concert pianist, and suddenly we were reading electronic mailboxes at the Naval Investigative Service Command. "Thing is," Wonder explained, momentarily slowing his byte-size glissando, "I logged in as the system manager, so I get to go through every fucking file in the damn computer." He giggled. "That's what I did in Iraq, too."

I watched as he scanned notes from investigators, scrolled through memos, E-mail, and reports. He found—and printed out—a copy of SECNAV's itinerary from the NIS security office. They hadn't even bothered to password the goddamn file—it was available to any twelve-year-old hacker who could get inside the NDW computer. Finally, after half an hour of eavesdropping, he sat back, stretched, and cracked his knuckles. "Bingo, Dickhead."

I squinted at the screen. Wonder had isolated a single message—a note from one NIS gumshoe to another that had been written six days ago.

BILL—I'LL BE OUT OF TOWN FOR THE NEXT THREE WEEKS TAD NAPLES, SO YOU'LL HAVE TO PICK UP THE PIECES ON THAT COUNTERESPIONAGE THING I'VE BEEN WORKING WITH WMFO [he used the acronym for the FBI's Washington Metropolitan Field Office at Buzzard Point]. THE BUREAU FILES ARE ALL IN IL. USE THE VAGRANT ACCOUNT FOR ACCOUNTING PURPOSES. ACCESS IS THROUGH TOPHAT, AND THE COMPARTMENTED STUFF IS IN LIMETREE. HAVE FUN. JIM.

"They can't be that stupid."

Wonder grinned and swiveled his head. "Sure they can—they're NIS."

He wrote the passwords down, disconnected from the Navy Yard system, then dialed the Department of Defense's Intelink network access number—which, incredibly, can be found in the DOD locator—in civilian terms, the phucking phone book.

The system answered on the second ring.

********** DODNET INTELINK 6.2 **********
*********** ACCESS RESTRICTED ***********
Trying . . .
DODNET INTELINK 6.2 CONNECT
welcome to DODNET INTELINK
log in:

When the log-in prompt came up, Wonder typed the word *vagrant*.

He was immediately asked

password:

Wonder keyed in the word *tophat,* and was greeted with "password accepted."

So much for classified systems and restricted access and all the rest of the security mumbo-jumbo. He took a pull of Coors, and grinned at me. "Watch."

Wonder typed "@intelink"

The computer bleeped a couple of times.

He hit the return key and typed: "intelink>open FBI intelink"

It took less than a second for a message to appear.

********** FBI INTELINK **********
******* ACCESS RESTRICTED ********

log in:

Wonder typed the word *guest.*

invalid password, try again

Wonder typed the word *visitor.*

welcome to FBI Intelink

Restricted, my ass. The damn thing was wide open. It was time to ask a technical question. "What the fuck?" I inquired of Wonder.

"Ah, Sir Dickhead," he said, "most system managers know that there are always going to be visitors. Like, say, an agent from Butte is visiting for a couple of days, and needs to use the computer to check something. Now, said agent doesn't use Intelink more than once a year in Butte. So he's forgotten his password, and his access code, or left it in his desk back home. So, said system manager can either spend his time programming new passwords every time a transient user passes through town, or he can just program a permanent one—something that's easy to remember, like *visitor,* or *guest.* That way, he doesn't have to worry about new passwords."

"But that's insane."

Wonder smiled. "What's your point? Of course it is. But as we all know, people talk about security a lot more than they practice it."

Chapter 4

TWO HOURS LATER, I WAS LOOKING OVER MORE THAN A HUNDRED PAGES of printout. We'd extracted the FBI's counterintelligence files on Alpha Detachment/Armed Militia, as well as dug up their internal memos on the group—a treasure trove of information that told me La Muchacha—you remember my favorite SAC from Miami—had lied through her expensively capped teeth when she'd said the Bureau had no files on those tangos. They'd had a sheaf of 'em hidden away—they just hadn't wanted to share any with me.

Then I realized that perhaps she hadn't lied. It was more likely that she hadn't been told anything about these files.

Why? The answer lay on the table in front of me. See, in the days after Oklahoma City, the Bureau had requested more lenient guidelines in order to operate against domestic terrorism. Those requests had not been granted by a Congress that remembers such FBI disasters as COINTELPRO—the mostly illegal COunterINTELligence PROgram instituted by J. Edgar Hoover against homegrown, left-wing subversion in the midfifties—and other domestic escapades that broke dozens of laws.

Regardless of congressional stricture, the Bureau still needed intelligence in order to operate against domestic terrorism. So what it—or at least one element of it—had obviously done, was to go covert.

And judging from the contents of the memos in front of me, ADAM had been the subject of several black-bag jobs over the past year or so. Now, as we all know, black-bag jobs are highly illegal. My conclusion was that the Bureau's panjandrums in Washington had decided to play dumb when La Muchacha requested background information on ADAM, because if they'd divulged what they knew, someone might ask how they'd known it.

I read on. There was no doubt about it—the memos indicated that the Bureau had evidence ADAM was one small element of a larger, informal network of crazies—domestic malcontents, fringies, psychos, and terrorists who advocate the violent overthrow of our government.

Now, let me digress here for a little while. There have, as you are all very well aware by now, arisen a number of what are known as citizen militias. These groups, whose membership may exceed a quarter of a million Americans by now, are linked together in more than thirty-five states by fax, computer network, shortwave radio, desktop publishing, video cassette, and cellular phone. Unlike the far-right-and-left-wing kooks, ethno-terrorists of all backgrounds, and KKK white supremacists, most of these new militias have a broad-based constituency, not to mention the support of many in local law enforcement.

Most of the groups share common values. They believe, for example, that the government is no longer a government of, by, and for the people, but has become a huge, expensive, national bureaucracy that has spun out of control. They believe that most of the laws and regulations concerning gun control, abortion, education, and welfare are misguided, irresponsible, or just plain wrong. Come to think of it, they sound a lot like many of those Republicans elected to Congress in 1994.

There is a feeling, among many militia members, that Americans are just not in control of their lives anymore—that government has hijacked control, and that if you object too loudly to that fact, you will get stepped on and squashed. The evidence they cite includes the Internal Revenue Service's confiscation of property, the SWAT-team tactics of the Bureau of Alcohol, Tobacco and Firearms, and the foreclosure on large numbers of family farms and homes in the Midwest and Northwest by banks that turn out to be fronts for huge corporations that wrecked the land.

Some in these militias are convinced that the New World Order is the most dangerous threat America has ever faced. According to these folks, there is a huge, secret conspiracy involving the United States government, the World Bank, the International Monetary Fund, and the United Nations, all of which will somehow combine to bankrupt the United States, then take over the country and occupy it with U.N. troops.

Now, I don't hold with the latter conspiracy. And I've spent too much of my life working for the government to believe that it can act as one entity. But I respect—and would defend—the rights of these militia members to educate themselves, to speak their minds, to defend and protect themselves, and to train as they see fit to do.

Having said that, I must also tell you that, since we are a nation of laws, I believe that anyone who actively conspires against the government to bring it down by violence is nothing more than a terrorist—and should be treated as one, just the way we've dealt with the perpetrators of Oklahoma City. The sons of bitches ought to be fried. The Constitution, which I have taken an oath to preserve, protect, and defend, guarantees all of us the right to protest. Well, protesting is one thing. Sedition is another.

The groups cited in the FBI's memos were not the lawful, law-abiding militias I have just described. Alpha Detachment/Armed Militia was one of the nasty-boy fringe groups. It had, so the files said, ties to the white supremacists of the Aryan Order, the Waffen Strike Force, and the White Hand of God. Even more astonishing was its apparent ties to certain other, equally dangerous groups coming from the opposite political direction.

One counterintelligence memo, citing a confidential informant code named Lancer, said that our deceased pal T. D. Capel had been seen by a friend of the CI's in the company of an assistant to Imam Fouad el-Yassin of Dearborn, Michigan. I knew who the Imam was—because he'd been tied into the network of tangos who'd bombed six locations across the country last year and set into motion the chain of events recounted in *Green Team.*

Imam el-Yassin's weekly audiocassette sermons are played in hundreds of mosques all across the nation to a growing audience of Islamic fundamentalists. I've heard 'em. The sonofabitch brazenly advocates terrorist tactics—"American blood must flow," he shouts. "American limbs must be cut off. Mothers must mourn their sons; wives must become widows . . ." But we can't do anything about him because, according to the Michael Kinsley look-alikes at the ACLU, which has sued successfully on his behalf, he's simply a humble cleric, exercising his First Amendment rights.

Don't get me started on that one.

Another memo detailed contacts between an ADAM asshole named McNabb—I knew that name, too: he was one of the bad guys we'd waxed in Key West—and Rockne Washington, aka Shaquile Shabazz, aka General Mayhem, the supreme leader of the Zulu Gangsta Princes, America's largest street gang, whose 25,000 members control vast portions of Chicago and Detroit, and sell their drugs along the interstate highway corridors running all the way to LA in the West, and Tampa, on the East Coast. It was, I read, the FBI's "conjecture" that ADAM was selling guns to the Zulu Gangstas, as well as plotting terrorist acts.

Now, you may ask why so much of this FBI counterintelligence information was being couched in such panty-waist language as "likelihood," "probable," and "conjecture." The answer is two-fold. First, confidential informants, or CIs as they're called, are chronically unreliable as sources of information. Since they are often selling information for either cash or a reduction of sentence, traditionally they will—and they have—say almost anything they think the Feds want to hear, whether it is true or not.

In fact, there have been half a dozen cases recently in which the Federal government has had to pay millions of dollars to the innocent victims of CI fiction. Therefore, judges, of late, have been reluctant to issue search warrants and other investigative paper-work based solely on CI information. It also meant that the FBI's intelligence work had to be larded through with disclaimers, in case of a lawsuit. The wishy-washy language also told me they hadn't been able to get a single judge to issue a search warrant, phone tap, or grant the Bureau permission to plant passive monitors—which was why they'd had to resort to covert methods.

Back to the point I was making: in other FBI cases, however, ones like ABSCAM, in which they caught USG—that's U.S. government—officials including senators and congressmen taking bribes, the Bureau must observe all the legal niceties. Corners cannot be cut. If they are, your bad guy will walk.

That was the case here. In fact, the FBI was caught in a catch-22. The Bureau needed the kind of inside information that could most easily be obtained through phone taps, monitors, and other electronic observational techniques. But the judge had insisted that, since there was no specific charge leveled against the group, such devices and techniques were *verboten.*

So the Bureau had simply gone out and done it anyway. But then, they couldn't use anything they'd collected. Crazy, right? I think so. But that's what happens when the bad guys have more rights than the good guys. Good guys have to play by the rules. Bad guys don't. Guess who wins most often.

I read on. I saw that the FBI's efforts were further stymied because ADAM was a small, tightly knit group. It had probably been formed very much like a cell of the Islamic Jihad—a nucleus of people who had known one another for years, who augment their circle very slowly. It is difficult to penetrate groups like these because all strangers are regarded with suspicion. Now, ADAM, which was a small cell of tangos, had been decimated. But the weapons they'd sold in the Detroit area were still in circulation.

As I read on, I realized that the FBI had not only screwed up the investigation, but it had also covered up its tracks. The most damning documents Wonder had discovered—the ones that had obviously been gathered through covert means—were filed in what might be described as an electronic wastebasket. The only reason he'd scooped them up was that he'd searched the FBI's files using a rational data search program, which scanned the Intelink for any files or fragments of files that mentioned the word *ADAM,* or Alpha Detachment/Armed Militia.

The ADAM files had been electronically "shredded," much the same way Ollie North and his colleagues "shredded" the computer records at the National Security Council after their activities came under scrutiny back in 1986. But just as in that case, shredded did not necessarily mean destroyed. So, Wonder was able to reconstruct more than 80 percent of them—enough to give me a pretty good idea of what the Feds knew.

Sure they'd shredded everything they could—their ADAM files wouldn't be able to withstand any scrutiny. They'd obviously been gathered illegally, which would mean any case against ADAM would be thrown out of court. Well, with the Alpha Detachment/Armed Militia out of business because of termination by yours truly, a court trial was not part of the equation anymore.

There was something else as well. When I looked at all the memos, I realized that the Bureau had been running into walls when it came to working against these seditious domestic groups, and had virtually been forced to work against them by covert

means. You couldn't tell that from reading them one at a
you sort of had to lay them all out and look at the patterns. A
patterns seemed to indicate that every time the FBI made prog
it got knocked backward. It was almost as if the bad guys had b
receiving inside information about what the Bureau was doing.

Was there a mole inside the FBI? It was improbable, but no
impossible. Like the CIA and NSA, the Bureau has had its share of turncoats in recent years, too. Well, internal security was a Bureau problem, not mine. I had other things on my mind.

One of them was the Texas billionaire. We ran LC Strawhouse's name. Wonder was able to retrieve and recompose the shredded FBI MEMCON—that's MEMorandum of CONversation—telling us that Strawhouse himself had told the FBI's assistant director for operations that he had "no damn interest whatever in talking to that damn expletive deleted bunch of fly-off-the-handle Michigan crazies acting on their own down there." Hadn't the FBI's Miami SAC told me he was unavailable? This was more than "unavailable." This was straight-out refusal.

Wonder discovered another bunch of files that mentioned Strawhouse, buried in the Department of Justice's Intelink bank. But he kept receiving "access denied" messages every time he tried to break and enter. He gave up after four attempts so as not to raise any suspicions. "This stuff is really restricted—they've probably got a random password that would take me months to find," he said.

"Can we do anything?"

A wicked grin spread over Wonder's apple-cheeked countenance. "Yeah—I have an idea or two."

He dropped off the Intelink long enough to get back into the NIS system. There, he used his superuser status to write a short program, which he managed to insert just under the Intelink's skin. He called the damn thing a Trojan Horse. What he did was to create a bogus request for everyone who wanted information on LC Strawhouse, or the ADAM group, to enter their account names and passwords.

It was a KISS program. Users would be asked "Enter your account" and then "enter password." The system would then make them repeat the information—only this time it would be diverted to a ghost file that only Stevie Wonder could access.

He looked at the lines of computer gibberish critically, then rewrote the last few, adding my name to the list of requests.

I asked him what the program was all about.

he explained, "when you type your password into a system, that password is encrypted into a nonsensical code. ., for example, I typed *tophat* on the keyboard, the system .'t use those six letters to allow me access. It encrypted them— o something that might look like this." He typed *gqri@vcr* on ie screen. "Then it compared those letters and symbols with a master list of accounts and passwords, logged the entry, and approved it. That's when I got the green light to enter Intelink."

"So?"

"So, I entered the system as Jim, the NIS investigator."

Ah—now I saw what he was getting at. Jim the NIS asshole didn't have access to files on LC Strawhouse. To get inside those, we'd need other, more highly compartmented account names and passwords.

The program Wonder had just written did two things. First, it would hand us a list of working accounts and passwords in nonencrypted English. That would allow us to use Intelink as any number of users—making it harder for us to be traced. Second, we could also see who was searching for the same sort of information about the things we were interested in. It was a way of breaking in, and looking back over our shoulders—checking our six, as the pilots say.

Chapter 5

WONDER TOOK THE REST OF THE WEEK OFF. ME? I SPENT MY TIME pondering the possibilities while taking out my aggressions on the one-ton weight pile that sits on a ten-by-ten concrete slab in a little hollow aft of the deck and outdoor Jacuzzi, and just port of the pond.

Pumping iron out-of-doors was a habit I'd acquired in prison. You remember I did a year in stir back in the early nineties after a Federal jury—after two trials and despite a distinct lack of evidence—found me guilty on one count of conspiracy to defraud the government on the pricing of some special-ops grenades. I served my time at Petersburg, Virginia, about forty miles south of Richmond.

Anyway, the weight pile at Petersburg Federal Bad Boy's Camp and Mayoral Blow Job Facility is about 200 yards downhill from the dorm, on 150 square feet of concrete slab, right next to the South Bronx–style basketball hoops. Every morning at six sharp I'd walk past the guard tower, throw the hack (hack is prison slang for Horse's Ass Carrying Keys) a friendly salute, then begin my PT routine. My outfit was always the same: a pair of nylon running shorts, a pair of Nikes, and a headband. I wore the same clothes whether it was fifteen degrees out, or ninety. I'd arrived at Petersburg on April 16. In November, the guards started taking a pool as to when I'd start wearing sweats—or at least a T-shirt. By February, as they watched me trudge back from my workout up to my hairy ankles in slush, ice crusting my matted beard and eyebrows, steam rising off my naked body, they realized there would be no winner.

So I worked out and I came to some conclusions. The first was that, given the information we'd gleaned on the computer, I'd have ample material with which to fight SECNAV's decision to have me disciplined. I knew I was right—and that her decision had been politically motivated. Second, I wanted to look deeper into the ADAM matter. There was a cover-up afoot, and I wanted to know why—because, given what Wonder and I had discovered, I realized I was being made the *bouc*—that's zee French fall guy—for both the Navy's intelligence lapse (SECNAV's itinerary falling into ADAM's hands was a major fuckup) and the Bureau's illegal surveillance of the tango group.

On Thursday afternoon, having set a plan in motion, I played back the tape. I had five calls from the deputy CO of the Navy Yard, a four-striper who always used his full name ("Captain Marcinko, this is Captain Steve Otway, United States Navy, calling . . ."), demanding to know where the hell I was, because I sure wasn't sitting at my desk. Well, he was right about that.

Half Pint Harris called to report that he'd been released from the hospital and the concussion had been a mild one, all things considered. Piccolo Mead called to say that Half Pint was a fucking liar—it had been a serious concussion and that he'd been lucky not to have broken his back and cracked his skull.

Doc Tremblay phoned from Quantico, where he'd gone with a couple of his sniper friends, to try the new Stoner semiautomatic .308-caliber sniper rifle currently favored by SEAL Team Six's shooters. He said he was having no problems making one-and-one-half-inch groups at five hundred yards. I thought of a couple of people into which he could put them.

There were more than two dozen calls from assorted reporters, all asking for just a few minutes of my time, and one message from a Major General Harrington, who identified himself as being with the Defense Intelligence Agency. He said he was calling on Thursday at 0930 on a matter of some urgency and would call again sometime in the next twenty-four hours. He didn't leave a number.

I shrugged. I didn't know any Major General Harrington. I did, however, know a Rear Admiral Pinckney Prescott III, and there were also thirteen—count 'em, thirteen—messages from *his* office. That was a nasty surprise. Pinky and I hadn't spoken in almost two months. Not that speaking would be easy for Pinky these days, because his jaw is wired together and he sounds like shit talking through clenched teeth. Come to think of it, he sounds like shit even when his jaw's not wired.

I hear you all out there. You want to know why Pinky's jaw was wired. Well, it's wired because I broke it in two places, just about nine weeks ago, in London.

Now you might think that breaking a two-star's jaw would be sufficient conduct to warrant a court martial and a long sentence of breaking big stones into little ones at the federal prison in Leavenworth, Kansas. Under normal circumstances, it would be. But I have an insurance policy that protects me from such unhappy consequences where Pinky is concerned.

Just over two years ago, I discovered that the Admirals' Gestapo—which is what they call the Naval Investigative Service around here—had launched a highly classified investigation of Pinky. I came upon his file the night when I broke into NIS headquarters during a security exercise I was conducting at the Washington Navy Yard. If you want to learn more about why I was there, you can read about it in *Red Cell*. Anyway, the file, code named Foxhunter, was in the offices of SLUDJ, the top secret NIS Sensitive Legal (Upper Deck) Jurisdiction witch-hunting unit whose investigators are known as Terminators, because they never quit until they win.

Since I always play for keeps, too, I took the file for safekeeping.

Eight weeks ago, about six hours after I flew back from London, I went to visit Pinky, who was recuperating at home. I brought with me a single photograph from the Foxhunter file. It was a grainy but completely identifiable likeness of the good admiral in flagrante delicto—that's Latin for "during flagrant pussy-licking"—with a known Japanese foreign agent.

The night I visited Pinky in his Ashcroft town house I never said a word. Explanations weren't necessary. Neither were threats. I just slid the eight-by-ten black-and-white across his eighteenth-century Williamsburg reproduction coffee table, watched his face change color, and then bid him a warm *"Sayonara."*

So, no way was I going to return Pinky's calls. Let the son of a bitch wait. Ditto all the reporters, the NIS lawyer, and the XO of the Navy Yard, Captain Steve Otway, U. S. Navy.

That left Major General Harrington from DIA. I called the main number there and asked to be connected with his office. The operator said there was no Major General Harrington at DIA.

Hmm. A DIA project code named TFB, whatever that meant, had been mentioned in half a dozen of the FBI's electronically shredded memos. Now a two-star from DIA, who the operator had just told me didn't exist, had come a-calling. Happenstance? Coincidence? What do you think?

I double-checked by perusing the current Defense Intelligence Agency telephone book and discovered that just as I'd been told, he wasn't listed anywhere. That said Harrington was a spook of some sort. The question was—I sang this to myself as I pondered the possibilities—what sort of spook he was, who wasn't listed there.

There are *beacoup* ways to find out about spooks without alerting the subject of your interest. The easiest way is to ask someone you trust. In my case, I dialed my old friend Tony Mercaldi's ninth-floor office at the Defense Intelligence Agency. If anybody knew about Harrington, Merc would. After all, he's an Air Farce colonel who works some of DIA's spookiest projects. During the Gulf War, Merc was tasked with directing all U.S. covert ops against Saddam Hussein. He himself was part of the seven-man team that got caught in Baghdad just after Saddam Hussein invaded Kuwait and had to be smuggled over the Turkish border by agents of the Polish intelligence service. In December 1990, Merc was the guy who told me that if I volunteered, he could get me out of prison long enough to lead an op somewhere in the greater Baghdad metropolitan area and reduce the mustached son of a bitch to a cinder. Since Desert Storm, Merc has had to learn a lot about the former Soviet Union for reasons I can't go into—unless you readers all have top secret clearances.

Anyhow, maybe Tony knew who the fuck Major General Harrington was, and what the fuck he wanted. I dialed. His phone rang four times and then switched me over to his DIA telephonic mailbox and message service. That meant he was out of town. Doom on me.

I thought of calling Irish Kernan at No Such Agency, which is what we SEALs call the National Security Agency. But calling Irish is like talking to your tootsie-wootsie on a Hell's Kitchen party line. You whisper sweet nothings, and the whole fucking neighborhood knows.

Well, that left me on my own. It's amazing how much information about supposedly classified subjects—or people—you can find if you know where to look. The Soviets (remember them?) understood that. In fact, that is precisely why they used to ship more than 450 tons—almost a million pounds—of books, magazines, newspapers, as well as congressional reports, committee transcripts, and oversight investigations, as well as thousands of U.S. Government Printing Office documents back to the USSR every year.

They bought just about everything that was published. Then they packed it all off to Moscow, where they analyzed it, word by word by word.

What did they learn? Well, from publications such as the *Biographical Register of the U.S. Department of State,* they could pretty much discover who was a career diplomat, and who was using State as his (or her) CIA cover. By tracking telephone listings and office assignments from one phone directory to another, they could follow government workers' careers. They simply checked the room numbers against the building schematics they'd been able to buy from the General Services Administration.

By looking up home addresses in the *Congressional Staff Directory,* KGB or GRU agents could find out where staffers from the Select Committee on Intelligence lived—and maybe burgle a house or two to see if classified materials were being brought home on the sly. Unlisted home telephone numbers of senators, congressmen, and other prominent Washingtonians (including many top spook WASPs) are often available in *The Green Book,* Washington's annually published social list.

I used the same technique. From my collection of *Congressional Staff Directory* books, I discovered that a Stonewall Jackson Harrington, Lieutenant Colonel, USA, had been assigned to the Senate Select Intelligence Committee just over a decade ago. His listing was starred—which meant his biography was included in the back of the book.

I flipped to the biography section and perused the listing.

Harrington, LTC Stonewall Jackson, professional staff member, Senate Select Com. on Intelligence. Born Feb. 25, 1944, in Rice, Virginia. Married 12 June, 1968, to Pamela Lynn Elliott. Children: Jebediah,

Jennifer. Georgetown Univ., 1962–1966, B.A. (magna cum laude), Phi Beta Kappa; Yale Univ., 1966–1969, J.D. Career record: entered active duty as 2LT, US Army in 1969. Assignments include: 82d Airborne Division, 173d Airborne Division, 5th Special Forces Group. Decorations include: Silver Star, Legion of Merit, Bronze Star with Combat V (3), Purple Heart, Vietnam Campaign Ribbon, National Defense Medal.

So he'd been a shooter in Vietnam. I wondered where he'd served—he'd probably gotten there just after I'd left—and if we knew some of the same people.

The bio sent me scrambling to a dozen other books. I checked my Special Forces files and came up dry. Then I got out my old intel contact files—a dog-eared looseleaf notebook filled with names and numbers. Sure enough: there was a Harrington, MAJ. SJ, attached to the U.S. Army Intelligence and Security Command at Fort Belvoir at the same time I was pigging out as a Sweat Hog at the Pentagon. Had I ever called him back then? Nope.

Sweat Hogs are the small group of staff pukes who work eighteen-hour days in the Navy Command Center dealing in factoids and info bits. They're the Navy's answer men. Some admiral needs to know how long it'll take a carrier task force to go from Diego Garcia to Oman. He asks his aide, who asks *his* aide, who picks up the phone and calls the NCC, where a Sweat Hog gives him the right answer.

Well, just prior to the clusterfucked Iranian rescue attempt, I was the NavSpecWar Sweat Hog, or more precisely the Sweat Frog. As such, I compiled a thick contact book of sources who'd help me get the answers I needed. My network ran the gamut from E-6 grunts at NRO—the National Reconnaissance Office—who slid me satellite recon photos or SIGINT—SIGnals INTelligence—target assessments at a moment's notice, to LANTFLT (AtLANTic FLeeT) master chiefs who knew how to body-english the system in my favor. I learned as a Sweat Hog that most often, it wasn't officers who helped. They were too interested in keeping their information close to the vest, just in case it might help their career tracks. So instead, I developed lots of friends in low places—the enlisted folks who actually got the work done—who were more than willing to help out when a four-star was scorching my back and the answer better be the right one—*NOW!*

Enough about me. Back to the case at hand. I'd discovered that my man Harrington had been on the intel side back as far as the late seventies. Which meant he was probably running some pretty heavy stuff these days.

Okay—now let's see if I could find his address. I called the main numbers at Fort Leslie McNair, and Fort Myer, asked for Major General Harrington's residence, and was told that the general did not live on base.

Next, I pulled the last five editions of the Washington, suburban Maryland, and Northern Virginia phone books down from their shelves, blew the dust off, and thumbed through them. Nada. I dialed 411, and received a recorded reply that "At the customer's request, the listing you have requested is nonlisted."

Next, I retrieved the current edition of the *Green Book.* There were two Harringtons on page 202, but not a Stonewall Jackson Harrington. I pulled the previous edition from the shelf, thumbed through it, and drew another blank. I tried a three-year-old book. There, the home address and telephone number of the current Director of Central Intelligence was listed (back then he'd been a socially prominent think-tanker). The address and phone number for the current Chairman of the Joint Chiefs of Staff was listed, too. Three years ago, he'd been the Marine Corps' three-star deputy chief of staff for plans, policy, and operations. And guess what. On page 204, there was a listing for one Harrington, Brigadier General and Mrs. Stonewall Jackson, with an Alexandria, Virginia, address and phone number attached, along with the notation that their daughter, Jennifer, was a student at Harvard University.

By now, it was after six: late enough for him to have left the office, and for me to have a Bombay. So I poured myself a drink, put my feet up, and dialed his home number.

The phone was picked up on the first ring. "Harrington."

I like a general who answers his own phone so promptly. "General, this is Dick Marcinko," I said. "You called."

There was a momentary pause as he shifted mental gears. Then: "Good to hear from you, Dick." His voice was even, strong, and no-nonsense brisk—what I like to think of as a good radio voice. "I'm glad to see we're starting off on a first-name basis."

I laughed for the first time in a week because I had, in fact, called him by his first name—General. I sipped on my Bombay. "What can I do for you, sir?"

"Since you've discovered where I live, you can come over here for a drink—Bombay, isn't it?—and a talk. I have a proposition that will probably interest you."

I was about to hang up, when he added: "Do me a favor—don't park in front of the house."

Since it was well past rush hour, it took me only slightly longer than an hour to shower, throw on jeans and a polo shirt, and drive the fifty-eight miles from the Manor driveway to the general's Old Town, Alexandria, town house. I parked my car three blocks away and—as ordered—strolled aimlessly up, down, around, and through the narrow streets for about fifteen minutes just to make sure I wasn't under some kind of surveillance.

When I'd determined that it was all-clear, I circled back on my trail one more once, just like Major Robert Roger, the first American SpecWarrior and founder of Roger's Rangers, had told his men to do more than two centuries ago, to make sure they weren't being followed by the French or the Indians.

So I slipped through the narrow, trash-filled alleyways between Pitt, Fairfax, and Lee streets, made a wide loop, checked my six (and nine, and twelve, and three), and when I was satisfied that it was all clear I found my way to the intersection of Duke and Royal.

Fifty feet off the corner I paused in front of a narrow doorway and checked the brass numbers on the dark green Chinese lacquer. Then I stepped back and admired the house. From the look of it, it was one of the newer ones—which meant it had been built in the *late* eighteenth century—a three-story, step-gabled red brick structure that sat on Duke Street's uneven brick pavement, three short blocks from the river, next to an old church.

The general greeted me at the door. He was shorter than I, and athletically trim. His handshake told me he worked out. He'd slipped out of his kind of uniform and into mine—a pair of jeans, work boots, and a black polo shirt that bore the embroidered logo of GSG-9, Germany's top counterterrorism unit.

I followed him inside. The long hallway floor was made of random-width, golden-colored pegged pine that was probably as old as the house itself. We turned right into a small sitting room. There was a comfortable velvet couch up against the window wall. On a butler's table in front of the couch, an elegant Georgian silver tray held a bottle of Bombay Sapphire, an insulated bucket of perfect ice cubes, a pair of delicate silver tongs, and a cut-crystal double Old-Fashioned glass. Flanking the fireplace were two eighteenth-century gaming tables. On each was an antique chess set. Both were in play.

I went to examine the games in progress. One that looked as if it was in its final stages must have been a Spanish set, because its well-used ivory pieces depicted El Cid fighting the Moors at Valencia. White seemed to be winning—at least white had more pieces on the board than black. The other was a Victorian English set; the magnificently carved chessmen represented warring Scottish clans. There, it appeared that black had the upper hand. I caught the general watching me examine the boards and turned toward him. "Nice sets."

"Thank you." General Harrington nodded. "Do you play?"

I shook my head. "Nope." I indicated the Spanish set. "Who's winning?"

"Black wins—in seven moves."

"And the other game?"

"White—nine moves."

I stared at the boards. I couldn't see it. "How do you know?"

He shrugged. "Because I *know*—same way you look at a building or a bridge and you know just how to bring it down. Same thing goes for me—except I work on a chessboard."

"What happens if nobody wins?"

"That's called a stalemate," S. J. Harrington explained. "Except I don't believe in them. I always play to win—even if I have to force the game one way or another."

I liked that thought and said so. The general grinned, and indicated for me to sit on the couch, which I did. He plucked up the tongs, dropped four perfectly clear ice cubes into the tumbler, filled it to the top with Bombay, set the glass atop a linen cocktail napkin, then handed it over to me.

I tasted. "Thanks."

"No problem." General Harrington turned toward the fireplace. He took a brass poker from the fireplace set, jabbed at the burning logs, added a cleanly split length of red oak to the fire, then set the poker back precisely where it belonged. He sat opposite me in a richly upholstered Queen Anne wing chair with matching ottoman, took a monogrammed crystal mug of amber beer from the English wine table that sat next to the chair, lifted it in my direction in an informal toast, then swallowed it down. "Ah, that's good."

He wiped a small mustache of foam from his upper lip with the back of his index finger. He picked up an inch-thick file that sat on the ottoman. When he turned it over I saw that it had the distinctive orange tab that proclaims the contents inside to be top secret. He shook the file in my general direction, then gently laid it on the table in front of me. "Well, Dick, as a professional intelligence officer, my assessment of this material is that you're in deep doo-doo again—and this time it may actually stick to you. What's your opinion?"

Chapter 6

There is an old Chinese proverb that goes, "Steal not a single link more of chain than you can swim with." From the number of links contained in the thick file General Harrington laid in front of me, I was well into the drowning phase of chain-theft.

I guess my problem is that I never give Pinky enough credit. He is, after all, primarily a bureaucrat. Thus, I tend to pigeonhole him that way, when I know from bitter experience not to, because he is more than a mere paper-pusher. This character flaw of mine is something I should know better than to indulge. After all, I'm always bitching that others look at my thirty-five-inch arms and my thirty-inch inseam and think of me only as the archetypal, shoot-from-the-hip knuckle dragger, when in fact I have a master's degree from Auburn, speak a trio of languages fluently (and another half-dozen passably), and have three *New York Times* best-sellers under my belt.

Well, I should keep that sort of thing in mind when I deal with Pinky, too. Why? Because he is a smart and cunning son of a bitch —you don't get to be an admiral without a healthy dose of smart and cunning—not to mention the fact that he knows how to wage political war better than most.

I now understoood that the whole UT/RUS assignment—in fact the unit itself—had been his doing—even though he hadn't left even a single faint fingerprint. I'd half-believed that my orders had come down the chain of command from the White House, perhaps as payback for the job I did in London, and no one tried to disabuse me of that notion. In point of fact, all I knew for sure was that the mission profile for UT/RUS had come from CNO's cabin, passed to me by Rear Admiral Don Layton—Pinky's Annapolis classmate.

From behind the scenes, Pinky had dangled the bait in front of me, and I'd snapped it up faster than a great white shark goes after chum. I thought I'd keep him at bay with the pussy-licting picture I'd, ah, laid on him. Well, doom on me—he'd been more subtle and effective than I ever expected him to be.

Worse, he'd predicted my subsequent actions pretty well, too. He knew me well enough to know that sooner or later I'd stage a UNODIR—UNless Otherwise DIRected—operation, which is my standard, Rogue Warrior modus operandi when I think the system is getting in my way and the can't cunts are asking me to say, "May I."

Damn it. For an unconventional warrior, I'd acted pretty damn conventionally—predictably, that is. So, I'd stormed the fucking plane in Key West without signing any of the rules of engagement sheets, and, more significantly, without obtaining a *written*—that is faxed—"go" order from the National Command Authority in Washington. You will remember that I'd been given a verbal okay. But now, I discovered from reading the file I'd been given, that despite what SECDEF had said on the phone, nothing had subsequently been put in writing.

Why is that significant? The answer, friends, is because, just as I'd explained to SECNAV, unlike a police SWAT unit, my shooters are not trained to take prisoners. We are trained to kill our targets. But before that can happen legally, the chain of command has to formally unlock our cages, and let me and my other SEALs of war out to prowl and to growl.

To put it simply, once we get a "go" from Washington, we do not have to provide Miranda warnings, announce ourselves, or worry about the consequences of shooting bad guys who've raised their hands in surrender. If, however, there is no record of that uncaging sequence—no written order from the president or the SECDEF—then, friends, it turns out that we can (and it appears that we had) become subject to the same laws that you are.

So, guess what? Even though all the hostages had been rescued, and all the bad guys subdued, I was now about to be fucking indicted for depriving SECNAV's stupid, pistol-waving NIS bodyguard of his goddamn civil rights, by depriving him of his goddamn life.

And that was the good news. The bad news was that the nine enlisted men who'd stormed the plane with me were to be charged under the goddamn RICO laws (those are the Racketeering Influenced Corrupt Organizations statutes), the same ones designed to be used against organized crime. How, you ask? Well, because they were about to be charged with conspiracy. They'd conspired against the dead NIS agent because they didn't stop me from killing the son of a bitch. They were, I read, to be indicted as accessories to murder.

The Navy was not going to protect them, either. Because they were being charged by the same government they served, they'd have to hire their own defense attorneys, at $500 an hour. Fat fucking chance of that. So they'd be defended by a bunch of overworked public defender types, which means they'd go down. And if that happened, they'd lose their rank, their retirements—not to mention their freedom. Their whole lives were about to be forfeited, because of me.

Let me explain what was going on here. These sorts of charges—most of 'em anyway—were bullshit. But they were exactly the blood-and-guts stuff that makes great reading in the newspapers. And what happens in cases such as this one is that the prosecution—in this case, NIS—leaks one nasty allegation after another, in a series of drip-drip-drips. And by the end of two months, my men and I would be seen as a bunch of child-molesting, mad-dog serial killers. The facts would have nothing to do with the case. Neither would truth. And meanwhile, my investigation into the root causes behind the Key West fiasco would be sidetracked.

No—better to attack than parry. So, instead of trying to explain myself, I looked evenly over at General Harrington, drained my Bombay, set the glass down on its coaster with an appropriate, roguish thwock, and said, "Okay, now that you've got my attention, what is it you want?"

He looked at me over the top of his glasses. "Just your help, Dick."

That struck me as odd.

"It's complicated," he said. "But the bottom line is that I've been waiting for someone just like you to come along. Come with me."

I followed him out of the living room, down a narrow passageway past a galley kitchen, past the dining-room doors, to a small office that looked out on a tiny brick patio and English garden. General Harrington opened a small document safe that had a DIA inventory control number engraved on its front, placed my file inside, and retrieved another orange-tabbed folder.

"Read this," he said.

He handed me a thin, blue-tabbed confidential monograph from the Army inspector general concerning a huge discrepancy between the number of weapons and ordnance in the military's current inventory, and the number it could actually lay its hands on. More than ten thousand fully automatic M-16, CAR-15s, and 633HB assault rifles were missing. So were twenty-five thousand grenades of various types, three million rounds of .223, 9mm, and .308 ammunition, and several hundred sniper rifles. Claymores, detonators, and C-4 plastic explosive had also been stolen.

I already knew that ADAM had been using stolen USG weapons. But the numbers I saw here were surprising. I went back and read them again. The news was still bad.

After I finished, Harrington handed me two single sheets of paper. The first was a top secret code-word note, handwritten on the buff-colored, four-starred, engraved letterhead of the Chairman of the Joint Chiefs of Staff:

CHAIRMAN OF THE JOINT CHIEFS OF STAFF

WASHINGTON, D. C. 20318-9999

TOP SECRET

WAYFARER

PRIEST—

READ ENCLOSED PAGES.

TAKE CARE OF THE PROBLEM—SOONEST.

METHODOLOGY UNIMPORTANT, RESULTS CRITICAL.

Gunny

TOP SECRET

WAYFARER

"Gunny" was the informal, first-name signature of the current Chairman of the Joint Chiefs of Staff, General A. G. Barrett, USMC. Unlike many of his predecessors, Gunny Barrett had a close personal relationship with his commander in chief. The JCS Chairman was a regular jogging companion and golf partner to the president. In fact, according to the newspapers, the CINC saw more of A. G. Barrett, General, USMC, than he did the head of the CIA, or the secretary of defense—and their relationship had gone far beyond a professional one. If the Priest worked for Gunny, then he had the kind of clout that comes straight from the Oval Orifice.

Thanks to Wonder's arthroscopic B and E, I had seen the second sheet before. It was a photocopy of a portion of a classified fax from the FBI Miami field office to the counterterrorism intelligence unit, at headquarters. It was a portion of the inventory of all the belongings taken from the hijackers of Flight 1252. Halfway down the list was the LAW I had stripped from the tango under the jet's tail. A handwritten notation next to the weapon's serial number read "Lincoln Weapons Stowage Depot—St. Louis." A second LAW was also listed just below it. According to a note in the margin, it had been taken from an armory in Rhode Island. The rest of the sheet had been blacked out. But I knew what was underneath: a note that the tangos' Colt 633HB submachine gun serial numbers had also been checked, and that two had been stolen from the SEAL Team Four weapons locker at the Naval Special Warfare Command in Little Creek, Virginia, two came from an arms stowage depot outside Baltimore, and the rest were from an Air Force Reserve security unit in Florida.

"You have a big problem—and I have a big problem," General Harrington said. "But between us, we may be able to find a common solution."

I kept a poker face while Major General Harrington threw my big Br'er Slovak behind right back into the briar patch.

He was, no doubt, a terrific and dangerous poker player, because he knew how to bluff. But I've been down that road before, too. So, when he showed me FBI files and DOD E-mail, I looked surprised, even though I'd read them all before. I even learned a lot from reading them again—learned, because the Priest had redacted them artfully. See, intelligence is often discerned not from what you are shown, but from what you are not shown.

An example? Okay. General Harrington had erased all evidence of FBI illegality. These were not the shredded black-bag memos I'd seen. Moreover, any suggestions that the Bureau might have been compromised had been redacted, too. That told me he was, at the very least, sharing intelligence with them. Which then told me I'd have to filter what I told *him.*

He'd kept many of the references to the Zulu Gangsta Princes, to Imam el-Yassin, and to LC Strawhouse. That told me his inquiry pointed toward the Texas billionaire. Fine: it was a direction in which I'd been headed, too.

He had solid background on the Zulu Gangsta Princes. That was good. I hadn't seen much of this information before, and the Princes' connection with ADAM might be significant. So might ADAM's relationship with an imam who advocated war against the United States.

While I was happy with what I read, there were also some niggling questions that were left unanswered. The material on LC Strawhouse was little more than I had been able to uncover using unclassified sources. Given the Priest's obvious connections and position, that was a bit curious.

You see, I knew from reading *Forbes* that Strawhouse hired only ex-generals and ex-admirals to run his companies, so there might be an ulterior motive here. Maybe LC had already offered the Priest a job after he retired—or, more ominously, he'd offered him one *before* he retired. It had happened before. Indeed, perhaps S. J. Harrington, Major General, USA, had a buddy or two already working for the California billionaire.

Finding out the truth would take more research on my part—and in the meanwhile, I would be careful about what I did and said within the Priest's earshot. I have been in this business for too long to believe in coincidence.

Within an hour, I came to realize why he'd been nicknamed the Priest. When I asked (he answered in such a beautifully offhanded manner that it had to be a studied move) he said it was because his initials were SJ, the same as the Society of Jesus, the Jesuitical order that had inculcated him in philosophy and logic at Georgetown University.

Maybe. I would have thought it was because he had the ability to make a true believer, even out of an apostate like me.

He must have been a hell of an intelligence officer because he was goddamn persuasive on behalf of Mother Army Church. The Priest's sermon was simple. He wanted me and my men to work for him. Our objective would be to find out who the hell was stealing the military's goodies and help take them down. He doubted that the job would take longer than a couple of months, during which time we'd be detailed to DIA—well, sort of detailed.

His homily continued: our mission was to be a Priority One. It was being undertaken at the personal behest, and under the protection, of the Chairman of the Joint Chiefs of Staff. The chain of command was magnificent in its catholic austerity. The Priest was the Chairman's acolyte; I was the Priest's altar boy. That ecumenical chain of command, he promised, overrode anything the secretary of the navy, the Justice Department—or any other authority—might want to do to me or to my men. No matter that we were about to be indicted for murder—he said he could fix it.

But what about afterward, your fixerdom? Do my guys still get hog-tied then deep fried?

Ah, the Priest continued, if things went well he would guarantee that the Navy and the Department of Justice would grant us all complete absolution for the sins of body, mind, and soul we had committed in Key West. The slate would be wiped clean.

That's when I realized he was speaking for the White House. I'd seen the clue—the handwritten note from Gunny Barrett—but the significance of that heavy, engraved stationary hadn't seeped through my thick skull until now.

It has been said that the best time to get a great deal from the government is before you sign anything. And since I realized that my men and I could still be harassed by the legal system—that we could be made to shell out hundreds of thousands of dollars to defend ourselves against specious charges—this was the time to fixee-fixee.

Clean slate forever, I asked? Deep-six all the charges stemming from Key West? Nothing in our records? No hidden agendas?

Absolutely, positively, 100 percent clean, pledged the Priest. Better than if you'd come from confession with the pope.

And do I get a copy of that piece of paper? Absolutely, said the Priest. Copy for the files. This is all on the up-and-up, after all.

Well, that being the case, I decided I'd be silly not to play along. After all, the Priest's goals and mine were similar. We both wanted to put the bad guys down. And until I knew he could be trusted, when it came time for a visit to the confessional I'd deal with this priest the same way I'd dealt with all those others back at St. Ladislaus Church in New Brunswick when I was an evil-minded, teenaged boychik, thinking impure thoughts and doing impure deeds—I'd lie through my teeth.

We sandbagged Pinky da Turd in the Chairman's office. When he came through the ornate wood door I was sitting behind the Chairman's antique desk in a huge, black leather high-backed judge's chair—the same one used by Bill Crowe, Colin Powell, and John Shalikashvili. The Chairman's flag, the Marine Corps flag, and the Stars and Bars were arrayed behind me. I was turned out in dress blues with all my ribbons. The Priest was standing behind my right shoulder. The Chairman, General A. G. "Gunny" Barrett—the first Marine four-star ever to be appointed—was behind my left. General Tom Crocker, the lanky former West Point wide receiver who was deputy chairman and Gunny Barrett's chief confidante, stood dead center.

The secretary had buzzed a warning, so we knew the Pinkster was coming. He strode into the office as if he was about to get a medal. He was two yards from the desk when he actually perceived our living tableau.

I caught his eye. "Yo—Pinky, guess who?"

In the great Tom and Jerry cartoons of the forties and fifties, whenever Tom the cat saw something absolutely horrifying, his eyeballs would look as if they were on springs—they'd go *boy-oy-oy-oy-oy-inng,* right out of their sockets. Well, that's exactly what happened when Pinky saw me.

I thought the son of a bitch was going to have a heart attack. He went absolutely livid. Then he went completely sallow. His hair, which has a remarkable tendency to cowlick at times of stress, did a full Dagwood Bumpstead. Pinky clutched his throat, made a braying sound that resembled "Wha-wha-wha?" then he turned and started running for the door.

The Priest stopped him in midstride. "Come in, Rear Admiral Prescott. Have a seat." He pointed at an uncomfortable, battleship gray metal-framed straight-back chair we'd had brought to the Chairman's office especially for Pinky's scrawny behind.

Pinky stopped in his tracks. He turned. I could see him counting stars—the Priest's two stars, General Crocker's four, and the Chairman's four. That made ten stars to Pinky's two. His whole body sagged. It was as if his bones had turned to Jell-O. He gritted his teeth—which must have been painful, because his jaw was wired—and then he trudged back and parked his bony butt exactly where the Priest had indicated.

I rose, and Chairman Barrett assumed his rightful place. "Thanks for coming, Tom," he said, flicking an index finger at Crocker as if he was pointing a Colt 1911.

Crocker cut for the door. "Nada, Gunny. I'll let you people get down to business." He stuck his thumb in the Priest's direction and smiled. "Besides, Major General Harrington here says this is need-to-know business, and when the Priest insists I don't have any need to know, I don't wanna know—because then he'd have to kill me."

The Chairman waited until his deputy had left. Then he fixed a steely eye on Pinky Prescott. He didn't say a word. He let Pinky sit there and stew for a full ninety seconds. If you don't think that's a long time, try timing it right now. If you don't want to take the time, then take my word for it. Believe me, it is a long pause, especially when the fucking Chairman of the Joint Chiefs is staring you down as only an angry Marine general can stare.

Finally, he spoke. "Rear Admiral Prescott," he said, underlining the word rear, "Major General Harrington and I would like to borrow Captain Marcinko and put him to work for us on an assignment of some considerable sensitivity and importance. Would that be all right with you, Rear Admiral?"

Pinky nodded in the affirmative.

"I can't hear you, Rear Admiral Prescott," said the Chairman, doing a real passable imitation of a Parris Island boot camp drill instructor.

"Yes, sir," said Pinky.

"I can't *hear* you, Rear Admiral Prescott," the Chairman said again, making Pinky repeat himself, too.

"And I need nine of Captain Marcinko's enlisted SEALs as well. Is that a problem for you, Rear Admiral?"

Pinky was actually sweating. His hair was now completely messed up. "No, sir," he said loudly and clearly through his wired jaw.

He must have said it loudly and clearly enough this time, because the Chairman didn't make him repeat himself again.

"Now, Rear Admiral Prescott," Chairman Barrett said, "is there anything you'd like to know about Captain Marcinko's assignment?"

"Well, I'd—" Pinky began.

The Chairman cut him off. "I don't think you want to know anything, Rear Admiral. What do you think, Major General Harrington?"

The Priest shook his head. "I don't think Rear Admiral Prescott has to concern himself with the particulars of Captain Marcinko's new assignment, sir. He probably has more important things to do than bother with bureaucratic minutiae emanating from this office." He smiled. "Isn't that right, Rear Admiral?"

"Well, n-n-no—" Pinky began. I was delighted to see that he still had his stutter. Some things should never change, and that was one of them.

General Barrett cut Pinky off. " 'No need to deal with minutiae.' Quite correct, Major General Harrington." The Chairman paused and quite transfixed Pinky with an ominous glare. The asshole looked like a fucking jacklighted deer sitting there.

The JCS Chairman's lip curled malevolently and he inclined his body toward Pinky's. "What I am saying, Rear Admiral Prescott, is that you will not interfere. You will not talk about this. You will treat this as a code-word sensitive matter. In fact, Rear Admiral Prescott, you look somewhat peaked right now. Perhaps the next month or so would be a wonderful time for you to take your family and go off on a camping excursion. Someplace where there are no phones or faxes."

"B-but," Pinky b-began.

"Take the fucking vacation," Gunny Barrett said. "If you don't, and if you meddle in this assignment I have for Captain Marcinko, you will be a very, very sorry person."

He gave Pinky an offhanded salute. "That will be all, Rear Admiral Prescott." The Chairman swiveled his chair away. "Dismissed," he said.

Chapter 7

WITH PINKY OUT OF MY PONYTAIL FOR THE NEXT MONTH, I ASSEMBLED my troops, then the Priest led us all back to his office at DIA to deal with paperwork. He had a corner suite on the fourteenth floor, which gave him a panoramic view of the whole national capital area from Catholic University and the Anacostia River on the east, to the U.S. Capitol, the mall, the White House, and all the memorials. To the right of the doorway, where the room number and section-slash-department placard are normally posted, there was a small white-on-blue printed sign that read NDBBM.

When I asked what it meant, the Priest said, in all seriousness, "Nobody's Damn Business But Mine."

The doors were equipped with electronic digital and hand-print-analysis lock systems. You could break into them, *if* you had a computer, a digitally correct bogus palm print with accurate body temperature—and a couple of uninterrupted hours in which to play with the dial. Then I noted the floor sensors, passive monitors, and heat detectors. While nothing is impossible, I decided that breaking into the Priest's offices would be a nasty, nasty chore.

Inside, we walked up three steps into his office proper—that meant the floor had been insulated and a vacuum air-void installed so it could not be bugged. I looked around casually and saw that the windows were made of triple-paned glass, with white-sound pipes between the two outer panes to foil electronic eavesdropping. I'd seen the same type of curtains that framed the Priest's windows before, too—in a bug-proof bubble room inside the U.S. embassy in Moscow. They were made of a space-age fabric that made them impervious to infrared and laser penetrations. I was impressed. Despite the million-buck view of Washington, we were sitting in a state-of-the-art bug-proof room that made the SCIFs back at the Pentagon—the acronym stands for Special Classified Intelligence Facilities—as leaky as old mobile homes.

The Priest settled behind his desk, checked his messages, and leafed through the half dozen pages that had come across his secure fax. He pointed us toward the small, comfortable settee on the far wall, the two armchairs, and the four metal straightbacks that had been left by the door. "Coffee?"

"Sure."

He pressed a buzzer on the phone console twice rapidly, paused, then repeated the signal. Thirty seconds later, an Air Force staff captain carrying a luncheonette-size tray with eleven blue-and-white DIA mugs, eleven spoons, a carafe of coffee, a bowl of sugar, and a pitcher of milk came through the door, set the tray on the coffee table in front of me, poured the Priest a mugful, topped it off with milk, stirred thrice, placed it gently atop an antique Portuguese tile that sat on the starboard side of the general's desk, then withdrew as efficiently and quietly as any proper Brit butler. God bless Air Farce staff—they *are* good for something after all.

I waited until my guys had all served themselves, then I poured myself a mug and sipped. It was good coffee—the kind of rich, smoky stuff that's brewed from expensive beans. This guy had style. I saluted the Priest with my mug. "Thanks."

"Time to get down to business." The Priest withdrew a thick sheaf of papers from a two-drawer, fireproof safe that sat behind his desk, and laid them out one by one so that we could inscribe, sign, and initial them paragraph by paragraph, page by page.

"Think of this as if you were joining a religious order," he said, a sardonic smile on his face.

I used to be an altar boy and I know the routine. So I dipped my finger in blood and took the fucking vow of silence. Then I put a dollar sign next to the fucking vow of poverty. I signed the fucking vow of chastity with a pecker-track, and put my thumbprint at the bottom of a document that warned me to think only pure thoughts in order to perform God's work on earth.

The last sheet was interesting—and brought back a lot of memories. What I did, essentially, was to sign myself on indefinite release from the Navy and transmogrify my nasty Slovak SEAL butt into a private, civilian-type person who had no overt tie to the military, the government, or anything official while simultaneously promising to obey, observe, and glorify all the manifold commandments of the Priest's somewhat Jesuitical intelligence-gathering order.

I've done this sort of thing before—but not quite so totally. As CO of SEAL Team Six, I actually transferred my entire command out of the Navy. See, the Navy still denies that there is a SEAL Team Six. To give that denial credibility, we were listed on the books as civilian employees of a MARESFAC, or MArine RESearch FACility. We all had, in fact, signed papers removing ourselves from the Navy's books and placing ourselves in MARESFAC. But since SEAL Team Six was a clandestine, not a covert, unit, we still got USG checks—just not from the Department of the Navy.

The Priest was going a few steps further. We were essentially being sheep-dipped, the way SEALs who go to work for Christians in Action are sheep-dipped out of the Navy and into a spooky netherworld.

We, too, were going to disappear from the Navy. We'd be run the same way DIA runs its network of deep-cover agents all over the world—no link to the government at all. Our code-word designation would be Task Force Blue. We would all be covert operators.

Task Force Blue. I'd seen the name before. That was the TFB mentioned in the FBI's electronically shredded memos. Which meant the project had been in the works for a while.

I pored over the papers in front of me. The fact that we were being sheep-dipped was good—and it was bad. Why the yin-yang? Well, first of all, there are laws that prevent the military from engaging in anything that might resemble actions taken against Americans, unless nuclear weapons, or CW/BW weapons are involved. Yeah—I know that in those Hollywood thrillers you often see Delta Force or SEALs doing the dirty dance against domestic bad guys. But that's so much bullshit. Fact: the Posse Comitatus laws make it illegal for me to dismember dirty dudes domestically. So by removing us from the books, the Priest was, in effect, giving me a hunting license.

Second, a thorough sheep-dipping would prevent the kind of

security leaks the FBI was currently experiencing, and the kind of corridor gossip that always eventually finds its way into the public media. DIA has run covert networks and programs for years without any embarrassing disclosures. It has been successful because it keeps its secrets. One way to do that is to make sure there is absolute deniability.

The Priest was emphatic about security: there would be no ties to the military. None. No calls to old friends at the Pentagon asking for favors. No master chiefs slipping their old pal Mr. Rick any goodies. No playing with switches and dials at satellite receiving stations.

Our single, authorized POC (Point Of Contact) would be with the Priest. Communication would be handled through a special cellular phone, on a special number, with code words. Contact would be only when necessary, or appropriate. In essence we would be on our own: jumping blind with no backup.

His decision was just fine with me—in fact, I prefer to operate on my own. Solo flight is perhaps the most effective way to control leaks and assure the safety of me and my men.

That was on the up side. The down side was that cutting my DOD umbilical cord removed us from the SEAL world—and the support networks within it. I was uneasy about that. There'd be no assistance from old friends at the Pentagon; no quiet help from my Fifth Column of SpecWarriors scattered all over the world; no support from the Safety Net of chiefs I've spent so many years building up. It also meant that, unless we begged, borrowed, or stole, we'd be forced to make do with whatever we could buy off the shelf in terms of equipment, weapons, and other supplies. No problem there—I'd done much the same when I first equipped SEAL Team Six, and when Green Team took off on its transcontinental odyssey from London to Afghanistan and back, we stole what we needed from POMCUS (Prepositioned Outside Military Custody of the United States) caches in Germany, and bought the rest.

But covert has its risks, too. Let me list just a few:

- *Item.* I am a convicted felon. As a Navy captain, that fact doesn't matter. Overseas, who gives a rusty you-know-what. But as a civilian, I cannot possess a firearm. And what if I had to carry one whilst on this merry assignment? The answer: I would be goatfucked if I was caught, because there was no one to whom I could run and cry, "Daddy, daddy, come save my ass."

- *Item.* In the military, I am allowed to do the things I like to do best—e.g., kill, maim, loot, pillage, and burn with no (or few) repercussions. As a civilian, these activities are generally frowned upon by the populace in general, and law enforcement in particular. In my current assignment, the Priest said, I could do whatever I could get away with—just so long as I didn't get caught.

  That, too, was troublesome. At SEAL Team Six, we'd had paperwork that allowed us to train—although not to operate—in-country. When the local sheriff showed up hot and bothered because there was a bunch of armed and dangerous dirtbags in his jurisdiction, I had a walletful of proper credentials. If he still wasn't satisfied, there was a toll-free number in Washington he could call and be told by someone wearing stars that I was as kosher as an Essex Street, New Yawk, dill pickle.

  My current status allowed me nothing like that. If caught, it was my ass that would get pickled. That's the way things are when you're covert. Just ask any NOC—Non-Official Cover—CIA operator how it feels to be dangling out there all alone. It don't feel good, believe me.
- *Item.* As CO of SEAL Team Six, Red Cell, and Green Team, I had access to your taxpayer dollars—as many as I needed to get the job done. That meant buying the best equipment I could find, obtaining the latest communications devices, weapons, and other goodies. Task Force Blue was for all intents on its own. Oh, the Priest promised I'd have access to a small cache of cash—but I knew it would be nothing close to what I'd need to mount any kind of meaningful operation. What the hell did he want me to do—rob a bank? I asked and he gave me the kind of look that told me such acts might not go beyond the realm of possibility.

And, there was the usual, niggling doubt that tickled the skeptical meter that hangs in the back end of my brain. What if this was all one big humongous clusterfuck and I was being—yet again—set up by the powers that be, so that they could put me and my guys behind bars, and be rid of us once and for all.

It was a possibility. Face it—so far as the Priest knew, he was holding all the cards. He could cast me out into the big, bad world, then cut the line and watch me disappear for good.

That was all on the one hand, and it made a lot of sense, too. But, on the other hand, I'd seen the Chairman's note. And the Chairman had slammed Pinky nice and hard, and the Priest certainly seemed to have the clout at Justice to get the putative indictments quashed. Moreover, the problem was real, the threat was unmistakable—and besides, what's life *sans* challenge?

So I signed, and initialed, and pecker-tracked my life away while the Priest looked on, happy as Torquemada in his nasty basement, while his newest converts joined a new, blue brotherhood.

I called a head-shed at Germaine's, a pan-Asian restaurant in upper Georgetown, run by a former Marvin (that's what we used to call our ARVN, or Army of the Republic of Vietnam, allies) parachute nurse named (appropriately enough) Germaine. I needed a good plate of *tom ram Nha Trang*—Nha Trang-style shrimp—to clear my brain. Besides, Germaine knows me well enough to give me and my guys a lot of elbow room when we need a quiet place to collude, conspire, and cogitate. The way she runs her restaurant—and the way she slaps me around—reminds me of all my favorite bistro owners, from Mama Mascalzone out in Huntington Beach, California, right back to Old Man Gussy, who ran a lunch counter just around the corner from the Rutger's campus when I was a hairy-palmed kid in New Brunswick, New Joyzey.

We left the Priest's sanctum singly and made our way to upper Georgetown. I parked back on Thirty-seventh Street, checked my six a couple of times, then sneaked up the steel back stairs, picked the fire door lock, and skulked through the storeroom, threading my way between stacks of five-gallon cans of cooking oil and hundred-pound bags of rice. I hung a left and slipped through the steamy, bustling kitchen (plucking a bottle of Hue Vietnamese beer from the cooler behind the permanently simmering kettles of beef and chicken stock that form the basis for so much of Germaine's wonderful cooking). Then I came through the swinging service door using a waiter named Huong as cover, and jumped Germaine from behind, sweeping her up off the floor in a big bear hug as she worked unsuspectingly on the big, chock-full reservation book.

It is impossible to surprise a parachute nurse. She knew exactly who it was. "Still coming through the back door, huh, Dick—just like when you surprised Mr. Charlie on Ilo-Ilo Island and give him big headache."

She dug an elbow expertly into my ribs—for a woman just over five feet tall she packs a hell of a punch—then swiveled neatly, caught my left wrist, and turned it inward into an effective come-along.

She gave me a wonderful, warm smile, patted my cheek, and applied just enough pressure to make me wince. "Now, please,

Dick, follow me to the bar. I have several of your friends here waiting for you and they're beginning to cause a disturbance."

We took a big table in the back room. Germaine kept the other customers far enough away so that we could get our talking done in private.

We finished off big bowls of *pho*—Hanoi beef soup laced with the Vietnamese fermented fish sauce called *nuoc mam,* hot peppers, spicy basil leaves, and fresh lime wedges. Then we moved on to *tom*—shrimp. We had it Nha Trang style, and also *nuong voi bun*—grilled Saigon-style with noodles. To clear our palates, there were huge plates of shredded green papaya with beef and hot Thai pepper, and mango salad made of shrimp, mangoes, lime and—you guessed it—vast quantities of Thai red peppers. Face it, gentle reader, if you're not sweating, you're not eating, and Germaine's is the best place in Washington to do both.

I watched paternally as my nine shoot-and-looters worked their chopsticks and drained their brewskis. If you read their fitreps, you'd think they were unruly, tumultuous scum who had no respect for officers—or anyone else. Well, they *were* unruly—if they didn't respect the officers they worked for. They did look like unkempt dirtbags—but in the field, the dirtbag look is the sort of camouflage that helps keep a man alive. No—these irreverent, playful, and dangerous Frogs were exactly the kinds of sailors I always look for when I put my units together.

Doc Tremblay and I have known each other since Christ was a mess cook. We've hopped and popped, shooted and looted, maimed, raped, pillaged, and burned together all over the globe. Doc was about six months short of finishing up a two-year, government-sponsored tour in Egypt when someone from the ambassador's office leaked the fact that he might have been a part of the extraction and subsequent death of a tango named Mahmoud Azziz abu Yasin—yeah, the one from *Green Team*—to the Egyptian Foreign Ministry. Anyway, the Egyptians declared him persona non grata, he lacked an assignment, and I snatched him up just in time for our little Key West fiasco. Ain't life grand?

I don't have to tell you about Stevie Wonder—not, that is, if you've read *Red Cell* and *Green Team.* In case you haven't, he's known as Stevie Wonder (his real name is neither Stevie nor Wonder) because he wears opaque, wraparound shooting glasses, and he swivels his head left-right-left, right-left-right, in a passable imitation of—you guessed it—Stevie Wonder. He's not a SEAL—he's a former member of Uncle Sam's Misguided Children (that's USMC), who enlisted in the Navy a few years back. But he is as tough and resilient as any SEAL in the world—and smarter than 99 percent of 'em. There are lots of operators who can jump and dive and patrol when ordered. There are fewer and fewer these days who live to kill. Wonder is one of them—a true hunter. Indeed, Stevie'd killed more Japs than anyone in the room except Doc and me.

The senior chief I call Nasty Nicky Grundle is about the size of an NFL linebacker, and twice as mean. I selected Nasty for SEAL Team Six when he was a young, energetic pussy-chaser at SEAL Team Four. He and I lost touch for a while, but I got him back when we reconstituted the Naval Security Coordination Team to hunt for the stolen nuclear Tomahawk missiles we wrote about in *Red Cell*.

Sitting next to Nasty was Duck Foot Dewey. Allen Dewey is a short, barrel-chested farmboy from the waterfowl marshes of Maryland's Eastern Shore. He won his spurs in Iraq, where he'd been attached to SEAL Team Five. His assignment was to infiltrate Kuwait City and bring communications equipment like cellular phones and video cameras, intelligence materials, and ordnance for booby traps to the Kuwaiti resistance. In fact, Duck Foot is the only petty officer third class who holds the Exalted Order of the Eastern Star, the highest military decoration the Amir of Kuwait can bestow.

Next to Duck Foot, Cherry Enders worked his chopsticks on a big bowl of *muc xao ha-long*—that's Vietnamese for spicy calamari cooked with leeks and tomatoes. He'd added three tablespoons of Germaine's best chopped fresh green chilis to the plate because he, like I, believes that if you're not sweating, you're not eating. Cherry (nicknamed for the tattoo on his left tit) was the youngest sailor who'd ever been selected for SEAL Team Six—he was six weeks past nineteen at the time. Cherry had been out of action for about a year. He'd taken a round during our sneak-and-peek of Grant Griffith's office in Beverly Hills and the damn wound had taken a long time to heal. In the meanwhile, he'd gone to mountaineering school—he could scamper up sheer rock walls or apartment houses better than Duck Foot, Half Pint, or Nasty these days.

Across from Cherry sat Half Pint Harris, his concussion just a dim memory in that hard little head of his. Half Pint's one of those five-foot-four squidges who believes he can slam-dunk a basketball —and does, out of sheer will to succeed. Aside from making us money on the court, he also speaks fluent German, passable French, and a smattering of Spanish, he can fix just about anything mechanical he ever comes across, and there's not a building anywhere he can't break into, being (as he is) a graduate of the Eddie the Burglar School of Lockpicking and Alarm Silencing.

For the last fifteen years, Half Pint's played Mutt to "Piccolo" Mead's Jeff. The Pick is the tall, thin drink of water who was assigned as Half Pint's swim buddy at BUD/S—that's Basic Underwater Demolition/SEAL training—by a master chief with no sense of humor. Well, doom on the chief, because they've been inseparable ever since.

Rodent is another squidge of a SEAL. He's served with SEAL Teams One and Two, SDV—for Swimmer Delivery Vehicle—Unit One, and a Special Boat Unit during the Gulf War. Rodent is a master scrounger—a real pack rat—whose commanding officers never seemed to appreciate his . . . irreverence. Well, irreverence is a quality I look for in my men, so since *Green Team,* he's been with me. In fact, let me digress for a minute or two so I can tell you why I choose the men I choose.

The godfather of SEALs, Roy Boehm, used to tell me that he'd rather get his men from the brig than from anywhere else. "Look, asshole," he used to growl at me affectionately, "if you can motivate a man others call a loser, he'll follow you to hell and back if you ask him to. Isn't that the kind of man o' warsman you want with you?"

I took Roy's tutelage to heart. I have by and large lived by that philosophy and it has served me well. When I form units—something I've done three times over my career, with SEAL Team Six, Red Cell, and Green Team—I don't look for men who live by the book. I look for men with a little larceny in their hearts; men who think for themselves, who are willing to take risks—and will suffer the consequences in silence if they, or I, fuck up.

What, after all, is the job of a SEAL? It is—when you come down to it—to annihilate, destroy, obliterate, kill, maim, and terminate. Sure, we sneak and peek. Sure, we chart harbors and clear the way for amphibious landings. Yes, we spot targets, gather intelligence, and check tankers for contraband. But that's not why we exist. We were created by Roy Boehm as guerrilla warriors who could hit from the sea, land, or air in order to counter the

Communist-inspired insurgencies that President John Kennedy faced in the early sixties. He created us to be warriors—killers—and that is how we will stand or fall.

These days, SEALs don't get to be warriors very often. In fact, they are most often used as an extension of the State Department, where they teach Haitian cops to be polite, show Salvadorans how to conduct road blocks without killing anybody, run after cocaine smugglers in Peru and Bolivia, or train a professional presidential bodyguard corps in Turkey or Indonesia. Shit, in Turkey they were pulled off bodyguard training so they could go help locate earthquake victims.

Well, so far as I'm concerned, if you want to train cops in San Salvador, join the Agency for International Development. If you want to chase cocaine smugglers in the Andes, apply to the DEA. And if you want to deploy as a rescue worker, become a goddamn Boy Scout.

When I created SEAL Team Six and brought Naval Special Warfare (kicking and screaming, I might add) into the world of counterterrorism, I followed the Roy Boehm dictum again. I looked for men who could shoot to kill without saying "May I?" So, instead of recruiting the able but by-the-book Sailors of the Year who were offered to me, I hunted through stacks of officer fitness reports and enlisted evaluation sheets until I found the rogues—evil-minded, nasty-boy, loot-pillage-rape-and-burn shooters who I knew would get the job done no matter what the consequences, and follow me into hell if that's where I led them. And guess what—we went to several places that made hell sound pretty good. But we got the job done. And we came back safely. Endeth the sermon.

Gator Shepard was one of the few exceptions to my dirtbag recruiting habit. But then, Gator came to the Teams through the back door. He's a former Special Weapons Teamer from the Broward County, Florida, sheriff's office who was bored with drug busts and barricades. So he enlisted in the Navy at the age of twenty-five and went through BUD/S at the age of thirty—that's Methuselah old, in case you were wondering—and made it by the graying hair on his balls. He's a buzz-topped, lean, mean motherfucker—one of those assholes who doesn't have more than about one percent body fat—and he loves his HK MP5K-PDW (that's his Heckler & Koch MP5K caliber 9mm submachine gun Personal Defense Weapon for you nonweapons aficionados out there) more than he loves anything else except his Miller GDB—

that's his Genuine Draft Beer—and all the ladies he can fondle. He's good with it, too—no, that's his *HK* I'm talking about. God, you readers all have dirty minds.

Anyhow, Gator can shoot a quarter-size pattern at thirty yards, day or night, hung over, or hung out. He's a little clean-cut for my taste, and he hasn't had the kind of military combat experience folks like Rodent or Wonder have had. But hell, a clean-cut guerrilla can infiltrate places a dirtbag can't go. And, if serving high-risk warrants to Colombian drug dealers and outlaw bikers, or hopand-popping escaped killers isn't the same as going over the rail, I don't know what the hell is.

My only problem with Gator is—as you have seen—he keeps wanting to shout, "Stop—police!" at bad guys when he should just shoot the motherfuckers dead and warn them later. He'll learn, or I'm going to boot his ass into next week.

They already knew that our situation wasn't good—hell, they'd only had to read the papers they'd signed up in NDBBM to know we were out in the cold—operating on our own, *sans* backup, *sans* even the support of that informal safety net of chiefs I'd spent so many years building up.

"What's your point, Skipper?" Cherry wanted to know. "Look—we're fucking SEALs. We're supposed to operate on our own."

"Besides," said Wonder, "they're gonna goatfuck us anyway, sooner or later. What the hell do we have to lose?"

"You're forgetting the most important element of this whole exercise, Captain Dickhead, sir," Doc Tremblay said in his broad New England drawl.

He drained the last of his twenty-two-ounce bottle of Asahi Dry, slapped it on the table loud enough to draw attention from a waiter and signal for a refill, then looked us all in the eyes. "Hey—let's take for granite the motherfuckers are trying to ambush us. Okay—so what? That means our only possible fucking choice is attack. We go balls to the wall—hit 'em before they hit us."

I just love it when he talks dirty. He was absolutely right, of course. It was time to take the initiative. As Roy Boehm, the godfather of all SEALs would say, it was time to fuck the fucking fuckers, whoever they were.

I decided that we'd HQ at the Manor. So after we left Germaine's we convoyed out and set up shop. I can bunk up to twenty without a problem, and there's always enough beer on hand for an entire company of infantry—or a platoon of SEALs.

Saturday morning we got down to work. I had the boys read every page we had skimmed from Intelink. While they read, Stevie Wonder made music with his keyboard.

Guess what? In the last seventy-two or so hours, there had been eight requests for information about LC Strawhouse, the ADAM Group, and/or Richard (NMN) Marcinko. That gave us eight new account and password codes to use.

Wonder printed them out. Then he asked the computer to backtrack the requests, so we could see what had been asked for.

The first had been for the FBI afteraction report from Key West.

Another had been a detailed request for all military operations relating to the ADAM Group.

The third was a probe checking to see who had asked for information about LC Strawhouse.

And five were directed at finding out about me—where I worked, who I worked for, what my most recent fitness reports said, and what my current assignment was.

People were nosing around.

I set my coffee down on the computer table. "Can we trace these queries?"

Instead of answering, Wonder removed the offending mug. "Liquids and computers don't go together," he said, sounding very much like my third-grade teacher, Miss Shoemaker, for comfort. Miss Shoemaker used to rap my knuckles with a thick wooden ruler, and I looked around to make sure that Wonder had no similar weapon within reach.

Instead of a knuckle rap, Wonder gave me a dirty look. "Go busy yourself elsewhere and let a man work." I know when I'm not wanted, so I left him to his tapping and typing while I stripped down and went outside for a bracing workout on the weight pile.

Half an hour later, he appeared with a single page of printout. "You'll just love this," he said.

I rolled off the bench, found my half glasses, and perused.

The query on LC Strawhouse had emanated from JSOC—the Joint Special Operations Command at Fort Bragg. That made no sense to me. JSOC is not tasked with any domestic missions—certainly not political ones.

The ADAM probe originated at DIA. That made no sense either, because I knew that DIA already had the FBI materials on file.

And what about me? Every one of the requests for information about Marcinko, Richard, had come through the Special Operations Command at MacDill Air Force Base in Tampa. They had been made by Vice Admiral G. Edward Emu, SOC's vice chief of staff, and the nation's highest-ranking SEAL.

I found that *real* surprising. Why? Because Eddie Emu knows all about me—we've been at loggerheads for years. As ensign G. Edward Emu, he tried to get me court-martialed. Just over a year ago, he tried to get my SEAL Team Six mementos removed from the UDT/SEAL museum in Fort Pierce, Florida, because he believes that I am not a "proper" sort of SEAL.

Thus, it made absolutely no sense for Eddie to start a computer search for my whereabouts, my assignments, or my fitreps—because he had all that information right in his files.

I told all of this to Wonder, who said, "That's what I figured, too. So, my eval is that somebody's using Admiral Emu's passwords, just the way I am."

It made sense to me. But who was tapping into Intelink? Could we trace the calls coming in?

Wonder frowned. "Not really," he said, "unless we have access to phone lines and phone company equipment." Which we did not have—yet. "It can be done, but it's gonna take me a few hours to play."

Time? He needed time? We had a lot of that. Besides, we knew someone out there was sniffing. That was helpful. It would be more helpful to find out who.

I pumped some more iron, then took a sauna and a shower while I gave the problem some thought. The answer came as I was soaping my nuts. Come to think of it, a lot of things come to while I soap my nuts.

The solution lay in following Major Robert Roger's Standing Order number seventeen.

Don't tell me you haven't heard of Robert Roger. He was the founder of Roger's Rangers, and is the father of all SpecWar. His buckskin-clad, flintlock-and-hatchet carrying warriors tore up the French and Indians back in the seventeen fifties.

Well, in 1759, Roger wrote nineteen Standing Orders for his men—maxims that still form the tactical backbone of all SpecWar operations. Number seventeen goes like this: "If somebody's trailing you, make a circle, come back onto your own tracks, and ambush the folks that aim to ambush you."

Except the circle we'd make here would be an electronic one—a program that would allow us to see where the requests were coming from. We'd do it by laying a false trail. The trail would force the pursuers to move slowly, working their way down a path they hadn't anticipated. While they scrambled through the unfamiliar territory, we'd come around from the back—and be able to identify them.

While Wonder composed his computer gibberish, I constructed the bait. I wrote out a bunch of bogus memos and E-mail messages from made-up DIA gumshoes and spooks, NIS investigators, and Pentagon bureaucrats. One series of messages gossiped about a new, code-word secret intelligence-gathering program, involving LC Strawhouse's American Phalanx. Another skein mused about a back door tie-in between LC and the ADAM Group. And a third vein of E-mail dealt with the nasty particulars of my upcoming court-martial. I planted "evidence" of improper behavior and financial chicanery. I left broad hints that SECNAV was going to appear and testify against me. The way I wrote it, my case did not look good.

Wonder then injected all of my missives under the skin of the DIA system, using bogus mailboxes and fake file folders. He even made it appear as if they'd been written at different times over the past day or so. And he left enough flags around so that anybody doing any serious hacking or cracking would stumble across them.

Then we sat back and drank Coors for three hours. At 1700, Wonder fired up the computer. Nada. No one had nibbled yet. Since we were in the mood for light entertainment, we put a laser disk of *The Terminator* on big screen, popped a microwave load of popcorn, and went back to our beer.

We stayed up most of the night, checking periodically. Nothing. Maybe these hackers worked five-day, forty-hour weeks. Then, at 0400 Sunday morning, just as we were about to hit the computer's ON button, we lost all power at the Manor.

What the fuck? I got on the cellular to VEPCO's emergency line, and after twenty-five minutes on hold, was told that some humongous transformer just outside Quantico had gone ka-boom, and hence we'd be without power for at least eight hours while they reconstructed the grid.

Well, I keep a gasoline-powered generator on hand for just this sort of emergency. You don't live out in the boonies without one. So, while I wasn't about to fire up the computer, at least we kept the beer cold and the coffee hot for the next seven-plus hours.

Just after noon on Sunday we were finally able to log in. And guess what? Having not watched the pot for all those hours had made things come to the boil: there'd been another query. This one had been routed through the Naval Special Warfare Center at Coronado. But now, Wonder was able to track it back down the line—or in this particular case, up the line. Why up? Because the it had originated just outside Rancho Mirage, California.

Guess, gentle reader, who lives just outside Rancho Mirage? The answer is that Lyman Clyde Strawhouse does. On two-thousand-plus acres of what used to be scrub, sand, and cactus.

It was time to travel. I wanted to pay old LC a visit—my kind of back door, sneak-and-peek, snoop-and-poop visit. I gathered the troops and told everybody to pack for the high desert. When I told them why we were going, Doc Tremblay raised his hand and objected.

"What's your problem, asshole?"

"Well, Skipper,"—Doc waved a copy of the latest issue of *American Sniper* magazine at me—"seems that the object of your research won't be in California. Says here that starting tomorrow, he's gonna be in Detroit. They're gonna honor him at the Special Operations Association annual convention, and he's scheduled to speak at their big banquet."

That changed things. Rancho Mirage could wait—Detroit was the primary target. It was an opportunity to see this guy LC Strawhouse up close. Moreover, we'd discovered all those damn FBI reports about contacts between the ADAM Group, fundamentalist tangos, and Zulu Gangsta Princes in the Detroit metro area.

And there was something else, too—a puzzle I had the pieces to but no solution for. My late and much lamented sea daddy, CNO Arleigh Secrest, was a great believer in looking at information in unconventional ways. We tend to categorize things—and in doing so, we overlook significant data. His advice to me was to overlay all my information, and see what develops. Sometimes it's as impenetrable as a Jackson Pollock oil. Sometimes, however, it's as clear as Canaletto.

I said a silent prayer of thanks to CNO, grabbed Wonder by the ear, walked him toward the computer, and watched as he turned it on. "Make me a database," I said.

"Okay—you're a database."

"Be serious, asshole."

"Mr. Dickhead, sir," he said, spelling it with a *c* and a *u,* "I am serious. I need material to input into a database."

And so he did. So I gave him material. I went to my files and read off to him the dates when LC Strawhouse had made his public appearances over the past year or so. Then I pulled the list of sites of stolen weapons compiled by the Department of Defense's inspector general. Then I found the locations for as many of the fringe militias, white supremacist groups, Islamic fundamentalists, and huge street gangs as I could.

"Now—juxtapose everything."

Wonder played with the keyboard and printed his results. Guess what. Of the thirty-three LC Strawhouse speaking engagements I'd come across in magazines and newspapers, nineteen of them occurred in, or near, cities cited in the IG report where arms thefts had taken place. Baltimore, Virginia Beach, and St. Louis were all on the list.

Now, if it had been me, gentle reader, I'd have made sure I was nowhere near the site of any weapons thefts—the less to leave any kind of trail. But then, I didn't have LC Strawhouse's ego, either. And from my research, I knew he had an ego the size of my dick.

There was more, too. Of the thirteen nasty organizations I'd had Wonder enter, seven of them were in places where LC Strawhouse had made speeches or appeared at a convention. And guess what—all seven were also listed in the IG report.

Now I don't know about you, but I found that information pretty damn significant. Enough to make me want to skip Go, skip the $200, and go straight to the Motor City.

Chapter 8

OVER CENTRAL WEST VIRGINIA I BROWSED THE SPECIAL OPERATIONS Association of the United States' convention schedule, which Doc Tremblay had clipped from his sniper's magazine for me. Yeah—there's even an association for the special operations community these days, complete with membership cards, roster booklet, and an annual get-together-cum-trade show. And guess what—anybody can join. You don't have to be a SEAL, or a Ranger, or any other form of Blankethead, Recon Marine, or Pave Low chopper pilot. You can be a goddamn lobbyist or a four-eyed wanna-be and you can still obtain a gold-embossed card that says you are a member in good standing of the Special Operations Association of the United States.

No bona fides checked—all you have to do is pay $160 per annum, and you get a card that identifies you as an "Operator" in SOAUS. What horse puckey.

There was no need for the whole team to go on this little jaunt—after all, there were budgetary considerations now that we were in the private sector. So, I brought only my personal zoo—Gator and Rodent. It's not the first time in my life I've traveled with animals. As an enlisted Frog, I was once in a platoon along with a Rabbit (as in John Francis), a Fox (Jim), and an Owl—Everett. We were a bunch of wild party beasts, too—constantly on the prowl for more livestock—for example, wild pussy and tame beaver. Anyway, because I booked at the last minute, there were no direct flights available to Motown, so we flew commuter: Dulles-Cleveland-Detroit.

I never saw the passenger manifest, but it became obvious by the time we landed in Cleveland that Mr. Murphy had accompanied us on the trip. Thus, a half-hour layover turned into a two-and-a-half-hour delay while mechanics probed and poked all around the port wing landing gear well of our aircraft. Then, having lost our takeoff slot, we waited on the runway behind twenty-three fucking jet aircraft. Did I mention the heavy ground fog and quarter-mile visibility? No? Well guess what—I was in a terrific mood when we touched down on Detroit Metro runway 33-N almost four hours behind schedule.

We rented a car and drove past a five-story Uniroyal tire, east on I-94, some twenty-five miles into the city. Detroit is something of a physical anomaly. It actually sits to the *north* of its Canadian sister city, Windsor, because of a knob of land around which sluices the Detroit River, carrying the waters from Lake St. Clair thirty-two miles south and east into Lake Erie. Fanned around that knuckle lies the city of Detroit, spreading north, west, and south from the water.

Of all the Rust Belt cities, Detroit is the roughest, toughest—and least revitalized. Much of the place has never recovered from the race riots that took place almost three decades ago. We came in from the west—driving past prosperous suburbs, malls, and shopping centers.

Suddenly I got a glimpse of a sign that said INKSTER. That was where T. D. Capel lived. "Hey—"

We swerved off the highway and turned north, cutting through blocks of nineteen twenties and thirties one-story, gray, stone chalets—middle-class housing built for the folks who'd worked at the assembly lines at Cadillac in Warren, or Ford in Dearborn. I pulled a note from my wallet and checked the address against the AAA street map. "Turn right."

We drove past the city hall, turned east, then south, then east again until we found ourselves on a quiet suburban street that backed up onto a small park. I checked the number on the street sign. "Pull over—we should be pretty close."

Gator edged up to the curb. I peered down the street. The house was about 150 feet ahead of us—it had to be the place, because it was all strung with bright yellow and black police crime scene tape. It was a blackened shell, completely gutted by fire, just past the still-smoldering stage. Obviously, Mr. Murphy had gotten here ahead of us by a few hours.

I got out of the car and looked, dejected. I saw a woman on the opposite side of the street coming toward us, walking an immense Rottweiler. "Excuse me—" I waved and smiled at her. "Excuse me?"

"Yes?" She stopped. She had a friendly smile. The dog didn't, and I kept my distance, remaining in the middle of the street. "I was just wondering what happened here. I'm looking for a friend of a friend's house—guy named Capel—and I think it may be the one that's burnt down—"

"A fire. Yesterday. They think it was arson."

"Anybody hurt?"

She shook her head. "Nope—nobody home. But look at the house—such a shame. These old places are wonderful. Great to restore. That one was done only a year or so ago. Now look at it—totaled."

So much for any evidence we might find at Capel's house. And the nice lady'd just said they thought it was arson, too. And guess who was in town. That's right—LC Strawhouse himself.

Coincidence? Happenstance? What do *you* think?

"Thanks." I waved and climbed back into the car. We found our way back to I-94 and continued into the city. It didn't take long until the road surface got noticeably worse—I caught a sign designating the city limit—and the eight-lane highway descended into an uncovered trench, with the city streets running above us. Looking up, I could see acres of burnt-out houses that resembled Bihać or Sarajevo more than a midwestern American city. Indeed, the occupants of the few blue and white police cars we saw on the road sat hunched and apprehensive—very much the same body language as U.N. peacekeepers in Bosnia. They probably had as much effect on their surroundings, too.

We peeled off I-94 onto I-96. I was looking down at the map and so we missed the turn onto the Fisher freeway. We got off the highway, looped around Tiger stadium twice to get our bearings (we didn't), cruised across Michigan Avenue, then turned south and east, heading, according to the map, toward the river.

Shit—even much of the downtown area looked deserted. We drove by a graffiti-covered building named Cobo Hall, a rundown Civic Center, and finally the huge Ren Cen, formally called the

Renaissance Center, a tall, riverfront complex of modern glass office buildings, a hotel, and a conference facility, where the SOAUS convention was being held.

We pulled over and I jogged into the Ren Cen hotel, asked for two rooms, and was told they were booked full up. I asked for alternate accommodations, and was given the name of a hotel about eight blocks north on Woodward Avenue.

Rodent drove while I played naviguesser, which meant that it probably took us an extra quarter hour to find the place because of the confusing series of one-way streets that sent us driving in circles. Well, no matter—we were already behind schedule. We claimed our rooms and dropped our bags.

Rodent, Gator, and the road map climbed back into the car and headed for Ypsilanti, which, Wonder had learned by checking his computer database, was the regional headquarters for the Sixth Michigan National Guard Infantry Division. I changed into real clothes, then went to the back of the line of guests waiting for taxis, as the downtown weather was currently halfway between mist and drizzle.

The taxi line wasn't moving—no cabs to be seen anywhere. I rocked on my heels for ninety seconds or so, then made what for me was an incredibly polite inquiry of the doorman. And how long is the wait for a cab? I asked. He cast a practiced eye along the queue, swiveled, peered up and down the empty street that ran in front of the hotel, and told me half an hour. I slipped him a fin for his honesty and cast off on my own.

Fuck it—even though I'd never been here before, I knew I could walk eight blocks to the Renaissance Center in fifteen minutes or less. And I wouldn't have to contend with one-way streets, either.

Big mistake. Four blocks into my stroll it began to rain in earnest. Half a block later, with Mr. Murphy right at my side—*he* was wearing galoshes and a Burberry—earnest rain turned to total downpour.

Now, gentle reader, as I am a SEAL, I do not believe in umbrellas. I am supposed to operate in maritime environments. But let me say here and now, that when I am dressed in my English-cut double-breasted blue flannel blazer and Oxford gray trousers (all from Marks and Spencer of Oxford Street, London), a distinguished, gray-striped shirt, and a fashionable paisley silk tie, I do not enjoy being rained upon. If I wanted to look rained-on, I'd wear seersucker.

However, I once took a physics course and hence I understand the laws of nature. Therefore, I hauled balls for the last two blocks. The law of nature I was thinking about goes, The quicker you move, the fewer raindrops will hit you. You can find it in your illustrated high-school textbooks under Marcinko's Third Principle of Maritime Physics. It holds true about 50 percent of the time. This time, it didn't hold true at all.

By the time I made it across eight lanes of traffic (not to mention over a five-foot-high concrete divider), and through the Ren Cen's heavy plate-glass revolving doors, I was soaked clear through my nice Egyptian broadcloth from the inside as well as the outside. You see, one can, and one do, sweat buckets when one sprints four blocks. *If,* that is, one be as large, as hirsute, and as intrinsically, genetically, inherently, sweat-conducive as I am. This was not a good development. Certainly, it was not the sort of appearance I wanted to cultivate.

So I threaded my way through the *moderne* lobby, past the bar (I saw they displayed a big Bombay poster and vowed to return shortly) and found my way down a series of corridors to a secluded *double-vay say,* as they say in French, where I could improve my soggy condition without too much interruption.

I sloshed my way up to the lavatory door. It was obstructed by a big youngster wearing a Secret Service-style radio earpiece, blue pinstripes, and a fifty-dollar haircut standing dead center in front of said door, arms crossed.

Did I mention that he was big? Let me rephrase. He blocked the light. Six foot seven. Three hundred pounds. No noticeable body fat. He looked like one of those ex-football players. Belay that—he looked like a whole fucking football team.

I stepped around him. "Excuse me."

He dropped his arms. "Sorry—this room's in use."

I stepped back so I could see the sign above the door. I shrugged. "Seems to me that's the universal sign for Men's Room up there—it doesn't say anything about 'private.'"

Señor football team wasn't overtly impressed at my ability to interpret nonverbal imagery. He simply stood there and repeated himself.

I sighed. This conversation, I realized, was going to go nowhere. And it was, after all, a public rest room. So I feinted right, cut left, and went for the door.

He put his hand on my chest to stop me. This was not a wise choice—even for someone his size. Not when I was in my current mood. You will remember, gentle readers, that it has not been a good week for Dickie.

So I trapped and pressed his hand against my chest, bent his wrist backward, nearly breaking it (I could hear the tendons and cartilage popping), and while he was thus preoccupied I kneed him smartly thrice in the groin, lifting him four or five inches off the floor with each impact.

It's amazing what a good knee in the balls will do to take the wind out of a BAW—that's a Big Asshole Windbag. So, since said BAW had been properly deflated, and wasn't offering any resistance, I sat him on the floor next to the doorway, removed the little microphone dangling from his wrist, and stomped it—the better to keep him from summoning more of his ilk (I'm not big on ilk), then I walked into the men's room.

Inside, the place was empty, except for what appeared to be a pair of real expensive, pale gold-colored ostrich cowboy boots, with a pair of equally expensive soft wool trousers and an extravagantly expensive pair of boxer shorts, both of which were draped down around the ankles of someone sitting in stall number three.

I see all of you out there. You people are shaking your heads, wondering how I know those boxer shorts around those ankles were—in my own words—"extravagantly expensive."

Well, friends, it was because they had three snaps on the fly front and they didn't have any elastic. Now, the kinds of boxer shorts most folks wear—they come in packs of three—have elastic waists and no front closure. The real good ones—the kind you buy if your last name is Rockefeller or Harriman and your underwear costs more than most people's suits—are made by individual waist size, and they have little snaps on the front so your pecker doesn't fall out and embarrass you in the dressing room of the Union League, or the New York Athletic Club.

You're probably wondering where I got all of that. Hey, bub, ain't it amazing, the trivia you pick up after a life in unconventional warfare?

"Don't mind me," I said in the direction of the fifty-dollar skivvies. "I just need to dry off a bit, then I'll be out of here."

I received no answer, so I shrugged, then went to work. I peeled off my blazer and jury-rigged it across two of the hot-air hand dryers, with the nozzles shooting down the arms. I used a third machine on my shirt and tie. After five or six minutes, steam began to rise from my blazer and I pulled it off the hot-air machine because I realized if I didn't, it would begin to shrink on me soon.

I'd just hung the jacket on a stanchion, when I saw old Mr. BAW in the mirror as he came huffing and puffing through the door. He had a collapsible spring-steel baton in his hand and murder in his little round pig eyes.

I tossed my shirt over a stall door, then wheeled to face him. I thought about extracting the Emerson CQC6 on my trouser waistband and simply killing him. But frankly, I didn't want any blood on me today. It would be impolite when I met LC Strawhouse.

So, as Mr. BAW feinted left, I countered right. He weaved. I bobbed. I weaved. He bobbed. We both feinted again, our feet and shoulders going in opposite directions. Then his eyes focused, and I knew the next move was going to be for real.

His feet went right, he went left, and the baton came around like a baseball bat, aimed right at the side of my face. I swiveled. But I didn't move quite fast enough—the grip of the shaft caught me upside my ear hard enough to make me see stars. Shit, those things hurt.

He knocked me into a stall door and followed after me. I reacted instinctively, moving as the baton dented the gray steel panel with a nasty thwock.

I was growing sick and tired of this motherfucker—it was time to put him away. Besides, he was using the baton like a baseball bat, swinging it, not chopping with it as I prefer to do.

That was a big mistake. I pulled back and let his swing go by me—strike one—then exploded forward, using my shoulder to hit him in the lower rib cage.

He grunted, and tried to bring the wand down on my back.

Except, I'd caught his wrist and he couldn't move very well. That was strike two.

I moved him backward—kind of the same way a defensive lineman works with a tackling dummy, except I wasn't playing by any rules. I really put my shoulder into it, and I heard his ribs break as he hit the six inches of exposed nozzle on one of the hot-air machines. It must have hurt like hell, because he dropped the baton.

That was strike three. I whirled, snatched it off the floor, and chopped him about the face four or five times. His cheekbones and nose were going to need medical attention soon. But that wasn't my concern. My concern was putting the cocksucker *o-u-t.* So, I wheeled him around, set him up about a foot away from the wall, and using my right forearm, knocked him—*whaaaap*—up against the heavy tile as hard as I could.

Heckler & Koch's International Training Division offers an intensive, week-long SWAT course called Tactical Team for police officers, as well as spooks and other sundry government types. One full day is spent studying and practicing what is known as "Active Countermeasures." That is a way of saying it is the day the trainees get to beat the shit out of one another. See, unlike SEALs, cops can't always kill an *armed* suspect. Unless they're in imminent danger of being killed themselves, their rules of engagement say they have to subdue the bad guy, not shoot him.

Now, if that subduing is done badly, you get the Rodney King case. If it is done well, it is over in a matter of a second or two, the perp hurts like hell for a week, and no one gets accused of police brutality.

The instructor for the Active Countermeasures segment of Tactical Team is a tough, impassioned, zealous lieutenant from the Milwaukee County Sheriff's Department named Gary Klugiewicz, who has held the U.S. National title in full-contact karate. You can get hurt doing full-contact karate. (I can identify with Gary because he, like I, believes that pain exists to tell you you're still alive.)

Anyway, Gary insists that one of the best weapons police officers have at their disposal is the common, everyday brick, masonry, tile, or concrete wall. He has, in fact, refined a wonderful technique by which you can knock the bejeezus out of anyone with one blow by using the laws of physics, a fast-traveling projectile (the perpetrator), and an immovalble object—the wall. You don't have to send the bad guy very far. Six inches will do (although a couple of feet is better). But you have to hit him decisively, so he bounces off that wall—hard. In training—and I had all my guys from Green Team study this technique with Gary until they had it down—you see stars. How do I know you see stars? I know because we used to practice on one another. In real-life situations, you can use Gary's technique to coldcock some son of a bitch better than any sucker punch, and with less potential damage to you.

In the current situation, for example, Mr. BAW came off the wall with his eyes rolled back in his head like a fucking slot machine gone TILT. By the time I slapped him against the wall a second time for good measure, he was gone for the week.

There was still not a peep from the occupied booth, and I hoped that whoever was inside hadn't had a heart attack during my little fracas. But that wasn't my concern. My concern was creating a resting place for Mr. BAW. So I dragged him over to a stall, sat him on the seat (leaning him against the back wall for support), and closed the door. If there'd been an OUT OF ORDER sign available I would have hung it to complete the aesthetics of my still life creation titled, *Big Asshole Windbag Recumbent.* Then I sat down on the cool tile, tucked my head between my knees, and tried to calm myself down both physically and mentally.

One of the things you should understand about violent interludes—gunfights, knife fights, and free-for-alls—is that they don't go on for very long. This one, for example, had probably taken less than twenty seconds from the first feint to the time I dragged Mr. BAW into the toilet stall. But even though the duration is short, they are nonetheless incredibly draining, both on the body and on the mind.

Yes, the mind. Now don't go accusing me of pseudomacho psychobabble here, because I know from what I'm talking about. The bottom line is that in those few seconds or minutes during which you are putting your life on the line, not only your body is challenged, but your mind is also working at warp speed. The combination is tremendously debilitating. When that mind drain is coupled with the 1,000 percent you have to give physically, the result is total exhaustion.

But sometimes, you just have to keep going. And this was one of them. So, while I wanted to stop at the lobby bar, down a couple of double Bombays, and strike up a conversation with something blonde and buxom, I wiped my face, straightened my clothes, and made my way down to the convention floor to do some serious recon. I had a billionaire to find.

Three hours later, walked and talked out but without having made contact with my target, I was finally perched atop a faux-leather stool in the smoked Plexiglas, neon-accented bar just off the main lobby, nursing Dr. Bombay, simultaneously fascinated and horrified as the bartender, a short-haired person of indeterminate gender who wore four earrings and bore the name tag KIM on . . . *i-t-s* black tunic, concocted a martini by adding three parts cold vermouth to one part warm gin and then dropping a maraschino cherry into the glass.

I sipped my gin and tried my damndest to figure out why

martinis hadn't been programmed into the humongous back-bar computer, which siphoned, mixed, poured, and then rang up everything from draft beer, blush wine, and scotch-on-the-rocks, to Long Island iced teas and tequila sunrises—each drink precisely portion-controlled down to the last milliliter.

Probably, I decided, because the goddamn thing had been designed by some freaking twenty-five-year-old Harvard MBA dweeb scum who'd been brought up on Santa Fe margaritas and Jell-O shooters and had never heard of martinis.

Why am I carrying on like this about a fucking machine? Because, friends, there is a parallel situation going on right now at the Pentagon—yes, the Pentagon—where they are taking SpecWar away from platoon chiefs with combat experience and turning it over to machines—computer-driven simulators. Just like the fucking hotel manager here had turned quality control, portion control, and total control over to a goddamn Rube Goldberg contraption made of rubber hoses, stainless steel nozzles, and shiny chrome gizmos.

Oh, yeah—SpecWar is now firmly in the hands of the portion-control crowd, too. And with what results? With bad results. Currently, for example, portion control dictates that each SEAL gets precisely one hundred rounds of ammunition per month. And what if he wants more? The answer is that he can buy it himself. My SEALs used to shoot one hundred rounds of ammunition in ten minutes. My SEALs used to shoot more ammo in a year than the entire U.S. Marine Corps.

Not today's SEALs. Portion control says one hundred rounds per month. And that's what they get. Portion control also says they get twenty-four parachute jumps per year. And how do you build confidence with such a low volume? The answer (I'll bet you knew this already) is that you don't. Which means that under combat conditions, SEALs will spend too much of their precious time worrying about whether they'll survive the drop, and not enough time figuring out how they're gonna kill the bad guys.

And what does portion control do? It saves money, so that the Navy can buy toys, such as their new Cyclone class ships. (Cyclones are officially designated PCs, which stands for Patrol Coastal, but the more roguish sailors have renamed them Politically Correct-class ships). Anyway, PCs are 170-foot craft designed to work in brown water—that is, the shallow waters in which more and more conflicts (Cuba and Haiti come to mind) take place these days. They are CALOW—Coastal and Limited Objective

Warfare—ships, as opposed to blue water, or mid-ocean craft. They were designed to patrol and interdict. A secondary role is SpecWar operational missions, because the PCs can hold up to nine SEALs.

But there's a basic problem here: we SEALs don't need a dedicated, 170-foot ship to do our work. We can insert and extract from any kind of craft—from a dingy to a goddamn ferry boat, to a fucking sampan. So it's not SEALs that need these ships—but the goddamn Navy hierarchy.

Why, you ask? Because it means thirteen new commands for young line officers, so they can be promoted and become captains, then admirals, which will ultimately put them in the position to buy more ships.

Now, the funding for these PCs has come from the Special Operations Command. So far as I am concerned, the money would have been better spent on two or three new kill houses and a few million rounds of ammunition. Kill houses allow SEALs to practice their deadly craft under stress and with some danger involved. But the people who run SOC don't think the way I do. They'd rather have their toys. So, these days, SEALs shoot electronic bullets at big-screen TV sets, and the Navy has thirteen new ships.

But when the *merde* hits the *ventilateur,* some young SEALs are going to get themselves killed because they won't have spent enough time shooting real bullets in real-life environments where ricochets can ding 'em, and where seemingly impenetrable concrete walls suddenly look like Swiss cheese. They won't have learned how to take cover under fire, or shoot under stress.

The new regime doesn't like live-fire exercises because people might possibly possibly get hurt. And an injured SEAL can ruin an officer's chance at promotion. And in today's Navy, promotion, not leadership, is what being an officer is all about. Which is why my way of doing business—the old-fashioned, in-your-face style of operating—is out the window. And it is why simulation, not live-fire exercises, now provides "experience" for operators.

In fact, most of today's missions are conceived, designed, and executed by war gaming and computer database statistical models. Then, after suitable deliberation by a bunch of managerial assholes (during which time the situation on the ground changes by 100 percent, of course), the shooters are, by the grace of these systems-analyst-Piled-higher-and-Deepers, allowed to go out and try to accomplish a small percentage of their mission—without hurting anybody, of course.

And how do these portion-control war gamers set real-life mission requirements? The answer too often is: by using still more toys. Example? You want an example? Okay. Today, instead of sending SEALs, Blanketheads—SEALspeak for Army Special Forces—or Force Recon Marines to snoop and poop, the portion-control crowd do reconnaissance by using RPVs—Remote Pilotless Vehicles—ditsy model airplanes with TV cameras in their bellies flown over the target area to send pictures back.

But what happens when a remote-controlled, pilotless plane takes a picture of a beach and it looks like sand, but it actually is quicksand, your four-starred panjandrumcy?

A clusterfuck similar to the Bay of Pigs happens, my son.

And what happens when the Chairman of the Joint Chiefs of Staff says, "Please, fellas, be careful not to wax any Iranians, and by the way that's an order and if you disobey it you'll get court-martialed," your six-striped worship?

Desert One is what happens, my hairy-assed Frogman.

And what happens when the computer database statistical model says there'll be calm seas and no winds, your flag-frocked grace?

Mr. Murphy of Murphy's Law fame will hijack your operation and four SEALs will drown off the shores of Grenada, my child.

And what happens when the secretary of defense, the Chairman of the Joint Chiefs of Staff, and the four-star CENTCOM commander believe in their hearts and souls that SEALs and Special Forces are just a bunch of kill-crazy cowboys, and besides, they're apprehensive about absorbing the 40 to 50 percent SpecWar casualties the statistical models predict because it would look bad for them politically? What happens then, your scrambled-egg-hatted majesty?

Saddam fucking Hussein gets off easy is what happens, you worthless shit-for-brains numb-nuts no-load geek, and nothing changes inside Iraq.

My roguish reverie was interrupted by a slow, low drawl. "Captain Marcinko, I see you're as handy with your fists as ever."

I swiveled on the bar stool. I recognized the beautiful gold-colored ostrich boots—as well as the face and the voice.

Chapter 9

"I'VE ALWAYS LIKED SITTING ON THE CAN ALONE," LC STRAWHOUSE said as matter-of-factly as if we were old friends. "When I was a kid, the outhouse was the only place I ever got to go to think."

Not very many of us remember outhouses anymore. I do. We had one in back of our first house in Lansford, Pennsylvania—a ramshackle row house owned by the coal mining company where my father, my uncles, and my maternal grandfather, Joe Pavlik, all worked. "Was yours a one-holer or two-holer?"

"Aw, hell, we were too poor to build more than a one-holer, Dick—ya mind if I call ya Dick, Captain?"

I shook my head.

"Good—and you just call me LC, okay? Well, then, Dick, the bottom line is that sometimes the fellas that work for me get a little overprotective, y'know, and when I tell 'em I want to be alone in the crapper so's I can think, they take me absolutely literally. Willy Bob—that's the one you banged up some—was that way." LC Strawhouse shook his head. "Young people. No sense of proportion. In fact, proportion was what I talked about today at the Association luncheon. Didja get a chance to hear me?"

I told him that I'd arrived almost five hours late and missed his lunch appearance.

That didn't appear to bother him. "Well, just so long's you're around for the banquet tomorrow—I'm gonna get 'em so worked up they're gonna be runnin' through walls to change things in Washington."

I must have seemed skeptical, because he smiled the kind of ingratiating smile you see on great salesmen and clapped me on the shoulder. "You come by afterward, too. Bunch o' people been tellin' me the two of us should get together and chaw the fat."

I wondered who the bunch of people were, but wasn't about to ask. "Sounds good to me," I said noncommittally.

LC continued his monologue. "They say you got big balls, you ruffle lots of feathers, and you get things done. I like those qualities. I like the way you dealt with them tangos over in London, too—decisive. You're a man o' war, Dick—and there aren't many like you anymore."

"Fewer and fewer shooters all the time," I said.

He grinned. "That category could include you, too, right?"

I didn't understand what he was getting at, and told him so.

"Well, considering the fact that you're always in deep shit with the Navy, you might want to be thinkin' about a new line of work sometime in the near future. That's why we should talk—see if we can work something out."

"Maybe." I asked where he was staying.

Strawhouse smiled. "Got me the penthouse suite upstairs—kinda like livin' in my foyer back home, but it'll do. There'll be a few folks droppin' by for vittles and fat-chaw. Why don't you come at, oh, 'bout twenty-two hundred or so. Just tell the young fella at the door I'm expecting you."

"LC, there's something about the young fellas you hire to stand in front of doors that makes me nervous," I said.

LC Strawhouse laughed. "Point taken," he said. "But you won't have no more trouble—I'll see to that."

He reached over, grabbed the bar check that sat behind my Bombay glass, and handed it to someone behind him without even looking. Now that, friends, is confidence—just the fact that he knew someone would be there was incredible. It's the kind of close-knit, small-unit behavior I try to encourage in my men.

I looked around—a quick recon—because it had occurred to me that I was with someone who was about as famous as anybody in America, and we were standing at the bar, and nobody was asking for his autograph, or barging in on our conversation.

I saw that we were in the middle of a protective bubble. There were three yards of air between the two of us and anybody else at the bar. All the other patrons had simply been moved away—so quietly and efficiently that I hadn't noticed until now.

I congratulated LC on his security, which brought a smile to his craggy face.

"I tend to hire ex-Delta troopers and SEALs, Dick. And they stay current because I make sure they enroll in Special Forces reserve units, and they train at my place in the desert. Besides, they got a damn good boss."

He stuck a long finger in the air, then crooked it vaguely in our direction. "Yo—Deppity Dawg, front and center."

A heavyset specter in an ill-fitting gray pinstripe suit, blue button-down, and thick-soled brogues emerged from the shadows. "Hello, Dick," Major General Elwood T. Dawkins growled ominously. "Long time no see."

The second year I commanded SEAL Team Six, Dawg Dawkins became the CO of Delta Force.

When Charlie Beckwith led Delta, I had an open invitation to send my SEAL platoons down to Bragg regularly so our men could cross-train. That is a polite way of saying my guys and Charlie's guys would fuck with one another for about a week. They'd stage live-fire hostage rescue exercises, compete fast-roping off choppers, and hold one-on-one sniping contests. The final events, which Charlie and I habitually led from the front, were the ten-mile pub crawl, followed by the two-day hangover.

Then Dawg took command of Delta. He got the job because his rabbi, a four-star, grade-A, U.S. government-inspected, ruby red sphincter named Jacques Malone, took over the Special Operations Command at MacDill Air Force Base. Dawg had been Frère Jacques's chief of staff and head ass-kisser. In return for his loyalty, he was given command of Delta.

Within days, the mood down at Fort Bragg changed. It was as if a thundercloud had suddenly blown over the Stockade. Dawg was one of those officers who'd spent more time on staff than in combat —he'd been in Vietnam for less than six months, and out in the field for less than eight weeks—and he just didn't think like a warrior. As a CO, Dawg was a lot less willing to share information with me, and with other SpecWar commanders, than Charlie had been. It was, we began to think, as if he saw us more as adversaries than colleagues.

Well, friends, there's a problem with that. SpecWarriors have got to stick together, because we already work at a huge disadvantage. The conventional military—and it doesn't matter whether we're talking Army, Navy, Marines, or Air Farce here—doesn't particularly like snake eaters of any pattern, stripe, or spot.

Another thing: I have always taken the point of view that as a SpecWarrior, I should have no future except as a SEAL—an operator. I wear my scars proudly. I've never wanted an admiral's stars the way others have. When I was a rowdy UDT enlisted man, I once told a four-striper that I'd rather be a chief in the Teams than an admiral—because I'd get more done and have more fun. When I became an ossifer, the most important job I believed I could ever get would be to command a SEAL team and lead men into battle. God has been good to me—he has given me that opportunity not once, not twice, but more than half a dozen times.

But Dawg Dawkins, I realized soon after he'd assumed command of Delta, had never earned scars. All he'd ever wanted were stars.

Our relationship defined itself when he grudgingly accepted my challenge for a head-to-head competition just like the ones I'd done with Charlie. After a month of negotiation, I flew a platoon of my very best dirtbags down to Bragg, and we went at it for a week.

It was nose to nose right up until the last day—that was when we were scheduled to do live-fire, dynamic room entry in Delta's five-story, modular kill house. In Special Air Service fashion, Dawg and I played hostages. The theory goes that if you're not comfortable letting your men shoot in your direction, you don't deserve to lead them.

The rules allowed me to set the scenario for Delta, and for him to do the same for SEAL Team Six. Since the home team bats last, we went first. He gave us a pretty conventional problem: three hostages in an upper-floor embassy office, held by six hostage takers. Dawg and I were positioned on the floor, next to a desk. Frankly, it was pretty much a mediocre variation of the SAS assault at Princes Gate in London, and my men, who'd debriefed the SAS Pagoda troopers who had performed the rescue, breezed through it.

They did their preliminary search well. They used silent drills to position tiny cameras so they could see where everybody was. They ran miniature mikes up through the walls and crawl spaces, so they could keep track of the "tangos."

Then, after they'd checked, double-checked, triple-checked, and locked Mr. Murphy in a closet, one squad rappelled off the roof and came through the windows with flashbangs and CS gas; the other blew the door. It took them seven seconds to complete the mission from the "go" signal.

It was our turn. I gave Dawg a real nasty: five hostage takers and three hostages on a Gulfstream-III jet. It was a bitch of a scenario because the interior of the Gulfstream's fuselage is small and narrow, and visibility—hence target acquisition—becomes a huge problem for the assault force. Then I made the situation worse: two of the tangos and one of the hostages, I dictated, would be women.

Why did that make things tough? It is because no matter how well your guys have been conditioned, no matter how much they have worked at it, it is harder to shoot a woman than it is to shoot a man. In point of fact, terrorists know this—and female tangos have been tremendously successful, because in that tenth-of-a-second delay when you hesitate because they are women, they will wax your ass.

Moreover, Dawg's entry teams would have to make a split-second decision about which of the females they encountered were the tangos, and which were the hostages. I didn't tell him that the nasty "girls" (actually, they were mannequins) wouldn't be carrying guns. Instead, they'd be holding small, electronic detonators.

My guys played the tango role well. They frisked us thoroughly. And guess what? They discovered a tiny radio transmitter in Dawg's clothes.

Oops—that's breaking the rules. Of course, in SpecWar, there are no rules. So, my command master chief, a brazen, copper-topped dirtbag I'll call Two Dogs, appropriated the transmitter efficiently and quietly before Dawg had a chance to say anything untoward.

From the playful look on his face, I knew what Two Dogs was about to do. He was going to broadcast all sorts of false information to the opposition. Well, all's fair in war and war—and if you're a hostage rescue team, you'd better factor disinformation into your game plan.

My men tied Dawg and me in adjoining seats, facing forward. Opposite us they placed a dummy representing a female tango holding a detonator. In the rear-facing seat directly behind Dawg's head was the female hostage—another dummy—clutching a small, rectangular purse. Directly behind me was the second lady tango mannequin, a detonator that resembled a handbag in her lap.

It took them only about half an hour to do their recon. That is a very short time, and it occurred to me that perhaps Delta was relying on information from the transmitter. Except, it wasn't Dawg broadcasting to them, but Master Chief Two Dogs.

Now you're probably wondering why the folks on the receiving end couldn't tell the difference between their own CO, and my master chief. The answer is because these minimikes are normally concealed under layers of clothing, and hence you don't get much voice quality. What you hear is intermittent. It's not the kind of information you should base a mission on—it is simply an ancillary intel source that can be factored in to help you understand what you're up against.

Then they hit. Ka-bloom—hatches and windows blew and the tear-gas flashbangs went off. Despite my eye and ear protection I was blinded and deafened. I knew if I hadn't been wearing anything, my eardrums would have ruptured from the concussion.

They came in well—swarmed just like they'd been trained to do. Then the CS gas got under my goggles and my eyes began to tear. I could hear the blam-blam, blam-blam of double-taps.

Fuuuuck—a round cut through the seat between me and Dawg, and my right shoulder and neck burned like hell. Some son of a bitch had shot me.

It was all over in seconds. They brought in fans to vent the CS gas, and a medic to stop my bleeding. The good news was that the fat .45-caliber round hadn't hit any tendons, bones, or nerves—it passed through the flesh of my neck, leaving a big, ugly, painful hole. And although it hurt like a son of a bitch and bled like a busted dam, it wasn't serious—I'd cure it later with a hefty double dose of Dr. Bombay on the rocks.

In fact, I told everybody it was more critical that Dawg's Delta troopers had "killed" the female hostage and rescued the baddie with the detonator, than that some dumb asshole had put a shot through my neck while missing the tango dummy altogether. Of course, if it had been a SEAL who'd screwed up like that I probably would have killed him. But then, I've always demanded more of SEALs than I have of Blanketheads.

The other crucial point was why they had fucked up so badly. One reason was because they'd relied on the bad information Master Chief Two Dogs had slipped to them on the purloined radio transmitter. Instead of sneaking and peeking and getting their intel the hard way, they'd taken a short cut—and it had led them astray. Remember when I told you they'd taken too brief a time doing their recon? Well, they had. And that's what I said to Dawg, too.

Dawg was furious. He didn't like the results at all. He insisted that we do it all over again so his guys could score better.

I, however, was having none of it. He'd tried to cheat, we'd caught him at it, and skinned him alive. And anyway, these mission profiles were supposed to resemble real life—and in real life, there's no going back.

So, I gave him my opinion in my normal, diplomatic bedside manner. "Fuck you, cockbreath—you lose."

As you can imagine, SEAL Team Six and Delta never joint-trained again. And Dawg? He built himself a *command.* Charlie Beckwith's Delta had been lean and mean: 200 men, all of them shooters. By the time Dawg vacated the CO's office, there were 475 Delta troopers, and another 300 support types. His empire was complete with bureaucrats churning out hundreds of useless memos, studies, and reports that worked their way up the chain of command. He must have impressed a few people, because Dawg got his star. In fact, he finished out his career as the JSOC two-star —the major general in charge of the Joint Special Operations Command at Fort Bragg. And when the Navy came after me back in the late eighties, Major General Elwood P. Dawkins made sure that NIS was given access to every bit of unflattering information about me contained in JSOC files.

He'd aged badly. He'd gone from burly to beefy—the sort of suety look you get from too many expense account steak lunches and not enough exercise. It was accentuated because he'd kept the whitewalls and the buzz haircut, except for the fact that it had gone gray and was pretty sparse on top.

The Dawg stuck a paw in my direction.

I looked at it but didn't do anything.

LC's coyote eyebrows went up about six inches. "My, oh my," he said, "I guess you boys have a *past."*

"We've had our ups and downs," Dawg said dryly. He paused. "Hear you're the one who's killing hostages these days, Dick."

I couldn't let that pass unchallenged. "Waxed a fucking unknown who was carrying a fucking pistol. You never could get the facts straight, could you, *Elwood.*" I turned away and finished the last of my Bombay.

Dawg curled his upper lip. "Well, asshole," he growled, "here's a fucking fact for you—my friends at the Pentagon say you're about to be court-martialed over your fuckup—and that SECNAV's gonna testify as a prosecution witness."

Oh, did he know that for a fact? I'm glad he did, because, as you'll remember, gentle readers, it was *moi* who'd composed that lovely factoid, that info-bit, that depth charge of disinformation, and buried it in the Intelink.

It was gratifying to come eye-to-eye with at least one of the folks who were grazing in forbidden territory. But I didn't move a muscle. I just looked at him evenly. "I don't give a shit what your friends at the Pentagon say. Besides, your friends are wrong. I'm out of the Navy—I was separated three days ago."

From the look on Dawg's ugly face, I had just surprised him.

From the look on LC Strawhouse's face, I'd surprised him, too. But he wasn't the type to stay surprised for long. "Need any work to keep the wheelbarrow filled, Dick? Now, I don't usually hire nobody who ain't got at least one star. In fact, I got so many stars around me it's like living in a goddamn planetarium. Got me"—he toted the number on his bony fingers—"a total of twenty-two stars on the payroll right now, including two former Chairmen of the Joint Chiefs. Got another half dozen in the pipeline, too—soon as they retire."

Then he looked at me with an expression that was so absolutely sociopathic that it made the hair on my neck stand straight up. "But in your case, I might just make an exception." He gave Dawg the sort of ruthless smile villains in spaghetti westerns reserve for peasants just before they loot, pillage, rape, and burn their village down. "Elwood, you give Dick a business card—the one with the *private* number, so he can get in touch with me anytime he wants."

The Dawg reached inside his coat and withdrew an embossed card. He put the card between two fingers and extended it in my direction.

My mama, Emilie, raised me to be polite. So, I told Dawg, "Fuck you very much," took the card from him, and gave it a quick glance. It read, PAJAR INDUSTRIES, LA QUINTA, CALIFORNIA.

Oh, how I love it when pieces of puzzles come together. I slipped the card into my shirt pocket.

"Havin' him around'd sure keep things interesting around the bunkhouse, huh, *Elwood?"* LC Strawhouse grinned and stuck me in the chest with his thumb. "See ya tomorra, Dickie."

I made a call from a pay phone on my way back to the Woodward Plaza. I'd given my word to the Priest that I'd stay away from the Safety Net of chiefs I've established over my career. Priest's request that I do made sense—security had been breached. If Dawg Dawkins was able to read secret code-word messages, then I didn't want to risk the slightest chance of being compromised.

But I hadn't promised Priest anything about *retired* sailors. You see, my friends, there exists a small, tight, nationwide network of old UDT/SEAL shipmates who stay in touch via fax and phone. They are veterans of World War II, Korea, Vietnam, and the Cold War—quiet, unassuming heroes, most of them, whose highly classified missions, thank God, have not been uncovered by prying writers. They're still closemouthed, too—except amongst themselves.

These are the same tough Frogmen who mined North Korean harbors and assassinated Chicom generals in the fifties, salvaged code books from sunken Soviet nuclear subs and retrieved live atomic weapons from downed B-52 bombers in the sixties. Some of them disappeared from the Teams to work with Admiral Hyman Rickover's secret projects. Others were sheep-dipped by the CIA or other, more covert agencies. They don't see one another in person very often. But they stay in touch.

A few—very, very few—ex-officers have been invited to become a part of the network. But the majority of this informal, irreverent, national society of former Frogs are "retarded"—that's Frog slang for retired—East Coast fleet sailors—former UDT platoon chiefs much like my old UDT-22 platoon chief, Ev Barrett; gunner's mates, snipes, and boatswains who kept their boat crews in order by using what was known in the old Navy as "rocks and shoals" discipline. "Rocks and shoals" meant miscreants were treated to a swift boondocker or a sucker punch, instead of a written memo of demerit. Believe me, it worked better than any bureaucratic form of punishment—and it made better sailors, too. I know, because that's how I was trained.

Anyway, I pulled a thin address book from my wallet, dropped the requisite number of quarters in the slot, and dialed a number. The phone rang once, twice, thrice, and then a Froggish growl answered, "Hello?"

"Mugs, you are a worthless asshole—nothing but a pencil-dicked pus-nuts crap-eating turd-faced shit-for-brains moth fucking little cocksucker."

There was an immediate roar of laughter at the other end of the line. Then: "Oh, hi, Rotten Richard—long time no hear. Still up to your ugly puss in horse manure?"

I left a note in the hotel room that I'd be gone overnight, rented a car, and drove northwest on I-75 through the fashionable Detroit suburbs—Royal Oak, Birmingham, and Pontiac—then on to Flint, where the big interstate turned just about due north. If Michigan is shaped like the human right hand held palm up, then Saginaw is just below the point where your thumb gets meaty. A few miles north of Saginaw, I veered off the interstate onto a two-lane state road, followed it for twelve miles as it cut northwest. At an intersection marked by a stop sign I turned left onto a black asphalt county road that meandered due west across creeks, between huge fields which, during the growing season, must have held alfalfa, wheat, corn, and soybeans.

Right now, they were probably barren, with remnants of crops poking up from the plowed, furrowed soil. But I couldn't see anything anyway—it was too dark. I drove on, under black night sky, following the directions I'd been given. I checked my six. The road was empty behind me. If anyone was following, they were doing it with their lights off.

Just to be sure, as soon as the road took a bend to the left, I pulled over, shut off my own lights, and waited for fifteen minutes, listening to the radio. Nothing passed by.

I resumed my journey, coming to a tiny town with an unpronounceable Indian name and a single main street of shabby, shuttered stores, crumbling sidewalk, and no traffic light. I drove through it slowly. Two miles on the far side, I turned onto another black asphalt road and drove five miles north until I came to a town named after a woman named Charity.

The greater metropolitan Charity area was comprised of a closed-down gas station, bare, water-pocked concrete slabs where the pumps had once stood, and an empty storefront that had in the past displayed farm equipment. The few houses, set back from the road, showed evidence of their age and the region's harsh winters.

The speed limit was still posted at twenty-five miles per hour when my headlights caught the huge white anchor set in concrete, his battleship gray wood mailbox bolted atop the shank. Just past the anchor I swung left and eased off the road and onto a gravel riveway that ran straight up alongside the small, white frame house that I knew had once belonged to his parents. At the head of it sat a recently washed and waxed, gray four-door Buick of indeterminate age.

He was waiting for me—behind a front door impatiently cracked open—with a fridge full of ice cold beer and a warm bear hug. He'd been known as "Mugs" in the Teams. "Mugs," because his big, Mick ears stuck out ninety degrees from the side of his head, not to mention the fact that Aloysius Sean Sullivan was not the sort of moniker you kept in the Underwater Demolition Teams, circa 1950. Not if you wanted to make it through UDT Replacement Training—which was what they had before they invented BUD/S—alive.

He was all alone now—his wife, Alice, had passed away; his kids and their families had moved west and south, doing well in Texas and California. Why not go and be with them—live in the sunshine; play golf? The answer was that this place was his roots, and he'd be damned if he'd leave it again. He'd gone to sea more than half a century ago. After twenty-one years of deployments, he'd retired, moved back to Michigan, and worked as a Detroit cop. Fifteen years after that, he'd pulled the pin, which is what cops call retirement, and come back here—and here he was going to stay.

I noted the shipshape living room, the neat, well-policed galley, beyond which was a small guest room he'd turned into an office—his phone, computer, and fax machine sat on a desk he'd made himself.

Just for fun, I bounced a quarter off the tightly tucked bed cover and watched Mugs's grin as I caught it a foot in the air. Once a fleet sailor, always a fleet sailor.

Even in his mid-sixties, he still had the rolling gait and bowed legs of a cartoon sailor man (in fact, Mugs had always kind of reminded me of Popeye in size and shape). He had the sort of face that God must have had in mind when He invented the Dixie cup hat. Mugs dropped into his well-used armchair and ran a hand through his thick, red-turned-white hair. I took the corner of the sofa. He'd chunked a bunch of Swiss cheese and spiked each piece with a toothpick, surrounded them with Ritz crackers, then set the cut-glass serving plate on the coffee table in front of me. I plucked a cube, set it on a Ritz, ate the whole thing at once, and washed it all down with a swallow of beer.

It was good—read reassuring—to see him. Mugs represented

the Navy I had joined as a seventeen-year-old: the tradition-bound fraternity of wooden ships and iron men—not the opposite, which is what it's become. And, like many chiefs of his era, Mugs Sullivan followed the precept I have come to call Ev Barrett's First Law of the Sea—which comes down to the idea that we all have a responsibility to pass our knowledge and traditions down to each succeeding generation of sailors. Finding chiefs who practice Barrett's Law is getting harder and harder these days. But when Chief Mugs Sullivan served, living by it was the Navy way.

He let me sit and decompress for two beers worth of time. When he couldn't take the silence any longer, he leaned forward in the chair and tilted his bullfrog jaw somewhat petulantly in my direction.

"Okay, Rotten Richard," he said, "what's the fuckin' problem? You didn't drive all this way just to eat my damn Wisconsin cheese and drink my damn supermarket beer."

I was back in Detroit just before noon. Rodent and Gator were waiting with news. Well, actually, they were waiting with a huge, smelly bag of Coney Islands. The Coney Island is generic Detroit food. It is a pork-and-beef-and-who-knows-what-else hot dog on which is piled chili, mustard, relish, and onions, all served up on a soft, chewy-cum-gooey frankfurter bun. Two of them will provide you with enough natural methane gas to heat your home for a week. As I am a true environmentalist, I ate three. Then, since the boys wanted to show me, not tell me, what they'd discovered, I hauled my butt (not to mention my exhaust pipe) into the backseat of the rental car and we headed for Ypsilanti—with all the windows rolled down.

The date on the Ypsilanti National Guard facility cornerstone read 1958. It was a truly ugly huge, two-story building built in a style that might be called *faux castle—not* the nautical term, either. The place had been constructed of cheap red bricks punctuated by blocks of unidentifiable gray stone and accented by battlements on the roofline, and four turret towers complete with crenels and merlons. Of course, the facility's medieval appearance was somewhat reduced by the amount of graffiti on the walls. The ungainly structure sat inside an unlocked, three-to-four-acre chain-link fence compound. In the front, a pair of Korea-vintage 20mm antitank cannons stood mute sentry duty, flanking a nicked, dented steel flagpole.

As we drove up, I saw a dozen two-ton, canvas-topped trucks parked haphazardly in a potholed, macadam parking lot in the rear. We left the car a block away so as not to draw attention to ourselves, and walked up to the front door. There, a glassed-in bulletin board listed the post's officers and monthly schedule. Although the place had been originally built as a National Guard armory, it was now, I read, a dual-purpose facility. It served as the regional headquarters for the Sixth Michigan National Guards Infantry Division. (From the artwork, I discerned that they called themselves the Wolverines.) It was also a secondary-level storage depot for U.S. Army ORDCOMSOMICH—ORDnance COMmand, SOutheastern MICHigan.

I rattled the front doors. They were locked. I pressed my nose against the glass. No lights were on inside.

Gator and Rodent walked me around the rear. We cut between the trucks and wandered toward the back fence, which was an eight-foot-high chain-link affair, lacking even the most rudimentary barbed-wire top. I checked the view on the other side. The parking lot backed up on what appeared to be a mammoth fenced truck park, where scores of huge tractor-trailers sat, unattended.

Rodent pointed at the ground. I looked. "So?"

He shook his head. "Ya gotta look carefully, Skipper."

Now I saw what he was getting at. There were faint but distinct double-tire tracks that backed up to the fence line—tracks that seemed to go under the fence itself.

I stepped back, turned, and inspected the landscape. Then I looked closely at the chain-link fence. Taking my time, I wandered back to the building, moving like a point man—which is to say, paying attention to everything around me.

I peered up at the roofline. When I saw what I'd wanted to see, I turned my gaze to the ground and examined the macadam carefully. I paced slowly along the facility's rear wall, looking at the uneven seam between macadam and brick.

This wasn't working. I walked to the center of the building, where the heavy steel rolling rear door (which had been thoughtfully decorated by a bunch of spray-painted, stylized white crown graffiti) was secured by a hasp and a heavy padlock, and began all over again, methodically executing what in the water would have been a pattern search.

I went inch by inch, moving right, until I'd covered the entire area from the doorway to the starboard corner. Then I did the same thing on the port side, stepping carefully over small shards of glass and other detritus, gazing intently at the ground, missing nothing.

After half an hour of concentrated effort I walked back to the fence, checked the angles, then went back to my pattern searching. It took me another forty minutes to find all the elements and piece them together.

The story was all there: you just had to know what to look for.

- Someone who wasn't a very good shot had used a slingshot to take out the two high-pressure sodium security lights that illuminated the parking lot. I had evidence of the sloppy marksmanship in my hand—nine ball bearings. It had been done recently, because the bearings showed no sign at all of rust or encrustation.
- Someone who was talented at camouflage had very cunningly parked the facility's two-tonners in what seemed to be a haphazard pattern in the lot. But actually, what had happened, was that the trucks formed an effective screen, preventing anyone casually driving by in the street from observing what was going on at the rear door of the place.
- Someone had very carefully removed the bolted straps that held a ten-foot-wide section of chain-link fence in position and replaced them with nylon ties, which could be stripped off and replaced in a matter of seconds.
- A double-rear-axled truck had been backed between the fence posts, just far enough to make sure that it cleared.
- All of the above improvements to the real estate had been done while LC Strawhouse resided in nearby Detroit. What a coincidence, huh?

I told Gator and Rodent what I thought. They nodded their heads in agreement. I pawed at the surface of the parking lot with my shoe, rolling a pebble under my sole. "What's inside?" I took it for granted that they'd broken in to find out.

"Well, the National Guard's got its own weapons and ammunition in lockers," Rodent said. "But the big stuff belongs to ORDCOMSOMICH. They've got maybe three dozen lightweight 81-mike-mike mortars and fifty M-60 bipod rigs in storage crates, plus fifteen, maybe sixteen hundred M-16s, five hundred of the old M-92 Beretta pistols, and lots of ammunition—a hundred-and-fifty thousand rounds of 7.65 on links, a hundred thou 9mm, a hundred boxes each of frag grenades, CS, and Willy Peter, a few hundred mortar rounds, and five hundred cans of 5.56."

"And no one around to watch, right?"

Gator shook his head. "The hatches to all the weapons stowage lockers were disabled—good job, too. Unless you look close, you don't see the locks have been opened."

"It's all set to be moved," Rodent said. If anybody knew about load-outs, it was Rodent. He could pack anything from a semi to a C-5.

"And no sign of any security, right?"

Gator turned his palms up and shrugged. Of course not.

Hey, don't be surprised. Let me give you a little background here. As of late 1995:

- The goddamn Department of Energy can't seem to lay its hands on twenty-two kilos of misplaced weapons-grade plutonium. Oops.
- The Department of Defense seems to have lost track of eleven Alpha Units—you know about those, don't you? They are man-portable nuclear weapons, which were designed to be carried by SEALs and Blanketheads on infiltrations behind enemy lines. Sorry about that, folks.
- The folks in charge of destroying all of our chemical/biological/nerve warfare supplies have misplaced 276 containers of assorted nerve agents, including Sarin, an odorless, colorless, deadly nerve gas (which you should remember from the Tokyo subway incident a couple of years ago), its more powerful cousin, Tabun, as well as two new and highly classified agents, TSB-12, and SRQ-44. Well, nobody's perfect.

So, given the above facts, why the fuck would the Army bother to secure a paltry few thousand weapons and half a million rounds of ammunition?

That information makes you feel real secure, doesn't it?

Yeah—me, too. Anyway, I knew exactly how the assholes who were about to rip off this place were thinking: they could take a hundred, maybe even two hundred of the M-16s, eighty or ninety pistols, five mortars and half a dozen M-60 machine guns, and it would be months—perhaps even years—before the losses were discovered.

Why? Two reasons. First, because they knew that nobody ever does administrative inspection—the kind that requires a CO to check out every nut and bolt, count every round of ammunition, and fieldstrip and check each weapon under his command. That process takes time. It also takes effort. And there's all sorts of nasty paperwork that has to be filed when you come up missing something. So the simple answer is that admin inspections are seldom performed—even though the Army's inspector general knows that weapons are being stolen.

Second, it is common knowledge that mortars and machine guns are not used by National Guard infantry units very often. See, the 81-mike-mike has an effective range of 5,800 meters—that's just under four miles. The M-60 can reach out 1,100 meters. Neither is used in the Guard's trimonthly training cycles, when platoons go out to a nearby 200-yard rifle range. In fact, only when the full division trucks down to Georgia, or up to Marquette, or wherever the hell it holds its yearly two-week combat exercises at a base with adequate space and a huge fire-impact zone, would the mortars and machine guns actually be distributed.

This place was about to be plucked clean, and I wanted to be around when the motherpluckers showed up.

It was time to assemble the troops. We drove to a cellular phone store and I used a Visa card I keep under a pseudonym to buy three Motorola digital cellular phones. As soon as they were enabled, I dialed Rogue Manor.

"Yo—" Wonder's voice came through loud and clear.

Ain't technology great? *"Fuuuck* you. Eat shit and bark at the moon, Wonder."

He laughed. "And the same to you, Mr. Dickhead."

"Get my message?" I'd faxed him from Mugs's house with half a dozen short memos to plant in various Intelink compartments.

"Yup—all taken care of."

"Good." I told him to get all the merry marauders out here on the double—things, I said, were about to get interesting. I told him what I needed him to do. Wonder gave me an aye-aye, sir, threw me a verbal middle-fingered salute, and rang off.

Next, I called Mugs to give him my new cellular number. He took it down, then started asking questions like the chief he was. He listened to my sit-rep, then growled that he'd be on scene in two hours.

I started to tell him not to come until he interrupted and told me—let me put this in his precise words—"Sometimes, you're such a perfect fuckin' asshole that I see why they made you become an officer instead of promoting you to chief. Hasn't anybody ever fuckin' told you that you need to learn how to take 'yes' for an answer?"

When I spent more than two seconds thinking about it, it was, of course, a great idea. He was a retired cop who knew the turf and many of the players. And, more to the point, he had a huge safe full of firearms and a concealed weapons permit.

Of course, I didn't have to bring *that* subject up. "Don't worry your ugly face about the small stuff, Rotten Richard, I'm bringing the toys."

From the car I called the northern Virginia number the Priest had given me as a point of contact. A female voice answered. I gave her the code name I'd been assigned. She said nothing, but seconds later I heard the electronic beep of a phone ringing.

The Priest answered after four rings. "Hi, Dick—what's the score?"

Since I was talking on a nonsecure line, I brought him up to speed in a general way (no pun intended). I told him we were planning to stake out the ORDCOMSOMICH facility in Ypsilanti, and he agreed that was a good idea. From the way he asked questions about what I'd discovered, I could hear him taking mental notes.

When I'd finished, he paused, then asked, "Need anything?"

You bet. I was going to need a bucket of bucks for this operation.

Not a problem, said the Priest, he'd make sure to pass some cash to Wonder at the airport. Was there anything else? Any concrete developments?

You bet there were concrete developments, and they all concerned one LC Strawhouse. But I wasn't about to say anything—yet. I told him I'd be in touch, then hung up.

By the time I rang off, Gator had just about made it back to Detroit.

I'd left Rodent behind to keep watch—my *raton en la hierba,* or more accurately, *en el aparcamiento,* which means my rat in de parking lot. Gator'd drop me at the hotel, then flip back to join him. And soon, my two young animals would be joined by an old Frog. What a nasty fucking menagerie.

And me? I had to shower and change my clothes. There were other feral creatures to deal with tonight.

Chapter

10

AT 2225—ALMOST HALF AN HOUR LATE—I WENT UP TO THE HOTEL'S penthouse on a special elevator, which was operated by the same big bad BAW I'd tangled with the day before in the men's room. He wasn't so impeccable now—his wrist was splinted, his nose was taped, his lip was split, the skin of his cheek was purple-green, and his fifty-dollar haircut had been ruined when some emergency room doctor had shaved the side away so he could put stitches—ten or so from the size of the bandage—above the poor asshole's ear.

I threw Mr. BAW a shit-eating grin and a solid right to the shoulder as I came through the doors. "Request permission to come on board, guy." He didn't say anything. "Finally got that plumb assignment, I see—moving up in the world. Congratulations." I popped him again.

He winced, then turned his back so he could punch his buttons (I'll bet you he was thinking about punching other things), and we rode up the forty-six floors in silence, staring at the ceiling and listening to an elevator-music version of "I'll Be Watching You." How appropriate.

The doors whooshed open and I stepped out. "End of the hall to your left, sir," said Mr. BAW through gritted teeth.

"Watch yourself on the way down, fella. It's a big first step." The carpeted hallway curved gently away from the elevator bank. I strode to a pair of huge, double wood doors, in front of which stood yet another BAW in blue pinstripes, radio earpiece, and wrist mike.

This one couldn't have been nicer. "Good evening, sir," he said, careful to spell it with an *s* and an *i.*

I nodded toward the stratosphere. Where the hell did Dawg find these guys?

He opened the right-hand door and stood to the side. "Please go on in. Mr. Strawhouse is expecting you."

I'd anticipated a crowd, but he was waiting for me alone in the living room. There was a fireplace and a fire—cherry from the sweet smell of it—and a long, white couch flanked by two pairs of armchairs. The art was litho, but it was good litho. The carpet was impressively sumptuous. The servants had obviously come and gone, because the place was spotless—not a cocktail napkin, discarded hors d'oeuvre, or empty wineglass in sight. On the inch-thick glass coffee table was a bottle of Bombay gin that had been frozen into a block of ice the size of a cinder block. It was wrapped in a linen napkin and sat on a salver.

Next to the Bombay was an ice bucket, in which sat a half-pint Mason jar filled with golden liquid, and an open can of Coke. Next to the bucket was a single cut-crystal double Old-Fashioned glass and a single cocktail napkin. I *was* expected.

He was standing looking out over the huge terrace at the lights twinkling across the river in Windsor, Ontario. Over those fifty-dollar skivvies he was wearing a well-cut tuxedo. The trousers fell onto a pair of benchmade, black lizard cowboy boots. Above the collar of his ruffled shirt was a blue-and-white ribbon choker, suspended from which was his Congressional Medal of Honor.

He held a highball glass down to dregs and melted ice in his left hand. He must have seen my reflection in the glass because he turned and toasted me with his glass. "Howdy, Dick. Welcome to the spread."

"Evening."

"Missed cha at the shindig."

"I had commitments."

"Too bad. It was a real lollapalooza. You shoulda seen my table —had me some senators, a passel of active duty generals and admirals, some local bidnessmens—captains of industry and all that horse puckey. It was a real kick-ass group of folks."

"Sorry I couldn't make it."

He nodded. "Me, too—coulda meant some mean bidness for you, now you're a civilian again."

I didn't say anything, so he turned back toward the view and changed the subject with a sweeping gesture. "Nice, huh?"

It was better than nice, and I told him so.

He laughed. "You're right," he said. "It's amazing what six thousand seven hundred and fifty bucks a day exclusive of room service will buy." He laughed again. "Hey, know what? I need a refill, and you need a drink."

"Thanks." I looked around. "Where's Dawg?"

"He's off prowlin' and growlin' somewhere," the Californian said noncommittally. "You know Dawg—he gets so damn restless. Sometimes I think he's bored with me." He strode over to the coffee table, picked up the half-pint Mason jar, carefully tilted some of the liquid into his highball glass, added three ice cubes, and filled it to the rim with Coke. "G'wan—he'p yourself."

"Thanks." I put a handful of ice in my glass and reached for the Bombay.

Before I got to pour any, LC Strawhouse interrupted. "Smell that." He passed the Mason jar in front of my nose.

The aroma was definitely moonshine. But different, somehow.

"G'wan, g'wan, taste it—it's okay—sip it right from the bowl, boy." He handed it to me. I took a small gulp and handed the jar back to Strawhouse. "Smooth."

"Damn right it's smooth. That's *melon*shine, boy—melonshine. And you ain't ever had nothing like it before. Two hundred proof, and smoother than any damn twenty-year-old single-malt scotch in the whole damn world. I got me a good ol' boy from west Arkansas, makes it up for me twice a year. Five-gallon lots. And ya know the secret? Tomatoes. He adds damn tomatoes to the mash, along with his melons and other shit."

The thought brought a crooked smile to LC's face. "Well, go on, son, pour yourself some of that damn expensive Limey gin you like so much, then park your fanny on the divan so's we can chaw some fat."

I don't know how it is for you out there, but so far as I was concerned, his folksy, redneck, sawdust-on-the-floor, sit-around-the-cracker-barrel-and-put-your-feet-up-on-the-pot-belly-stove crapola was getting just a bit too thick for me.

"Hey, fuck you, asshole," I said by way of a wake-up call. "You're not standing there wearing goddamn bib overalls and shit kickers. So just cut the phony redneck accent and the "aw-shucks" backwoods crap and deal straight, huh?"

That brought him up short. He looked at me as if I was crazy. Then he took a good-size swallow of melonshine and Coke, slapped the glass back on the table, wiped his mouth with the back of his hand, and laughed. "I guess there's no shitting a shitter, eh, Dick?"

That depended on who was shitting whom. "You said it, LC, not me."

He paused. From the way he looked at me I guessed that few people ever spoke to him the way I just had. "Well," he said finally, "I like that. I like a man who's straightforward. My first ten deals were made with spit-on-your-palm handshakes—and they made me rich." He sipped his drink. "Now I got me two hundred damn lawyers on staff to draw up contracts, got me another hundred at four firms in Los Angeles, New York, London, and Washington—and those sons of bitches bill me five hundred an hour plus expenses to have some damn paralegal look over the heretofores and whereases and forthwiths my staff guys write—and I still get my ass sued all the damn time for breach of this, or lack of that, or failure to whatever. Shit, I'd rather go back to those old-fashioned handshake deals."

I could relate to that. But I wasn't here to talk about lawyers or deals—I wanted to know why he thought a bunch of tangos hijacking an airplane in Key West wanted to talk to him so bad. So I asked.

"Hell," he said, "probably because they knew I'm a straight shooter." He sipped his drink and watched me react. "I get all kinds of calls like that. Man went crazy last year, took his wife hostage. I was on *Larry King*—the sonofabitch called me up and I talked him down, right there live on the TV show."

He shrugged. "Bottom line? I got no idea why those hijackers called for me, other than *I'd* rather talk to me than the president, because between the two of us, I'm the one with the most honest answers." He sipped again and gave me a wistful look over the top of his glass. "Y'know, I wish the FBI had called me—I probably coulda done something so you wouldn't have had to wax them dumbass fellas."

But the FBI's assistant director for operations *had* called LC

Strawhouse—and he'd turned the Bureau down flat, complete with deleted expletives. I'd seen the MEMCON.

So much for LC Strawhouse and his honest answers.

I don't know if you've realized this yet, gentle readers, but so far as I was concerned, there was something distinctly unkosher going on here.

Let's look at the situation from where I stood.

- *Item.* LC Strawhouse, or someone close to him, was reading the files I'd planted in Intelink.
- *Item.* If he could read my bogus files, that meant he could manipulate the whole damn system—just like Wonder was doing.
- *Item.* If he could manipulate the entire system, then he could also move evidence around, pilfer information, change the substance of documents, even "shred" the contents of files. All electronically. All without leaving any fingerprints—unless we knew what we were looking for and set a trap for him, the way we'd done.

No wonder the Priest had wanted me and my men sheep-dipped. No wonder he had insisted that we stay out of the military loop. I had to take for granted that there was nothing in the Intelink system that LC Strawhouse couldn't lay his hands on if he wanted to.

No wonder Gunny Barrett's memo to the Priest had been handwritten—if it had been put on the computer, then LC would probably know about it already, and my ample Slovak behind would be incipient grass.

Okay—I know that one of my SpecWar commandments says that Thou shalt never assume (because to assume makes an ASS of yoU and ME). But let's break that commandment. Let us assume that LC Strawhouse was dirty. The question then becomes, what kind of dirty? Was he skimming inside information in order to get business? Was he selling it—and if so, to whom? Or was he using his access to help him run for president—creating a private intelligence network that could spread chaos, confusion, and disinformation inside the government.

Well, friends, there are several ways of finding out. One way would be to confront him—the old Perry Mason–style straightforward in-your-face accusation.

That, I knew, would never work. LC Strawhouse had spent the past year and a half on TV talk shows. There wasn't a question he hadn't been asked—from the ridiculous on MTV ("Have you ever dropped acid?"), to the sublime on *Larry King* ("LC, some people call you a pseudofascist—how do you feel about Mussolini?"). No—old LC had been to TV school. He knew how to deflect questions with humor, wit, or sarcasm. The direct approach was not going to work. I was going to have to hit him through the back door—that's my SEAL shorthand for using unconventional warfare.

In this case, however, I wasn't about to shoot and loot literally. What I wanted was to create a psychological edge for myself. I chose to do it by attacking his sense of self-esteem and sowing confusion.

But I could not accomplish that goal in an overtly intellectual manner—he'd see right through me. Instinctively, I knew I'd have to be damn subtle. In fact, I'd have to be fucking inscrutable. (That was probably the only way I could give him the screwting he deserved.) So I fell back on the fundamentals of unconventional Warriordom—teachings I'd studied as a Tadpole.

It was Roy Boehm's idea to take young Frogs and inculcate them—us—in the mysteries of Oriental philosophy. We all thought it was a lot of bullshit at the time—and God knows we gave Roy a lot of grief when he made us memorize snippets from Sun Tzu, Chang Yu, Miyamoto Musashi, and a bunch of other ancient warriors. In fact, he had literally to pound the knowledge into us, often with the help of his fists. But guess what—later, in battle, when the *merde* was hitting the *ventillateur* and lives were at stake, those words of wisdom and philosophy came back to help us win; to help us kill our enemies in great numbers.

So, now, did Roy's advice come back to me, once more—this time in the words of the great Chinese tactician Chang Yu, who tells us that the Warrior controls his enemy by causing frustration, aggravation, confusion, and harassment.

But isn't that advice just a tad obvious, Master Marcinko-san?

Sure it is, Tadpole—but it's precisely the kind of Keep-It-Simple-Stupid advice that works.

I accept the wisdom of your experience, Master Marcinko-san. But then, how is such a formidable yet simple goal accomplished?

Well, Tadpole, listen up. I take my lesson today from the well-read precepts of a master swordsman known as Fudo, who was a seventeenth-century disciple of the great Miyamoto Musashi.

Fudo was born in Kyoto in 1627. (He was known as "The Immovable One" for those of you who are interested in such trivia, and like Cher, Roseanne, and Halston he had only one name.) Orphaned at the age of twelve, he became an itinerant Shinto priest. At twenty-one, he had an epiphany and turned all of his energies to learning the art of the blade. By 1652, he had already invented the controversial Bushido fighting method combining Kendo and Fujitsu that has come to be known as Statue technique. It was probably best summed up in Fudo's famous 1654 haiku on swordsmanship:

Air cut through by steel.
The blade stops: from silent stone,
Death is preordained.

Now, if you have followed the Way of the Warrior, Tadpole, you will know that this Haiku can be interpreted in several ways. The "silent stone" of which Fudo writes, for example, can mean the enemy, or it can mean the Warrior himself.

Come off it, Master Marcinko-san. This is just so much macho psychobabble horse puckey, and I ain't buying it.

Impudent Tadpole, you have much to learn. Listen and I will impart wisdom.

See, if the enemy has become silent stone, that means he has been robbed of all ability to defend, plan, and resist because the blade, stopped in its deadly path, has reduced him to fear and confusion. But if it is the Warrior who has turned into silent stone, then he becomes as impenetrable as granite. His motives cannot be fathomed, and he will create confusion and disorder.

But that is contradictory, Master Marcinko-san. You can't have it both ways.

Of course it is contradictory, Tadpole. But you forget, as Master Boehm has taught, that the essential discipline of Mindfulness requires everything to be everything, and in equal degrees of being. The endless interaction that affects the destinies of all creatures and things. Think of it as the balance represented by black and white. Yin and yang. Laurel and Hardy. Abbott and Costello. Clinton and Gore.

Oh, Master Marcinko-san, I fear you have gone off the deep end here.

Fuuuuck you, Tadpole, get out of my goddamn temple—you're beyond help.

But *I* wasn't beyond help. Because, I remembered something else significant about Fudo's haiku: I recalled that Statue technique can form an effective basis for interrogation.

For those of you who are now totally confused, let me explain. Silence is a great and effective weapon when used during interrogation. Simply put, you stare the asshole down until he feels compelled to speak.

Yeah, I know you're dubious, but it works, damn it. As a matter of fact, it's even been adapted as part of the CIA's current interrogation doctrine. Christians in Action even printed Fudo's haiku in their training manual.

I know it works because I saw it used by Toshiro Okinaga, my old friend from Kunika, the Japanese national police counterterrorism unit, during a joint operation we conducted a few years back. Tosho captured a Japanese Red Army suspect, on whom interrogation seemingly didn't work. Kunika's toughest agents tried to break the guy—but he wouldn't crack.

Then, Tosho had the tango brought to a tiny cell. There, the two of them sat, face-to-face. Tosho stared intently at the prisoner for forty minutes without moving, without blinking, without seemingly even breathing. The JRA tango found Tosho's penetrating gaze irresistible—it was as if he suddenly found himself compelled to speak. Ultimately, he confessed his sins willingly.

It would be interesting to see how long LC Strawhouse could hold back when he was faced with the combination of Musashi and Fudo—channeled through me. I took a sip of my Bombay, then set the glass on the table, and stared at the billionaire, focusing on the Congressional Medal just below his Adam's apple. I didn't blink. You couldn't see me take a breath. Just silence. And patience.

LC Strawhouse, no inscrutable Oriental, lasted less than a minute and a half. At first, he looked puzzled. Then he set his glass down and fixed me with an ingratiating smile. When I didn't react, he picked his drink back up, sipped it, and put it down again. Then he drummed his bony fingers on the table brrrrrm, brrrrrm. Then he coughed. Then he looked at me again. He started to stand, sat himself back down, and smiled once more, nervously.

"Not that they didn't deserve what they got," he blurted. "Assholes—they were stupid assholes."

Once again, he waited for me to say something. When I didn't, he began again. This time I got the full, boilerplate campaign speech. "Dick, you've gotta see what I see—which is, the world has gone crazy and it needs to be fixed." He retrieved his drink, took a sip, and replaced it carefully on the coffee table. "We've lost our sense of responsibility—the kind of independent, pioneer spirit our grandparents had. Take these damn lawsuits today. You make anything these days, you get sued.

"The damn gummint's no better, either. I own a company makes bricks. So last year OSHA—that Occupational Safety and Health Administration—they sued me. Some thirty-five-thousand-dollar-a-year bureaucrat wanted me to put damn warning labels on my bricks because he'd ground 'em up and fed 'em to rats, and the rats *died.*" He slapped his hand on the arm of his chair. "Hell, boy, you'd die, too, you ate ten pounds of ground brick.

"And that's the bidness end of it. Look at what's happening in the military. You walked the floor at the convention—it's all simulators and war games now. Damn toys. Nobody wants to hump through the mud anymore down and dirty, the way you and I did. And that's the least of it. We got no gumption. Got no pride, no esprit—you get that from the top down, and there's no 'top' around. Hell, Dick, we ain't got but a few man o' warsmen left—and they're getting rid of 'em as fast as they can."

His well-rehearsed monologue went on for another half hour and two more melonshine-and-Cokes. He talked about downsizing the military and lack of preparedness, the rising crime rates, the proliferation of welfare fraud, coddled criminals, and our over-bearing government. I let him babble on. I never changed my expression. I never let him catch me breathing or blinking.

When he ran out of canned speechifying, he blustered and flustered as he tried to probe this way and that, exploring for some sign that would allow him to get past my implacable presence. Finally, he began talking about me.

First, he recited my whole curriculum vitae. It was obvious from what he said that he'd been given access to all my fitreps—even the classified ones from SEAL Team Six and Red Cell. He quoted from NIS internal memos, written during the Navy's $60 million investigation of my activities. He even recounted Pinky Prescott's memos damning me for operating UNODIR.

I took his words in stony silence. I knew what he was doing: he was trying to build a case against the Navy. Why? Because he was trying to recruit me.

It's an old intelligence officer's trick. You turn the target against the people for whom he works. You flatter. You cajole. You make nicee-nicee. And then, before he knows it, you've set your hook, and he's dead meat.

True to formula, his tone and demeanor changed—it went from patriarchal to seductive.

He insisted that he needed my help. The Navy had screwed me and I owed it nothing. Even if I was out of the Navy, the government could still come after me. After all, they'd done it before. But LC would help me—if I supported him. After all, he said, I still had my network of friends—lots of them—and he wanted me to use my influence in the SpecWar community to help him achieve his goals. It was in my power, he said.

That had to be the core of it. The real shoot-and-looters weren't behind him—and he wanted them. Obviously he knew I still had some influence in that quarter, because the s.o.b. was going all out now—little flecks of spittle flicking past my shoulder as he prattled on about if he won the White House, I would be assured of a top administration job. "You'd be the president's personal shoot-and-looter," Strawhouse said, a lopsided grin spreading over his face. "Think about it, Dick—think about it."

My face was a mask.

He spread his arms, palms up, as if in supplication. His tone changed again, from coy to conspiratorial. "The truth, Dick, is that you gotta run the country like a bidness. That's the only efficient way to give the people their money's worth. But in bidness, there's room for only one CEO; one chairman of the board.

"One point of view," he said again. He waited for me to respond. "One way of life. One set of values—"

That sounded like totalitarianism to me—Stalinist, in fact. But I remembered Fudo's haiku, bit my tongue, and didn't say anything.

He looked at me for confirmation. "Right? Well—am I right? I'm right. No doubt about it." You could just see how the silence provoked him.

Which is exactly what I wanted. And finally, just as the immortal Japanese warrior had predicted, my behavior caused him to act precipitously.

I watched as his face took on a wild-eyed expression that was abhorrent, malevolent, and indescribably frightening. "Know what's gonna happen, Dick? I do. The country's gonna come apart at the damn seams. First they'll disarm us so all the guns'll be in the hands of criminals. Drugs? They'll be everywhere, and nobody stoppin' 'em. Domestic terrorism. That's the next step. Oklahoma City was nothing—nothing, compared to what's gonna happen soon. It'll be total anarchy—the animals in control and no way to stop 'em. The whole social fabric will come apart at the damn seams." He paused. Caught his breath.

"And y'know what? It was you who showed me the way."

I fought the impulse to move, to respond. What the hell was he saying? I knew the only way I'd find out was to keep him talking. I remained mute.

"It was you," he said. "I read all that stuff about London—that fucking asshole Brookfield. He had it all wrong. Tried to organize the shit out of things." His face was red now—his eyes fucking crazy. "See, that's the mistake they all make. They organize—they leave tracks. They make patterns. Patterns are bad, right? They're fucking conventional, Dick. You can trace a pattern. But you can't trace chaos. Chaos just happens. No pattern. Just action."

I stared at him, silent. He continued babbling. "There's nobody to stop the chaos—nobody except me. *Me.* Do it my way, too—which is the same as your way. You know what to do—hunt 'em, and kill 'em. Kill 'em all—the animals, the dissenters, the damn bureaucrats. Think of it as taking out the garbage."

He looked over at me for some sort of endorsement. He got only my blank Zen stare. He responded by taking another sip of melonshine and Coke, gulping his words as he continued. "But you know what *that* takes, 'cause you been there. Strong fist. Absolute power. Now, you call it what the damn hell you wanna call it, boy—I think of it as dynamic gummint. Them assholes got other words for it—autocratic, fascist, totalitarian—well, screw 'em. Shit, it's what this country needs. Dose o' salts. Political enema. Fresh start. Know what I think? I say, to hell with the Congress—all those self-important bastards who take your rights away; to hell with the judicial system—goddam pussy-assed judges who won't take a hard stand on anything. And to hell with all those damn checks and balances—which haven't worked in fifty years anyway. We don't fucking need 'em—any of 'em."

He drained his drink and filled it up again. He'd gone glassy-eyed, and I wondered how many he'd actually had. "Know why I'm gonna be president?" he asked rhetorically.

No response.

It didn't matter—he couldn't wait to tell me. "'Cause I got the balls to do what's got to be done—to force America to realize how bad it needs me. And it does need me, Dick—it needs us—needs our kind of leadership."

He paused long enough to catch his breath and sip his drink.

"Y'know, when I look at that weak-kneed, pussy-whipped fella up there in the White House," he slurred, "I get sick. I wanna throw up. He's nothing but a draft-dodging, pussy-whipped, pot-smoking womanizer. A coward, Dick—the man's a coward. You know what that means? It means he's not my commander in chief, and I'm not beholden to obey his damn orders, follow his damn directives, or respect his damn laws."

Well, friends, that's not true. The president *may* be a cowardly, pussy-whipped, draft-dodging, pot-smoking womanizer—and if he is, then impeach the sonofabitch, or vote him out of office (or better yet, don't vote him *in* in the first place).

But the president *is* the commander in chief. Full stop. End of story. And I understood now what LC Strawhouse had in mind for us. All those missing weapons—they'd go to drug gangs, crazies, paranoids. And while the FBI and the rest of 'em looked for structure, for patterns, for some kind of master plan, all those thousands of armed and dangerous asshole crazies would be out there shooting and looting—courtesy of LC Strawhouse.

LC was right about one thing. It would fucking turn America inside out.

But LC wanted to do more than that. He was looking to encourage the same kind of bottom-up revolution Charlie Manson hoped to bring about by his random murders back in the late sixties. Manson called it helter-skelter. Of course, Charlie Manson was nutball crazy. Loony. Psycho. Sociopathic.

But then, I told myself, so was LC Strawhouse. What he'd do was pass out a lot of guns and explosives to a bunch of dangerous crazies—and innocent people would end up getting killed. Killed so he could make a political point. Just like the tango assholes who bombed the Murrah building in Oklahoma City. They'd wanted to make a political point, too. They did—but not the one they'd intended to.

He was sweaty now and wheezing, moisture obvious around the edge of his collar, his face flushed from the booze. From the look of it he'd talked himself out. But he'd gone too far. He had left the back door open and I'd snuck in—gotten a glimpse of what he had backstage. Yeah, I knew what he wanted—and the most incredible thing was that he'd thought I might want to be a part of it.

Don't be fooled, friends. I may fight the system with every molecule of energy and strength I can summon up. But I struggle not to destroy the system but to make it better. I want admirals who lead, not manage. I want shooters who can kill. I want a fucking Navy that can go to war and win. I want a nation that will always persevere. Fucking LC Strawhouse had made the same mistake Grant Griffith had—he misread my anger. He thought I could be bought.

Well, he—like Grant Griffith before him—was wrong. I may be a rogue—but I am a patriotic rogue. So now—*now* it was time to act. I fixed LC in my sights, walked up to him real close, fingered the Congressional Medal of Honor that hung round his neck and let it plop back atop his throat.

Then I took both his lapels in my hands and put my nose about an inch from his. "Listen, you worthless pencil-dicked sack of shit, you were a member of the armed forces—just like me. And when you're a member of the armed forces, you take an oath to preserve, protect, and defend the fucking Constitution—just like I did. And you know what that means, *cockbreath?* It means you don't have to *like* the man who is president, or even *respect* him. You just have to be willing to *die* for him. That's your fucking job. That's what the fucking oath you took is all about."

He wasn't used to being spoken to like this. "I'll deal with you, talking to me like that," he slurred. A globule of spittle was caught in the corner of his mouth, giving him a slightly demented appearance.

He tried to say something else but I flipped the medal back onto his shirt, pushed on his chest, sending him back onto the sofa, and stepped away. "Now *you* get *this* straight, *asshole.* Yes, the fucking Navy has screwed me in the past. And, yes, the fucking Navy would probably try to bend me over and jam the big banana up inside again if it ever got the chance to. But it is *my* Navy, and *my* country, and no peckerwood-talking sonofabitch billionaire cockbreath is going to steal it out from under me without a hell of a fight."

My friends, it was absolutely clear to me right then that this moonshine-sipping schmuck was nothing more than another tango—no different from the goddamn IRA child killers that Mick Owen chased in Ulster, the Japanese Red Army assassins Toshiro Okinaga tracked in Tokyo, the ADAM assholes I'd waxed in Key West, or the Islamic Jihad fundamentalists I'd hunted in Afghanistan, Libya, and wherever else I could find 'em and kill 'em.

They deserved to die because they brought violence into the political arena. Simply put, when things weren't going their way, they hijacked planes, blew up buildings, and left car bombs on busy streets—killing innocent people to make their point.

Well, LC Strawhouse was a tango, too. But he had set his sights on a bigger target and more hostages than you could find on an aircraft in Key West, the World Trade Center in New York, or downtown Oklahoma City. He wanted to hijack the whole fucking country.

"Y'know," I said, "I think you better look for a different kind of bad boy to help you out. Because you're precisely the kind of asshole I like to go hunting for. And y'know, LC—your fucking head's gonna look just great stuffed and mounted on my wall."

I let myself out past the blue, pinstriped BAW, rang for the elevator and descended in silence as Band-Aid Billy Bob or Bobby Bill or whoever the fuck gave me the cold shoulder. There was a bar in the lobby, and it occurred to me that a Bombay on the rocks might help take the nasty taste of LC Strawhouse away. I started across the sculptured carpet but stopped abruptly—just as if I'd sensed a trip wire and booby trap.

I have a very good instinctual sixth sense. It has kept me alive. I have stopped, foot poised on jungle trails, and seen land mines right where I was about to tread. In Libya, a tango shot straight at me—the bullet shattered a wall directly behind the spot I stood. I hadn't heard anything—but I sensed that he was there and I ducked away in time. Last year in London, my instincts kept me from being scooped up by NIS Terminators because, as I approached Grosvenor Square, where they'd set up their ambush, I sensed that all was not right and took evasive action.

Here, too, something made me pull up short—to not enter the bar. Instead, I stopped and sniffed the air, just the way I do when I am hunting tangos. The scent of danger was palpable to me.

I stepped back, out of the light, and observed from the shadow. There, across the room, a cellular phone just like the one he'd given me sitting at his elbow, and engaged in deep conversation with someone whose face I couldn't see, was the Priest.

It was, I decided, time to regroup.

Chapter

11

It was snowing by the time I changed into jeans, running shoes, and a Michigan State Rose Bowl sweatshirt, checked out of the hotel, packed up the car, and hauled balls out to Ypsilanti. The drive was slowed by nasty weather—slippery highway with ice patches, and big, fat, wet snowflakes, the kind that clot on your windshield no matter how hot you run the defroster. Then they catch on your windshield wipers and burn out the motors. I had a lot of time to think about my situation, and I didn't like what I came up with at all.

If the Priest and LC Strawhouse were connected, then everything I was doing had been compromised from the very start, and I was dog meat. But—and this means a lot with me—I had liked the Priest. He'd struck me as one of the good guys, and I am not often mistaken about that sort of thing.

So, perhaps he had good reason to be in Detroit and not to tell me he was here—he was, after all, the guy whose door read NDBBM. Maybe he'd come out to visit the SpecWar convention, and not to see LC Strawhouse. Maybe. And maybe not. I sighed and watched the windshield wipers struggle with the wet snowflakes. Shit—I was fucked.

* * *

There wasn't a whole lot to do at the armory. Wonder and the rest of the crew had gone to Rent-A-Wreck, leased two cars for a month (and charged them on one of Freddie the Forger's best pieces of rubber plastic—standard operating procedure when you're operating undercover), then driven direct from Detroit Metro about two hours before. Mugs had wasted no time in deploying them. When he ascertained from Rodent and Gator that the bad guys hadn't shown up yet, he had the two animals take everyone on a growly prowl so nobody would get lost in the neighborhood and fuck up. Then he handed out weapons and flashlights. Then he broke the group into two five-man watches—eight hours on, eight hours off.

He'd brought extra batteries for the flashlights, AAA maps, and two two-gallon thermos jugs of hot coffee with him. There was a portable digital police scanner on the dashboard of his car, and a CB radio in the glove compartment. God bless all chiefs. (Yes, friends, you have seen this material before, and you will see it again. And again.)

Wonder had packed a few supplies, too. He brought a pair of Night Enforcers—range-finding, three-power night-vision binoculars he'd managed to liberate from the United Nations during one of his four covert trips to Iraq as a bogus nuclear weapons inspector. He'd remembered my favorite—not to mention well-worn—leather sap, as well as a handful of nylon restraints, a couple of rolls of duct tape, and the wallet of false IDs I keep in the secret compartment beneath the Rogue Manor kitchen floor next to Pinky's NIS file. Ever conscious of my need to dress well, he'd also packed a set of black BDUs. (I wished he'd remembered my boots, though. My toes were getting real cold in nylon running shoes and cotton socks.) Still, in his suitcase there *were* eight scrambler radios with four sets of spare batteries and chargers, and a battery-powered direction-finding beacon/receiver that we'd stolen from NIS's Technical Security Division, located in Building 22 at the Washington Navy Yard, when Red Cell had performed a proctosopy—that is to say, a security exercise—about two years ago.

And Christmas came early for Dickie this year. I forgot all about my cold feet when Wonder handed over a Heckler & Koch P7 9mm pistol with Trijicon night sights, two magazines, and an SOB—I know what you're probably thinking, but the acronym stands for Small-Of-the-Back—holster that he'd all brought especially for me. I didn't want to know where he'd gotten the P7, but Wonder volunteered the fact that no felony had been committed while obtaining it. (Knowing him, I checked to make sure he wasn't crossing his fingers behind his back.)

Actually, I wasn't worried about firearms and ammo—there was a damn building full of lethal goodies sitting right in front of us, ready for a mean motherplucker like me to do some plucking. I turned to Wonder. "Okay, so you brought me a gun—but if you really loved me you'd have brought your lockpicks." He swiveled his neck left-right-left, right-left-right, smiled behind the yellow wraparound shooting glasses, reached inside his parka and retrieved a small leather case. He unfolded it and proudly showed me his American Express card—and his precious burglar tools. "Don't even think about telling me what you won't leave home without," I told him. "Just take some of your brothers and go to work."

Nine minutes later, he, Doc, Nasty, and Duck Foot returned with enough firepower to violate most if not all of the weapons laws in the United States. They brought out six Beretta M-92 pistols—old ones that were made in Italy in the late eighties and pawned off on National Guard units about five years ago—and 1,000 rounds of 9mm ball ammo. They also retrieved a pair of M-16 assault rifles—*real* assault rifles: the kind that are fully automatic, not the wanna-be semiautos they argue about in Congress—thirty 20-round magazines, two 840-round cans of 5.56 ball, and one can of 5.56 tracer.

Duck Foot and Wonder had filled their ample pockets with grenades—ten riot control grenades that spread CS tear gas, a dozen concussion grenades—these are *grenades,* friends, not stun devices. They are lethal—and eight white smokers.

Doc Tremblay carried out two Remington 870 riot shotguns, a hundred rounds of double-0 buckshot, and four shot-shell bandoleers—shit, he'd look like Pancho fucking Villa with his big droopy mustache if he wore 'em crossed over his chest. And for some unfathomable reason he appropriated a couple of hundred 5.56 training blanks—the kind of ammo National Guard units use for demonstration purposes. When I asked why the hell he'd bothered, he told me that he was going to pull the plugs out, dump the powder, and use the virgin, primed cases for some of his handmade hot sniper loads. Brass, he explained in his broad Rhode Island accent, was getting "mo-ah and mo-ah expensive these days."

And Nasty? He had found one LAW, and somehow also discovered a one-kilo block of C-4 plastic explosive, half a dozen pencil detonators, three M-1 spring-loaded firing devices, and fifty yards of OD tripwire. Where the hell does he come up with this stuff? I tell you, if the asshole ever retires, he can find work as a bomb-sniffing dog.

We had four rental cars, so we broke the equipment down between them and returned Mugs's goodies to him—under protest.

The snow was still coming down. That was a catch-22 problem. See, if you sit in a warm car with your engine idling and your wipers slapping, you're gonna look like you're on a stakeout. But if you turn the engine off, then your windshield freezes over, your side windows coat up with snow, and you can't see fuck-all.

Moreover, it's much easier to spot car tracks in the snow—and if the armory was going to be cased, I wanted it to look as if no one was in the area—which precluded any cars close at hand.

So, I made an executive decision. A quarter mile from the armory I rented two rooms for us at a Motel 6 where they'd kept the lights on for us. One watch would hole up. They'd be on call but free to grab combat naps, hot showers, and food. The other watch would set up in positions on the armory perimeter and keep their eyes open.

The first night we froze our behinds without any tangible results except frozen behinds. It snowed right on into the morning—six and a half inches by daybreak—which did wonders for my nylon running shoes. Well, at least I wasn't wearing sandals. It stopped snowing by midafternoon, and the roads were plowed before rush hour. (It actually works like that in the Midwest.) Since we'd had eight hours rest, Wonder, Nasty, Duck Foot, Cherry, Mugs, and I took the night watch—1800 to 0200. We set Nasty in an observation post behind a convenient trash Dumpster. He protested, but it didn't matter. He was the youngest and besides he couldn't smell much because his nose had been smashed almost flat when he'd taken a bad—read seventy-foot—fall at the end of a HALO exercise some years ago.

Nasty was positioned at green eight on the armory's left side.

Green eight? Yes, that means he was sitting on the armory's left side, in the fore-quarter.

Let me explain. In CT—counterrorism—operations, you generally have teams coming from all sides when they stage the assault. In the heat of battle, when things get confused—the nineteenth-century philosopher Karl von Clausewitz called it *"la friction*—the fog of war"—what is on the right to me, may be on the left to someone else. If I say, "Take the guy on the right out," and we are talking about opposite sides, the clusterfuck quotient progresses upward geometrically all the way to FUBAR.

To prevent such situations, I have adapted what the SAS calls the Colour Clock Code. (Yeah—in this instance I even spell *colour* with a *u* just like my Brit pal Captain Mick Owen, who runs SAS's Special Missions detachment of tango hunters, does.)

Looking at any target from the front, the colour clock goes like this: front side is white, left side is green, back side is black, and right side is red. The middle of the white zone is six o'clock; the middle of the black zone is twelve. Nasty's Dumpster was at eight o'clock green. See—now everybody including you knows exactly where he was positioned.

Duck Foot scaled a drainpipe and sat on the roof with the night-vision glasses—out of the wind, I might add—roving between white five and seven. Cherry and I hid out in a couple of tractor-trailers in the adjacent lot to make sure we could close the back door if necessary, and Wonder played CTC—that's chauffeur to the chief—cruising the neighborhood in Mugs's Buick. How does Wonder always manage to get the plum assignments?

At 2010—that's just past 8 P.M. civilian time—Duck Foot's voice came over the radio. "Big Ford Crown Victoria with four assholes inside just stopped at white six."

I poked my nose out of the trailer. "Copy that."

"They're moving off now, passing green eight."

Mugs's voice broke in. "Get a license number?"

There was a pause. "Juliet Foxtrot Whiskey eight-nine-nine," Duck Foot's voice came back at us.

"I'll run it," said Mugs's voice. "I still got friends in low places and I've never used one of these here cellular phones."

God bless all chiefs. See—I told you you'd see it again.

Duck Foot's voice came on-line. "They turned around and came back. They're sitting on the other side of the street, opposite white six."

Wonder said, "I got 'em. Lemme take a look."

Damn him—"Shit, Wonder—hold off." It was too late. I saw the car cruise by. That meant the Buick was no further use. If he came by again, he was blown. Wonder's voice came through loud and clear. "Yup—four assholes. Two salt-and-pepper teams."

"Thanks for nothing." We didn't have the resources to play around like that. "Damn it, Wonder, wait until I tell you to fucking act, okay?"

He actually sounded chastened. "Sorry, Skipper."

After five minutes, Mugs's voice came back to me, "You're not gonna believe this."

Frankly, I was cold enough to believe almost anything. "Go on."

"It's registered to the fucking FBI Detroit field office."

Feds? That gave me pause. Who knew I was here? Well, LC Strawhouse knew I was in Detroit. But only the Priest—who had snuck into town—knew I'd been snooping around Ypsilanti. Well, maybe it was coincidence—the Bureau was just checking up on armories because there had been a lot of thefts lately.

Friends, you know as well as I do that coincidence doesn't happen in my line of work. It even occurred to me that they weren't interested in stolen weapons at all, but in armed and dangerous ex-felons like me who might be lurking in the vicinity.

But I had the edge here. "Mugs—"

"Yo."

"Can you check on them with the scanner—see what the hell they're doing here?"

"You got it."

The wind picked up. I hunkered down just inside the trailer while I waited.

Twelve minutes later, Mugs called back. "We're fucked. They've gotta be on some kind of scrambled tactical frequency, because I can't get a handle on 'em worth a damn—and I've been wearing the fuckin' keys offen the scanner."

So much for technology.

"Skipper—" It was Duck Foot again.

"Yo."

"Second car—station wagon—just pulled into the top of the red alley just below me, facing one o'clock. I think it was four guys inside, too."

I started to say something when Duck Foot interrupted in a hoarse whisper. "Third vehicle. Van. Two visibles. They're working their way toward the black eleven, coming up past you."

It was a fucking stakeout. Had to be. "Keep me posted." I dropped back deep inside the trailer just in case the assholes in the van were also carrying night vision.

Damn—it was going to be a long, cold night. Let me clarify that.

It was going to be a long, cold night—for us. For the FBI, it was going to be a long, warm night.

Why do I say that? Because they sat in their goddamn cars with the engines idling and the heaters on and the windows up, which of course made them stick out like the sore Dicks—as in Dick Tracy—that they are.

Now frankly, friends, this is not how you conduct a stakeout. Not, that is, if you actually want to catch the bad guys. Why? Because Mr. Perp, if he has an IQ of more than 10, is gonna drive by and case the joint. When he does, he's gonna see a bunch of assholes sitting in idling vehicles with lots of antennas in strange places—vehicles which, as I've already explained, are real easy to spot in the wintertime—and he's gonna take the well-known powder.

I checked my watch. 2035. It was still early—there was steady traffic moving on the four-lane avenue in front of the armory. The 7-Eleven down the street was doing a brisk business. If I was a bad guy, I wouldn't hit this place until after midnight, when things quieted down. That gave me some wriggle room.

Something else occurred to me, too. "Mugs?"

His voice came right back. "Yo, Richard, you rotten asshole."

Ah, he still loved me. "Anything else playing on the scanner, Chief?"

"Not really. The usual traffic. A state copper grabbed himself a stolen car down near Milan. There was a fistfight at a pizzeria in Ann Arbor."

"What about our pals here in Ypsilanti?"

"There's a lot of Code-6 activity over by the KFC on Route Twenty-three"—Mugs was using cop-talk to tell me a bunch of blue shirts were grabbing their dinners at the Kentucky Fried Chicken stand—"and some idiot drove his car over a patch of ice onto somebody's front lawn—they've got a wrecker on the scene. But other than that, nada. It's all quiet."

"How does that strike you?" I asked Mugs.

He paused and thought it over before replying. "Now that you mention it, it strikes me as strange, Richard. Very strange."

It had struck me exactly the same way. Let me explain why. See, the FBI usually coordinates all of its moves with local law enforcement. That is because in the past there have been some nasty testicular confrontations between local cops and Special Agents, when the left ball didn't know where the right ball was swinging. These days, Bureau SOP was to advise local law enforcement of all activity, and to request backup—except in those few cases in which the locals are thought to be part of the problem.

Then there's the secondary fact that most cops are notoriously talkative sons of bitches. During stakeouts, they're always on the radio—ragging one another, gossiping, telling their corny cop jokes, and making small talk. It's like listening to a damn party line. Even if Bureau cars maintain radio silence on their secure tactical channels, locals tend to chatter.

But there were no gabby cops tonight. I changed frequencies and rousted Doc Tremblay back at the Motel 6. From the tone of his voice he must have been having his bimonthly erotic dream.

He grumbled. He groused. He griped. He called me *behayiem*—Cairo street slang for so fucking stupid you can't even move—but he got himself out of bed—and woke up the rest of my merry marauders, too.

I wanted to take no chances. Wonder and Mugs had cruised past the Ford. A second drive-by might give them away. But we had four rental cars. I wanted my guys to pack up quick—no use taking chances just in case the motel manager thought we were suspicious-looking assholes—and scour the neighborhood for local cops. If there were backup teams, that would tell me one thing. If there weren't, then maybe these agents were acting on their own.

Was this a black op? Was this a rogue maneuver? Or were these guys just security conscious and shutting out the locals because the locals would give 'em away?

I had one answer in seventeen minutes. There were no locals on scene. If anybody could spot a police officer, it was Gator Shepard, because he are one—and Gator declared the square mile around the armory 100 percent cop free.

That meant it was time to get a sit-rep on the current condition—in technical SEAL language, a what-the-fuck.

"Duck Foot—"

"Skipper . . ."

"I'm gonna recon these assholes. Check the black eleven van."

"Roger that."

I waited.

"Still sitting at black eleven, about fifty feet from the back door."

They'd moved way past me. "Facing?"

"Facing the back door, Skipper. Dead on. Perpendicular."

"What about the station wagon?" I couldn't see the damn station wagon either.

There was a momentary pause. "Red four," Duck Foot whispered. "Parallel to the red wall, facing the rear fence line."

That was no good—if the sight lines were right, they'd see me as I made my move.

Except if I was real careful. I crawled to the trailer doorway, which faced the rear fence. Although I couldn't see it, I knew the van was behind me and to my left, about twenty-five yards away. The station wagon was thirty-five, maybe forty yards across the parking lot.

I checked the starboard side of the trailer. A second semi—a huge reefer—was parked parallel to my semi, six yards away. I poked my nose around the sidewall and saw nothing wrong.

"I'm moving. You guys watch my six." I gave thanks for small blessings, because a third semi—this one was a flatbed steel hauler—blocked the station wagon's direct view. Well, at least the first few yards of this little jaunt were going to be easy.

I checked my watch. It was 2115. I patted myself down to make sure the Emerson CQC6 was securely clipped to my waistband and that I didn't have any miscellaneous junk rattling around to make noise when I moved. Then I slid the radio into my BDU thigh pocket, and oh so carefully I rolled, dropped to the ground, and waited in the shadow next to the right-side tandem wheels to see if there was any reaction from the station wagon. I perceived none.

Good. Cautiously, I crabbed my way across the aforementioned six yards of frozen slush to the adjacent reefer, slamming my knee on a melon-size chunk of ice as I went. So much for easy. I rolled underneath the starboard mud flap in considerable pain, crawled between the double axles on elbows and knees—uttering silent oaths and curses all the way—and, using the deck of the semi-trailer as cover, progressed another ten yards. I lay under the deck, just aforeships of the support leg crank and aft of the front wall, listening to my knee throb and my heartbeat race, thinking, Ain't life grand.

There was a two-yard space between the nose end of the flatbed and the next semi, a platform steel hauler, which sat on a diagonal angle, directly opposite the station wagon but thirty yards away. If I kept to the far side and moved v-e-r-y slowly, I might be able to crawl unnoticed.

I slithered across the six feet of space using my elbows, slid under the tail, and holed up between the huge tandem axles. That's when the interior lights in the station wagon went on—because somebody was opening the front passenger-side door.

Oh, shit. Doom on Dickie.

I looked for an exit. There were none available. I looked up. I saw three cross members in the axle area, and I pulled myself up, wrapping my arms and legs around them until I was hanging upside down like a fucking tree sloth.

The door closed and the ambient light shut off. I heard the scrunch of shoes on hard-packed snow, coming in my direction. I tried to make myself invisible.

Movement stopped. Then I heard another sound—it was familiar but I couldn't identify it. Until, that is, the son of a bitch took a leak on the rear fucking tire, less than a yard from where I was hiding.

I held on until he walked back to the station wagon and climbed inside. As the door opened and the interior light went on, I moved —fast. There'd be about ten seconds when they'd lose their night vision because of the dome light. As it came on I dropped off the cross members and snaked my way along the back side of the flatbed until I was out of sight of the station wagon. If I couldn't see them—they couldn't see me, either.

Now I had another ten yards of open space to crawl. I went slowly, carefully, foot by foot, until I found refuge behind a two-ton transporter, perhaps fifteen yards behind the driver's side door of the van.

The good news was that I'd positioned myself in the van's blind spot. The bad news was that if I wanted to get any closer, I'd have to move into an area where the driver could see me.

How did I know that? It's simple. I could already make out the shadow of his face in the rearview mirror. And if you can see someone in a mirror, they can see you.

I hunkered next to a huge tire, pulled out the radio, turned it on —carefully, so that the squelch wouldn't give me away—and whispered into it. "Nasty."

"Yo."

"Can you move on the van passenger?"

There was a momentary pause. "Affirmative."

"On my signal."

"Roger."

See—I'd learned something during my long crawl. It was that all these stakeout vehicles were out of sight of one another. The van couldn't see the station wagon, and the Ford out front couldn't see either the van or the wagon. It was a huge tactical error, which allowed me to take them one by one—if that was what I'd wanted to do.

In this case, however, I just wanted to see what the hell was inside the van—and who these assholes were.

I came up directly behind the van, moving slowly, cautiously, silently on knees and elbows. Any ambient noise I might have made was being thoughtfully covered by the two assholes in the driver's and passenger's seats—because the motor was purring nicely, and the heater was turned on full.

From where I crawled, I could see Nasty. He'd moved from his position behind the trash bin and come up under the van's nose—in the blind spot. I dropped flat. So did Nasty. I displayed my leather sap for him. He displayed his right middle finger for me.

I signaled back with circled thumb and forefinger—a sign that told him everything was okey doke in London, and that he was an asshole in Rio. Then I raised my head and put my ear to the door. They were talking to each other, although I couldn't make out anything specific because they also had the van's radio on and music drowned out the words. What were these guys—amateurs?

I dropped again, pointed to the radio, and as soon as Nasty put it to his ear, I pressed the SEND button. "On three—"

He gave me a thumbs-up and moved around the nose of the van just behind the passenger door.

"One." I slid my own back against the side panel and reached toward the door handle with my right hand while my left held both the radio and the leather sap I'd retrieved from my BDU pocket.

"Two." I put down the radio and set myself, so that as soon as I'd flung the door open I could reach inside, grab the driver, and quiet him down.

I stage-whispered "Three—" loud enough so that Nasty could hear me, then reached up, took the latch in my hand, and opened the door.

Talk about total surprise. I took the scumbag by his fucking throat before he could react, sapped him twice before he saw my face, knocked him cold, and pulled him down onto the ground. Mission accomplished.

Except it wasn't accomplished, because Nasty hadn't whopped the upside of the passenger's head yet. In fact, he was nowhere to be seen.

How did I know that? I knew it because said passenger was coming at me like the fucking Twentieth Century Limited, his elbows and legs working like steam engine pistons as he hurled himself across the bench seat in my direction.

I looked past him and saw Nasty—absolute, shit-eating frustration all over his face—working at the door. The door that was, of course, securely locked from the inside.

And then I saw the passenger's face as he hurtled toward my throat, arms outstretched. It was Dawg Dawkins. And he didn't look happy to see me at all.

Chapter

12

IT WASN'T THE FIRST TIME THAT THE DAWG AND I HAD TANGLED. BUT I don't have time to give you a history lesson about that right now because he was moving fast and he had murder in his eyes, and I had to put this asshole *d-o-w-n* before he sounded any kind of alarm.

I fell back and let him come, waited until his body was fully extended but his feet were still caught up in the steering column, then I advanced like the *picaron picador*—that's a rogue picador *en español*—I are, and as he tried to seize me I stepped between the bull Dawg's deadly arms—*Hola!*—and slapped the back of his head with the sap, whaap!

The whack stunned him. It also made him mad. But it certainly didn't stop him. He bellowed in pain, then growled, struck wildly in my direction, and caught me just below the heart with a ham-size fist—a wallop that had a lot of shoulder power behind it.

The blow caught me good—it knocked me backward. And, being the suave, unflappable asshole that I am, I tripped over my own two feet and went down—absorbing most of the impact right on the point of my throbbing right knee.

As I regrouped, he scrambled, pulled his legs free of the steering column, lurched out of the van headfirst, tumbled and stumbled all fours onto the ice, found his footing, came at me with his legs windmilling just like a fucking linebacker going after a quarterback. He sacked my ass, too—clotheslined me in the Adam's apple, and took me onto the ground. It was definitely Doom on Dickie time. Dawg is a heavy sucker. He threw me down hard, and my friends, there is absolutely no "give" at all to a frozen macadam parking lot.

I heard nasty things popping in the vicinity of the small of my back—it felt like he'd broken it for me. But there was no time to worry about vertebrae, ribs, cartilage, or muscles, because this asshole was trying to kill me. He wrapped my ponytail around his hand and yanked backward, snapping my neck nastily. I twisted away, but he had me by the long-and-straights. I sucker punched him in the solar plexus. He wheezed, wrenched at my hair again, and chopped at my exposed throat with his free hand.

I parried, caught it just above the wrist, and bit him—I hope I gave the son of a bitch rabies—and he yanked it away, simultaneously releasing my hair.

That tiny break gave me a way in. I poked him in the eyes, grabbed his ears and head-butted him, drove him back against the van like he was a tackling dummy and kneed him in the balls. Then I jumped on him and we rolled around doing a passable imitation of a bar brawl free-for-all no-holds-barred gang bang. Okay, so it was finally getting to be fun. But to be honest, there was no time for fun right now. Besides, while the Dawg might have had no qualms about screaming his damn head off, I certainly didn't want him making any noise—there was absolutely no reason at all to disturb the occupants of the other two vehicles. So in addition to trying my best to disable the cocksucker—not to mention fending him off—I had to keep the sumbitch quiet, which would have been a lot easier if I'd come equipped with a third arm.

Speaking of which, it occurred to me as Dawg was trying to reconfigure my face to look like a pound of ground chuck, to ask myself where the hell Nasty was, anyway—still pulling on the fucking door?

I wrestled Dawg to my left, then my right, escaped his grip and flipped him onto the ground with a satisfying thud. Then I wrapped my legs around his thick torso and, using my knees, elbows, and belly weight, I finally managed to come up on top of him—more or less straddling his chest. He poked me a good one in the balls, but I got him back, slapping him in the whitewalls—that is, just above his ears—with the sap, whap-whap, whap-whap.

That slowed him down some. Finally, Nasty decided to drop by. He jumped Dawg from the back, choked him around the carotid artery, and the asshole finally went limp.

"Where the fuck were you while I was getting the crap kicked out of me?" I wheezed. I was lying flat on my back on the cold asphalt, too tired to get up. Damn it, I was tired and I was sore. "I'm getting too old for this kind of *merde.* If I'd had a gun I would have shot the motherfucker."

Nasty was having none of that. "You *have* a fucking gun, Skipper. Besides, you looked like you were enjoying yourself."

See how I am treated, gentle readers? I get no fucking respect. They treat me like the Rodney fucking Dangerfield of SEALs. I might as well be an ossifer.

Nasty bound and gagged Dawg and the van driver while I went through their pockets. One thing was certain: the van man was no FBI agent. I recognized the name on his California driver's license and concealed weapons permit: he was a retired SEAL from Team Three in Coronado—a CPO—chief petty officer—nicknamed Johnny Cool (it was because he wore sixties-styled sunglasses, loved dirty dancing, and played volleyball, as I remember) who didn't have either the brains—i.e., the book learning—or the smarts—i.e., the streetwise edge—to make senior chief.

He'd wanted to join Red Cell, but I'd turned him down. Despite the fact that he had a hell of an overhead serve and the hips of a disco pro, he didn't have the heart or soul of a Warrior.

The weapons permit and driver's license told me he was probably one of Dawg's mutts. And tucked inside the left-hand waistband of his jeans, snug in a nylon holster, was the blue steel French-made Walther PPK/S known as a Manhurin, with seven of Federal's best 95-grain Hydra-Shok jacketed hollowpoints in the mag, and one in the pipe. Since the CWP was legal only in California, I gave the pistol to Nasty as a souvenir just to show him I wasn't mad.

Then I searched Dawg. He wasn't armed, and he wasn't carrying anything of interest, either. There was no list of phone numbers in his wallet. There were no discreetly marked maps in his pockets. In fact, there was nothing incriminating at all. Boring. There was a cellular phone sitting on top of the gearshift console. I took it, dropped it onto the ground, and stomped it flat.

It occurred to me that maybe I'd want to have a little chat with the retired general—perhaps attach a field telephone wire to his pecker and ask him a few questions about what he was up to. But any interrogation would have to come later. Why? Because right now, Nasty was gesturing frantically at me—pointing toward Duck Foot's position. I looked up and saw him. He was furiously silent signaling—enemy approaching. Take cover.

Shit—they were coming, and here I was with two unconscious assholes on my hands. Doom on me. Okay—first things first. Camouflage—the fucking van had to look normal. Moving quickly, Nasty and I hefted Dawg into the passenger side of the van, seat belted him in position, and taped him in place so he couldn't shift around and hit anything that would make noise.

Next we placed the driver behind the wheel, running tape around his ankles, which anchored him to the tubular frame. Then we wrapped a long X around his torso, mooring him firmly to the seatback.

I turned the motor off and pocketed the keys. These sons of bitches were about to get cold until I could come back and grab 'em. I sent Nasty back to his Dumpster and made my own way back to the semi-trailer.

I hadn't been there more than five seconds when I got the first report from Mugs—an anonymous-looking twenty-two-foot, gate-lift panel truck drove past the building. It went clear around the compound, circled back for another look-see, then cruised around the block to the truck storage yard, where it stood, engine running and lights off.

Duck Foot gave it a once-over with his night vision and called the plate numbers in to Mugs. As he was whispering, a man dressed in dark clothes and wearing a knit watch cap jumped out of the truck cab, sauntered over to a tractor-trailer, climbed aboard, and turned the engine over. As the huge diesel revved, two more men, these guys dressed all in black, slipped out of the panel truck, ran up to the chain-link fence separating the armory parking lot from the truck park area, and snipped the nylon ties out of the ten-foot fence section that had been precut.

As the fence came down, the tractor-trailer eased carefully through the opening. It passed out of my sight line, and I got on the radio to Duck Foot.

"Sit-rep?"

"They're backed up to the door." He paused momentarily. "They're inside."

"Dick—" Mugs's voice.

"Go, Chief."

"The step van. It's registered to an address on the East Side."

"Roger that."

They'd gotten in ORDCOMSOMICH effortlessly. Ah, Army security.

We all waited, silent. Even though they'd prepared everything in advance, it was almost half an hour before the huge semi rolled slowly past me and back into the truck area. Then the panel truck backed through the fence to be loaded.

"Duck Foot—"

"Yo."

"Is the semi moving?

"No—it's idling."

That was good—and it was bad. We had two trucks to deal with, not to mention two cars of bad guys, plus the van. I had to know where they were all going.

That meant splitting up my forces.

Okay, what did I know?

First, I know that tractor-trailers are used more often for long-haul than short-haul trips. They're cumbersome and hard to handle in the city.

Lift-gate panel trucks, on the other hand, are perfect urban camouflage, which meant that we'd deal with it first. I got on the radio and made assignments. Doc, Half Pint, Pick, Gator, and Rodent would follow the tractor-trailer. Mugs, Duck Foot, Nasty, Wonder, Cherry, and I would deal with the locals—then we'd bat-out-of-hell it to catch up with the other guys. We'd stay in touch via cellular. I'd miss my Q&A session with Dawg and Johnny Cool, but life is full of little disappointments and this would be one of them.

And what if I was wrong?

Well, then it would be doom on Dickie time one more once, as Count Basie used to say. Ain't life grand?

While the bad guys load up, let's you and me spend a few minutes talking about automobile surveillance techniques. You know how, in the movies or on TV, you see all those video cops wheel out into traffic and U-turn, tires all a-screaming, to stalk the bad guys?

Well, friend, that's so much bull puckey. I mean, don't you *notice* those assholes who drive like Bullitt when you're eking your way through rush hour traffic?

Let me put the gist of it in a simple, declarative sentence for you. Shadowing a bad guy is a tough job. A successful surveillance op can take as many as a dozen vehicles, a couple of bottles of Bufferin, and a bunch of empty wide-neck bottles with tight-sealing tops. There are untold variables, which include weather and road conditions, traffic flow, time of day, and number of assets available. Then there's Mr. Murphy, the constant backseat driver who's always trying to screw you up. Other goatfuck factors include countersurveillance—that's when the bad guys use their own vehicles to check that they're not being followed. Or overt ambush—when they set up a roadblock to keep you from following the target.

So you see, surveillance is not as simple as it's made out to be in the movies or on TV. But it can be done—and done well. The easiest way is through the use of electronic beacons. The old devices were hard to track and gave off such a big call that they often interrupted the AM/FM radios in target vehicles and tipped off the bad guys. The most recent generation of passive beacons combines secure transmissions, lithium batteries, and a miniature package. They beam a signal that can be accessed by a trailing vehicle, from an aircraft, by a satellite, or through the use of telephone land lines. (Yes, friends, just like the AT&T ad says, you actually *can* reach out and touch someone.)

If you can't plant a beacon, then you have to do it the old-fashioned way—out where the rubber meets the road. The two most effective vehicle surveillance techniques are known as leapfrogging and paralleling.

In leapfrogging, you use five or six cars that constantly surround the target vehicle, all the while changing their relative positions. The cars run ahead of the target, then fall back—just the way real traffic flow moves. If the bad guy turns left or right, the cars in front race to the next street, track on a parallel route, then fall back in line. If the subject U-turns, the cars at the rear line pick him up.

If leapfrogging is done well, the target never sees the same surveillance car in his rearview mirror more than once—even though he may be driving for hours. On the plus side, it's hard to spot a leapfrog tail. In the minus column: it takes a lot of vehicles to do it right.

Paralleling is where one chase car remains far enough behind the target so as not to alert him, and four or more other cars travel on parallel streets, bracketing the target. Plus side? It's an almost invisible technique. Minuses? Well, for one thing, if traffic lights run against you, you get screwed. For another, if the target does a quick turn, and heads back the way he's come, you can lose him.

Both techniques require good communications—preferably secure, so that the bad guys, who probably have police scanners and other countersurveillance devices in their cars, can't eavesdrop on your conversations. It also helps to know the area in which you're going to operate. When I ran SEAL Team Six, I used to play a game called SEAL tag. SEAL tag entails long, fast car chases and clandestine surveillance exercises in European cities. It was played against a series of Naval Investigative Service security details—the people in charge of protecting our flag officers overseas—to give them a chance to see how terrorists would behave when under observation.

NIS wanted to play in Washington—they like to wage war on a nine-to-five schedule at NIS. I preferred cities like London, Lisbon, Rome, and Naples for a couple of reasons. First, Europe, the Middle East, and Asia were where the game would be played for real, anyway. And second, because each of those overseas locations has the kind of environment that makes shadowing bad guys a real nightmare: a lot of traffic and confusing traffic patterns, ongoing construction, crowded squares, gridlock, and *beaucoup* one-way thoroughfares, dead-end streets, and anonymous cul-de-sacs—the sorts of places you can easily lose, confuse, and abuse your baby-sitters.

My men and I played the nasty boys. (Type casting, right?) And we always decimated the good guys because we took the time to learn the city and use it to our advantage when we played. That's true guerrilla warfare, folks. Remember Mao Zedong's famous exhortation: "The revolutionary soldier should move through the masses like a fish through water."

Tonight I'd be moving through those masses like a fish through molasses. Oh, I had secure comms. But you will note, gentle readers, that both of the surveillance techniques I've just described above demand multiple vehicles. Tonight, I had two targets, and a mere five cars to run against them, while the bad guys had two countersurveillance vehicles. Most significantly, tonight, *I* was the one who was driving blind.

They knew what they were doing, too. The Ford let the panel truck go first. Then it fell in behind, driving slowly eastward on a four-lane county road that had almost no traffic. The station wagon paired off with the tractor-trailer, and headed south on Route 23.

I called in the cavalry as soon as they pulled out, and made quick assignments. Wonder checked the armory and came out white-faced. "They picked the motherfucker clean," he reported. So much for my ideas about the genteel pruning of weapons. These guys had gang-banged the place.

Now, we really did have to keep up with 'em. Two cars of my lethal leprechauns took off after the tractor-trailer. Nasty and Wonder took one of the remaining rental cars, Cherry and Duck Foot the other. I retrieved the night-vision glasses from Duck Foot and rode with Mugs.

As the ex-chief pulled out of the armory lot I could see that Dawg and his SEAL pup had come to—they were struggling in the van, smashing themselves against their duct-tape bonds to break free.

Mugs hooked a thumb in their direction. "In my day we didn't leave witnesses," he said. "Loose ends, y'know. Messy."

It actually had occurred to me that I should have killed the sons of a bitches when I'd had the opportunity—except I'd wanted to interrogate 'em. But as usual, Mr. Murphy had interrupted me before I'd had the chance.

"Yeah, well, if we weren't otherwise engaged right now . . ." Mugs was right. And if we weren't in such a hurry, I'd have pulled over and waxed 'em now. But there was no time. There were vehicles to follow. We headed out after the Ford.

They took their time getting back into the city. Which made problems for us. Because they were on Route 12—a four-lane state highway that turns into Michigan Avenue once it passes the city limit—there were a series of traffic lights. The damn Ford would drop back and let the panel truck get a quarter mile or so ahead—after all, *they* knew where the fuck they were going.

Just outside Greenfield Village the panel truck turned south onto the Southfield Freeway access road while the Ford kept moving east on Michigan. It stopped suddenly on the freeway overpass.

Mugs slipped into the right-hand lane as I hit the SEND button on the radio. "I got the truck—Wonder stays with the Ford. Cherry—you drop way back—pull over and wait till we see what the fuck, over."

"Yo, roger that," Wonder's and Cherry's voices overlapped back at me.

I peered at the truck, which was accelerating now. "C'mon—move," I told Mugs. "Keep up with 'em."

He shot me a dirty look. "Patience, Rotten Richard, don't be so blankety-blanking impetuous." He steered gently into the access road curve. "What lane are they in? My eyes ain't what they used to be."

I peered at the truck a quarter-mile ahead knowing that Mugs could still spot a dime at a hundred yards. "Curb."

"Thought so." He smiled knowingly. "They're checking their six. Curb lane don't go to the freeway."

He kept us moving slowly. "The guys in the Ford are probably eyeballing us to see what we do."

They were running Robert Roger's Rule Nineteen on us. Instinctively, I turned around in the seat and looked through the rear window. Of course, I couldn't see anything.

Right on cue, Wonder's voice came through the radio. "Guy's jumped out of the Ford—looking at where you are."

Dammit—were we blown? "Go past 'em and get the fuck out of sight," I radioed back tersely.

"I know, Dick—I know." Wonder's voice had a taut edge to it and I was sorry I'd snapped at him. He was as good at this game as I and didn't need to be told what to do.

Now, the panel truck turned right at the first intersection. Mugs kept rolling. "Duck," he said.

I ducked. I know when to take yes for an answer. It is when a chief tells you to do something.

Mugs drove steadily past the intersection, checking the rearview mirror. I sat back up. We came to an intersection. I expected he'd turn right. Instead, he drove through it.

"Mugs—"

"They can still see us from the overpass, you asshole," he explained, his exasperated tone sounding much like Ev Barrett on a good day. We rounded a right-hand curve. "*Now*—" he said, and floored the accelerator. He hit sixty on the straightaway, then braked sharply as we came to a second intersection, and veered the car in a tight, controlled skid right-hand turn, one-handing the steering wheel with the confidence of an old patrol-car driver.

Just after we made the turn he shut down the headlights. "We're taking the long way around the Ford proving grounds," he said by way of explanation. "We'll pick 'em up on the back side—they have a fifteen-miles-an-hour limit going through the village so we'll be there before 'em."

And we were, too—by forty-five seconds or so. They came out of the Greenfield Village road, turned right, drove three-quarters of a mile back to Michigan Avenue, and turned right again. Mugs and I shadowed them to the intersection. I jumped out of the car, ran to the corner, peeked around and watched through my night-vision glasses as the truck chugged slowly past the Ford and continued eastward.

0220. They worked their way around downtown, moving east, circling Lafayette Park, and working their way onto a wide avenue called Gratiot. The truck and the Ford both pulled off the main road onto a narrow street into a huge, crowded open square, chockablock full of trucks and hundreds of stalls, all lit by floodlights.

"What the hell?" I asked Mugs.

"Eastern Market," he explained. "The city's main wholesale food center."

"How many exits does it have?"

"Half a dozen, maybe," said Mugs. "Not counting the alleys."

Shit. The traffic conditions reminded me of Cairo on a bad day or a Rubik's Cube—continually confusing permutations of vehicles, pedestrians, and hand trucks, all moving in a flow that had no seeming logic. Our target was six vehicles ahead of us—at the moment. But yet another van was now backing up, blocking our way, and keeping us from the quarry.

"Wonder—"

"Yo."

"Let's check 'em on foot."

"Roger."

I swiveled in the seat and saw Nasty slip out of Wonder's car, which was hung up three or four cars in back of us, and make his way through the chaos past Mugs and me. He stopped long enough to toss some money at a food vendor and grab a shwarma, dump hot sauce on it, snatch a handful of paper napkins, and continue onward.

Now, you may think he was wasting time. I knew better—what he did, was camouflage himself. You use what's at hand. And in a market, that's food.

Another van cut in front of us, bumped the car in front of it, and everything stopped while the fucking drivers got out to examine the damage.

"Cherry—"

"Yo."

"Where are you?"

"Back at the turnoff, Skipper. Sitting on"—he paused while he looked—"Gratiot Avenue."

"Hold where you are. It's impossible to move in here." I turned to Mugs. "Can he get around the perimeter of the market?"

"It's possible," Mugs said. "There's an access road back there—it leads to I-94, or I-75. But I'd keep him where he is—more choices from Gratiot than around the back."

"Where does I-94 go?"

"West to Chicago, north to Huron."

"And I-75?"

"North to me, and south to"—he thought about it—"Florida."

I threw my thumb in the panel truck's direction. "And what if they're headed for Florida?"

Mugs shook his head. "That doesn't make sense," he said.

Sense? What the hell was he talking about sense for? Nothing made sense. I chewed on my mustache. There is an accepted military technical term for my present tactical condition: clusterfucked.

Well, if that was going to be the case, I needed some good news. I dialed Gator Shepard on the cellular. He answered on the third ring.

"Fuuuck you—"

He laughed. "You, too, Skipper."

I asked for a sit-rep. And I got one—with good news for a change. They were in a truck stop on Route 23 right near Dundee, on the way to Toledo, Ohio. The semi and the station wagon had pulled in, parked, and the crew had gone to breakfast. One man had remained on board the semi.

"Keep me advised."

"Aye-aye."

"And slip your DF beacon on that semi first time you get a chance." They had the passive direction-finding beacon Wonder had brought from Rogue Manor.

"Will do." The phone bleeped and he was off-line.

"Skipper—" Nasty's voice on the radio.

"Yo—"

"Moving north. They're heading for the aft port side of the square."

I looked at Mugs blankly. "So?"

"The interstate," he said morosely. "The fuckin' interstate."

And here we sat, gridlocked. We'd been bottled up as neatly as I'd ever managed to screw with the NIS security teams in Europe.

It was déjà screw all over again—except here, I was the déjà screwee.

These assholes were good.

Mugs grabbed the radio from me. "Cherry," he said, "It's Mugs."

"Go, Mugs."

"Where are you?"

Cherry told him.

Mugs thought for a minute. "Make a U-ee, hang your first right, go until the street dead-ends, turn left, go half a block, it'll dead-end again. Then go right again."

"Come again?" Cherry was confused.

Mugs hit the radio's SEND button. "Don't worry, asshole—I'll talk you through it."

Cherry and Duck Foot watched the panel truck move past them on the I-75 access road. The Ford was rear security. Once it moved past them, they swung out, *sans* lights, and followed. It was risky, but necessary.

They were moving blind, too—Mugs had to talk them through a maze of one-way streets, because the panel truck turned off the access road and made its way through a warren of decrepit crack houses, onto a two-lane street of boarded-up storefronts.

0255. Mugs pushed through the market as best he could. Then, playing catch-up, we made our way to Cherry's location. Mugs wrinkled his nose as we drove past stripped cars and burnt-out tenement shells, on streets whose lighting had long since been shot away. "We gave up on this whole part of town twenty years ago," Mugs said. "Look—" He pointed to a series of crude white crowns spray-painted on the doors and walls of the charred frame houses that lined the street. "That's how the Zulu Gangsta Princes mark their turf. It used to be, you'd see the goddamn things over a twenty-square-block area on the East Side. Now, you see 'em all over the city—even the fuckin' city hall is covered with graffiti." He dropped his window, spat, and raised it again. "They're in charge, I guess—because we sure ain't."

I looked at the crown. It was the same design I'd seen spray-painted on the back door of the armory.

I have told you before that I don't believe in coincidence.

There was no traffic. Mugs drove without lights. Wonder followed close behind. We came on Cherry's position after half a dozen blocks. He'd parked on a side street behind the shell of a burned-out car that sat perched on cinder blocks.

We talked by radio. The panel truck, he told me, was in an alley that backed up to the rear of a delapidated Alabama pit barbecue storefront. The Ford, he said, had pulled abreast of it.

We came up on Cherry's car quietly. Wonder dropped back half a block, then cut round the front onto Mack Avenue. Mugs gently slipped the nose of his car into the head of the alley. The target vehicles were about a hundred yards away—dark shadows in darkness.

I peered through my night-vision glasses. There was somebody kneeling at the rear of the Ford, working on the license plate. He unscrewed it, put it on the ground, then replaced it with another plate.

The man—a tall, black guy in a suit—picked up the discarded plate, opened the Ford's front driver-side door, and tossed the plate inside. Then he opened the trunk, removed a set of coveralls and a sweatshirt, discarded his suit jacket and his tie, pulled on the sweatshirt and coveralls, then slid into the driver's seat and turned the ignition over.

Mugs set his jaw. "You take a hike, Richard. I want to see where the hell that son of a bitch goes with those plates, now I know they're stolen."

It sounded good to me. I wanted to move, too. The Zulu Gangsta Princes were a minor problem that I could solve quickly and efficiently. The huge semi, which contained tons of weapons and ammo, was more significant.

"Call me on the cellular when you learn something." I grabbed my bundle of goodies and started to move.

"Whoa, shit for brains." Mugs reached up and turned the dome light switch off. "No need to broadcast our position—" He tapped me on the shoulder. *"Now* go, Rotten Richard."

I rolled out of his car and, staying out of sight, worked my way to Wonder's rented Chevy, which he'd pulled up behind Cherry's car.

By the time I slipped into the backseat and turned around to look, the old Frog had disappeared.

Chapter 13

DUCK FOOT TOOK MY NIGHT VISION AND CREPT INTO THE ALLEY TO SET up a one-man OP (that, you'll recall, is an Observation Post). Meanwhile, working very *q-u-i-e-t-l-y,* Nasty, Wonder, Cherry, and I removed the backseats of the rental cars, wormed our way into the trunks, and retrieved some of the lethal goodies we'd taken from the armory.

The Zulu Gangstas weren't off-loading, which told me they were going to truck their booty elsewhere for distribution and/or sale. No they weren't—not if I did my job right tonight.

To make doing my job right more difficult, they had posted two sentries in the alley—a pair of urban hip-hops wearing bulky padded cotton jackets, poor-boy caps turned backward, sweatpants, and the brightly colored, high-top cross-training athletic footwear that has come to be known as felony shoes. The pair fondled a couple of the stolen CAR-15s with 40-round magazines. Telltale bulges told me they were carrying pistols, too.

Let's stop here while I explain to you about sentry duty. And don't skip this part because you're going to see it again. First, sentry duty is like PT—you don't have to like it, you just have to do it. Moreover, it is tough work. It demands concentration, attention to detail, and unfailing vigilance. In the field, a good pair of sentries can mean the difference between life and death. Yes, I said a pair of sentries. Unlike all those war movies you've seen, in real life you almost never allow a sentry to work alone—especially at night.

Most people, however, consider sentry duty the tactical equivalent of KP. They use it to do everything but keep watch. They don't realize that war is 99 percent waiting, and one percent fighting. Sentries like that are inviting targets for people like me. It would have been easy to eliminate the hip-hops. But tonight, that wasn't my job. I had to get in and get out without being spotted. So we'd simply wait 'em out.

The situation was tilted in my favor because the Zulu Gangsta sentries were unwilling participants—they didn't like it, and they weren't gonna do it. It was cold, it was damp, and it was boring. So, after just four or five minutes, they began shifting their feet. A few minutes later, the shifting turned to stomping. Then they began talking—losing their concentration. Soon they lit cigarettes—thus ruining their night vision. And after three-quarters of an hour in the cold, the pair decided they could watch things just as well from inside the building.

That, as they say, was our cue. You remember all those wonderful Warner Brothers cartoons where Zeke the Wolf or Wiley Coyote sneaks and peeks? Y'know—the character sneaks up behind a tree on tippy-toe, then suddenly peeks his nose out from behind an adjacent tree—which is twenty feet away across the field. Well that, friends, is how SEALs move, too. Except we don't do it on our tiptoes like Wiley or Zeke, because our feets are too big and we have opposable fingers, and besides we have a harder time than they do breaking the laws of physics.

On a more serious note, part of becoming a SEAL is learning how to move stealthily. From the early days in Vietnam, when SEALs conducted silent, nighttime snatch ops against Mr. Charlie, to the clandestine forays I ran against tangos all over the world, the goal was the same: to come, to do our jobs, and to leave, all without anybody knowing we'd been there.

Accomplishing this goal has always been easier in the countryside than in the city. In the country, you can infiltrate by using the terrain to your advantage—rivers and streams allow you to slip up on your enemy undetected. Foliage affords great cover, aiding in your covert movements. In the city, access is generally confined to streets, alleys, rooftops, or sewers. There is less natural camouflage available—and a much higher probability of being spotted by a random civilian as you're making your way to your objective.

Still, if you follow my three basic rules for nighttime urban operations, you will probably succeed in getting where you want to go, and getting there in one piece.

- Rule One. Always keep low, because a silhouette offers the enemy a great target.
- Rule Two. Avoid open spaces unless absolutely necessary. I may not be the world's most touchie-feelie guy, but when I'm in situations like this, I become a big devotee of wall hugging and cement sucking.
- Rule Three. Move slowly. The less attention you attract, the less attention you'll attract.

Because I believe in my own commandments, I volunteered Wonder and me to stage our little foray, with Cherry, Duck Foot, and Nasty providing backup. That was because, over the years, I've worked so closely with Wonder that we don't really have to talk anymore—we're like a couple of old marrieds who read each other's body language and breathing.

Wonder, being a former Recon Marine, led the way. He squirreled up the alley on knees and elbows, moving slowly but deliberately as he squirmed along a ragged, rotted picket fence, using the darkness to his best advantage. I followed, two yards behind, content to play catch-up.

One reason I was happy to let Wonder take point is that our crawl was not going to be a pleasant one. A plethora of nasty items tends to collect in alleys such as this one. So our expedition was enhanced by the addition of broken glass, rotting garbage, and other more colorful substances that are best left undescribed but not unimagined. Since he was first, Wonder would go through them, moving carefully, and I, noting his discomfort—remember how well I can read his body language?—could work my way around the bad stuff. Our passage tonight was made more challenging by the fact that our path led through piles of soot-and-dirt-encrusted snow, which camouflaged the above-mentioned goodies.

We'd writhed our way down about thirty nasty yards when the door opened and one of the hip-hops stuck his head out of the doorway, as if he'd heard something. He walked outside and closed the door in back of him, shutting out the light. He stood there, his eyes getting accustomed to the darkness, sucked on his cigarette, took a peek down the alley—and looked straight at me. There is only one way to react when that happens. You avert your eyes slightly, so as not to make any contact. You do not move, or breathe, or blink. And with every molecule of your heart, soul, and brain, you believe, I am invisible.

Ah, Marcinko-san, you say, more of this psycho-warrior b.s. you're always trying to foist on us. Come off it already.

No, Tadpole—read, and learn. One of the first lessons at the SERE—Survival, Evasion, Resistance, and Escape—schools to which all SpecWar operators regularly go, is how to react when it appears that you have been discovered.

The instructors will tell you that *if* you have paid attention to the three basic tenets of concealment—shape, shine, and silhouette, *and* you don't draw attention to yourself by moving—in other words, believing in your own invisibility—the man who is looking straight at you, probably hasn't seen you yet, and won't see you at all.

The reason for that lies not in the metaphysical, but in the physical laws of nature. Remember biology 101, when you studied the principles of vision? No? Well, let me give you a little refresher course.

The reason you won't be seen is because most of us discern most of what we see through our peripheral vision, not by looking straight on. Example? It's easier to see a deer in the forest when he's to your left or right than when he's straight ahead, because your peripheral vision picks out his movement. Ditto a car coming at you as you're crossing the street in heavy traffic.

At night, the situation is compounded because of the way we see. The human retina is composed of two kinds of cells. There are cones, which help us see during daylight, and rods, which surround the cones, and help us see at night. The rods are very sensitive to light. But since they are not at the center of the eye—remember, they surround the cones—they do not pick up anything emanating from the center of one's vision. They work best when your sight is directed slightly off-center. I knew, therefore, that if the hip-hop was staring right at me, he couldn't see me.

So instead of panicking, I simply froze where I was—which was in midcrawl. My gloved hand had just hit something definitely rotten. My left leg was hyperextended. My right knee—the one I'd mangled back at the armory—was atop something uncomfortably sharp. But I did not move. I knew that my *S*-words were okay. My shape was low, and indistinct against the fence. There was no shine, because my face was blacked out and the rest of me was covered in old, dirty, black gear. And my silhouette, softened by the picket fence, garbage cans, and lack of light, was indistinct.

I focused my eyes on the hip-hop's feet. That way I'd know if he was approaching me, but I still would not make eye contact.

I made myself breathe so *s-l-o-w-l-y* that I wasn't apparently breathing at all (there are real assets to being a SEAL and having learned how to hold my breath under water for three minutes at a time).

And I waited. And waited.

Two yards ahead of me, Wonder was in the exact same mode. He'd learned his stuff at the same schools I had—and put it to use in the same uncomfortable places, from Afghanistan to Libya, from western France to Eastern Europe, over his two-decades plus in the Marines and the Navy.

I heard a flick, and a hiss, and the cigarette landed between us. I raised my eyes slightly, just in time to see the hip-hop adjust his Malcolm X cap, spit, and saunter back inside.

I moved for the first time in some minutes—my knee joint cracked loudly enough to make Wonder react with a dirty look. We waited to make sure we weren't going to be interrupted again, then continued to the truck undisturbed.

Wonder wormed his way forward, under the motor. He loves to play with motors. He played with this one by taping a two-ounce wad of C-4 plastic explosive to the manifold, rigging it with a pencil-detonator, then running the detonator wire up into the ignition system.

Turn the key, and ka-boom.

Meanwhile, I was having my own fun. I picked the padlock on the tailgate and slid the gate up just enough to make sure we had the right truck. (Yes, friends, I follow my own commandments—especially the one that says, "Thou shalt never assume.") I saw weapons and ammo crates, and that was good enough for me. So I closed the tailgate, clicked the lock shut, and squirmed underneath the chassis.

There, I took a chunk of C-4 about the size of a large can of shoe polish and rolled it out between my hands until I'd made it into a long, narrow-shaped ribbon charge just over three feet in length. Using duct tape, I taped the charge underneath the truck bed in an uneven rectangle. I reached down to my thigh pocket to retrieve my Emerson CQC6 and cut the tape. The knife wasn't there. That pissed me off.

I lay on my back and went through all my pockets. The damn

thing was gone. Five fucking hundred dollars' worth of handmade, personally inscribed knife, a gift from Ernie Emerson, who designed it for me. I lay there and tried to figure out what had happened and decided that it must have come loose when Dawg and I were going at it.

Well, there was no use crying over spilt steel. I dug in my breast pocket for the lightweight Benchmade folder I always carry as a backup, and sliced the tape. Then I ran a piece of trip wire around an exposed bolt head in the rear door, brought the wire under the bumper, past the exhaust, tied it securely to an M-1 trip-wire firing device I'd attached to the plastic explosive, and cut off the surplus OD wire.

I unrolled a second piece of trip wire, which I handed to Wonder. He secured it to the manifold, after which I stretched it taut and attached it to the M-1's detonator ring too.

I like M-1s because they're Keep-It-Simple-Stupid detonators. Sure, there are more elaborate gadgets available today—electronic detonators complete with semiconductors and computer chips, as well as sophisticated radio-controlled contraptions that cost hundreds of dollars per unit.

But when you're jumping out of planes, locking out of subs, or crawling through the mud in hostile territory, you want something that Mr. Murphy can't screw with, no matter how hard he tries. And the M-1 is guaranteed Murphy-proof. Believe me, these things work. In good weather, or bad. Wet, or dry. Hot or cold. They are foolproof because they are old-fashioned, KISS devices with very few moving parts, no complicated electronics to go awry, batteries to run down, or miniconnectors to come apart.

Basically, the M-1 is a metal tube—a cylinder-shaped device about four inches long. At one end is a coupling assembly and protector tube. That's the business end, where you attach the firing device to the explosive. Just behind the coupler lies the primer which, when it explodes, detonates your C-4, your Semtex, or whatever other payload you've chosen. Immediately fore of the primer, is a cotter pin safety device, which physically separates the firing pin from the primer.

The firing pin and its heavy-duty compression spring are held in position by two additional cotter pins. When the explosive has been attached, and the device has been installed *and* secured in position—this is very important—a taut trip wire is then stretched and attached to the firing-pin-release ring. At that point, you remove all the cotter-pin safety devices (being careful to drop them in your pocket so you don't leave a telltale sign that you've come a-calling), and clear the area.

The results? When our friendly Zulu Gangsta Prince hip-hops unsuspectingly opened the rear hatch of the truck, they would yank the trip wire, which would pull the ring, which would release the firing pin, which would ignite the primer, which would detonate the C-4, which would explode, which would dismember said hip-hops into thousands of separate, fragmented, and hard-to-identify pieces. Moreover, the explosion would detonate whatever explosives were inside the truck—ammo, grenades, mortar rounds, they'd all go up. The earth would move.

If, however, the bad guys decided simply to drive away, the sequence would be slightly different. They'd climb aboard and turn the ignition key, which would detonate the C-4 taped to the manifold, which would then move enough to trigger the M-1 and the shaped ribbon charge of C-4. Result? Death and destruction. And, once again, the earth would move. As you can probably tell, I love to make the earth move.

Kind of gives you goose bumps, too, doesn't it?

We exfiltrated smoothly and were well on our way south toward Toledo when we heard the explosion in the distance. I low-fived Wonder. Another job well done. Another evening well spent. It's not a career—it's an adventure.

It was still well before dawn when we linked up with Doc, Half Pint, Gator, Pick, and Rodent just north of Cincinnati. We chatted by secure radio. Gator told me he'd been able to plant the passive beacon on our target. That made me breathe a little bit easier. Maybe we'd left Mr. Murphy behind for a while. I sat back and sipped hot coffee from the huge jug Mugs had left us. Shit—life was pretty fucking good. We'd roasted the Zulu Gangsta Princes, destroyed the stolen weapons and ammo they were going to sell or use, and by now, Mugs probably had a line on the asshole who was stealing FBI license plates.

I call that a good night's work. I peered through the windshield at our little convoy. In the adjacent lane Gator Shepard touched the brim of his ball cap in a ragged salute, which I raggedly returned. Sixty yards ahead of me in the dim predawn, Doc Tremblay caught my eye and threw me a shadowy finger. I tossed it right back at him.

Let me pause long enough, gentle reader, to tell you a simple yet profound truth. There is no emotion so strong, no satisfaction so deep or fulfilling, as the incredible high you experience when you lead a great body of warriors into battle. If you've ever done it, you know exactly of what I speak. If you haven't, then you never will.

It was getting light as we crossed the Ohio River on the 275 bypass, and we followed the semi southward at a steady seventy miles an hour. This was getting boring already. I had another cup of coffee, sat back, and grabbed a combat nap.

"Skipper—" Nasty tapped my shoulder and I shook myself awake.

"What's up?"

"They're pulling off the Interstate."

"Where are we?"

"About a dozen miles north of Lexington. Place called Sadieville. They're about two miles ahead of us."

I stretched and yawned. It was time to go to work.

Everybody needed a potty break, but we'd have to do it in shifts. Our crew would follow close, while Doc in his car and Gator in his would run backup. When me and my guys had returned our rented coffee to the men's room, we'd switch places.

I turned to Nasty. "You overtake Gator. We'll go in behind the truck." I picked up the radio, pressed the TRANSMIT button, and told Duck Foot and Cherry to stay with the station wagon—but give 'em some leeway. I didn't want anybody spotting us. Not here.

We performed a smooth transition and watched as the semi lumbered into the huge parking area reserved for tractor-trailers while Gator and Pick coasted their Chevys into the gas lines to top off their tanks. Nasty slid our sedan into a convenient slot, from where we could see the rest rooms, the fast-food joints, and the truckers' shops, and keep an eye on the semi.

Once, when I was working a one-car surveillance in Italy with SEAL Team Six, I got burned because me and my guys all followed the driver and backup as they went to breakfast at the huge rest stop near Ponte corvo, on the A2 *autostrada* between Rome and Naples. We watched them eat their *uovi*—eggs—munch toast and *marmellata,* and drink their *café latte* as if they had all the time in the world. Which they did. And why?

Because a new driver and assistant had been waiting in the wings, and as we followed the old crew into the *ristorante,* the new boys watched as we left the scene, then they slipped on board and drove merrily away, leaving us well fed, and holding our limp *salsicci* in our sorry SEAL paws.

So I'd learned my lesson—and I wasn't about to get singed again. I always keep both the crew and the truck under surveillance now. And there would be backup, just in case Mr. Murphy decided to put in an appearance. Gator and Rodent, who'd filled their gas tanks and were parked by the southward exit, and Doc, Half Pint, and Pick, running on full, were doing sentry duty on the north-bound side. No way were these assholes going to slip away from me.

I tucked my hair under a ball cap, ambled toward the men's room, drained my lizard, then made good use of the sink, soap, and paper towels to wash the residue of the black camouflage cream I'd worn last night off my face and hands. Then, clean (and mean) I dried myself off, went into the sundry shop, where I bought a newspaper and a dozen lithium batteries for the cellular phones and secure radios, and wandered back out to the car to relieve Nasty. While he attended to business, I rolled the car into the gas line and filled 'er up.

Our crew finished its break and we shifted with the others. The look on Half Pint's face as he headed for the head was nothing less than anguished. I watched through binoculars as he emerged three minutes later, a humongous, relieved smile on his face. He gave me a quiet thumbs-up, and headed back to his car.

Two minutes later I scanned the restaurant area through my 7X35s and picked up Doc Tremblay coming through the door. There was no relieved smile on his face, though. Doc and I have known each other since we were fleet sailors—a couple of enlisted pukes whose idea of a good time was a case of beer, a night of pussy, and a good bar brawl. I have seen Doc in all kinds of circumstances. But I have never seen him look so frantic and distraught as he looked right now. He came out of the rest area, his eyes wild—searching everywhere. When he didn't see what he wanted to find, he ran for the car.

I picked up the radio. "Yo, Doc—what's the prob?"

"Dick—where the hell are you?"

I told him.

"Turn on the news. Turn it on now."

I reached over and flipped on the car radio. I got full-bore country and western on the FM band. I switched to AM, and scanned until I got an all-news station.

The voice was familiar, but I couldn't put a handle to it for a few seconds. Then I realized that it was Dawg Dawkins I was listening to. He was talking about me—not nicely, either. Then a correspondent came on and summed up the story. "Marcinko," he said, "whose bloody assault knife was found at the scene, is thought to be armed and dangerous. The FBI, which believes he has left Michigan, has issued a warrant for his arrest on charges of interstate flight from felony murder. Billionaire businessman and undeclared presidential hopeful LC Strawhouse, whose security employee Marcinko allegedly executed, has issued a half-million dollar reward for information leading to the rogue ex-Navy captain's capture."

Part Two

ESBAM

Chapter

14

DID YOU KNOW THAT WITHIN THE LAST YEAR AND A HALF A GOVERNMENT contractor has developed devices that allow us to pinpoint the locations of cellular phones in a matter of seconds? Well, it has, and they arc out there. That's how the FBI tracked down Herman Slotnik, the computer terrorist who'd been at large for more than two years. Slotnik was able to elude both the Bureau and civilian computer security experts because he employed a modem attached to a cellular phone to place the calls he made to break into secure computer systems. He knew that it was virtually impossible to trace a cellular phone unless you knew its precise phone number.

Enter S_3 Systems. For those of you who've never heard of it—and I'd venture to say that most of you haven't—S_3, for Stealth, Security, and Surveillance, is the nation's largest corporation devoted exclusively to black-ops and Skunk Works projects. It is based in the center of an anonymous, five-hundred-acre industrial complex twelve miles outside Dallas, Texas. That is, it's anonymous if you give it a quick once-over. If you look closely, you'll see that the entire five hundred acres make up, in fact, only one artfully designed compound, which in turn is monitored by a formidable assortment of sophisticated antiintruder arrays.

There are UGS—Unmanned Ground Sensor—systems, advanced, short-wave pulsing lasers, infrared, and high-frequency monitoring devices to name only a few. And they are supplemented by an energetic staff of competent ex–Green Berets and former CIA security types. I know they are competent, because as a favor to S_3's CEO, I once took Red Cell to Dallas for a surprise security exercise against them. It took us more than a week to break through all their defenses, and in the process, we "lost" our whole crew of ersatz tangos doing so. It's nice to know some people take corporate security seriously.

When I ran SEAL Team Six, S_3 Systems crafted dozens of toys for me. They modified the Motorola radios I bought, making them totally secure against intercepts—even from NSA earwigs. They developed the miniaturized silent drills I used to insert mikes and video cameras through walls and into airplane fuselages. Then they built the tiny mikes and video cameras.

More recently, as intelligence-gathering priorities have evolved, S_3 has become increasingly involved in computer-based or generated espionage. It has developed software viruses that hide in massive corporate supercomputer networks, seeking passwords and pulling out the sorts of data that spooks look for. (Just between us, incidentally, it did very well in France a couple of years or so ago until three S_3 employees on loan to the CIA and working under embassy cover got careless, got caught, and were expelled for industrial espionage.)

Anyway, in March 1993, the friendly folks at S_3 Systems developed a cellular phone tracking system that allows agencies to trace calls without having to know the cellular number of the phone. They sold the system—really it is a computer-based software program—to the FBI, as well as to the folks at No Such Agency, Christians in Action, and DIA. Six months after that, Herman Slotnik was arrested in Raleigh, North Carolina.

There is, however, one tiny flaw in S_3's cellular-tracking computer program. I'll tell you what it is, too—if you promise never to reveal it to anyone. Okay—the defect is that if you put your cellular phone on call-forwarding, it is the "forward" phone that the program locks onto, not the originating unit.

How do I know this? you ask. I know it because it is my job to know about back doors and hidden entryways and nasty, spooky, downright unfair ways to win. That's what makes me the unconventional, hirsute, loveable, Bombay-quaffing rogue that I am—that and the fact that I'll kill you before you kill me.

So—first things first. Wonder pulled the car into the farthest corner of the rest area. No need to sit out in the open and get spotted by some observant civilian who'd like to retire on a cool half-mil stipend from LC Strawhouse.

Then I reviewed my options. To be honest, I didn't have a lot of options—not obvious ones, anyway. Dawg and LC had set things up pretty fucking well. But I wasn't without recourse, either.

Let's go over the situation. You know and I know that I didn't off Johnny Cool—the dirty Dawg done did da deed, and he dood it with my very own Emerson. But the fact that you know and I know wasn't going to help me out with the FBI, or any of the hundreds of local cops between here and wherever we were going, who'd see wasting me as one way to get their ugly faces on *Top Cops, American Detective, Unsolved Mysteries,* or any of those real-life infotainment shows, not to mention land themselves a lucrative book deal out of it.

So where did that leave me? It left me out in the cold. But I'm a goddamn SEAL, bub—and out in the cold is nowhere I haven't been before.

Besides, I knew exactly what Dawg and LC Strawhouse were doing. LC was pissed—he'd opened the door about his goals to me, asked me to come aboard, and I'd slapped the shit out of him. As he'd said at the time, I was a dead man. Dawg was pissed, too. I knew they'd be willing to go to any length to put my ugly Slovak ass *en echarpe*—which is a sling, if you're in Paris. They knew damn well where I was, too—which was tracking their precious semi-trailer full of toys. They were probably waiting for me to make some kind of move. (Which, in point of fact, was why I wasn't doing anything but watching, right now. Frogs who make precipitious moves get gigged. And I wanted both my *grenouilles,* for kicking ass and taking names.)

Moreover, Lyman Clyde and Elwood P. had their own set of ESBAM—that's Eat Shit and Bark At the Moon—problems. Incidentally, do not forget this acronym or these conditions—you will see them all again.

- ESBAM One. Sure, they wanted to waste me. But they had to do it themselves. They couldn't allow the possibility that I'd tell some local sheriff about the precious load of stolen weapons in that semi when he clapped me in cuffs. They also had to assume—I certainly would—that I'd told someone up my own chain of command about what they were doing. Bottom line? They'd probably try to take me down themselves. But they would do it only when they had total advantage. Which in turn told me it wouldn't happen on the road: interstates are reasonably public places and they wouldn't want to be interrupted. The fact that they had to hit me themselves gave me *beacoup* wriggle room.

- ESBAM Two. They also had no idea how many people I had working with me—unless, that is, they had access to the documents we'd signed that sat in the Priest's safe. Which wasn't out of the question, given what I'd seen in Detroit. But even if they discovered who was in my crew, they'd have a hell of a hard time finding everybody.
- ESBAM Three. They had no idea about Mugs Sullivan and his network of retired chiefs. Mugs was my Mick in the hole—the hub of my underground Safety Net.
- ESBAM Four. My camp included Stevie Wonder and his durable laptop computer—which meant I had an arthroscopic access to Intelink no one knew about. Wonder's ability to seek and disseminate information gave me a heads-up about the opposition's thinking and tactics.

Hell, the more I thought about it, my situation was better than theirs. For sure. Right on. I guar-ron-*tee*. (Yeah—and have I told you lately that I still believe in Santa Claus, and that Kermit and Miss Piggy will actually get married?)

Go-to-work time. I retrieved our second cellular phone from Gator Shepard and called Mugs. He hadn't gotten home yet, so I left a message on his machine.

Then I punched the call-forwarding code into my own cellular and dialed the secure line at Rogue Manor—it's an S_3 Systems programmable cellular phone I kept as a souvenir from Green Team. It works all over the world, and it can't be tapped—at least not easily. The phone rang three times, then a gruff, tough voice said, "Manor."

That's Brud's voice. Brud is an ex-Camp David Marine who works buildings and grounds and security for me three days a week, patroling my two hundred acres of snakes and lakes, and watching over my house with the same flawless attention to detail with which he used to guard the president's weekend retreat. The other two days, he pulls much the same duty at a secure site called Ground Zero, which sits atop a certain hollowed-out Blue Ridge mountain, code-name Ark Waterfall, up on the Virginia–West Virginia border.

"It's me. Sit-rep?"

"Slicker 'n you-know-what," said Brud. "Got me a bunch of Revenooers out by the front gate, steaming up their windows, just sittin'."

"Yeah—I figured you might. Stay cool."

"No prob. One of them gray phone company vans came by, too, about an hour ago—stopped and talked to the steamy window crowd then drove off. I went out the back door, came up through the wood—y'know, just past where the crooked spring comes up and feeds the creek—and took me a peek. Guess what? They be playing with the phone lines out there, Dick."

That was to be expected. But they couldn't play with the line I was on. "Sounds about right."

"Well?" He waited. I knew what Brud wanted to hear. He was waiting for me to tell him it would be all right to head for the EOD locker, take some C-4, put it up their exhaust pipes where the sun don't shine, and watch the Feds go boom. Brud comes from a part of West By-God where they don't have a lot of respect for Revenooers.

But that wouldn't happen—at least, not today. I told him what I needed. I didn't have to say it twice, either. Brud's a good man that way.

I hung up and gave him fifteen minutes to program the phone. He hadn't done it before, but it was simple, if you followed the steps carefully. Nine minutes later, my own phone rang.

"Hi—it's Brud. I got it—you're set to go."

"Great." I rang off. Now I could call the Priest—not on his scrambled phone (which could be tracked), but through the Manor's lines. But I wasn't about to talk open-ended. If I did that, he'd know right away I'd breached the tracking program. But I still had to know what the hell was going on, because this was turning into a clusterfuck the proportions of which even I had never seen before.

I punched the Manor's number into the phone. I waited as the line opened and the S_3 cellular began the relay sequence Brud had programmed into it.

The Priest's line br-ringed. I gave my password, and was connected. The clock was running.

I got the first words in. "It wasn't me."

The silence on the other end told me either he wasn't convinced or there was somebody close by. I kept a close eye on the second hand on my watch. A preliminary trace takes about forty-five seconds—*if* you're set up to do it. I took for granted the Priest would be set up. Finally, he spoke. "Where are you?"

Was he crazy? "Someplace safe." A bulb went off in my head. "Where are *you?"*

"Office."

That had to be a lie—unless he'd flown back last night on a military plane. I knew all too well that you can call-forward cellular phones—wasn't that what I was doing? The absurdity of the situation struck me. Given the technology, we could have been sitting in adjoining cars, lying to each other about where the fuck we actually were. "Sure," I said. "Sure you are."

His tone got wary. "Okay, Dick, tell me what happened—what the hell you were doing."

Nine seconds. "There's no time right now—it would take an hour to explain it all. You know what I was looking for? Well I found it. Now, you tell me what's going on back there. I need support."

"Do you have proof positive?" Suddenly he was all-business. Where the fuck was this guy coming from?

Still, I gave him a straight answer. "No." I didn't, either. I had LC Strawhouse making a speech in yet another location where a weapons heist and subsequent distribution took place. I had a dirty Dawg on scene. I had a stolen FBI license plate, a bunch of Zulu Gangsta Princes in lots of pieces, and a dead retired SEAL who'd worked for LC Strawhouse. But take-it-to-the-bank proof that absolutely implicated LC Strawhouse? Nada.

"Then there's nothing I can do for you right now," the Priest said tersely. "Look—you haven't completed your assignment. I need hard evidence. Something I can take to court. When you get it, then we can talk about support. Until then, you've been designated a target of opportunity. You're officially cannon fodder, Dick."

I was clusterfucked. BOHICA'd. I told him as much.

"If you had something concrete, we could deal." He paused, and his tone softened just a bit. "Look, you have to understand that my hands have been tied—tied way up the food chain, if you catch what I'm saying."

Twenty-three seconds. Food chain, as in chain of command. Yeah —I'd caught it. And I didn't like the sound of it either. "You have any suggestions?"

The tone of his voice told me that he was upset about this nasty turn of developments, too. "I'll try to do what I can. In the meantime, keep hunting."

Thirty-one seconds. "And?" I was growing very tired of this crap.

"And—you must not fail, Dick. You *will* not fail."

The phone went dead. What he'd said was significant. He'd repeated the very same words to me as Admiral Black Jack Morrison, the day Black Jack, then CNO, ordered me to create and command SEAL Team Six.

"Dick, *you will not fail,"* Black Jack had said. Now the Priest had said the same thing. I scratched at something that had taken up residence under my beard. He was sending me a message—no doubt about it. I just wished I knew what the fuck it was.

I called Mugs. He picked up the phone and singsonged oh, so sweetly, "I told you so."

I could have strangled the son of a bitch. But he didn't give me a chance. No—*he* had to state the obvious. "Rotten Richard, my boy, are you in a pile of it this time."

"I never would have guessed. C'mon, what's the real bad news, Chief?"

That made him laugh. Actually, it was good to hear someone laugh.

There were developments. The FBI license plate had been stolen from (and subsequently replaced on) a car in the FBI motor pool, which was located in an unsecured corner of the underground garage at the Federal office building on Michigan Avenue, which is where the FBI's Detroit field division headquarters is located. You, like our obtuse editor, are probably wondering what the significance of that fact is.

Well, let me explain. It is common tango practice to do this. In *Red Cell,* if you will remember, we actually stole a Navy security vehicle to use during our raid on the Washington Navy Yard. That way, if another cop drove by, he'd see nothing untoward—no strange vehicles, no out-of-state plates, no rented Ryder vans with cargoes of fertilizer-and-fuel-oil bombs. Same thing applied in our current situation. Remember, when Mugs had first checked on the car, he'd been told it belonged to the FBI. Who'd ask any further questions? Anyhow, the old chief told me the switch had been pulled by an asshole named Patterson, who worked as a laborer on the contract maintenance crew. Patterson had ties to the Zulu Gangstas.

Does this strike you as strange? Yeah—me, too. But you have to understand that, unlike FBI headquarters, where even the people who clean the building are full-time FBI employees, the bureau's field offices, which are often located in federal office buildings, use contract labor for cleaning. The FBI is not alone in this lunacy, incidentally. At American embassies and military installations all over the world, building and vehicle repair, food preparation—even secretarial help—are performed by local contract employees. To be honest, we could not run our overseas facilities without local contract labor. Domestically, we use contract services for everything from cleaning our federal office buildings, to auto pool maintenance, to providing security at such sensitive sites as nuclear weapons stowage depots and operational military bases.

And what kinds of security checks are done on the people who go to work for these contract services? If you have answered "few or none," give yourself an *A.* Example? Mugs had checked up on the aforementioned Mr. Patterson. Who, it turned out, had spent eight and three-quarters of the last ten years incarcerated at Marquette prison on the beautiful shores of Lake Huron, on Michigan's Upper Peninsula. He had done his time for aggravated assault (now that is a charge that puzzles me—I mean, have you ever heard of *un*aggravated assault?) and armed robbery.

The old chief had some other news, too. The Detroit police were rounding up Zulu Gangstas by the dozens. They'd picked through what was left of the panel truck, seen the automatic weapons fragments, and went bonkers. The downside was that—courtesy of Dawg Dawkins—the cops believed I was the one who'd been selling the Zulu Gangstas their weapons.

I shook my head and added another black mark next to Dawg's name in my brain. Sooner or later, we'd settle the score.

Meanwhile, Mugs continued, he'd just faxed a retired PO1 named Hinton who'd been in the Teams Vietnam. If the target continued down I-75, Hinton would help us out—pick us up just south of the state line and convoy with us to Atlanta.

That concerned me. "Is this guy trustworthy?"

"Don't be an asshole, Richard."

"Hey, Mugs, no offense, but I *am* wanted for murder."

"What's your point?"

That shut me up.

"Look, Richard," he snapped, "when you are in a situation with which I am not familiar, then you can worry. For now, S^2, okay?"

I know when I'm outranked and outflanked. "Aye-aye, Chief."

"Good." From Knoxville south, Mugs continued, he could fax a contact in Birmingham—a Vietnam-era SEAL who'd recently retired from the police department there—if the semi turned west. If it kept moving south, toward Atlanta, he knew another old Frog we could count on. If they went to New Orleans, our butts would be covered by an old Frog from the bayous. If they drove to Tampa, there was an old Frog with a forty-two-foot Grand Banks Mugs Sullivan knew. He had put his list at my disposal. "You just tell me what you need, Richard."

Would I ever.

Now, you all may be wondering why I wasn't all that nervous about being spotted, since I was a fugitive with a bunch of Feds looking for me. The answer is that during my time with SEAL Team Six, Red Cell, and Green Team, my men and I had regularly practiced going underground. To play the role of terrorist, you have to learn how to think and act like one. The best way to do that, is to do it.

Remember how in *Green Team* we were able to make it from Pakistan to London even though we were on the Interpol wanted list? Well, the same principles applied in my current situation. In fact, the United States may be the world's most receptive and hospitable environment for terrorists. One of the most positive facets of American society is that it is virtually an open one. As a people, we are friendly to a fault. From the very first, these qualities have been a part of the American character—they've been chronicled by writers from de Tocqueville to James Fenimore Cooper; from Henry James to Ernest Hemingway. And they are reflected in every aspect of our lives, from the laxity with which our military bases are guarded, to the freedom with which people come and go in the U.S. Capitol. On the downside, that very openness which makes us special, also makes it possible for tangos and other no-goodniks to exploit us. It also made it easy for me to disappear.

We'd rented our cars and bought the phones under false names. We had enough cash for a few weeks—if we maintained budget discipline. The warrant was for me, which meant that my boys could move more or less undisturbed. The one major problem I had to solve was my own well-used, overabused, and currently contused Slovak face, which growls out from the cover of more than two million book jackets these days, as well as being blanketed over TV news shows and newspapers, courtesy of the Federal government.

So, I had to change my appearance. Next to my dick, my face is my strongest feature—and my eyes are my face's strongest element. So what I had to do was draw attention away from them. Sure, I could start by shaving my beard, trimming my eyebrows, and keeping my hair under a hat. But those alone wouldn't be enough to make me invisible. People would look at me—and recognize me by my eyes.

I know what I am telling you is true because of an incident that took place a few years back, when elements of the PKK—the Kurdish Workers' Party, a small, Marxist terrorist group of ultranationalists supported by Iraq and Syria—attacked an NSA listening post masquerading as a NATO radar installation in Mardin, Turkey, which is close to the Syrian border. Two of No Such Agency's earwigs were killed by an RPG—a rocket-propelled grenade. In those days, we had a president who allowed us to retaliate when our people were murdered, and Red Cell, which was conducting a security exercise at the NATO base in Sigonella, Sicily, was uncaged to neutralize the perps.

So much for background. I left six men behind to continue the exercise, packed my cut-down, suppressed Ruger Mark-II .22-caliber pistol and fifty rounds of Eley's best subsonic hollowpoint ammunition, took Doc Tremblay along for moral support (he brought his lightweight, mini-sniper rifle in case I needed anything more), and went hunting.

Well, I didn't go hunting right away. This, after all, was the Middle East, which operates within the parameters of its own particular traditions and customs—not to mention a certain, shall we say leisurely, *ma'lesh,* or *mañana,* way of doing business. So it took six long weeks for our own intelligence organizations to nudge the Turks in the right direction (convincing them every inch of the way that everything was their idea), and finally track the PKK's Lord High Executioner, a cretin named Cetin Abbas, to a small Syrian border town (populated mostly by Kurds), called Ayn Diwar.

We finally got to climb aboard a NATO C-9 and flew to Diyarbakir, where we were picked up by two carloads of MIT grads. (No, not computer dweebs from Cambridge, Massachusetts. The acronym stands for *Milli Istihbarat Teskilati,* which, as anyone in Anatolia can tell ya, means "Turkish Intelligence Organization.") During the drive, they handed us their files. Their thin files. Their painfully thin files. Cetin the cretin may have been on Turkish intelligence's most wanted list for a long time, but MIT didn't know a lot about him. And they hadn't actually seen him in almost a decade—ergo the only photos they had for me were a grainy, eight-year-old surveillance picture, and a passport portrait taken when he was seventeen—more than thirteen years before.

The lead MIT case officer told us that they'd sent agents familiar with the photo across the border into Ayn Diwar—a fact that made me very nervous, because it meant that our quarry was already on guard—but Cetin was nowhere to be found. Doc and I, he said apologetically, had probably come on a wild tango chase.

Not according to *my* information. But to play the game according to the local rules, I threw up my hands and commiserated. Of course, I added, we'd infiltrate anyway, and *Inshallah*—whatever happened would be Allah's will. That made the MIT men happy. We drove south to the small city of Midyat, where we sat over tiny cups of sweet Turkish coffee followed by huge tumblers of arak—which is high-test, anise-flavored liquor. After six hours of arak and coffee, and coffee and arak, and arak and arak, we convinced MIT to let us drop out so we could infiltrate anonymously. Somehow, two Mercedes 500 sedans and eight guys wearing matching brown suits in a region where the average yearly wage is less than $988 tend to attract unwanted attention.

Doc and I checked into a no-star hotel for the night. The next morning we bought ourselves local attire at a convenient old-clothes kiosk. Then, after a breakfast of sweet tea, yoghurt, garlic, and cucumber, we caught an ancient bus on which we ruined our kidneys as it jounced, bounced, and bumped down the pot-holed road to Cizre, a town of two thousand or so, 250 yards across the border from Ayn Diwar.

The first night, photos in hand—well, okay, not in hand, but safely folded in the waistband of my rough Kurdish clothes next to my Ruger—I slipped under the razor wire-topped fence that ran along the border and went to work. Ayn Diwar was your archetypal north Syrian one-camel town. There was a single main street and three side streets. The flat-front, balconied, two-story houses (shops below, living quarters above) had the sort of TV antennas that are fashioned out of wrought iron and look like the Eiffel Tower. The main drag was unpaved. Half a dozen soldiers, their arms folded over AK-47 assault rifles, lounged on the street or in doorways in the same stoop-shouldered, angular slouch they achieve in every Third and Fourth World country from Paraguay to Pakistan. Where the hell do they give the goddamn posture lessons for this kind of thing, anyway?

There were three grill shops, featuring goat and lamb on the spit. Nearby, were two shabby cafés filled with men sipping tea, reading week-old newspapers, smoking *nargilah* in water pipes, and gossiping. In the second of them, sitting on a low, square stool and playing *mahbouz,* a local variation of *shesh besh,* or backgammon, I saw my target.

He looked almost nothing like the man whose pictures sat in my coat. Almost. He'd cut his long hair short, in the style of the Iranian Shi'ites. He had removed his long beard, trimming it back to Yassir Arafat stubble. He had lost weight—the round, cherubic face in the photograph had been replaced by an angular, ascetic countenance.

All of that had changed. But he couldn't camouflage his eyes—his bright, burning, mesmerizing eyes. The eyes of a leader, a visionary, a fanatic. Cetin Abbas's eyes may have been the windows to his soul—but they were also his undoing.

By the time I rolled under the fence back to the safety of Turkey three hours later, Cetin was dead. And I had learned a lesson about hiding in plain sight that I'd carry for the rest of my life.

The bad guys sailed around Atlanta, blew through Valdosta, and stopped long enough to buy microwave hot dogs, drain their lizards, and refuel in Lake City, Florida, forty miles south of the Georgia border. Then they put the well-worn pedal to the well-worn metal and shot around Gainesville, through Ocala, and by Trilby, coasting into Tampa's northern suburbs after three hours of hard driving enlivened by patches of thick, opaque fog and slippery highway. We kept a quarter to a half mile or so behind them, jockeying for position among ourselves, keeping our eyes on the passive beacon, and watching to make sure that we weren't being followed ourselves. The God of War does not look kindly on SEALs who allow themselves to be ambushed.

I was now beardless. I'd trimmed my eyebrows back so that I'd lost the beetle-browed, patriarchal sociopath Joe Stalin (or is it the matriarchal grandfather Joe Pavlik) look. And I'd dressed for the occasion in gear the guys had acquired piece by piece over the past eleven hours: a green John Deere ball cap, baggy jeans, a lime golf shirt with pocket, and—remember what I learned from Cetin the cretin—some fresh liver.

Don't laugh. Like my sainted mother, Emilie, says, liver is good for you.

She cooks it with onions and bacon. My recipe—slightly more exotic—goes like this. You take a piece of fresh beef liver about the size of a silver dollar, slap it up on the cheekbone next to your eye, wrap it neatly in gauze bandage—being careful to partially cover your eye, too—tape it securely, then let it alone.

The blood in the liver will seep through the bandage, then it will coagulate. You will look like you've been through some nasty surgery—the kind of surgery that tends to make people avert their eyes from your face. Which is, of course, exactly what I wanted them to do.

Especially in Tampa, where I probably knew five hundred people. I've always liked Tampa. It probably has more kinds of ethnic—real ethnic—food than any other city in the state, a holdover from the days before freeways and interstates when the place was a glorious, chaotic, melting pot of immigrants. There are still Cuban cafés in Ybor City, site of the old cigar industry. There's Greek, up north in Tarpon City. Downtown—if you can find anyplace to park—you can eat Salvadorean chorizo, Mexican fajitas, Puerto Rican *cuchifritos,* or Dominican *mafongo.*

There's a steak house called Bern's that boasts the best wine list on the East Coast. Over by Hooker's point, just south of Ybor City, Florida's largest fleet of shrimp boats—not to mention some of the area's best cheap eats sea food—can be found.

But the reason *I* know so many people is because, just south of the city itself and due east across the bay from St. Petersburg, is a peninsula shaped somewhat like a horse's hoof, measuring roughly three miles high and five miles wide. On that huge plot sits MacDill Air Force Base, headquarters to both the U.S. Army's CENTCOM—Central Command—and SOCOM—the nation's Special Operations Command.

It's not a bad place to serve. If, that is, you're the kind of nonwarrior professional staff puke who, like my favorite three-star admiral—G. Edward Emu, deputy chief of staff at SOCOM—likes your cammo BDUs starched, your jungle boots spit shined, and your day to end at 1630 *sharp.* Quality of life is great. If you're a senior officer like Eddie you get waterfront housing on Bayshore

Boulevard between Catfish Point and Gadsden Point—the kinds of villas that civilian snowbird retirees pay three grand a month to rent. If you're an O-4 or O-5 (that's a major or a lieutenant colonel), there are town houses with water views and nice backyards for the weekly barbecue.

There's a big O-Club over by Catfish Point on the base's easternmost coast—a sprawling, one-story World War II–era building—where the hot hors d'oeuvres are free during the 1600-to-1900 Happy Hour hours, and the O's feed like locusts until the food runs out. There's bingo and golf for the huge retarded community, a humongous commissary and post exchange. The visitors' BOQ is walking distance from the O-Club, and across the boulevard from the beach. All very convenient.

And where are the warriors, you ask? Ah, friends, that is a good question, and if I had a good answer I would give it to you. There are few warriors actually at MacDill. Warriors can't take the quiet pace, the golf, and the 0800-to-1630 hours. In fact, it has been my experience that when real shooters come to town, the folks at SOCOM, who have access to the base's 137 visiting officers, and 136 visiting enlisted units, actually house them up north in Tampa proper, as far away from the spit and polish, the manicured lawns, and the O-Club Happy Hour activities as possible, so said shooters' roguish activities will not cause discomfort to the base personnel.

You think I'm putting you on, don't you. Well, I'm not.

I may not be putting you on, gentle reader, but I *am* digressing. To get back to my point, the bottom line was that between retirees, hangers-on, wanna-be's, and active-duty staff pukes, I knew enough people in the area to make me nervous, liver or no liver. So I felt a lot better when the semi and its station wagon escort took the left-hand fork just north of the city and continued south on I-75.

Better, that is, until they turned off onto Interstate 4, drove west —the 0620 sun coming from the horizon directly at their backs—took a left at the university, then headed due south. I knew all too well where that road leads—it dead-ends at the MacDill main gate. Which was where the station wagon turned right onto Chisholm Avenue, and drove off in a westerly direction toward the port. Incredibly, the semi drove straight to the main gate. The driver reached down and handed the white-gloved, fourragèred, blue-bereted female Air Force cop at the gatehouse a sheaf of papers, which were once-overed and handed back. She saluted, and the truck was waved through as if it belonged there.

Yes, I was a wanted man. Yes, it was a reckless thing to do, but there was no way that the goddamn truck was going to get away from me. Not now. "Follow the fucking truck," I said.

Wonder shrugged. "Aye, aye, sir," he grumbled, spelling it with a *c* and a *u.* He floored the accelerator. We burned rubber, careened through a yellow light, sped across four lanes of honking traffic, and drove through the MacDill main gate with a wave and a hearty "Hi-Ho, Silver."

We'd left our shipmates in the other two cars behind. But that was okay—they could chase the station wagon. Nasty peered through the rear window. The gatekeeper didn't seem especially perturbed by our behavior—at least she hadn't picked up the phone. We slowed way below the twenty-five miles per hour posted limit, let a couple of cars get between us and our quarry, and continued. The semi took the main base road south for about a quarter mile, past warehouses and storage facilities. Before it got to the CENTCOM headquarters building where it might have attracted some attention, it turned left onto an access road that led past a series of double-wide trailers that sprouted UHF and VHF antennas, as well as eighteen-inch SATCOM receiving dishes.

From there, it crawled over a wide concrete apron that sat in front of a hangar I knew housed C-5 aircraft. Then it turned south again, and drove past a narrow perimeter road lined with warehouses and equipment sheds. There, it cut a wide left, tacking onto a two-lane asphalt artery that had OFFICIAL VEHICLES ONLY stenciled on its surface every hundred yards.

I knew that road, too. It dead-ended right on one of MacDill's two huge concrete aprons—the base's aircraft loading areas—which were directly behind the two-story SOCOM headquarters building. There was no place to hide anything there—but you could see people coming your way from any direction.

These guys were checking their six, not stashing the goods, and I wasn't about to get us caught.

There was a one-way street just ahead. "Turn left here," I told Wonder.

"It's the wrong way."

"What's your point?"

He groaned. But he turned. "Now what?"

"Follow this until we get to a half-moon drive. Cross it—there'll be a stop sign. Go straight on, then take your first right after the flagpole."

Wonder wheeled the Chevy as directed. We cut through a narrow passageway between two hangars, rolled past half a dozen comm trailers, turned right at a stop sign, and emerged next to the policed-thrice-a-day-and-mowed-twice-a-week lawn in front of SOCOM headquarters. The half-moon drive was directly ahead of us—and it was fucking blocked by orange fucking rubber cones.

They were resurfacing the goddamn driveway.

SNAFU. I pointed left. "Go around there—"

Wonder shot me a dirty look. He reversed, K-turned, and went back the way we'd come. We raced to the stop sign, turned right, turned right once more, and hit a dead end.

TARFU. He backed up, reversed direction, and came nose to nose with a base security vehicle.

FUBAR. Wonder stuck his head out the window, smiled graciously, and did what no real man ever does—he asked for directions to the road that ran in front of SOCOM HQ. He even said, "Thank you, and have a nice day," when he'd received them. He wasn't so polite to me.

Finding your way is simple if you know where you are going. Two left turns and a right turn later, we cruised past the neat palm tree groves that sit directly outside SOCOM's main entrance.

I glanced over and was happy to see they'd actually made an improvement or two since I'd been here last. The wide, covered portico—it's the kind of structure you drive an explosive-laden truck under and detonate, thus bringing down the whole building —was now blocked by two dozen concrete antiterrorist pylons that had been deposited between the driveway and the front doors. They were painted white and looked like two platoons of Munchkin swabbies in dress whites standing at parade rest.

I gestured with my thumb, and Wonder—skeptical but willing —turned right again at the far end of SOCOM. We drove down a narrow alley that ran parallel to the building, turned left, and wound up atop the neat, gravel pathway that ran from SOCOM's back door to the planetarium parking lot.

Planetarium, you ask? Yeah—planetarium. That's where the stars park.

We pulled to a stop at the back corner of the building. In front of us, the wide concrete apron stretched for a quarter of a mile. Beyond it were the hangars and beyond them, in the distance,

MacDill's 3,900-meter main runway and its adjacent network of taxiways, ramps, and aprons.

I smiled the smile of the lucky and the dumb. The semi crawled down the middle of the apron, approaching from our right. It turned a wide, lazy circle, then went back the way it had come.

I was reaching for the radio to let Gator, Half Pint and Doc know what they were up to when Mr. Murphy got my attention by pounding on the roof of our car.

No—I mean *literally.* Pound-pound-pound. Wham-wham-wham.

I dropped what I was doing, stared out the open window, saw the crotch of summer white trousers topped by a brightly shined brass buckle, kept going north and saw staff badge, jump wings, service ribbons, and a fucking Budweiser, all topped by three stars set onto open-necked collar points. I gasped, then looked up directly into the scrawny, indignant face of G. Edward Emu, vice admiral and deputy chief of staff, United States Special Operations Command.

"Do you people know where you are? Do you realize that this is a pedestrians-only area. What in heaven's name is this car doing in —*geeeezus!"* He stopped in midcaterwaul and stared intently at my bandaged face.

I was dead meat. There are only a few active duty people who remember me as a clean-shaven, geeky, enlisted team puke of a sailor, and Eddie Emu is one of them. He was a snot-nosed ensign at UDT 22 when I was a radioman second class working for Everett Emerson Barrett, chief gunner's mate/guns, in the Second-to-None platoon. Eddie didn't like me then, he don't like me now, and the feeling is absofuckingposilutely mutual.

But Eddie wasn't looking at *me.* He was looking at my liver. Which brought to mind one of the reasons I dislike G. Edward Emu so much: the good admiral has never been able to stand the sight of blood. The first time he saw a dead Viet Cong he fainted, which made him a bona fide SEAL legend (but not the sort anybody'd ever want to be). Anyway, Eddie sucked wind. He swallowed hard, his Adam's apple j-j-juggling *g-gulp, g-gulp.* His bug eyes swelled into an expression that combined revulsion, loathing, and nausea. He actually brought his right hand up to his forehead to block the view.

Simultaneously, he brushed the air frantically with his left hand. "You're not supposed to be here," he croaked, waving us away. "Drive on. Drive on."

Have I told you how I've learned to take "yes" for an answer lately?

Well, Wonder knows how, too—especially when I'm back handing him on the shoulder hard enough to leave knuckle-hair prints. He put the car in gear and hauled my profusely perspiring *betzim* outta there.

We rolled slow and easy, allowing the semi a long, long leash. It meandered back up the access road, crossed the main post road three hundred yards south of the main gate, stopped at the traffic light that regulated traffic moving across the main MacDill runway, and turned north, creeping parallel to the perimeter fence on an overgrown, obviously underused security path.

There is no vehicle gate at the northwest corner of MacDill. There is, however, a railroad siding. Actually, there are two railroad sidings. One runs north/south, the other, east/west. Access to both is through a pair of huge, sliding steel gates, each topped with barbed wire, that sit roughly seventy-five yards apart, twenty yards south of Chisholm Avenue—which runs parallel to MacDill's northern border.

We worked our way parallel to the semi about three hundred yards south of it and stopped. I climbed out of the Chevy and perused the sidings and gates through my binoculars.

In case you wanted to know, railroad gates are security sieves. Red Cell used the railroad gates at Groton, Connecticut, to infiltrate the Navy's allegedly secure nuclear sub base there—walked right through carrying big duffel bags, and no one ever stopped us. (Things were so lax that three of my better sneak-and-peekers actually sauntered aboard one of the Los Angeles class attack subs moored on the Thames river and cached a load of Improvised Explosive Devices right next to her nuclear reactor without being challenged. If the IEDs had been for real, they would have caused an atomic explosion big enough to vaporize greater metropolitan Groton.)

Anyhow, alongside these sidings (say *that* three times fast) were a series of three-story warehouses, in which were stored such essential but nontactical supplies as fifty-five-gallon drums of axle grease and other lubricants, huge tubs of floor cleaner for the hangars' concrete slab floors, bales of barbed wire, huge rolls of chain-link fencing—all the janitorial and mechanical odds and ends that are needed to support the physical well-being of the installation.

There was something else sitting on the east/west railroad siding, too. It was an industrial-size crane—the sort that is used to transfer semi-trailers on and off railroad flatcars. Which is exactly what took place in front of our eyes right now.

The semi pulled up parallel to the siding, directly under the five-story crane. The tractor disengaged its fifth wheel, and the driver unhooked the hydraulic, brake, and electric lines. Then he and his assistant attached four hawser-size cables to the trailer, and it was lifted gently up, and onto a convenient flatbed railroad car. I would have panicked, except I saw that it was the only railroad car on the siding. That told me it would have to be attached to a train if it was heading anywhere—and we'd get to it well before then.

I rousted Doc's car on the radio. He and the others had followed the station wagon which, he reported, had parked down at the end of something called A Road, right on the Port Tampa dock—one of the city's commercial shipping harbors—which I knew to be roughly two or two-and-a-half miles away, as the pelican flies.

As I spoke to Doc, a small switcher engine began moving backward from the north/south siding. It eased up to the loaded flatbed. I saw the platform car shift as the buffers retracted and the coupling devices engaged. I pressed the TRANSMIT button on my radio. "Anything interesting moored over where you are?"

"Well, since you asked, there are a half dozen old shrimpers—you should be able to smell 'em from there—and two nice trawlers—sixty, seventy foot. And there's one beautiful Hatteras moored just off the dock. I can give it away for a quarter mil, cash."

Doc began to chortle. I told him to quit—he's not the chortling kind. So he got serious. "And, as a matter of fact, there is also one of those dumbass supply ships—the ones we used for oil-rig boarding exercises when you and I were a lot younger and actually got some pussy every now and then."

Pussy, shmussy. I was about to call "bingo" because I had a full card. "Is it one of those supply ships that they use to carry platform modules?"

"Hold on a sec—" Doc paused long enough to take a careful look. While he does, let me explain to you the significance of my question to him. See, oil rig platforms these days are designed in modular fashion. In English, that means that prefab sections—often about the size of a semi-trailer—are shipped out to the rig, lifted aboard, and bolted into position. That allows the configuration of the platform to change. A drilling platform, for example, will have two or three living quarter modules aboard, because you need more folks when you're drilling than when you're pumping.

The pumping modules will house more computerized equipment than humans because once the well is drilled, and operational, it can be run by a skeleton crew and a computer.

"Yo, *muta khallef?*" Doc came back on-line, calling me a dumbshit in Arabic. "That is an affirmative."

There are few times in life, my friends, when one and one does, in fact, actually equal two. I had a gut feeling that this was going to be one of them.

I watched until the switcher and its flatbed moved north through the unguarded railroad gate. Then we hauled our butts, too, so we could monitor its progress as it made its way to the Port Tampa docks, where it traversed the cold sheds and transit sheds, slid under the container-loading bridge, and was gently laid across the foredeck of an anonymous-looking supply vessel. Just as Doc had reported, it was the precise kind of vessel used to supply oil rigs. But there was more. The name of the ship, *Helen G. Kelley,* was written in foot-high block letters across her wide, flat stern. Below the name, the single word GALVESTON was centered. Galveston, as we all know, is an oil-processing center. But there was more, too: on the *Helen G. Kelley*'s single gray stack was painted a stylized, medieval sheaf of straw on whose binding was emblazoned the words PAJAR PETROLEUM. The fucking thing belonged to LC Strawhouse.

So, the weapons were being shipped to an oil rig, from which they'd probably be dispensed or sold. That made perfect sense to me. What? You say you're confused? Okay, let me explain my thinking.

Oil rigs are isolated. Sure, they're hard to reach. But they're also more difficult to stake out than some warehouse in the middle of a big city. Moreover, you can mix and match your weapons. Steal 'em from Michigan, Iowa, California—and sell 'em to tangos from Florida (or anywhere else). That kind of miscellany makes them harder to trace—at least initially.

We had to follow the *Helen G. Kelley.* So, it was time to work the phones. While Wonder attached his modem to my cellular unit and routed the call through Rogue Manor so he could monitor the Intelink without being traced, I dialed Mugs's number with the other phone and waited for his welcome growl, so I could remind him that he'd offered to introduce us to a Frog with a boat.

Chapter 15

SINCE WE'RE ABOUT TO EMBARK ON OUR WAY TO AN OIL-DRILLING RIG out in the Gulf of Mexico, maybe I should tell you something about them. Okay—there are three types of oil-rig platforms commonly found in the Gulf. In relatively shallow waters, there are semisubmersibles, which float atop huge, tire-shaped pontoons and are secured with the aid of immense, winch-and-cable-operated sea anchors. There are jack-up platforms, smaller, skeletal steel structures whose height from the water surface can be controlled by a complicated raising and lowering procedure known —you guessed it—as "jacking." In deeper water, or where the currents are dangerous, there are fixed drill-rig or pumping platforms—huge towers of steel and concrete that ascend more than a hundred feet above the surface of the water from depths of three hundred feet.

The specific features, layout, accommodations, and creature comforts of each company's platforms may be somewhat distinct, but their structures, their dynamics, and what's on them are always more or less the same. The skeleton of the offshore rig—this is a fixed platform I'm talking about here, because it is really the most commonly seen rig—is made of steel pipes and girders set into concrete and steel pylons. The frame supports a series of grid tiers, on which sit the drilling, pumping, and storage equipment. Some rigs are drill rigs—they are actively searching for oil by running long probes into the ocean floor. Others are pumpers—drawing oil from below the surface and transferring it first to onboard storage tanks, then to seagoing tankers.

Normally, platforms have but two main decks, although there are a maze of passageways, catwalks, and ladders that connect them, as well as various terraced structures that protrude from the primary framework. There are also a plethora of miscellaneous tanks, vats, reservoirs, and steel Conex boxes, as well as various levels on the drilling or pumping platform, which is known as the derrick. These caches, stashes, hiding places, and mazed passageways make the takedown of a platform rig—this is a top secret U.S. Navy SEAL technical term I'm going to use here—a total potential clusterfuck.

See, roughly sixty feet above water level sits the first level. It consists of a series of interconnected catwalks and grates, on which sit the pumps, the separator tanks, and the bulk-storage containers. Also stored there are the piles of twelve-inch pipes that carry the oil from the ocean bottom. Twenty feet above and connected by a series of ladders and ramps lies the main deck.

There, you find a central work station, which includes the draw works, or "doghouse," where the oil-pumping equipment itself is housed. There is a control module, which houses the offices, the cellular phones and ship-to-shore radios and the weather equipment. There is a crew-bunking module, which includes a mess area and rec room, and there is a monitoring module, where the computers that oversee the operations are kept.

Along the perimeter of the main deck are a series of cranes, which are used to bring supplies aboard, boat-mooring stations, a helipad, and the long flare pipe from whose nozzle is burned off the natural gas that is separated from the oil by the oil/gas separating module that sits on the main deck.

Some rigs are larger than others. Some have huge, multistory drilling derricks that also house drill-string motion compensators —the hydraulic-pneumatic devices that move the derrick *up-and-down, up-and-down,* in rhythm with the sea to keep the pipe stationary in the drill hole while everything else moves. The semisubmersibles have enormous, doughnut-shaped pontoons fifty to sixty feet in diameter, which lie thirty feet below the surface and support the weight of the platform.

The tactics used to board platform rigs take up thirty pages of the current NAV-OPS manual. But since that document is classified, I can give you the gist by defining the strategy simply as SC/FD. That means you either Swim and Climb, or you Fly and Drop—or you perform a combination of both.

If you take the SC option, you can, for example, come off a ship safely over the horizon and transfer into smaller boats—Zodiacs or Boston Whalers—and then drop into the ocean eight hundred to a thousand meters from the target and swim the last leg. Once you reach the platform, your lead climber shinnies up the vertical brace until he reaches a secure position. Then he attaches and drops a caving ladder, and the rest of your shooters clamber aboard.

What I have just described is much more difficult than it sounds. As Desi used to say to Lucy, "Lemme 'splain you how come."

First, getting to the rig in a small boat can be a problem. Most of the time you will do the approach at night so that you won't be seen. In calm seas, no prob. But the Gulf is not known for its calm seas. Moreover, the wave and current patterns in the Gulf are different from those found in the Atlantic or Pacific. Sure, an Atlantic Ocean storm, with its twenty-foot seas, can be rough on the kidneys—I still remember all the fun we had (I am using that *F*-word in a literary application known as irony here, people) when SEAL Team Six practiced boarding exercises in February, thirty miles off the Virginia coast. And the Pacific's huge, thirty-foot swells make chasing down ships almost impossible. You will recall that in *Red Cell,* both our C-130 and our rubber ducky almost ran out of gas before we were able to chase down and board Grant Griffith's rogue tanker with its cargo of bad guys and stolen nuclear Tomahawk missiles. You don't recall? Then go out and buy the fucking book right now, it's still in print.

Okay—now, back to our story. I was talking about current events. Well, the swirling currents you find in the Gulf of Mexico resemble the kinds of riptides you see close to shore in other waters. So you are not only slapped in/out, but also right/left. This semicircular sweeping action can cause you to lose your sense of direction, especially if you are out beyond the sight of land—and believe me, many of the platforms are more than one hundred miles from shore.

Second, getting that first man up the platform can be tough. The braces are slippery. The currents are treacherous. The waves slap you up against the steel and you can break arms, legs—even back or neck—in the attempt to climb. Even once you have made the ascent and are in position, you have to deal with the caving ladder—the rolled-up steel-and-cable boarding device you've carried with you to make things easier for everyone else—which is a slippery, narrow son of a bitch, and as you put boondocker to rung, your sole slips, your soul flips, and you tumble ass over teakettle back down into the water. If, that is, it is indeed water you hit—and not concrete pylon.

Believe me—I have climbed a hundred or so of these nasty things, and each one is worse than the last. Of course, the good news was that we were in the Gulf of Mexico and not the North Sea, where the fucking platforms are coated with ice seven months of the year, and you can remove the skin from your hands trying to scale them.

So much for SC. For FD, you have two options. You can fast-rope from a chopper, which sneaks up on the platform at sea level and then rises, flares, and drops you off quickly. Or, you can HAHO—High Altitude High Opening—from a plane, jumping from twenty-five thousand feet and riding a flat chute down, forming up at about a thousand meters above the target and corkscrewing the rest of the way down onto the platform in formation.

The fast rope is good—but it makes you vulnerable during the approach, when the bad guys have about thirty seconds to see you coming and do something about it. Still, a chopper, which can deliver ten shooters in less than five seconds, is an effective insertion platform. Moreover, if you have an additional chopper—a Hughes 500 with a sniper team aboard—you can sit above the rig and pick off the bad guys while the main force fast-ropes.

The HAHO option, while the most picturesque in the Hollywood sense of things, is the most dangerous to the shooters. Landing on one of these motherfuckers in a crosswind can be lethal, because of the huge number of steel cranes, masts, wires, cables, and other goodies that can snag, snare, impale, entrap, and hook your vitals as you descend out of the sky at seventeen feet per second, which computes out to roughly twelve miles an hour. Moreover, a drop is hard to coordinate. There are too many uncontrolled variables—wind shear, descent rates, and unexpected thermals are three that come to mind right now—which can make the split-second timing that is absolutely crucial for these sorts of operations go awry.

When I commanded SEAL Team Six, we developed a coordinated swimmer/chopper approach that was particularly effective against tango-occupied oil rigs. First, we'd put a snoop contingent onto an adjacent rig. (Normally, you see, offshore oil platforms are built in clusters. That way they are easier to supply, repair, and maintain.) Once our "eyes" had established themselves and reported on the tangos' activities and schedule, we'd make our final assault plans.

Generally, we'd launch our swim team at night—darkness is great cover at sea. Once it had reached the target, made its ascent, and hunkered in position just underneath thc rig deck, we'd launch the airborne element. Only when the swimmers were locked, loaded, and ready to go, would the choppers head in. We would track their progress on the radio. The swimmers could also hear as the choppers passed through the three-minute perimeter, then two minutes, and finally one minute. Just before the aircraft hit, the swim team would go over the rail and head for the nearest tangos—identified by our snoopers who had night-vision equipment trained on the platform.

Bang—we'd swarm the rig and surprise the bad guys. And just as the tangos were being hit, the airborne team would arrive, fast-roping onto the rig's helipad. Our timing was always great. In fact, even when Mr. Murphy was at his worst—when the visibility sucked, or the crosswinds screwed up the chopper's approach, or the seas dinged the hell out of my swimmers—this combined assault technique always worked. I mean, it *worked.* I vass dere, Cholly.

I know, I know—you're sitting there asking why the hell I am providing you with all of this techo-thriller sort of detail. The answer, gentle reader, is because I was convinced that I was, quite soon, going to need to use all the various skills we had developed to board oil rig platforms—and when you are boarding an oil rig platform, you don't have a lot of time to talk about it or explain how. You just gotta do it.

Moreover, I want you to understand just how elaborate, complicated, tricky, and potentially disastrous such assaults can be under the very best of circumstances, because we were about to enter the Doom on Dicky Zone. We would operate *sans* equipment—no caving ladders, no swim gear, and no Zodiacs or Boston Whalers to bring us within striking distance. There would be no tactical intelligence to assist us. There would be no backup to haul our butts out of the fire if we screwed up—no choppers to drop a platoon of shooters; no Hughes 500 and sniper team to protect our six.

I found it somewhat depressing to realize that this was not the first time I have been in this sort of bleak, lose-lose position.

Mugs Sullivan directed me by long-distance phone to a beer-nuts-and-pickled-pig-foot joint just off the A Road at the end of the Port Tampa dock, told me to S^2, and wait to be contacted. How the hell he knew about these places was something I cannot fathom—except for the fact that he is an old chief, and old chiefs know everything.

Our man pushed through the door an hour and three-quarters (and three cases of Coors Light) later. I knew he was our old Frog by his faded denim cutoffs, thong sandals, and the way he walked—that rolling, roily, bow-legged, splay-footed gait common to fleet sailors and cartoon characters with big muscles and cans of spinach in their pockets. He stood five foot six or seven, with the round, mischievously cherubic face of a falling angel, a thatch of thinning gray hair, a barrel chest and rock-hard beer belly to match, tanned, muscular arms bedecked with faded blue tattoos that ran from brachs to biceps, and huge, wide scarred hands.

He walked right up to me as if he'd known me for years, put his big mitt out and shook my hand. His palm was as rough as forty-grit sandpaper, and his grip was strong enough to make me wince. "Fuck you, you worthless cockbreath," he said by way of greeting. "I'm Grose."

Grose. Grose—nobody had ever called him anything else but that; in fact, I'm not sure he even had a first name—was a legend in the teams. He'd joined the Navy in the early forties and seen action in the North Atlantic during World War II. He'd been a fleet sailor, a boatswain's mate, a hard-hat salvage diver—he'd even worked with Roy Boehm for a while. But diving wasn't enough of a challenge, so he'd joined the Teams in the early fifties—the oldest and meanest guy ever to go through UDT Replacement Training at Little Creek up to that point.

By the time I was an enlisted tadpole he'd already retired. But they all were still talking about him. He was, they all said, the roughest, toughest damn Frog who'd ever lived. Took on twenty nasty Corsicans in Bastia and sent them all to the hospital. Ate a whole live rooster—feathers and all—in Dominica. Blasted a mile-and-a-half-long trench in the Philippines—an explosion so big the desk jockeys at Subic shit and thought Mount Pinatubo had blown its top. He'd been an instructor at Little Creek when Ev Barrett went through replacement training, and Barrett's butt still bears symmetrical scars from the burnished tips of Grose's size eight, triple-E boondockers.

After retirement, he'd packed his gear and gone south. Dropped out of the Frog scene altogether. Rumor had him in Costa Rica or Mexico. Others swore they'd seen him in the Philippines, or Bali. In fact, he said, he'd bought (and currently lived aboard) a forty-two-foot Grand Banks—a trawler-hulled, twin Leland diesel fishing boat, which he berthed over in Clearwater, on the Gulf Coast. And, he added, he did keep up with Frogs—at least the few he respected—mostly old Frogs who also respected his privacy.

He was a loner, except for the tight circle of fax friends that included Mugs. He had never become a part of Tampa's huge Navy retired community. He didn't shop cut-rate at the commissary at MacDill, or bother with the free Happy Hour hors d'oeuvres at the Chiefs' Club. He never showed up at reunions, either. Never visited the SEAL Museum's annual Muster in November, or the Little Creek bash every July. But they still talked about him at both.

He made a good living, he said, sucking down a Coors Light. Mostly in construction-related areas. He paved driveways, roughed-in plumbing in new houses, or drove a concrete truck.

I watched the faces of my youngsters as Grose talked about the Navy—*his* Navy. They were rapt with attention; awestruck kids who hung on his words. And rightly so. Today's Navy is not the wooden-ships-and-iron-men Navy of yore. Today, it is the other way around. Sure, we have all the technogoodies. And the youngsters who make it through BUD/S these days are probably better educated than those who came before them. But Grose and the chiefs like him are veterans of a Navy whose tradition can be traced directly back from Bull Halsey through Farragut and John Paul Jones. They know the history that is too often ignored by today's four-starred manager-leaders.

We piled in our cars and convoyed back to Clearwater. I rode with Grose and on the way described our situation. He reamed my ass in a manner that would have made Roy Boehm and Ev Barrett envious, drained the last Coors from a big thermos cooler on the worn bench seat, wadded up the still-wet can with his left hand like an old paper napkin, tossed it over his shoulder through the open cab window into the scarred bed of his well-used but not abused dark green F-250 diesel, and backhanded me in the chest hard enough to take my breath away.

"Don't worry, son," he said. "I'll have you up and running in no time." It was said as a simple statement of fact—and I believed every word of it.

We sat in the well-appointed cockpit of his boat and went over nautical charts. The Pajar supply ship had departed Port Tampa Dock about the same time we'd left for Grose's pier in Clearwater. It had an average speed, Grose estimated, of just over six knots—that's just under seven miles per hour for you nonnautical types. The initial phase of its journey—clearing Port Tampa, sailing down the channel through Tampa Bay, under the Sunshine Skyway and clear around St. Petersburg into the Gulf, was a thirty-nine-mile haul, according to the lines on Grose's charts. Divide the mileage by the speed and you get 5.5 hours.

Grose's Grand Banks, which he'd named *FYVM,* had a top speed of just over eight knots and a range of six hundred nautical miles running its twin Leland two-hundred-horsepower diesels at a 6.5-knot cruising speed. When we did the calculations and figured in all the variables, we had two and a half hours from now to get ourselves under way, so we could intercept the supply ship as it cleared the channel, and follow it to its target.

A forty-two-foot Grand Banks can sleep eight under normal circumstances: two in each of the forecastle cabins, two in the amidships bunks, and two in the main cabin, which has a couch that converts into a double bed. We were eleven, and we'd have to haul a boat load of equipment. Well, we could hot-bunk if necessary. Ah—the editor asks me to explain that nautical term. Okay. Hot-bunking is when three shifts of sailors share the same bunk because there isn't enough space aboard ship (or sub) for each man to have his own bed. So as soon as one man rolls out, the next rolls in. The bunk stays warm, and the phrase "hot bunk" was born to describe it. Happy, editor dearie? Okay—back to the narrative—since this was the tropics, we could also sleep out on the foredeck and flying bridge.

The only weapon he had on board was his shark gun—a stainless steel Mossberg 12-gauge—and a brick—that's fifty rounds—of hollowpoint sabot slugs. That was okay—we had weapons from Michigan courtesy of the United States Army, and a shit-load of government-issue ammo.

We had a fair amount of equipment, too, for folks on the run. There were my night-vision glasses. I also had the pair of secure radios, and the cellular phones I'd bought. And Grose's boat had just about every electronic toy you could find. He had a SATCOM direction finder that allowed him to pinpoint his position and track a course. He had the latest VHF radio equipment. He'd installed the newest generation of radar and short-wave equipment. He had a computer and a modem. There was even a fax.

And even if all of that failed, we could still track our quarry. The NIS beacon was still working, so we could shadow the supply vessel from up to six miles—ten thousand yards away—which would give us good cover.

Of course, we had no boarding equipment, no swim gear, no Zodiacs or Boston Whalers, and no extra fuel bladders for the Grand Banks. But what is life without adventure?

So we improvised. Grose hit an ATM and came up with a fistful of dollars. Stevie Wonder handed over the last of the cash he'd received from the Priest, and we pooled it all. Then Pick, Half Pint, Gator, and Duck Foot hit the Clearwater Dive and Sport Shoppe and bought masks, fins, knives, and all the soft mountaineering rope they had in stock. Rodent, Nasty, and Wonder discovered the wonderful world of Surplus Sam's, where they bought ten five-gallon Jerry cans for extra diesel fuel, ten five-gallon red plastic gas containers, five wrist compasses and five Silva compasses on lanyards, ten sets of BDUs—those are the oxymoronically named Battle Dress Uniforms—belts, coral booties, and mesh assault vests, all in black except for the coral shoes, which were blue, and a dozen infrared Cyalume light sticks.

Cherry headed to the Winn Dixie, where he stocked up with a week's worth of rations—and, more important, beer. Doc Tremblay made a run to the drug counter at Piggly Wiggly, where he assembled an off-the-shelf tactical first-aid kit—everything from painkiller to splints—which he then broke down by category and stored in plastic Ziploc freezer bags. The bags were then crammed into the pockets of his combat vest. The Ziplocs would keep everything waterproof, he said. I hoped so—I hate soggy Advil.

Then, his Florence Nightingale imitation finished, he drove with Grose to the neighborhood Zodiac dealer, where they paid a wad of Grose's cash for the smallest rigid inflatable and forty-horsepower outboard in stock. I watched as they drove up with the goddamn boat sticking out the end of Grose's pickup. Where the hell we were going to store the damn thing I had no idea, but it was better to have one than not have one.

We sorted, stacked, and stowed for an hour until Grose was satisfied that everything was shipshape. He topped off the tanks and made sure the Jerry cans and gas containers were filled brimward with diesel and regular. Finally, Grose scrutinized his boat—and us. I'd always thought the term "stem-to-stern inspection" was a cliché. I discovered by watching Grose's attention to detail that it was not a cliché—it was a fact of life.

He pronounced us ready. He faxed Mugs a scrawled sit-rep that he signed S.I.Y.F.H.—for Shit In Your Flat Hat, an old Chief's curse directed at other chief petty officers—then assumed his position on the flying bridge and instructed Wonder to disconnect the electric and telephone lines that ran from the cabin to a box on the pier. That done, he started the twin diesels. After a minute or so of throaty growls, he shut them down, and rumbled at Wonder, who was now standing by the bow rail, to connect everything up again. Grose clambered onto the pier, roiled up the dock, climbed aboard his truck, and roared off without a word.

Twenty minutes later he was back. He drove up and retrieved from the back of his truck a heap of what looked like commercial tuna netting. He rolled it into a ball, slung it over his shoulder, carried it down the pier, then tossed it down into the Grand Banks's cockpit.

I looked at the pile of mesh and asked, "What the hell's that for?"

Grose ignored me. He lowered himself onto the deck, picked up the netting, wrestled it forward, and stored it in a locker next to the wheelhouse. He pulled himself back up onto the flybridge and checked all his gauges and dials in a full precruise inspection, even though he'd done it less than half an hour before. When he'd assured himself that all systems were "go," he started the engines and played with the throttles until he was happy with what he heard. That was when he waved at Wonder to disconnect the electric and phone lines, and signaled Cherry and Nasty to cast off their bow and stern lines.

They all obeyed smartly. He waited until the youngsters had coiled the hawsers neatly and jumped aboard. He flicked his throttle levers, edged slowly eight, nine, ten yards away from the dock, nudged the throttles again, spun the wheel, and reversed as effortlessly as if the Grand Banks had been attached to a pivot post. Then, pointed in the proper direction, he gave the boat some power and slid evenly into the channel.

Finally, he descended into the wheelhouse, plucked a Coors from the reefer, opened the port-side door, looked in my direction, and answered my question with a question. "Didn't you say you needed a caving ladder, asshole?"

Chapter

16

WE CLEARED THE MARINA CHANNEL RIGHT ON SCHEDULE, PICKED UP THE *Helen G. Kelley* as it sailed almost due west out from Tampa, then dropped way behind as it turned slightly to the north, its wake cutting a lazy swath across the wide, deep blue expanse of the Gulf. We'd dropped the Zodiac overboard as soon as we'd cleared the breakwater and were now towing her to give ourselves more room on the deck. It was Grose's idea. "Trawlers are always towing their dinghies," he growled. "Nobody'll give us a second thought." So we hitched a hefty fifty-foot line to the inflatable's bow, tossed it, and let it ride behind.

The Grand Banks with its big, flat trawler's hull and high cabin rode the swells with an easy grace. This craft had been built not for speed but for comfort and endurance—it was a real old-fashioned cruising boat. The main cabin settee was upholstered, not foam. The glass was thick and tinted. The appointments—down to the built-in bud vases, in which Grose stored his collection of swizzle sticks—had been individually crafted. The paneling, deck, and trim were real teak.

The galley was tiny but functional, although Doc and I would be cramped cooking for eleven. Grose had packed the boat with creature features. There was a microwave, a TV set, even a CD player and a rack of Montovani's greatest hits. Best of all were the two extra refrigerators he'd built into the main cabin, which kept six cases of beer at a constant thirty-eight degrees.

Grose, an omnipresent Coors in his big paw, sat like a proper *aristocratico* in his captain's chair and kept the supply ship between ten and fifteen thousand yards ahead of us, tacking us back and forth in gentle, random legs. We were too small for them to see us, unless they had the kind of equipment used by the Navy or the Coast Guard's drug interdiction forces. But they were big enough for us to make 'em out on Grose's state-of-the-art radar gear.

Navigation was no problem. We could track them on our charts by plotting their course in relation to ours by using Grose's satellite position finder in conjunction with the radar. Grose assigned watches—four hours on, eight hours off—just as if we were serving in a man o' war.

Which, as a matter of fact, we were. During the first watch we worked on equipment, loading magazines, rigging charges and improvised explosive devices (IEDs), cleaning weapons and storing them safely out of the salt air environment. These, after all, were U.S. Army issue Berettas, not our usual Heckler & Koch USPs, and they required tender, loving care so they wouldn't jam on us at the critical moment. If they'd been USPs we could have towed them astern for a week and still shot the hell out of 'em if we ran a patch through thc barrcl and used dry ammo.

With Doc at the conn, and me playing naviguesser, Grose and Duck Foot used some of the mountaineering rope and the length of tuna netting to fashion a jury-rigged caving ladder. Actually, it looked more like one of those old cargo nets on which Marines clamber down into landing craft than a piece of stealthy assault gear. But as you have probably heard before from your Brit friends, buggers can't be choosers.

When the watch changed again, I stretched out on the aft deck cushions to take a late-afternoon combat nap. From under half-closed lids I watched Half Pint work his way down the tow rope so he could sack out solo in the Zodiac. I smiled at his ingenuity. You need to find your own space aboard a ship—someplace you can crawl into, and leave the world behind. For some, it's the chain lockers. For others, it's the forecastle, or the athwartships passageways. On subs, I've seen sailors sneak into missile tubes in search of solitude. It's not a game. Serving in a ship is a stressful, sometimes emotionally difficult situation. There are always people around you. There is no privacy. Not in the head, not in the showers, not even in your bunk. So you carve out someplace that is yours—a private, quiet spot where you can be alone with your thoughts.

I lay back and filled my lungs with the wonderful, salty sea air. The weather was perfect—calm, following seas, easy easterly breezes, lots of sun and high clouds. As soon as we'd cleared the coast I'd pulled the bandages off my face and deep-sixed the fucking liver. Now, the sun felt great on my skin. I closed my eyes and dreamed SEAL dreams about cold beer and hot women.

Have I ever told you how detrimental a bucket of cold seawater is to a classic combat-nap hard-on? If not, lemme tell ya—it's wilt city, folks. I wiped the water out of my eyes, sat up, and peered at Wonder and Gator, the laughing perps who'd snuck up and doused me good.

I smiled back. After all, I can take a joke. So, I hoped, could Gator. Because I picked him up by the collar and belt, wrestled him to the rail, and tossed him overboard. Then I turned toward Wonder with good-natured murder in my eyes.

Wonder didn't wait for me—he relieved himself of wallet, watch, and wraparound shooting glasses, then jumped without any coaxing. He hit the water in a perfect cannonball. The man has talent.

It was suddenly playtime aboard the *FYVM*. From the main cabin, Nasty, Cherry, and Doc came swarming. Doc was screaming "Cast and recovery! Cast and recovery!" as the three of them gang-tackled me. We rolled around the deck. Rodent and Pick grabbed for a piece of me. There were three guys on my legs, and two on my arms, and for a while I was kicking, screaming, and wriggling enough to keep 'em off me. But by the time Duck Foot joined the party, there was nothing I could do but accept my fate with grace—and take as many of the sons of bitches with me as I could.

"Fuuuck you—" I nabbed Doc tightly around the neck with my right arm, and hooked Nasty with my left. My bare feet had trouble getting traction on the wet teak deck, but I windmilled until I made it to the rail, pushed up, over—and hit the water with my two unwilling hostages.

I let them go and kicked to the surface, spitting water, watching the *FYVM* move off. From the flying bridge, Grose tossed me the bird, then spun the wheel and came about.

The change of course disturbed Half Pint, who sat up in the Zodiac, shook himself awake, discerned the situation and windmilled his index finger like a B-movie ossifer signaling a cavalry charge. The Grand Banks came to life, the line drew taut, and Half Pint draped himself over the side, a human snare to grapple us swimmers into the Zodiac as it swept past.

Doc was the closest target. Treading water, he held his left arm above his head. As the Grand Banks went by, Doc kicked high, but Half Pint ignored his outstretched arm, one-handed him by the throat, and tossed him kicking and streaming aboard the Zodiac. Doc was heaved nose first over the gunwale. He bounced once off the wood floor-plate, careened mustache first into the heavy plywood stern transom, then disappeared. If the son of a bitch was knocked cold it served him right.

But Doc's as resilient as any other cartoon character. So, he recovered quick enough when Half Pint dumped a coffee can of water over him. Holding his head like a man with a bad hangover, he crawled to the bow on his knees, grasped the tow line, worked his way over the gunwale, hooked his legs securely around the line and, pulling himself hand over hand while hanging upside down, worked his way to the Grand Banks and struggled over the stern diving platform, arms and legs working to keep himself away from the screws.

That was the first pass. Grose figure-eighted and came back for the rest of us. Half Pint snared Wonder and Gator with ease. Gator managed to make the precarious trip back to the Grand Banks dunking himself only half a dozen times. Wonder wasn't that lucky. The line went slack, and the goofy-looking ex-Marine was dragged underwater for about two hundred yards before he finally hauled his body over the rail and collapsed in the stern, spitting water.

Now it was my turn. Grose circled again, skewing the Zodiac wide, then bringing it back on track. Just to make things interesting, he gave the Grand Banks some throttle. I saw Half Pint's paw, stubby strong fingers poised to clamp my throat, coming at me six inches above the surface.

No way. I *like* my Adam's apple and I want to keep it uncrushed. I snapped my head back, put my left arm up, grabbed his hand with my own, and flipped him backward. He wasn't expecting that. He'd been poised to lift and fling, except he was the one who was being lifted and flung.

Half Pint may have had the footing, but I had the weight. My body acted like a fucking sea anchor and dragged the poor asshole along the length of the Zodiac, smacked him against the stern transom, jerked him over the outboard (whose rudder handle, of course, caught him square in the nuts), and pulled him into the water.

Grose eased up on the twin throttles and the Grand Banks finally slowed, then stopped some two hundred yards away and wallowed in the gentle swells. I struck out for it, side-stroking through the water. Half Pint, sputtering and muttering unintelligible sweet nothings to himself—rude imprecations about my ancestors, no doubt—followed in my wake.

Our exercise session and playtime for the day finally over, we dried off, chowed down, and settled in to do some serious head-shedding. Now, if you are a careful and retentive reader, you will recall that, some pages back, I mentioned certain ESBAM conditions under which our old friends LC Strawhouse and Dawg Dawkins were operating. I want you to think back to ESBAM One.

If you want, check the Index under ESBAM, then go and look at the section. Okay, okay—you're lazy. Like the chief says to the dew-balled ensign, "Oh, please allow me to fill you in, sir." (In case you didn't realize it—the ensign never does—the chief is spelling *sir* here with a *c* and a *u*.)

ESBAM One is that while the bad guys want to waste me, they have to do it quietly and/or privately.

And now, gentle readers, having set the stage, allow me to bring you along with me and my thought processes as we quaffed our Coors and talked things over.

First, we'd had a real easy time shadowing our quarry all the way from Motown down to Tampa, hadn't we? I mean, Mr. Murphy'd hardly been along for the ride. But Mr. Murphy, as we all know, is *always* along for the ride. Hmmm.

Coincidence? Happenstance? What do *you* think?

Second, the *Helen G. Kelley,* which chugged fifteen thousand yards ahead of us, was strangely silent. No chatter on the radio, reported Grose, who'd been monitoring short-wave, long-wave, and medium-wave, plus the whole spectrum of UHF and VHF transmissions on his digitized, midgetized, police-band, aircraft-band, marine-band, weather-band, and fucking brass band radio scanner.

That, too was strange. After all, experience has shown me that sailors are a loquacious bunch, and especially when the ship-to-shore airwaves are free, they like to flap lip. But not here. Hmmm.

Coincidence? Happenstance? What do *you* think?

Third. Think of a perfect location in which to dispose once and for all of that nettlesome, aggravating problem yclept Marcinko. I mean, purge. Get *rid* of. Deep six. E-*lim*inate. Dis-a-*ssemble.*

Here are three choices for you to ponder: One, a busy, public interstate highway. Two, the middle of a crowded city. Three, two hundred miles out to sea, aboard an oil rig that you know well, and I don't know at all. Hmmm.

Coincidence? Happenstance? What do *you* think?

Yeah. Right. Me, too.

Chapter 17

GOING INTO COMBAT HAS ALWAYS MEANT SOMETHING SPECIAL TO ME. Combat is, you see, what I truly believe I was born to do—to hunt and to kill other men. But combat (just like marriage) is a state into which one should not enter lightly. The battle itself is not the thing. The battle is inhumane, chaotic, bloody—a frenzied, messy affair. But the battle is only the means. The end—winning—is what combat is all about. And so, as we sailed westward, a crepuscular moon peeking through the high clouds overhead, my mind focused on the mission ahead—and to what I'd have to do to make it successful. After all, *they* were out there, somewhere, setting an ambush for us—whoever *they* were. Their objective was to kill me.

Well, just knowing that fact gave me the advantage.

According to the current SpecWar field manual issued by SOCOM at MacDill Air Force Base—this is the bible on operations that is given to all SEAL pups and baby Blanketheads so they will learn what the military expects of them—*ambush* is defined as (and I am quoting precisely to you here): "Aggressive actions, usually mounted by surprise and generally initiated from concealment, which, when approved by the proper chain of command, can be used against both moving and stationary targets."

Have you ever heard such incredibly mealy-mouthed crap? I

mean, I couldn't make shit like this up if I tried. But this sort of spineless, obfuscatory crap, my friends, is what you get when your fucking field manual is written by a committee of pussy-ass can't cunts, and edited by some goddamn pen-pushing bureaucrat apparatchik manager puke, to whom *killing* is a dirty word that might offend someone, and *attack* is a politically unacceptable deed performed by murderers. Am I making myself clear yet, or am I still being wishy-washy on the subject?

Y'know, friends, today's SEALs are better trained, equipped, and educated than any SpecWarriors in history. They are, most of 'em, potentially first-rate shooters. And yet, the overall morale of today's SEALs is at an all-time low. You know why? The reason is because they are overseen by managers, not led by warriors. Oh, they have lots of intramural sports. They have *beacoup* creature comforts. They go through dozens of wonderful, Outward Bound-like training cycles all over the world.

But if they ever have one beer too many, get pulled over by some wanna-be cop, and receive a DUI, they are shit-canned. If they say *fuck* too often in public, they are shit-canned. If they are too loud, too boisterous, and too SEAL-like, they get shit-canned. Image is the topmost word in the current crop of officers' lexicons. Training —realistic, dangerous exercises in which SEALs can get themselves killed, has all but *quitter le droit chemin*—which means fallen by the ol' wayside in the Foreign Legion.

They want to train past the edge of the envelope—to get as close to combat as possible. But their requests are denied (and those promising junior officers who ask are told that their career tracks will be jeopardized if they make any more waves). The C^2s—that's can't cunts—in charge do not want anybody hurt. Why? Because it would screw up their chances for promotion to O-6—captain—and then selection to flag rank.

That is just plain wrong. SEALs, my friends, were created to be killers, not saints or social workers. I know this firsthand, because the mustang son of a bitch sea daddy of mine who created them, Roy Boehm, himself a shooter and a looter and a confirmed killer of men, told me he'd created SEALs in his own fierce, ruthless, savage Old Testament image.

So purge the bureaucratic crap you read above from your mind and let me give it to you straight. *Ambush,* gentle reader, is derived from the Middle French word *embuschier,* literally "to set in the woods." So, when from hiding you use a huge amount of well-directed firepower over an extremely short period of time to decimate-cum-exterminate-cum-annhiliate an unsuspecting enemy force, you ambush them. In the sort of plain English I understand, you kill the motherfuckers. You kill them fast and without mercy. And when you're finished, if there is time, you booby-trap their corpses, so that when enemy reinforcements arrive, they, too, will become your victims.

There are two general types of ambushes. The small-unit ambush can be conducted by groups as small as a single squad. Generally, the kill zone of a small-unit ambush is no more than seventy-five yards, and most of the killing is actually accomplished by a series of Claymore mines with overlapping fields of fire. Mopping up is done with CAR-15s or your assault weapon of choice.

The large-unit ambush can have a kill zone as wide as 250 yards—that's two-and-a-half football fields of corpses if you're good. For these sorts of ambushes, which were originally designed and implemented by Special Forces A Teams in Vietnam, using Montagnards, Nungs, or other indigenous troops, heavy machine guns augment the Claymores, and the thirty to forty ambushers can call in artillery and chopper gunships once the ambush has been initiated.

There are any number of ambush forms—actually, there are as many as there are shooters with imagination. In class, however, half a dozen variations are generally taught. There is the section linear ambush, in which you line up along a trail, road, or stream used by the enemy and concentrate firepower in a lateral, or hosing motion as they pass by. There are "T" and "Triangular" ambushes, which are effective when used against regularly traveled enemy routes. In each of these you must be careful to place security elements on your perimeters and at your six o'clock, so that the enemy does not follow Robert Roger's rule, circle around, and hit you from your blind side.

Other ambush techniques include static vehicle ambushes, which employ roadblocks or explosives on the road to disable trucks or tracked vehicles. They were used to great advantage by the Afghan mujahideen against Soviet armored convoys. During the Gulf War, SEALs used maritime ambush techniques—in plain language, clandestine boarding followed by shooting and looting, or assaults with limpet mines—against Iraqi shipping.

Now, you, like our editor, are probably wondering why I am telling you all of this, when we were sitting in the middle of the goddamn Gulf of Mexico on a forty-two-foot Grand Banks trawler, there isn't a Claymore or a limpet in miles, and we weren't setting up an ambush but chugging into one. An ambush, I might add, that was to be executed atop an oil-rig platform.

And how do I know they'll try to ambush us on the rig and not aboard Grose's trawler?

Because it's easier, Tadpole. To ambush us aboard the *FYVM,* they'd have to sneak up on us first. That's hard to do in the open sea.

But it's not impossible, is it? Master Marcinko-san?

No, Tadpole, nothing is impossible. But hear me out. Let me explain the basics, and you will understand. See, whether large unit or small, whether land-based, or maritime, the success of all ambushes is based on a trio of common principles.

Oh, Master Marcinko-san, I can't find this *material anywhere in the current field manual.*

Of course not, Tadpole. I learned this shit by doing, not by reading. See all those scars? Now S^2 and listen.

Okay—the first of these principles is intelligence. Ambushes do not just happen—they are designed, created, set up. To do this properly, you have to know where your enemy is coming from, approximately how many he will be, and how he is likely to be armed. If you know these things, a small force of ambushers will be able to decimate a large number of ambushees. Back in 1987, six of us shoot-and-looters were able to exterminate seventy-five Islamic Jihad tangos as they made their way across the Syrian border into the Bekkáa Valley near a Lebanese town appropriately named An Nabi Shit which, in Arabic, means An Nabi Shit.

We'd tracked them by satellite and were set up above the wadi they'd been using for months to go back and forth. We knew they had AKs and RPGs. Big deal—we did, too. We also had Soviet Claymores, Vietnam War–era Bouncing Betty land mines, and shaped Semtex charges. It took less than six minutes to cut the bastards into ribbons, after which we booby-trapped the bodies, and skedaddled out of Shit. And y'know the best part of all, it was the Israelis who got blamed.

Second, ambushes often take both patience and timing. In El Salvador, we taught General Juan Bustillo's special forces rangers how to line a trail with Claymores, then dig in and wait for the FMLN tangos to make their move. At first, the rangers resisted burying themselves in camouflaged ambush positions—they were used to more conventional means of assault. Then we had to convince them not to fire the detonators and exhaust all their ammo as soon as they saw the first guerrilla wending his way up the trail. *"Incorrecto,"* I told them. "You have to wait until the entire enemy force is contained within your killing field—*that's* when you wax the suckers."

But you can't wait too long. Because if you delay, and your opponent is a warrior, too, he will recognize the signs of ambush, counterattack, and kill *you*.

Which brings me to my third principle. Ambushes must be executed quickly and mercilessly. There must be no time for the enemy to regroup, or they will mount a counterambush—which could prove devastating to your small force if you have not made provision for hauling balls. I always create a back door out of which I can slip if things get hairy, and a back door "lock" (usually made of Claymores or other lethal supplies) that will make it hard for my enemy to follow me.

The most common image I use when I teach the art of the ambush is that of hammer and anvil. Your strike force is the hammer. You build your anvil using the terrain and your Claymores, and then, with your firepower and surprise, you hammer the enemy against the anvil until he is decimated. There is also, says Roy Boehm, the godfather of SEALs, a lubricant that is used during these hammer-and-anvil exercises.

That lubricant is your enemy's blood.

Now, let's go back to the statement I made above—the one in which I said I, not my enemy, currently held the tactical advantage. My reasoning was simple: I did not believe that any of the above conditions had been met by the bad guys. They could not take the offense and attack me on the open sea, because there was no way for them to approach my position by stealth—no matter how they tried, I would be able to defend and decimate. That left the oil rig.

Okay, let's go over the various peregrinations. They knew I was coming—and that I would probably come by sea. But they had no idea precisely how many were in my force. Neither did they know how I would make my approach.

Yes, they controlled the location, and the terrain. Yes, the choice of weapons and tactics was theirs. But they could not pick the time of the ambush—the time depended on me. To me, that meant that no matter what they might be thinking about their tactical situation, *they* were the ones who'd be on the defensive, not me. It was *they* who would have to be constantly vigilant while I could afford to rest and bide my time. It was *they* who would become antsy, jittery, fretful, irritated, while I sat quietly, making plans and sipping Coors.

The bottom line? Easy. This was going to be *my* ambush—not theirs.

The evening and the morning of the second day, as they say in the Old Testament, was spent mostly in quiet time. Wonder plugged his computer into Grose's cellular phone and grazed the Intelink for intel nuggets.

There wasn't much on-line, so Wonder signed off and plugged into the Internet. We cruised the bulletin boards, checking cyberspace for any new information we could find on the rogue militias. There was a bunch of it since we'd last looked. Most was off-the-wall stuff—conspiracy theories about Waco, Oklahoma City, and Key West. But there was a lot of new traffic as well—messages to and from right-wing crazies and white-supremacist groups. It was a crescendo of hate mail, directed at local, state, and federal officials.

We pulled some of it down and showed it to Grose. He read it, then balled the paper up and tossed it overboard. "What assholes," he said. "Fuckers deserve to be shot."

Wonder came up to the flying bridge waving a sheet of paper. "Yo, Dickhead, check this out—"

I looked. He'd somehow pulled a list of all the Pajar oil platforms registered in Louisiana off the Internet.

"How the fuck—"

Wonder grinned and swiveled his head left-right-left. "It's simple. Oil companies all have to file the locations of their rigs with the state that has jurisdiction over 'em. It's public information, too. All you have to do is plug into a state's utilities bulletin board, ask the right questions, and bingo."

"Can you get precise locations of all LC's rigs?"

"Don't see why not—I just need to query each state on the Gulf."

"What other information can you dredge up?"

"Don't actually know," Wonder admitted. "But let me see."

The guys sacked out, worked over their weapons one more time, checked gear, and kept themselves busy. I sat in the wheelhouse with Grose, looking at charts and keeping an eye on the radar systems. I punched the ON switch of the satellite position finder that sat on the wood console next to the radio and below the radar screen, peered at the readout, and plotted the position on Grose's chart. We were 217 miles off the coast of Mobile, Alabama, sailing in a westerly direction.

We'd identified the first of the oil rigs at 0620 that morning—a cluster of five showed up on the radar, thirty-five miles north and west of us, shrouded in the early-morning mist. Seventeen minutes later, we picked up a second cluster. Soon after that, we'd detected a third, then a fourth. I knew that between here and the Texas coast, there were hundreds more. I'd nudged Grose. He nodded in the affirmative, nudged the throttle levers, and closed the distance between us and our target from fifteen thousand yards to about nine thousand—just over five miles. He didn't want to lose the *Helen G. Kelley* in a cluster of rigs.

Nor did I. Despite the fact that Wonder had given me a list of all the Pajar rigs, I didn't want us so far behind the *Helen G. Kelley* that we couldn't determine exactly which platform in a particular cluster the ship was going to "service." Our top speed was just over eight knots—which would put us an hour from any rig if we were fifteen thousand yards behind the target ship. I knew that the trailer could be hoisted aboard a platform and camouflaged in about twenty-five minutes under calm sea conditions. If they accomplished that, we'd have to board and search every rig in the cluster.

But, of course, they wouldn't hide. Grose had predicted—and he was right, that they'd do everything right out in the open, so we could see where the *Helen G. Kelley* was going, and follow right into their trap. As if to prove his point, they cut south in a shallow arc, moving away from the oil-rig clusters and into the open Gulf, making it easier for us to shadow them.

I could have been mistaken, but I almost thought I saw Grose actually wink at me. I responded by reaching into the fridge and grabbing two Coors Lights. I tossed one to Grose and popped the other myself. I inclined the can in his general direction. "Fuck you very much for everything you're doing for us," I said. "I really appreciate it."

Grose took a long pull on the Coors and flexed his left arm so that the topless blue hula dancer tattooed on his big bicep wriggled her hips and stuck out her boobs.

It was truly rewarding to see him have so much fun.

1420. The *Helen G. Kelley* turned due north and cut her speed from seven to five knots.

1452. She turned west again, maintaining a steady 29.283 degrees latitude. Her speed dropped to under four knots.

1535. North again. Now she veered toward a cluster of oil platforms at 88.125 West, 29.301 North.

We went to eight knots and turned up the intensity of the radar. What had been a solid mass on the screen now separated into six separate islands, shaped in a rough crescent, running on a northwesterly axis.

I called an all-hands. From here on, there would be no more than three people visible at any time—and we'd all dress as much alike as possible. The old stage manager's rule applied here. That rule says, "If you can see the audience, the audience can see you."

1554. We closed to within four and a half miles. I pulled Grose's twenty- to sixty-power spotting scope out of its locker, went on deck, trained it on the *Helen G. Kelley* like an old-fashioned pirate's spyglass, and focused. I could make out the figures on her deck. "Let's back off some," I suggested to Grose.

He nodded in agreement, and we veered away, finally settling in six miles from the rig cluster. Grose let out a sea anchor, dropped two fishing lines into the water for camouflage, set a tripod on the foredeck and attached the spotting scope.

Have you ever used a sixty-power spotting scope? Well, it ain't easy. The image field is very, very narrow when the damn thing is turned up all the way. It's hard enough to keep things in sight when you're on dry land. Here, with the Grand Banks sitting in three-foot swells and humping up and down, it was nigh on impossible. I unscrewed the damn thing from its mount and played Blackbeard, keepin' me peeper on the nasty rascals whilst I thought of mischievous ways to make 'em all walk the plank, har, har, har.

1602. The *Helen G. Kelley* edged up to the largest of the drilling platforms—the one at the very top of the crescent. It approached from the easternmost side, where a huge, skeletal crane cantilevered over the water.

I dropped the power back to thirty and gave the platform a quick peek-peek. It was a drill rig, not a pumping station, and its huge main derrick had a wind wall over the middle third, right next to the monkey board, where the derrick man had his control-panel cubicle. On it, PP-22 was written in two-foot-high characters. Next to that was the same sheaf of wheat design the *Helen G. Kelley* had on her single stack—LC Strawhouse's company logo.

I began to look at things carefully—and realized that my work was not going to be easy. If you were a Navy or Coast Guard vessel sailing past PP-22, and you ran your glasses over it quickly, you'd probably notice nothing peculiar or unusual. It had all the bells and whistles common to these platforms. Two twelve-man motor-driven lifeboats hung in davits on the northeast side. The platform's explosives locker was isolated—suspended on the southeastern hull column and protected by a blast wall that would channel any explosion straight up. There were two-three-four cranes, and a long gas-flare arm that sat high above the water at the side of the platform farthest away from the chopper pad. I had to squint to see the blue-white flame burning hot in the afternoon sky. At night, it could probably be seen for miles. There was a basketball backboard and hoop attached to a bulkhead by the chopper pad. There was a dive locker—its door marked by the white square bisected by diagonal red stripe universal DIVER BELOW flag. Kilroy was even there, too—his face had been graffiti spray-painted on one of the steel oil-processing modules.

But there were things that made my neck hair stand on end—things I have trained myself to look for even when I am being my most cursory. Most rigs, for example, have one radio mast. This one had three. It also had a VHF antenna, and a small dish that could either be a direct-broadcast satellite receiver, or a SATCOM antenna, capable of secure communications. There were also two radar domes, as well as one rotating antenna.

I also noted that the modular units were built securely, and there was lots of defendable space. See, most oil rigs have lots of nooks and crannies. That makes it hard to take 'em down. But it also affords the assault force good cover. This rig had been designed for defense. There were only a few ladders from level to level, and the bottoms of those ladders were open—no available cover—while at the tops, there was ample defendable space.

The control module was also fortified. I saw that when the hatch was opened. The inside of the door had more handles than the outside—so it could be barred. I cranked the power to forty and looked carefully at the glass ports—windows, to you landlubbers. A quick glance would have told me nothing. But a close examination of the way they reflected light—they had an unnatural, green patina—gave away the fact that they were extra thick. Bulletproof. Class-III. They'd take an RPG at ten yards without shattering.

1614. The *Helen G. Kelley* edged to its berthing station on the platform's most protected side. A series of bumpers were thrown over the ship's low rails to preserve the rig's tubular members and hull columns. Then, mooring lines were tossed from the bottommost platform grate down to the ship.

1633. I switched to binoculars and watched as a huge crane swung around, and lines were dropped and attached to the container.

1638. The semi-trailer was hoisted aboard the main deck level of the rig. I went back to the spotting scope and watched as the huge steel box was gently set down between the chopper pad and the derrick, port of the oil-processing area and starboard of the crew modules. I passed the glasses and spotting scope to Nasty and Duck Foot, with instructions to keep a watch log of everything—and everyone—they saw. Then I called Gator and Wonder to the conn. It was time to start making sketches.

1822. The *Helen G. Kelley* departed, slipping away from the platform, turning north, then west, and disappearing into the low, red sun. We'd kept a constant watch on her, and knew she hadn't taken on any cargo. Nor, so far as we could tell, had anyone from the rig sneaked aboard. There was no way they could have without our seeing it happen.

1900. We gathered in the Grand Banks's main cabin and sitrepped. Our surveillance had indicated that the rig the *Helen G. Kelley* had berthed at was the only rig in the cluster that was inhabited. That made sense if you were using your oil rigs to camouflage other activities. Besides, every platform in this particular cluster bore the Pajar logo.

We discussed tactics. Some of my Leprechauns wanted to hit the platform as soon as it got dark. But I vetoed that. They'd be waiting for us tonight—and I wanted the enemy tired and on edge, not keen and alert. Besides, I wanted to probe the cluster—make sure the other rigs were indeed empty. And I wanted to send a boarding party to the closest rig—use it as an observation post during the night.

Gator and Duck Foot volunteered to sneak and peek. They took my night-vision glasses, the cargo net-cum-caving ladder and a climbing rope, adequate weapons, a radio, and drinking water, dropped into the Zodiac, and chugged off as soon as it got dark.

We watched them go from the wheelhouse. Grose pulled on his Coors and agreed that tactically, it would be better to wait. "Wear the assholes down," he said. "Good idea." He crushed the empty beer can in his hand and flipped it swish into a wastebasket across the cabin. "But there's another consideration."

I looked at him quizzically. "Yeah?"

"Weather. I checked the radio, and took a look at my Doppler radar. So far as I'm concerned, there's a good chance of a front coming through tomorrow. It's calm now—great shoot-and-loot weather. But tomorrow? No guarantees."

Sometimes you forget that Mr. Murphy is always in attendance. When that happens, you can count on him to remind you. Thing was, we'd have to chance it. No way was I going to go up against that platform tonight.

Every SEAL mission is divided into six separate phases: premission, insertion, infiltration, action, extraction and exfiltration, and postmission. Each of these steps is then further broken down into a separate sequence. Sure, SpecWar is often performed seat-of-the-pants. It is, after all, unconventional warfare. But whenever possible, you plan ahead. Remember Everett Emerson Barrett's Law of the Seven *P*s—Proper Previous Planning Prevents Piss Poor Performance. In other words, planning is crucial to success because it allows you to see what could go wrong, and fix it before it's too late.

An example? Okay—take our Zodiac. We were ten men. The boat's capacity was six. That meant two trips from Grose's Grand Banks to the platform. First, what would our transit time to the target be? Second, how much gas would that call for? And what would happen if we had five-foot seas, not two-foot seas to contend with? Five-foot seas require more energy, hence more gasoline. Third, how long would the first group be exposed, treading water under the platform while they waited for the second contingent to arrive—and what condition would they be in because we didn't have wet suits to help keep us warm. Would we, in fact, be better off on the platform, or in the water? It is a nasty fact that you get colder faster from wind chill than you do from water temperature.

Get the picture? These are the sorts of things that kept me up all night, making lists, designing flow charts, and asking myself questions I couldn't necessarily answer.

I made a list of all the EEIs—those are Essential Elements of Information—we'd need to complete this mission successfully. I folded in Gator and Duck Foot's report on the adjoining platforms—they were, in fact, deserted and had been for some time. I checked the position and phase of the moon, and its rise and set times. I checked Grose's charts for sunrise/sunset as well. No need to silhouette ourselves needlessly against the horizon.

At about 0410, Grose padded into the main cabin and reached into the reefer for a Coors. It was cool out—low sixties in the six-knot breeze, water temperature about seventy-four—but he was bare-chested, wearing only cutoffs, flip-flops, tattoos, and a fifty-year-old UDT Team watch—one of those old-fashioned, wind-up Mark II Mod 1 models with gray nylon bands they used to call "Big Watch Little Pecker" watches. He'd been out on deck, peering through the night-vision glasses, which he'd jury-rigged to his spotting scope. He dropped a small spiral pad on the table in front of me, rubbed his eyes with those big fists of his, yawned, and stretched. "Shit, Dickie, you got your work cut out for you. There are a lot of fucking people on that goddamn platform."

I looked at the pad he'd given me. Grose had toted up more than two dozen separate tangos. Eighteen carried descriptions. The others were noted by time and location.

Grose finished off his Coors as he brewed a huge pot of Cafe Bustello. Damn—it smelled good. I poured myself a mug and sipped while I worked his findings into my calculations. I scratched my cheek. The list showed thirty or so bad guys, but there could have been double that number. How the hell could I know? I didn't have any sensors. I had no parabolic mikes. No long-lens video cameras. I was goatfucked.

Weapons? *They* had a shitload from which to choose. I was limited in mine. I was goatfucked.

Defenses? I knew they'd have a bunch of things I didn't know about. I was goatfucked.

The longer my list got, the more I saw how much we lacked, and how much the bad guys had. The longer that list grew, the worse our chances became.

But, my friends, there is a point at which lists such as this, no matter how well thought out, become meaningless. And at 0540, sitting at the long table in the main cabin, hunched over the legal pad, I reached said point of no return.

You see, there are some mission elements that cannot be codified, listed, flow-charted, or annotated. They include all those wonderful, ineffable qualities my beautiful band of merry, murdering marauders had—their extraordinary combination of stamina, unstoppable will to succeed, and heart, all of which, when taken together and shaken, not stirred, combine to make truly great SpecWarriors.

I knew that, no matter how outnumbered and outgunned they might be, they would never be outmanned or outclassed. They would persevere. Keep on. Never quit. They would never leave a swim buddy behind. They would do what it took—whatever it took—until they'd won.

So, while the debit side of my legal pad had more annotations than the credit side, and while I was justifiably apprehensive about our chances, I knew deep in my washboard gut that we would overcome, and ultimately we would prevail. It was our destiny to do so.

The simple yet intriguing challenge we faced was to accomplish our goal before we were all dead.

At 1020, the wind shifted from westerly to southerly, gaining in intensity. By 1300, we had a twenty-five-mile-per-hour blast blowing the waves into a nasty four-foot chop. Much to my relief it died down by 1645, just as we began our serious preparations. Sunset was at listed 1952, and the moon was slated to rise at 2015—a workable window, although the three-quarter moon was somewhat worrisome to me. The moonlight situation was improved by the high clouds that blew in during the early part of the afternoon. It was unimproved by the winds that picked up again just after 1900 —an hour and a half before we began our insertion transit.

The plan I'd come up with was KISS-simple. We'd launch from our four-mile anchorage—a twenty-minute shot over open water to the platform cluster. The first Zodiac crew would include me, Wonder, Doc, Cherry, and Gator. Half Pint would serve as coxswain. He would drop us off six hundred yards east of the platform—the most "blind" side they had—and we would swim in, aided by the current. Once we'd swum under the target, we would lash ourselves to the pylons while Cherry climbed up and attached our improvised caving ladder. Then we would scramble up, hide in the rafters, and wait for the second boatload of shooters. We'd all stay in touch by radio. Grose would play night watchman with the spotting scope and night-vision device. He wouldn't be able to spot for us the way a sniper might, but it was better than nothing. When all ten of us had formed up, we would make our way topside, go over the rail, and take the rig down.

Obviously, no one had bothered to tell Mr. Murphy about this great plan, because he showed up with one of his own and imposed it on the rest of us. Oh, the launch went great. But we hadn't gone more than a mile and a half from the Grand Banks when the wind shifted on us, moving from south to west, and bringing an unexpected rain squall. That meant swimming into the current, which is a no-no. A swimmer cannot fight more than about one knot of current. We were also facing twenty-mile-per-hour gusts here, which were blowing us off course.

Was that a problem? You bet it was. See, we were in a small—read *t-i-n-y*—boat. We had no reference points by which to judge our position relative to the well-lit oil platform, which was now obscured by the rain squall. The SATCOM position finder was safely aboard the Grand Banks—now two miles astern of us in the dark. Now, we had our compasses, and we had the NIS passive beacon. Using them, Half Pint steered a course by dead reckoning while the rest of us bailed water, which was by now washing over the gunwales of our overloaded Zodiac.

Dead reckoning, you ask? Dead reckoning, friends, is the means by which you steer when you have no other way to judge your route. It is called dead reckoning, because if you reckon wrong, you will be dead.

We knew what our compass heading had been when we left the Grand Banks. Now, Half Pint tried to keep us straight on that course while adjusting for wind and waves. The problem, of course, was that we really had no idea where we were going. The rain picked up. We were all soaked through—it was probably colder out in the air than it was in the water. But I wasn't about to find out—yet.

We Zodiac'd through the chop for another sixteen minutes when Grose broke radio silence. "You assholes are way off course," he growled. "You're about two miles east of where you want to be."

I was cold and I was wet. Now I was two miles off course, too. How did he know?

"Because I'm watching you numb-nuts in the goddamn night-vision glasses, you shit-for-brains pencil-dicks. I can see you every five minutes or so, bobbing around like a fucking cork out there. I thought you were making a tactical sweep until just now when it occurred to me that you'd fucked up. Didn't any of you dipshits ever learn to navigate?"

A huge lightbulb went off right above my head. I grabbed an infrared Cyalume light stick out of my vest, bent it to activate it, then stood up, holding the plastic tube high above my head while I fought for balance in the heaving, pitching inflatable. "Grose—can you see this?"

"Affirmative—" Grose's voice came back at me loud and clear.

He might have said something else, but I couldn't hear him because I lost my balance and went butt over coffeepot backward into the drink.

I sputtered to the surface, still clutching the damn Cyalume stick and dog-paddled, talking trash to myself while Half Pint circled to pick me up.

Wonder and Doc hauled my butt over the gunwale, rubbing my face raw on the rough net that lay on the wooden deck-plate. "Don't be so anxious, Dickhead," Wonder said sweetly as I lay there, sweating. "You'll get plenty of opportunity to swim later."

"Fuck you." I ran my hands over my vest to make sure I hadn't dropped anything, then stood up *c-a-r-e-f-u-l-l-y* and waved the Cyalume above my head again. Grose reconfirmed our position. That meant he could guide us right where we needed to go. Talk us in like an airliner in one of those melodramatic movies like *Airport*.

Even so, the transit took half an hour longer than I'd planned. It was 2120 by the time we dropped into the warm Gulf water and sidestroked our way through five hundred yards of three-foot chop, swimming south now not west because of the wind change.

It was not an easy swim. First of all, we had no SEAL combat vests—only cheap, surplus store mesh-and-nylon imitations. SEAL vests are inflatable. They help support you in the water when you are carrying fifty or sixty pounds of equipment.

That much? You bet. Let's check out my load tonight. I had a Beretta 92 and three 15-round magazines of 9mm ammo secured around my waist and strapped to my right thigh. I had a CAR-15 strapped to my back and five 30-round magazines of .223 in vest compartments. Two grenades sat in vest-pocket pouches. I carried a radio. There was twelve feet of nylon climbing rope wrapped around my waist. My mask. My fins. My vest. An electrician's screwdriver, a pair of wirecutters, and a steel pry bar were all tied to me. A Mad Dog DSU-2 knife in its molded Kydex sheath was taped to my left leg. I had my leather-and-lead shot sap safely secured in a rear pocket. And I was dressed in black cotton ripstop BDUs, which, when wet, are goddamn heavy.

Hey, I'm fucking tired, I'm fucking cold, my fucking face fucking hurts, and we haven't even fucking begun our fucking mission yet—we're still in the second fucking stage, fucking *insertion*. (And trust me—if I don't get a chance to fucking *insert* my DSU-2 in somebody's neck soon, I'm gonna bust.)

Chapter 18

2200. THE PLATFORM LOOMED ABOVE US AS WE TROD WATER. IT LOOKED like something out of a science fiction movie. From the water, they're immense structures—skeletal, modernistic skyscrapers that towered over us. The arc lights played tricks on the water's surface. Oil rig platforms are lit up at night. The natural gas flares can be seen for miles if the weather is clear. Halogen and sodium work lights also abound, bathing the structure in a mix of cold white and warm yellow-orange light. The catwalks have perimeter lights. The rails are strung with safety bulbs. The tall derrick has red warning lights and white flashers to make approaching chopper pilots aware of its existence. Even tonight, with clouds, occasional surface fog, and driving rain, we'd been able to pick up the platform cluster from half a mile away.

I threw a line around one of the horizontal tubular members, looped it around my waist, and tossed the other end to Wonder. He attached himself and gave me a thumbs-up. I gave hand signals, and we removed our fins. Each man banded his swim buddy's fins together and attached them to the back of his neighbor's combat vest. Then we checked one another's equipment, fore and aft.

The water slapped my face with considerable force, and I

wrapped an arm around the steel support. The seas were getting rougher now—the wind gusts were way above twenty now. I didn't want anybody washing away. I wasn't being sentimental—I'd need every goddamn body I had to go over the rail and get the job done.

Doc and Gator had swum in dragging the netting, which probably weighed a fucking ton. Now, they clung exhausted to a support beam, washing up and down with the current. The netting, slung over a steel support, lay next to them. Eight feet away, Gator ran his own safety line around the steel. He tied a loop around himself with a bowline, threw the end to Doc, who looped it around his torso just under his armpits and tied off too.

I watched as Cherry adjusted the hundred feet of lightweight climbing rope he'd swum with. He had the toughest job tonight. He had to monkey his way up the wet, slippery steel, secure a position, lower the rope, pull the netting up, and tie it down so we could all make the climb.

I gave him a raised thumb. He saluted me with his middle finger, pointed skyward, and mouthed, "Piece of cake."

I knew he was a liar. I told him so and he tossed me the bird again. Then he went to work. Cherry edged his way along the support beam to Doc's position, moving in the lull between waves so he wouldn't wash off the steel. He removed his combat vest, which Doc attached to his own gear. Climbing was going to be hard enough. With the combat vest, it would have been nigh on impossible. Cherry kept only his knife and pistol belt. He threw the coil of rope diagonally over his shoulder, swam to a soaring, four-inch-diameter steeply inclined steel member three yards away, and pushed himself up and out of the water onto it.

Climbing is not an easy task. The steel is wet and hence slippery. It has very little adherent surface, so you are forced to support yourself by using your arms and thighs—pushing yourself up in tiny, painful, muscle-burning increments.

Remember when you were a kid and you tried climbing the slide pole at your neighborhood firehouse? The first five or six feet were easy. Then fatigue always set in, and you'd slide inexorably groundward. The same elements applied here. Except here, Cherry was also contending with rain, with wind, with the fact that he was wet and tired, and the knowledge that there were people above him who wanted him dead.

He'd already plotted his course over the past day. He'd spent hours looking at the platform through the scope, making notes. So he knew exactly where he was going to go, and how he'd get there.

Route was not a problem. But there were other obstacles—intangibles—tonight. Maybe it would be the weather. Maybe it would be the stress of actual combat conditions. The pucker factor is something that can never be discounted, even by those of us who have been there many times before.

He worked his way up, six, eight, ten, fifteen, twenty feet above the surface. Each foot cost him—you could see it in his face. But he was determined not to let the fucking platform win this one. He was going to make it.

And he did—by sheer force of will and muscle he made it—finally eased himself onto the last of the diagonals. It was a cylindrical pipe perhaps four inches in diameter, roughly thirty-five feet above the water. Cherry's pace was deliberate, now that he was almost within reach of his goal—a small ledge six feet below the first-level grate, where he could shelter, catch his breath, and then lower the rope to the rest of us.

He was directly above Doc and Gator when the fucking wind shifted—from the look of how it hit him it must have been a goddamn horizontal wind shear, forty miles an hour at least. The blast caught Cherry in full extension, and knocked him off balance. He swung precariously, caught the pipe with his fingertips and feet, fought until he'd almost regained his grip and footing, then slipped again, rolled topsy-turvy, lost his hold and came crashing down.

Wide-eyed and flailing, he glanced off the beam six feet from Doc, hitting shoulder first. He would have cracked in two—except his fall was broken by the roll of climbing rope he'd coiled over his shoulder, and the wad of fishnet that lay atop the steel. Nonetheless, he hit with a sickening, dull thud. Then both the net and Cherry disappeared into the churning water.

Doc and Gator both reacted at the same time. They immediately dove after their shipmate—and were nearly strangled by their safety rope. I already had my DSU-2 knife in my hand. I sliced through the nylon line, sheathed the blade, and launched myself toward the spot where Cherry had vanished. Wonder followed in my wake, trailing safety line.

Going down was not going to be a problem—I was weighted by my equipment. But swimming? I had no fins—just the mask—and getting the twenty yards to where I'd seen Cherry go down was going to be a struggle. Instinctively, I knew that it would be better to make my way underwater. I kicked below the surface and breaststroked toward where I thought he'd be.

The water was black and I had no light—Mr. Murphy again—I

simply hadn't thought to bring one. I descended by scissors-kicking with my legs while I probed the water in front of me with my hands. At about three fathoms I grasped something. Cloth. Combat vest. Body. I pulled it close as its hands grappled frenzied touchie-feelie with mine. We came mask to mask. It was Doc. We released, pushed off, and kept moving.

I ran out of breath, surfaced, inhaled a lungful of air and dove again. I was fucking frantic. I went down three, four fathoms, trying to pattern search as I kicked. Nothing. I fought my way back up. The ambient light from the oil-rig platform made the surface look like an antique silver mirror from below—and as I broke it and spat water I hoped I wasn't going to have seven years of bad luck starting now.

Wonder surfaced two yards away, wild-eyed. He coughed up a half-pint of seawater and shouted, "Anything?"

I shook my head, took a deep breath, and went under again.

I caught a glimmer, perhaps ten or fifteen yards below me—no way of computing distance in the dark—and swam toward it. As I got closer I saw light. Then I made out shape—shapes. It was Gator, and he was wrestling with something. I moved fast—kicking toward him with every ounce of energy I could summon. I came down to his position. God bless Gator. He had his shipmate. Cherry was unconscious—there was no movement. None at all. He was tangled in the netting and the rope.

Then I saw Gator's face—it had turned blue behind the mask. He'd run out of air and he knew he didn't have the strength to bring Cherry to the surface. But he wasn't going to let his buddy go until the cavalry arrived.

I grabbed Cherry's inert form and wrestled the light out of Gator's hand. I nodded vigorously to let him know I was okay and then pointed toward the surface—get your ass the hell out of here. Even then, Gator hesitated before kicking off—that's the bond between shipmates. I shone the light in Cherry's face. No sign of life. I waved it in circles, trying to attract attention, while I scissors-kicked to move us up, up, up.

God, he was heavy. The weight of the net and rope was pulling me down even though I was using all the strength in my legs to force us toward the surface. Then a second diver appeared out of the darkness—it was Wonder. He grabbed the net and began to work Cherry free of it. That allowed me to get the DSU-2 out of its sheath and slice the tangle from Cherry's body.

Wonder took the net and rope and kicked off. Now I began to

make progress. Doc found me—he got Cherry around the waist and the two of us fought our way up, toward the shimmery brightness above.

I thought my lungs were going to burst by the time we broke surface, but there was no time to worry about me. Doc and I made our way through four-foot chop and forty-mile-an-hour surface winds to the platform corner—where the horizontal members joined the huge vertical shafts. I began to lift Cherry out of the water, but Doc waved me off.

He threw his own arm over the beam to steady himself in the turbulent water. "Dick—hold him steady, now—real steady."

I propped an arm under Cherry's upper back to help keep him afloat.

"Don't get near his neck, goddammit." Doc fumbled one-handed in his vest pocket and retrieved one of his Ziploc bags. He looked inside, cursed, slid it back into the vest, and retrieved another. He opened the seal of this one with his teeth, and with one hand extracted a white, horse-collar-shaped piece of plastic about five inches wide.

There was a small tube and screw valve attached to one corner of the collar. Very painstakingly, he eased the collar around Cherry's neck, then gently blew into the tube. The plastic doughnut inflated, immobilizing Cherry's neck.

Doc closed his vest pockets, hoisted himself out of the water, and straddled the steel support. "Okay, okay—now we move him onto the beam."

Wouder and Gator had arrived, although I hadn't noticed them until now. The three of us floated Cherry next to the support, trying to keep him level in the choppy water.

Doc wasn't happy with the way we were doing our jobs. "Easy, dammit!" He reached down, took Cherry under the shoulders, eased him up onto the ten-inch-wide beam, and lay him flat.

Doc felt alongside Cherry's neck. His eyes told me we were in trouble. "No pulse," he said to himself. From another pocket he withdrew a second waterproof envelope. He unsealed it, and extracted a small penlight. Gently, he raised Cherry's eyelids and shone the light downward. He turned it off and pocketed it. "Fuck."

He rolled off the beam into the water. "Dick—get up there, hold his shoulders down. But don't screw with his neck."

I did as I was ordered.

Doc hand-over-handed down the beam, pulled himself aboard

two feet below Cherry's body, then worked his way back. He spread Cherry's legs, threw open his BDU blouse, and began cardio-pulmonary resuscitation. "One, two, three, four, five—" He did the chest compressions, counting cadence as he rocked back and forth. "Dick—c'mon. What the fuck are you waiting for?" He nodded toward Cherry's face.

I bent over, careful not to disturb the neck collar, opened Cherry's mouth, held his nose shut, and blew air into his lungs.

"One, two, three, four, five . . ." Doc counted the cadence. Five chest compressions. One blow. Five compressions. One blow. Five compressions. One blow.

We kept it up for half an hour with no result. Doc shook his head. "He's gone, Dick."

I wasn't willing to give up. "Come on—"

Doc put his penlight beam into Cherry's blank eyes. "C'mon, Dick—take a good look. He's had it."

I ran a hand over my sweating face and rolled into the water to cool myself off from the rage that boiled within. Then I took the safety rope from Wonder. Carefully, we lashed Cherry to the beam. I looked at the faces of my shooters as we gently tied him down. Their intensity was ineffable. Their resolution to win was palpable. They would take no prisoners tonight—their expressions told me that. Wonder placed his right hand on Cherry's chest in farewell. Gator and Doc did the same. So did I. We didn't say anything. We didn't have to. We knew what we had to do.

2254. Gator made the climb to set the net ladder. He didn't like it, but he did it. I was getting nervous and wasn't about to wait for the second Zodiac crew to arrive—I wanted to get up and ready to go. So I volunteered his ass to do the job. We watched from the water as he worked his way up the beam, shinnied across the diagonal support, and climbed the vertical. Sweating and nervous, he reached the shelf Cherry'd been going for, tied off, lowered the rope, and hauled the netting up.

It was a tough climb. Wonder went first, then Doc, then me. I'd slashed at the net to clear it off Cherry's body, and the DSU-2 had weakened it considerably. So instead of climbing, they had to pull themselves up, arm over arm, legs finding what toeholds they could. But their rage carried them up it, inch by painful inch.

I stayed in the water. I wanted to use the radio and I wasn't about to do it where I could be overheard by anybody on the rig. I gave Grose a sit-rep—he wasn't happy with my news, either—and asked him for one, too. He told me the Zodiac was on its way, and that he'd be standing by.

Then it was my turn to climb. I hate climbing. I am a big, dense motherfucker, and it takes a certain effort to get my weight up a rope ladder. By the time I arrived on the catwalk fifty feet above the water, I was physically exhausted, emotionally wrung out, mentally drained, and sore in every goddamn extremity. Even my fucking cuticles hurt.

2342. Nasty, Duck Foot, Pick, Rodent, and Half Pint made their way up the improvised caving ladder. They'd seen Cherry's body, and from the grim expressions on their faces I could see they wanted revenge. We would extract it, too. That is the Warrior's way.

Let me take just a minute here to explain about the Way of the Warrior. From the Old Testament warriors of Canaan, to the Spartans, to the Roman Centurions, to the Japanese Samurai, right down to my current generation of SEALs, all true Warriors have always had a few basic qualities in common.

Yes, Warriors have a deep-seated need to win. Yes, they must be proficient in the ways of death. And, yes, they must also be ready to die—at one with themselves, and with their world. Those qualities are perhaps the most obvious ones.

But Warriordom is more than skin deep—or "win" deep, for that matter. It is a code, a philosophy, by which you live your life. It is the unique way you inhabit and relate to the world around you, which separates the Warrior from everyone else.

All Warriors have a quiet, understated, yet profound sense of integrity. All Warriors are true to themselves, and to their sense of absolute honor, no matter what the personal or professional consequences. Warriors never rest: they are constantly looking for ways in which to improve their abilities and expand their minds. Warriors always trust in themselves to survive and to persevere, no matter what the odds.

There is more, too. A Warrior also never lets a comrade's death go unanswered. We follow the tradition transmitted by the Unnameable Name to Moses in the twenty-first chapter of the book of Exodus: "Thou shalt give life for life, eye for eye, tooth for tooth, hand for hand, foot for foot, burning for burning, wound for wound, stripe for stripe."

0010. I led the way. We went over the rail just port of the bulk-storage tanks, and split up into two-man hunter-killer groups, moving quickly across the metal grating of the deserted deck. Gator, who'd been swim-buddied with Cherry, insisted on working alone. I gave him Cherry's .223 magazines and turned him loose. You may disagree with that decision, but you're not here—and I am. See, there are times when rage becomes so great that a man has to be allowed to do certain things. This was one of them.

Wonder and I made our way along the perimeter rail, past the tank area, to the pump station. There, I attached an IED to the generator, and set the timer. The charge was large enough to disable, but small enough so that the damage would be confined. Next, we worked our way past the pipe-stowage area, and took one of the catwalk ramps that rose toward the main deck.

Our preassigned goal was the control module—that's where the offices, with their communications and security equipment, would be located. It was also where the bad guys would probably be waiting for us.

Now, you are probably wondering why I just didn't sneak aboard, set charges of C-4 that would drop the whole damn rig into the water, and haul my ass out of there. Well, first of all, PP-22 sat amidst a cluster of rigs, and even though they were deserted, I didn't want to draw a lot of attention to what I was doing. If we were gonna blow things up, we had to do it with discretion. Well, okay, we could use C-4, too. Second, I wanted to preserve evidence. We knew they had lots of illegal goodies on board, and I needed to be able to show them off without having to dive 150 fathoms for 'em. And third, while dropping a platform might be fun, destroying the rig would only make my personal situation more . . . shall we say . . . complicated.

It was awfully quiet out there. No sign of resistance so far—which only served to tell me that they were (1) all asleep, or (2) waiting in ambush positions to kick our asses. I wished we'd had radios with lip mikes and ear pieces, so I could stay in touch with my men. But we didn't. So we'd each complete our assignments and tell one another about it over brewskis at Miller Time.

I moved slowly. I forced myself to breathe evenly, keeping my rage in check. Cherry was the youngest SEAL I'd chosen for SEAL Team Six. He was a plank owner—one of the original seventy-two shooters I'd chosen to form a unit in my own image. I'd selected him because he was willing to learn; because he wanted to be the best; because he'd convinced me that he'd never, never quit. And he never had—right up until the end. Losing him was like losing one of my own children—and whoever was responsible for his death was going to pay for it.

But my rage was not going to make me act precipitously. I have lost men in battle before, and (although it has taken me some effort) I have learned how to deal with it. Instead of reacting badly —basically going berserk—I now channel my anger. I let it take me to new heights of action and destruction. I allow its energy to make me a more proficient, deadlier warrior.

Cherry's soul—his Warrior's spirit—was instilled within each of us on this oil rig platform tonight. Imbued with his energy, his talent, and his passion for war we would kill more of our enemies, and kill them better.

I saw the first of them as I pulled myself up by my fingertips over the top of the wireline-logging unit, which sat atop an eight-foot steel platform that was braced on the seaward side. Wonder and I had eschewed the easy route and worked our way around the outside of the platform, inch by painful inch. I gritted my teeth and pulled my nose level with the logging unit. He was dressed like a Ninja. Wearing body armor. Carrying a suppressed MP5. Stretched prone atop a Conex box just off the left side of the unit I was dangling from. A second Ninja lay at a forty-five-degree angle to the first; his field of fire would pick up anything Ninja One missed.

Cautiously, I lowered myself by my fingertips until my feet rested safely on metal grating. Using silent signals, I gave Wonder a sit-rep. I didn't have to explain what we'd have to do. Then, resting my back against the steel plate wall of the logging unit, I ever so gently set my CAR-15 on the deck. We had no suppressors, and I wasn't about to let them know we were in the neighborhood—yet.

Wonder carefully laid his own CAR on the deck, tapped the Marine-issue Ka-Bar on his belt, gave me the finger, and began to work his way around to the left, so as to move up behind Ninja Two while staying out of Ninja One's sight line.

As Wonder skulked off, I fingertipped myself back up onto the logging unit until my nose poked over the top. I hauled myself up inch by inch. Talk about fucking fatigue. *You* try this sometime when you're wearing wet BDUs, a heavy combat vest, and you've just pulled yourself up fifty-something feet of netting and wet steel pipe from a pounding sea.

Finally, I worked my way on top of the logging unit. But I wasn't in a position to rest. I had to slip my DSU-2 out of its sheath and, ever so *s-l-o-w-l-y,* begin to edge forward, toward Ninja One's back.

Remember when I told you about ambush techniques? Well, it appeared as if we'd come upon a rear-security position. Problem—for them—was, they'd expected us to emerge from a narrow channel between modular steel boxes. And instead, Wonder and I had instinctively come through the back door—slipped over the rail and worked our way hand-over-hand around the edge of the perimeter, dangling by fingertips from the nasty sharp grate decking. Sure I was sore. Sure my hands hurt like hell—especially because I wasn't wearing gloves—but the good news was that we had bypassed all the obvious chokepoints where the nasties had set their ambush and were now approaching the control module from the back door.

When you move against a position like this one you do it in increments of less than an inch at a time. Your muscles burn. Everything you do is amplified by a factor of ten. It felt as if it took me half an hour to creep the seven or so feet from my initial sighting, to striking distance, even though in real time it was less than a minute. You can't take longer, because at the sort of proximity I was operating, you give off vibes, and the son of a bitch is gonna feel 'em, turn around, and wax your ass dead.

I was lucky this time—I caught him unaware from behind and managed to cover his nose and mouth with my left hand. There are a number of what are known in the killing trade as high-payoff targets when you are attacking with a knife from the rear. First are the occipital and cervical nerves, which can be found where the occipital bone of the skull joins the atlas bone and meets the first of seven cervical vertebrae. In words of one syllable or less, I'm talking about the base of da skull. Also effective are the subclavian arteries—huge blood vessels originating at the top of the heart that carry the main supply of blood to the arms. They come out of the heart, loop over the lungs, and can be reached by striking downward through that soft, triangular area between neck and shoulder bones. There are the internal and external carotid arteries, which are also found in the neck area. (Those can be attacked by using the old carotid and stick technique.)

Now, those of you who are squeamish may want to skip the next three or four paragraphs. For those of you who are not, let's talk a little bit about death by blade, starting with what's known in Hollywood as throat slitting.

My first guideline on the subject has always been that it is better to cut the carotid and jugular from the side—sticking the knife blade edge-to-front—that is, facing forward, and cutting away from you—than it is to cut across the neck, blade facing the rear, as you often seen done in the movies.

Let me explain why. By plunging your blade into the side of your opponent's neck, you will not only sever your target's jugular, but the blood will immediately drain into the dying man's windpipe, making it harder for him to scream and raise an alarm. Moreover, if you cut backward through the front of his throat, you are going to get a lot of blood spraying in all directions.

Unlike those Hollywood movies, cutting a human throat in real life is not a quick, clean act. The front of the throat is tough—there are lots of sinews there, not to mention the sternocleidomastoid and trapezius muscles, which are harder to cut than pronounce. We're talking tough tissue here, folks. So, if you do not have a serrated blade—Roy Boehm actually used to take his USG-issue Ka-Bar and cut saw teeth into it before he went out and committed death by blade on his enemies—your knife will probably not slit deep enough and nasty enough to do the job.

Believe me, I have been there, and I can tell you from firsthand experience that it takes a real effort to sever a man's throat cutting front to back. And if you merely slash him without carving the jugular and carotid clean through, you will simply make your opponent mad. Another thing to think about is the fact that blood stinks when you come upon it in great quantities, and if you get it on you, you will stink, and thus your enemies will know you're in the 'hood. Doom on you.

Blood is also slippery—if it sprays, you may lose your grip on your knife, as well as your hold on the victim, who then staggers off raising what Shakespeare liked to call "stern alarums." Doom on you again. It only makes sense, therefore, to want to keep as much of the blood inside the bad guy's body as you possibly can.

That's why the subclavian assault works so well. You shut off the bad guy's air supply with one hand, then ram the knife down into the subclavian area, working it around nicely, so that you cut both artery and vein. Then you penetrate down, past the lungs, cutting as you go, penetrating toward the heart area. If your blade is long enough (and mine certainly was) it will puncture the aorta and cause terminal injury, while a majority of the blood stays in the body.

Now, since the asshole in front of me was lying prone, I had to make sure that I could wrap him up neatly before I stuck his subclavian. I came at him from his eight o'clock. The rain and water noise helped shield my approach. In fact, the first notice he took of me was when I looped my left arm around his neck, caught his nose and mouth, and stuck the blade—which is a full quarter of an inch thick and six and five-eighths inches long—up into his kidney area.

That sure got his attention. He sucked air—except there was nothing to suck because I had him by the mouth and nose. But he did exactly what I wanted him to do—he rolled away from me. That allowed me to get some leverage on him and work myself up to where I could pull the knife out of his back and get it nestled in the shoulder area.

Slight prob, people. The subclavian stroke requires a downward thrust. That means you gotta change your grip from the kidney thrust.

See, when I hit him in the kidneys, I was holding the knife blade forward—thumb and forefinger wrapped around the grip next to the blade guard. Now, I had to flip it so that I could hold it in a stabbing grip—blade downward.

Have I said that I wasn't wearing gloves? Have I told you that my fingers were sore and stiff?

I'm not making excuses here, except that in rotating the blade in my right hand while my left hand was busy snuffing the breath out of Mr. Ninja One, the DSU-2 came out of my grip and landed on the Conex box, whereupon Mr. Ninja—now struggling for some absurd reason as if his life depended on it—kicked the fucking thing off the edge.

The good news was that losing my knife freed my right hand. Which I immediately applied to his throat, trying like hell to crush his Adam's apple, thorax, and anything else I could get my sore Slovak fingers around.

We lay there thrashing for a few seconds. But I am a big motherfucker, and I was madder than he was, and I managed to hit him in the face with my forearm half a dozen times—which was enough to put him down. I broke his neck to make sure he wouldn't bother us again, rolled onto my back, and tried to stop hyperventilating.

Wonder tapped me on the knee. I looked down. He had hold of my knife by the blade, and handed it to me without a word but with a look so disapproving that it reminded me of the first time the priests caught me doing the dirty deed they'd guaranteed would give me the hairy palms I've got today.

I shrugged. Wonder, who has precious little tolerance for the dropping of any weapon, gave me the one-fingered salute, followed by the silent signal for, I've done my job neatly, and you've done yours messily as usual, so let's get the hell out of here, asshole.

Who was I to contradict such wisdom? I checked my corpse for intel (Wonder'd obviously already finished searching his because he was watching me impatiently), and finding none, I picked up my CAR and moved on.

0017. SHF—Shit Hit Fan—time. First, three big explosions. That would be Pick—our EOD specialist. His first job tonight was to take out the rig's antennas—radio, VHF, telephones, and anything else he found. We didn't want the bad guys telling anybody what was happening out here.

Right on the first explosions' concussion, came a second series of blasts—these somewhat more muffled. That would be Gator, disabling the rig's electrical generators. Almost immediately, I heard automatic weapons fire from the doghouse area—controlled bursts of staccato .223, and the slightly more resonant choppa-choppa of 9mm.

Well, with surprise lost, there was no reason to be stealthy anymore. Wonder and I formed up and moved quickly down between modules, our weapons covering opposing fields of fire. If the Ninja I'd killed was rear security, then the main ambush force would be spread out ahead of us.

I pulled one of my two grenades out of its pouch, pulled the pin, and held the spoon down with my hand. We moved quickly and made noise to draw attention to ourselves. Why? Because I wanted somebody to panic and fire before we'd entered the point-of-no-return killing ground. We'd see them before they saw us and we could counter—return force with force.

We came to a chokepoint—Conex box to our right, rectangular steel module to the left. Ramp ahead, leading to the crew quarters and control area access. I popped the spoon, counted two, then rolled the grenade down the grating as Wonder and I secured ourselves behind the Conex box.

There was an explosion and screams. We charged toward the sound. I went first, with left-hand field of fire. Something moved and I squeezed off a three-round burst, cutting it down. Muzzle flash at my ten o'clock. I answered it—and hit something. A ricochet caught me in the cheek and I felt blood on my face. Something else tagged me in the leg. I'd forgotten just how nasty oil-rig platforms are to fight on. Everyfuckingthing is made of metal, and rounds—especially ball ammo with its solid, copper-coated bullet—carom like goddamn billiard balls.

At SEAL Team Six we'd developed special, frangible rounds for assaults like this one. But that was then, and this was now, and we had to do with what we had to do, if you catch my drift. So I took my dings and kept going, firing at everything that moved.

Down the ramp and onto the control module access platform. A body to my left—inert. I put a round into its head anyway. Two more at eleven o'clock—heads and torsos and sub-guns coming up in my direction. I didn't think. I just reacted—my CAR spitting controlled bursts of three. Sight-acquire-fire, sight-acquire-fire, just like I'd trained my men to do, shooting at six-inch steel knock-down plates from five, seven, ten, and fifteen yards. And these assholes went down just like the goddamn steel plates did at the range.

"Cover—" I knelt and exchanged mags while Wonder gave me protection, then did the same for him. We moved another six yards and were within striking distance of the control module hatch when we were blindsided by a long burst of fire from above. I tucked and rolled to my left, sucking steel wall and flattening myself against the grating.

"Fuck me—" Wonder tried to make himself invisible, too, as well-aimed rounds from above clanged off the steel plates three inches above our heads.

I pointed skyward. "Derrick?"

"Prob'ly. Maybe the—*fuuuck*—monkey board." He winced as he caught a tiny fragment of ricochet above his ear and commenced bleeding. The monkey board was the protected cage where the derrick man worked. It sat attached to the derrick, about fifty feet above the deck, and directly to our left. It was a high-ground position that gave whoever was shooting from it a commanding location, from which they could fire almost directly down onto the deck. It had to be neutralized—and quick.

I pulled my radio from its pouch. "Anybody on the monkey board? Fire coming from there—we're pinned down just south of the control module and it's fuckin' time to move."

"Working the prob, Skipper—" Nasty's voice came back at me. "Duck Foot's on his way."

"Roger that." I was glad to hear the problem was being addressed, but I wished he'd get there already. We were way behind the schedule I was keeping in my head.

That schedule, incidentally, already had us opening the single hatch of the control module, which lay straight ahead of us. It was a watertight affair, with two handles. Now, if I'd been a Limey—that's British SAS—or a Frog—that's French GIGN—shooter, I would have simply cracked the door and tossed a concussion grenade inside, then followed up with full-fire automatic, raking the room side-to-side, and up-and-down. I think of it as O-K Corral technique—effective but very, very messy.

But, as you all have probably realized by now, I am a scrupulously neat and habitually tidy person. Besides, I wanted what was inside the control module to remain more or less intact—it's easier to gather intelligence that way, and we were suffering from a distinct lack of intel. Therefore, Wonder and I would do things the old-fashioned way. Instead of O-K Corral, we'd do Iwo Jima: we'd take the fucking room down inch by damn inch.

I looked at Wonder. A long rivulet of blood ran down behind his right ear, smudging and disappearing into the collar of his wet BDU shirt. He'd taken another fragment of something on his cheek, which now looked as if he'd cut himself badly while shaving. His eyes were red from all the saltwater, and his skin was puckered white from the cold.

He caught me staring. "Whatcha looking at?"

Well, he was beautiful and I was admiring him. So I said, "You're not only fucking ugly, you're a fucking mess."

He takes compliments well, Wonder does. Especially when we're being shot at. "What's your point? You look about half-past shit yourself right now."

"Yeah, well, that's because I left my tux at home." I ducked and scrunched my neck, so as to escape a new burst of fire from above. "We can't sit here all day."

Wonder nodded in agreement. "So?"

I pointed. "Six yards and we're home." And, in fact, there was a chest-high wind wall just to the right of the control module hatchway, which would shield us from fire. If we could make that six yards unscathed.

Belay that. We were already scathed. We just had to get there alive.

I smacked Wonder's shoulder. *"Après vous,* Alphonse."

"Fuuuck you, Gaston." He rolled his eyes, then rolled out on knees and elbows across the grate. I followed, trying to make myself invisible as sub-gun bursts cracked, dinged, ricocheted, and caromed by me.

Progress was also slowed by the surface upon which we were

traveling. The goddamn grate was sharp—it cut into your hands and knees as you crawled. Hey, pain is my middle name, so I just kept scurrying as fast as I could. Which turned out to be too fast. I came up directly behind Wonder—a burst of 9mm spurring me on —just as his right leg spasmed.

Mother*fucker.* The fucking sole of his coral boot slammed smack into my face, smashed my nose flat, then moved on and down, stomping my thumb.

For an instant, I saw stars. I mean, he'd really tagged me.

It didn't take him long to realize what he'd done. He reached back, grabbed the collar of my BDU shirt in a fist, and dragged me along with him.

It was not a smooth ride. But we got there anyway. Wonder released me, and rolled around the corner just in case somebody was there, waiting for us.

It was all-clear. I struggled on my own, made it to the protected area and lay there, arms akimbo and legs sprawled, doing a passable Gregor Samsa imitation, and tried to catch my breath.

There was, as I lay there, the proverbial good news and the proverbial bad news. Let's do that first. The bad news was that there wasn't a single part of me that didn't hurt. The good news was that the firing from the monkey board had stopped—which meant that Duck Foot was now up there, backstopping us all.

I rolled back onto my hands and knees, groaned, and tried to focus my eyes—which were slightly fuzzy, courtesy of Wonder's size ten foot. "C'mon. Let's go to work."

I pulled myself up and we stacked outside. Stack—hell, it was just the two of us. He took the bottom handle of the control module hatchway and tested it. It swiveled easily. Now he flipped the top one. It, too, pivoted opened without difficulty.

The door opened outward. We were well positioned, on the side opposite the hinges. I was crouched low. My CAR was in what's called the low ready position. That means its muzzle is slightly lower than horizontal, so I can look over the barrel, acquire all threats quickly, bring the muzzle up, and wax the bad guys brrrp.

Wonder reached above me, took the top handle, and swung the hatch open. "Go—"

I broke the plane of the doorway. The one thing that is perhaps the most difficult to learn about making these sorts of entries, is not to have tunnel vision as you go through the door. If you tunnel, you will see only one thing. You will fixate on it, and go toward it, and kill it. Which is good. Except, of course, if there is a second or third or fourth threat in the room, in which case, it will be Doom on You time, because your ass will be dead by the time you realize you've screwed up.

I went through into the room. No matter how many times you've done it for real, the whole sequence is always like a dance—a deadly series of choreographed moves—filmed in slow motion. *Space. Low light. Don't tunnel. Use peripheral vision. Move into room to allow Wonder entry. Eyes left-right. Keep* moving, *moving. Breathe. Angle left. Motion at nine o'clock. Sight-acquire-fire. Breathe. Look left-right-left. Breathe. Motion—two o'clock. Sight-acquire-fire. Breathe. Keep moving. Roll left. Use wall as protection. Peripheral vision. Wonder rolling right. His CAR bursting rrrip-rrrip. No words. Not necessary. Breathe. Target at eleven-thirty. Pistol coming up in his right hand. Target's weak arm wrapped around a sack of something chest high. Shoot through the bag*—no. *Could be explosives. Neutralize perceived threat. Shoot low. Groin shot takes him down. Bag falls away. Breathe. Second burst in asshole's chest takes him out for good. Peripheral vision. Breathe. Wonder's across room now. I move to rear wall, too.* Breathe.

"Clear," Wonder was shouting at me. The whole sequence had taken less than six seconds of real time. We'd killed four bad guys in that time.

I echoed "Clear" to let him know I was okay, too.

Then I raced to see what was in the bag. Grenades? Timer? Detonator? Radio we hadn't silenced?

The asshole I'd shot was gone—well, fuck him. He'd dropped the bag when I'd hit him in the groin, but its strap was still wrapped tightly around his wrist, the end clutched in his dead hand.

I put a foot on his wrist, which released his hand, kicked the bag across the deck, bent over, and picked it up. It was OD canvas, and about the size of a soft attaché case.

I opened the snaps and peered inside. "Holy shit!"

Wonder came up and stared over my shoulder. "What the fuck?"

Still clutching the case I sat down on the deck. Wonder gently removed the case from my grip, examined it, and whistled in amazement. The son of a bitch I'd shot had been holding a DCWO bag. The DCWO is a Divisional Chemical Warfare Officer. He's the medic in charge of making sure that you've received all the protection against chemical agents—mustard gas, as well as nerve agents like Sarin, Tabun, and SRQ-44. The way that is done, is to shoot you full of atropine, then give you a small dose of each nerve agent, as a way of making you resistant. The process works much the same as cholera, yellow fever, typhus, and typhoid shots—you get a small and controlled dose of the disease along with the protection, and you are immunized.

So what's my point? The point is this: I'd almost shot through the fucking bag of goodies, which would have broken some of the three dozen small glass vials containing Tabun. That would have released the odorless, colorless liquid into the control module atmosphere, and I'd have been dead within, oh, two or three seconds. So would Wonder. There was enough Tabun here to do the Tokyo subway five times over. It doesn't take much. One drop's enough to kill scores, maybe hundreds of people.

Now, if there was a good side to this, it was that, being a DCWO kit, the nerve agent therein had been diluted. After all, you don't want to kill your own soldiers. So, all Tabun used by DCW officers is watered down. It was still lethal—if I'd spilled any on me I'd have croaked. But it could be safely carried around—so long as you don't shoot through it.

"You keep the fucking thing," I told Wonder. "Maybe we'll find somebody to use it on—like good old LC Strawhouse."

Wonder grinned wickedly and slung the bag over his shoulder. His expression told me he'd been thinking the very same thing.

0134. We secured. There'd been a crew of twenty-two. Of those, sixteen were DOAs. The survivors—not an oil driller among 'em—was made up of the sorts of disaffected wanna-bes you're seeing on TV talk shows these days, dressed in camouflage fatigues, complaining about everything, but doing nothing positive to solve the country's problems. I don't have much patience with that kind of asshole under normal circumstances. I have even less when one of the best shooters I've ever worked with has just been killed. Nasty, Duck Foot, Gator, and Rodent handled the interrogations with the help of a twelve-volt battery and a bucket of saltwater. Hey, don't *you* be shocked, friends, just because they were. My men had just lost a shipmate, and they weren't feeling very compassionate. Frankly, neither was I. But I needed a couple of live bodies for evidence, so I finally intervened in time to keep the last two bad guys alive.

Wonder had wanted to be the chief interrogator—he and Cherry had bunked together after Cherry'd been wounded in the attack on Grant Griffith's office in *Red Cell.* But I needed him to diddle the laptop computer he discovered in the control module. It took him about an hour to break its password code, then extract what we needed: telephone numbers, messages, codes, and deleted files.

While he diddled, I searched. And guess what? The oil platform was being used as a goddamn Ordnance "R" Us. The container that had been brought aboard held enough toys to keep small underground groups like ADAM in business for years. There were hundreds of thousands of rounds of ammunition, more than a thousand firearms, hundreds of grenades, and dozens of Claymore mines, and other explosives. Elsewhere on the rig there were five Redeye missiles, two Stingers, and two Tows—late model wire-guided antitank missiles.

There were hundreds of field medical kits, MREs—Meals, Ready to Eat—wrapped in plastic, with expiration dates well into the next century. There were field radios, direction finders, even a pair of encrypted SATCOM suitcase transmitters. The SATCOMs were third-generation stuff—larger and heavier than the ones SpecWarriors carry into the field today, but still current enough so they had to have been stolen from a SpecWar unit somewhere. And there were three more DCWO kits. I turned those over to Doc Tremblay—who was the only one of us qualified to handle the fucking things.

PP-22 was, just as I'd suspected, a warehouse—a distribution point. It made perfect sense, too: weapons from all over the country were shipped here, then disbursed. Remember the list of goodies that ADAM had carried? They were from all over the country. No ostensible pattern to how they obtained 'em. Sow confusion, said Sun Tzu—and that's just what LC was doing by using PP-22 as a distribution point.

Sure, it was isolated. Yes, it was hard to get to. But that was precisely its strong point. You try to buy equipment like this at gun shows, or from underground contacts, and sooner or later you're gonna get burned by the FBI or the ATF. By employing the platform, LC had guaranteed himself anonymity. And what if an undercover agent showed up? Well, friends, there was a lot of water out there.

Wonder printed up what he'd found. Skimming the pages, I learned that the weapons and supplies we'd tracked was one of a dozen shipments that had been brought out over the past year. Those supplies had been given away piecemeal. A small boat would arrive, and weapons, ammo, explosives, and other supplies would be onloaded—he'd discovered computer records that confirmed the transfers. But there was no way to tell precisely who'd received the goods. That was to be expected: when you deal with tangos you don't ask for drivers' licenses or purchase orders.

But there were enough tracks so that we knew when, and where, the shipments had gone. They'd been scattered all over the map—there were thousands of weapons out there, and hundreds of thousands of rounds of ammo, tons of explosives and who-knows-what else.

I could have called the Priest, but I thought better of it. I needed someone I could trust, and the signals General Harrington was sending were definitely mixed. Instead, I got Mugs on the line. I gave him the facts and the figures. He said he'd query his Frog network and see if any bells of hell went ting-a-ling-a-ling out there.

I said I'd get back to him soon. Right now I had other things on my mind. First was Cherry. We weighted his body and buried him at sea—another Frogman to guard the gates of heaven. I looked at the resolution on the faces of my men as Cherry slipped into the dark water and knew they'd never give up until they'd avenged his death.

While they policed the rig, I took some time to do some thinking. More often than not, you end up acting on pure instinct. Most of the time, that's all right. But once in a while—and this was one of those times—you have to ponder all the possibilities, then act.

It took me a bit of time, but I finally realized that our current situation can be traced back to what happened in Key West. The problem is, I've been looking at Key West in one light, when I should have been using another, brighter beam.

Follow along with me, please. Fact: Virtually all of the fringe militias—crazies like ADAM—had gone underground in the wake of Oklahoma City.

Fact: To track them, the FBI'd had to resort to illegal means. That was why the chain of command at Key West had been so screwed up. The right hand had no idea what the left hand had been doing. I'd focused on those screwups, because the screwups directly affected the performance of me and my men.

That had been wrong to do. Aren't I the guy who's always talking about Mr. Murphy? Aren't screwups a normal part of my life? Sure they are. But at Key West, I had allowed myself to be distracted.

Well, doom on me. Instead of worrying about who screwed up and why, I should have been asking about the three principles upon which all crimes are based: motive, means, and opportunity.

ecause he'd been the one
f they'd met face-to-face (and
nt have been some disturbing

he ADO to whom he'd spoken
That document had somehow
already learned, it is harder to
e than one might imagine. The
absolute. And so, the shredded
Wonder, ended up in my hands. (It
st's hands—and I found it significant
thing.)

at hand. There was also incontroverti-
ound groups were getting support and
ds, the instruments by which to operate,
er two—means.

Let's go back to Key West again. That is
that ADAM employed current-issue weap-
ns of separate locations. The question was
oups such as ADAM were getting their toys.
er and I played with the computer back at
d discovered a remarkable coincidence: virtu-
Strawhouse spoke or appeared in a major city
e USG weapons stored nearby, some of those
olen. Final proof? The Dawg had been on scene in
even killed Johnny Cool to cover his trail. Now
d their distribution method—mix and match—out
ulf of Mexico.

ere was crime principle number three—opportunity.
e one the didn't fit the pattern. But don't exceptions
ule? Sure they do.

had received first-rate tactical intelligence. They'd
bout SECNAV's schedule. And how had they obtained
ely held information? I'd assumed they'd received it from
whouse. But I was wrong. At least one of the ADAM group,
Capel, had access to the military police's nationwide
uter network. That net was tied in with a bunch of others—
s among them. SECNAV's schedule wasn't classified. But it
n't been made public, either. It was, however, on the NIS
nputer. I knew that because Wonder had obtained a copy for

ow, having just laid out all of the above, let's add a couple of

Okay
Fi

wa
gan
said b

The A
outburst.
ADAM was
on their own?

He knew they
and what the Alp
said they were fly
because ADAM had
They were operating U

It all made perfect sens
unsanctioned operation. It
except ADAM's.

They'd been out in the Gulf
been told to go home and wait f
hadn't—instead, they'd gone to
SECNAV's plane.

Maybe it had started out as an exerc
SEALs once actually stalked "Hanoi Ja
security exercise that went awry. And wh
always made a habit of shadowing our targe
staged a hit. So the precedent was there.
original motive, however, the situation had gotte
had become real. Real bad. And when it had tu
Strawhouse decided he wanted nothing to do with it.

And why had he been so vehement about not me

other factors. The first was LC Strawhouse's vision of America. That vision—as paranoid a perspective as I've heard in some time—began with what sounded like a civil war, waged against the government by fringe groups that ran the tango gamut from ADAM to Zulu Gangstas—and everything in between.

That, too, made sense. See, among the more paranoid and sociopathic crazies, there exists a conspiracy scenario that goes as follows: the government will secretly arm youth gangs and domestic terrorists and use them as shock troops and cannon fodder, so that they can wage war against "real" Americans.

LC was running a fucking false-flag operation. What's that you ask? It is an old intelligence term for making your agent think that you are, say, a KGB guy, when in fact you are a CIA guy. So he, a dedicated Commie, thinks he's stealing secrets from his government to help the Soviet Bear, and all the while he's feeding the American Eagle.

Well, LC was doing much the same. He was selling his bogus patriotism to the masses, and at the same time he was stealing USG property and slipping it to ADAM, on the one hand, and the Zulu Gangstas on the other hand. The son of a bitch was playing both ends against the middle. That made him a real PUS(NUT) so far as I was concerned—that is, a Paranoid Ugly Shithead (Nefariously Unforgivable Tango).

Moreover, it is a fact that crazies tend to fixate on anniversaries. The Oklahoma City bombing, for example, took place on April 19, the anniversary date of the FBI's Wackos-in-Waco fiasco. Now, we were rapidly approaching the anniversary of the Oklahoma City bombing (a double whammy, if you catch my drift and pardon my pun). And from the records on PP-22, a huge number of lethal supplies had been delivered—and disbursed—in the past ten weeks.

My instincts told me that one clock—or, more likely, a whole lot of time bombs—were ticking away.

I had Wonder fire up the computer. He brought up everything we had: the FBI's shredded memos; the information the Priest had slipped to us. He added names, dates, places, and supplies from PP-22. Then he played "What if?" with his sophisticated spreadsheet program.

The answers he extrapolated were downright scary. And now, I had some precise locations. I got back on the phone to Mugs and read him the results.

His first response was, "Motherfucker." Then he began thinking like a chief. In fifteen minutes of jawboning he'd come up with a plan. He'd already alerted his network. Now it would go on overtime. He even solved the security problem. He knew a couple of dozen old Frogs who had ties to local law enforcement agencies all over the country. It was them Mugs would put to work. We knew that LC had his hooks into Federal agencies and departments. So we'd stay away from them, rely on Mugs's old-Frog contacts, and circumvent the system. I loved it—once more, I'd be going through the back door.

Mugs told me he'd need about two days to get things set up. The timing sounded about right to me—so I told him to get his ass in gear, and rang off.

Wonder and I played with the computer again, scrolling through hundreds of files and documents. Then we punched in the Trojan Horse program—the one that Wonder had written to capture passwords—and ran through it to see if anyone was playing the same game as I was.

Yeah—someone was. Wonder backtracked. The evidence was plain as my Slovak puss—someone was out there, tracking us. You could see it from the requests—requests that were duplicates of my own queries. A single password stuck out like the proverbial sore *szeb.* Oh, the password had been digitized, midgetized, and scrambled like an omelette. But Wonder's good-as-gold program reduced it to the letters typed by the original user. Those letters were NDBBM. The same ones that sat outside the Priest's office suite.

The s.o.b. was not only tracking me—he'd been able to get his hands on every piece of information I had. That meant the Priest already knew LC Strawhouse was every bit as dirty as I did. So why the fuck was he talking about hard evidence?

Let's give the man the benefit of the doubt here, folks. Maybe he was waiting for me to solve the one mystery I still couldn't figure out: the method LC would use to trigger everything—set his helter-skelter revolution in motion. LC couldn't use a SATCOM—not enough of 'em out there in private hands to make it feasible. Fax network? Nah—there are too many ways to intercept and otherwise screw up faxes. We'd gone over the rig top to bottom. There were no code books, no schedules—in fact, very little paperwork at all. And certainly, there was nothing that could be used to send a coded message to a hundred—or a thousand-groups, all at once, without leaving some sort of easily discerned pecker tracks.

"Oh, yes there is," Wonder said grimly, his hand fingering the telephone line plugged into the modem. "It's staring us right in the face."

I looked at him uncomprehendingly. "Internet," he said. "LC could use Internet. There are hundreds of freaking bulletin boards out there—you saw a few of 'em. He could use any or all of them. All he has to do is transmit on the World Wide Web, or send a simple E-mail message to one of the freaking Usenet news groups. There's no way to stop him, either."

Never tell me there is no way to do something, because I will find a way to get the goddamn job done. The bottom line is that I will not fail.

"Fuck you," I said. "There is no such word as impossible." I scratched at my face. "Let's think KISS."

"Okay," said Wonder. "What's the simplest solution we can think of?"

"Dispose of the problem at the source. Kill LC."

Wonder's head rotated in his trademark left-right-left, right-left-right swivel. "Oh, *that* would solve the problem, all right," he said, a malevolent grin on his lips.

It didn't take much research to discover where he was. The son of a bitch was a fucking egomaniac, and a simple search of the Nexis database revealed that LC had told a political reporter from the *Los Angeles Times* only two days ago that he was planning a—and here let me quote it for you verbatim, friends—"a kinda strategic think-tank, policy-wonk thing at my place in the desert while I sort my options electionwise." Translation: He was going to ground in Rancho Mirage in order to set his plot in motion and didn't want to be bothered.

I put Grose in command of the rig. We repaired some of the platform's communications gear, so that he and I could stay in touch. Over their vehement objections, I left Half Pint, Pick, Rodent, Gator, and Nasty with him to operate the rig. They wanted to go with me, but there was important work to be done here. They would act as PP-22's crew—and they'd detain, secure, and interrogate anybody who showed up asking for supplies. They didn't have to like it—they just had to do it.

I watched the old Frog as he took charge. From the determined look on his face, it was obvious that he was delighted to be back in real-world action.

Duck Foot, Wonder, Doc, and I spent about two hours packing gear and supplies. Then we lowered the thirty-foot, covered lifeboat from its davits just east of the chopper pad, cast off, and steered a course for the coast between Mobile and Gulfport. We had a vehicle to rent, a two-day drive ahead of us, and that goddamn second hand was tick-tick-ticking away ominously and incessantly in my brain, counting down the 264 hours until the double-whammy anniversary, second by second by second.

Chapter 19

HOUR 249. DOC TREMBLAY USED THE LAST OF HIS FREDDIE THE FORGER IDs and credit cards to rent an anonymous, tan, one-way step-van bound for Chicago at a Rent-A-Wreck depot. Then we drove due west. We stayed out of the big cities (as well as the small towns, and just about everything in between, too). We stopped only for self-service gasoline, paying cash from the cache of several thousand dollars Grose had handed us out of the safe he kept aboard the *FYVM*. We kept our ugly pusses out of sight, too. No 7-Eleven junk-food sprees. No beer stops. If we had to hit the head, we did it by pulling over on the road and finding a convenient thicket of bushes. No fucking gas station attendant was going to remember *this* nasty-looking quartet because one of us had to drain the old lizard and one of us resembled pictures he'd seen in the damn newspapers.

I see you out there. You're dubious. Well, don't be dubious. Remember the aftermath of Oklahoma City? Even with a nationwide manhunt on, John Doe Number Two proved almost impossible to find. And the man accused of being John Doe Number One was only captured because he was a stupid asshole who drove a vehicle *sans* legit license plates, carried a fucking pistol in an obvious shoulder holster, his cover story sucked, and he was stopped by one of the most effective anticrime instruments in existence: an alert state trooper. Knowing that, we drove a legitimately rented van, we cached our weapons out of sight, we proceeded at the speed limit, and we attracted absolutely no attention to ourselves whatsoever.

Which is why it took us a mere twenty-eight hours on I-10 (which traverses the southern route from Jacksonville, Florida, all the way to Los Angeles, California) to make the run from Gulfport, Mississippi, to Indio, two and a half hours west of LA. As we'd come across the southern part of Arizona I thought about stealing a C-130 from the old CIA air base at Marana, just northwest of Tucson. But we didn't need an aircraft, we'd BTDT—Been There, Done That—in *Red Cell,* and we do hate to repeat ourselves in these books. So we gave a nostalgic, one-fingered salute to the place as we passed the two dozen aircraft that sat behind the still-unprotected (!) fence line, and kept moving westward, ho, at a steady sixty-five legal miles per hour.

From Indio (which, incidentally, has a sign at the Indio Fashion Mall that says ELEVATION-ZERO), it was less than ten miles to Rancho Mirage. We found ourselves a motel about halfway between the two and slightly above sea level, checked in, then grabbed combat naps and showers. Let me be perfectly honest about the sequencing here and say that we grabbed showers first. We were pretty road ripe.

Hour 221. At dusk, Doc bought us the best map he could find, and we began our first recon of Rancho Mirage, and the well-heeled environs to the north of the city where LC Strawhouse had his hacienda and compound. I have played in the general region—the Marines have a huge air base at Twentynine Palms, north of the Coachella Valley, and I once took Red Cell there as part of an exercise. One hundred and fifty miles north and east is China Lake, home of the Naval Weapons Center, where we SEALs have developed some of the dirtiest, spookiest, nastiest explosive devices in the history of special warfare. I'll tell you about them sometime.

South of Palm Springs by a hundred miles are the Chocolate Mountains, a high desert area where SEALs—mostly but not exclusively the surfers, football players, and health-food dweebs from the West Coast's SEAL Teams—come to play and train with those wonderful Tinkertoy all-terrain vehicles that you saw during Operation Desert Storm. (Yes, I know they are modified Chenowths, and officially proclaimed DPVs, or Desert Patrol

Vehicles. But they still look like they're built out of fucking Tinkertoys.) The hot Chocolates are also where SEALs go to perfect their long-range (and I do mean *long*-range) sniping techniques. So, anyway, I'm familiar with the area. Of course, I'd spent no time in Palm Springs or Rancho Mirage proper. But WTF—you figure that one out on your own, gentle readers and diligent editor, or look it up in the Glossary—California high desert is California high desert, right?

Doom on me. Rancho Mirage *proper* is right on target. I expected another sleepy desert town. I got Beverly Hills in the Desert. They sold champagne at the fucking supermarket. French champagne. Dom *foutu* Pérignon, to be precise—at one hundred simoleons a bottle. They had goddamn cases of the stuff on display, right alongside the gourmet blue corn tortilla chips at six ninety-eight the bag, and the ever-popular candied popcorn in a big tin bucket at twenty-six bucks even. What ever happened to Great Western with the twist-off top and original recipe Cheetos in the ninety-eight-cent bag?

I counted sixteen golf courses between our motel and the biggest of the Rancho Mirage resorts—a hotel so large that the bellmen used golf carts to take guests to their rooms. There was no fast food—at least not on any of the main drags. We drove north on Bob Hope Drive, which intersects Frank Sinatra Drive and is only a few miles west of Gene Autry Drive and north of Marilyn Monroe Mesa and Jayne Mansfield Valley (or is that Jayne Mansfield Cleavage?). Anyhow, we cruised past the Eisenhower Medical Center—that's where the rich and famous go to change their lifestyles (and tame their substance abuse) at the Betty Ford clinic.

South of the Eisenhower, the houses that lined Bob Hope Drive and the streets that intersected it were tightly packed—most homes, even the ones on golf courses, had quarter-acre lots; the town houses sat on even smaller plots. But northwest of the medical center, the houses (and the golf courses) got bigger. We circled through a half dozen of the streets that backed up onto the fairways. Houses here sat on two- and three-acre lots. Placard signs for half a dozen security companies sat prominently on front lawns and next to the two- and three-car garage doors. The architecture was an unsettling melange of ersatz Mediterranean, pseudo-Spanish colonial, and mock Frank Lloyd Wright Mission-cum-Hollywood, all accented by palm trees, lush lawns, and small citrus groves. The place was a commercial gardener's dream.

We drove back southeast along Route 111 and passed the gate

house for Thunderbird estates, where ex-president Gerald Ford once rented a house. We continued into Palm Desert, where the houses were cheaper by a hundred thou or so, looped north past the College of the Desert (where Duck Foot and Wonder were denied their request to go chase coeds), turned west onto Country Club Drive, then north again when we intersected Bob Hope. We continued north, past the Eisenhower Center. Three or so miles north of the Eisenhower we turned east, then north again, cut across the Southern Pacific railroad tracks, turned left onto a ribbon of black macadam called Varner Road, and drove another three miles. There, a winding asphalt road had been cut into the desert foothills. We steered onto it, and climbed slowly through a series of tight S curves.

I was impressed. You see, I see things differently from most people. Most folks look at a building and wonder how they put it up. I look at a building and wonder how I can bring it down, or how I can get inside without being seen. Same thing here. We were on a road that had been designed by someone who understood good defense. It was narrow, so that two vehicles trying to pass would have considerable difficulty doing so. Its tight S curves precluded such high-speed driving maneuvers as bootlegger's turns —there just wasn't enough room to make a one-eighty without going off the steep shoulder.

I looked toward the summit, which was about a mile away as the bird flies—but probably three miles worth of curves, turns, and reverses. A single man with a .50-caliber sniper's rifle would be able to stop any vehicle on the road at will. You had to give LC credit—he knew enough to build on the high ground.

After another ten minutes of S curves, we reached the summit, which was in fact the edge of a wide plateau. The road widened here—enough so that two cars could actually run side by side. In the distance, I saw lights. So we extinguished ours and drove another quarter mile at a snail's pace.

There, we found ourselves in a kind of swale—a dip in the road where it would be difficult to see us. I asked Wonder to pull over. He did. I clambered out, walked along the roadside until I could see a long stretch of plateau ahead of me, then peered through the night-vision glasses I'd brought. It took a few seconds for my eyes to adjust. I focused the lenses. There, about a mile ahead of us, a high perimeter chain-link fence, topped with concertina razor wire, ran perpendicular to the road we were on. Across the road itself was a sliding electronic chain-link gate. It, too, was topped with concertina wire. Beyond the fence line by twenty feet or so was a gatehouse. I increased the magnification. Inside the gatehouse, I could make out a pair of figures. Beyond the fence, the road continued straight. There were lights, but it was impossible to make out precisely what they illuminated.

I turned up the power to full. Now I could pick up some detail on the gatehouse itself. There, on its side, was the same stylized, medieval sheaf-of-straw design I'd seen on the stern of the *Helen G. Kelley* and PP-22.

Yes, that damn clock was ticking away, but there wasn't much I could do about it. We couldn't crash the gate because we'd simply be shot down before we made it the mile and a half up to the house—and besides, the commotion would draw every cop in miles. The best SEAL operations are the ones in which you come and go and no one ever knows you've been there—except the corpse you've left behind. That was precisely my mission here—get in, get LC, destroy his trigger, and get out without anybody the wiser. So, it had to be a real stealth operation. Which meant it was going to take time. Which was something I didn't have very much of.

Moreover, it wasn't going to be an easy break-in, either. First of all, the place was immense—two thousand acres is a big spread. Okay—maybe not in Texas. But ten miles from the center of Rancho Mirage, it is.

What's the best way to do a target assessment on two thousand acres? From the air, of course. And so, at 0900 the next morning, Duck Foot, who is the most anonymous-looking of us, signed up (and paid cash) for a BluSky Tour at Palm Springs airport and took a ninety-minute Lifestyles of the Rich & Famous guided-tour flight.

The pilot was very accommodating. Duck Foot took all sorts of pictures with a video camera we'd bought. He got close-ups of Frank Sinatra's house, the old Bing Crosby estate, the house where President Ford currently lives, Ambassador Walter Annenberg's nine-hole golf course—and LC Strawhouse's humongous hacienda up on the plateau above Thousand Palms.

Hour 199. We screened his handiwork until we learned as much about the place as we could without actually being there. Duck Foot's no Vilmos Zigmond, but at least he kept the damn camera steady, in focus, and he zoomed in on the right stuff. The house itself—twenty-five-thousand square feet of living space built of stone and wood in a modernistic, quasi-chalet style—was situated at the end of that previously mentioned mile-and-a-half-long Spanish tile driveway, in the midst of a grove of manicured date palms. The area around the house was landscaped, but it had been done in shrubs and small trees, affording virtually no cover to an infiltration force. Next door sat a smaller structure—only six thousand square feet—of similar design. That was the guest cottage, Duck Foot was told on his tour.

The house and guest quarters were surrounded by a low chain-link fence, situated some five hundred yards away. It was nicely camouflaged, too, aided by the contour of the land itself—in fact, you wouldn't notice it unless you came right upon it. It was electrified, too, by the look of it.

Beyond the fence, about a hundred nicely landscaped acres distant, stood another, smaller compound. This one held a dozen small town houses, what appeared to be a good-size motor pool housed in a tan metal building, and a small office complex. Duck Foot's four-hundred-millimeter lens caught Dawg Dawkins, hand raised to his eyebrows, peering toward the BluSky Tour Cessna. You can hear Duck Foot's voice on the tape at that point—yeah, I know he broke cover, but it was worth it—saying, "Smile for the birdie, asshole."

We took what we'd seen and transferred the information onto paper. The security was impressive. Better than the White House, in fact. There were ground sensors behind the outer perimeter fence. There was infrared. And there was a well-paid, highly motivated guard force on duty twenty-four hours a day. They cruised the fence line (with its thrice-a-day ploughed-and-raked *chemin sanitaire*) in Land Rovers. They manned the gatehouses in pairs, spelling each other on the TV monitors and sensor dials, so no one got eye fatigue. And, dressed in blue blazers, gray slacks, white shirts, maroon ties, and packing side arms, they walked irregular patterns through the compound.

Like I said, it was impressive. And it was no doubt built to keep the riffraff out. But then there's me.

You see, back in the eighties, I'd broken into a 134-acre compound as well (maybe even better) protected as this one. It is called Camp David, and I had done the penetration at the request of the White House chief of staff, who'd read about SEAL Team Six and Red Cell in some classified report or other. How he found me was way above my pay grade. All I know is that one morning the phone on my gun-metal gray desk rang, and two hours later I was in civvies, sitting in West Wing One, as the White House chief of staff's office is called, listening to an offer I couldn't refuse.

It was explained to me that the numerologist who worked for the First Lady was worried about Libyan terrorists taking the president hostage or blowing him up. (You will remember that these were the days when Qernel Qaddafi's hit teams were actively prowling and growling.) Well, tea-leaf readers were well received in this administration, and so the First Lady had called the chief of staff and said she wanted the guards at Camp David to be tested, so she'd feel confident that they could, in fact, withstand a terrorist attack during their weekends up in Maryland's Catoctin mountains. Her husband had already been shot. She didn't want him taken hostage or blown up.

The First Lady had requested the help of Delta Force in the matter. But by then there was so much known about Delta that the story—and its origin—would have leaked to the press in a matter of weeks, which would not have helped the situation. Red Cell, however, was still operating in a wholly top secret fashion. And so, we were tasked, assigned, and entrusted to conduct our security exercise in the black.

It took us almost two weeks of work—intelligence gathering the same way terrorists would gather their intel. We hung out at the bars nearby. We took pictures. We probed the fence lines and the sensors. But thirteen days after we began, we managed to get three SEALs and two pounds of simulated C-4 to within five yards of Aspen—which is what the president's cabin is called. That was close enough for me—and for the First Lady's numerologist, too.

Once we'd accomplished our mission, we showed the Marines and Secret Service exactly how we'd done it, so they could take appropriate countermeasures. (I'm pleased to say, by the way, that the protective doctrine we Frogs developed a decade ago is still SOP up at Camp David—and there have been no subsequent penetrations, although regular exercises are still performed by Delta Force and SEAL Team Six.)

Hour 183. First thing we did was run a forty-eight-hour surveillance on the main gate. Wonder volunteered for the duty. After all, he first did that sort of thing as a baby-faced Force Recon Marine in the outskirts of Hanoi—and since he's still here among the living, he's gotta be pretty good at surreptitious surveillance. We dropped him off at night (actually, at 0430, when it is quietest and a guard's biorhythms are at their least effective). He dug himself a concealment position, burrowed in, and started his target assessment log. Yes, it was uncomfortable. Yes, he ached. Yes, the creepie-crawlies had nibbled on his nether parts. And yes, he was stiff, hurting, and stinky by the time we came to get him. But that is the way such things are done. Remember my Commandment: Thou has not to like it—thou hast just to do it.

A quick story. Do not skim over this, gentle reader, because you are going to see this material again. Okay. General Sam Wilson, as good a SpecWarrior and leader of men as ever lived, once assigned a five-man group of his Special Forces shooters an exercise against an entire company of the 82nd Airborne Infantry. He selected as his venue a high, old wooden railroad trestle bridge northwest of Rice, Virginia, just outside Appomattox. The bridge—known as High Bridge—dates back to the Civil War (although the current trestle was built in 1936). The SF's goal was to "blow" the bridge, which was being guarded by the paratroopers, just as a train came across it.

Now, the trains run only every two days on this particular spur of the Norfolk and Western. That told the colonel in charge of the 120-man 82nd Airborne contingent he'd kick the hell out of the Green Berets. No way could they get to the bridge without being seen. Especially since he'd be on scene thirty hours before the train showed up.

But General Sam was a take-no-prisoners kind of guy. "If you don't win this one," he told his A-Team, "don't bother coming back. You're professionals, and I expect you to behave like professionals."

So the A-Team went in forty hours early. At night. During a rainstorm. Four of them floated down the Bush river, using logs and other detritus as camouflage. They dropped off beneath High Bridge and concealed themselves in the mud of the river bank. One by one, they pulled themselves up the bridge and hid in the track bed and the thick oak supporting beams that ran under the span. They stayed put for almost two days, lying silent in the ninety-degree sunlight, and fifty-degree night, while unsuspecting paratroopers walked right over them as they patrolled in shifts.

General Sam's shooters stayed there until four minutes before the train came. At which point they got a signal from the fifth man, who'd been lying concealed half a mile down the tracks. They rolled off the bridge, hit the paratroopers from behind, detonated their IEDs and "blew" the trestle. Sure, they were uncomfortable during that night and two days. (And that, friends, is an understatement.) They'd pissed and shat on themselves. They'd been bitten by mosquitoes, ants, and spiders. They'd drunk their sparse water supply by the sip, not the gulp. But they *lasted.* They'd persevered. And they went back to Ft. Bragg with their heads held high—and the knowledge that they'd acted like the professionals they were.

And that's the way Wonder did his job, too. In forty-eight hours we retrieved him, cold, messy, smelly—and replete with information.

And while he'd done his job, we'd done ours. I'd been in touch with Mugs. His law enforcement fax-net buddies were coming through. They'd identified more than three dozen self-styled militias and armed gangs. And, better, they'd staked them all out without alerting 'em.

That's the great thing about local cops: they can sneak and peek without attracting attention to themselves because (1) they know all the back-door routes, and (2) they're part of the landscape. Ride some night with a state trooper or local country sheriff's deputy. There's not a Jeep trail or unpaved logging road they haven't traveled.

I went over Wonder's log while he showered and made notes.

- There were two regular deliveries to the hacienda: a Pajar messenger van that made the trip into town at 0900 and again at 1630, and (this being California) a greengrocer's truck that came at 1100 to deliver the day's salad greens. All the other vehicles on the log sheet had come and gone at irregular times.
- There had been a security company van that arrived to check a problem. The phone company came and went. An office supply house had delivered several cartons of goods. There had been a dozen visitors, including a TV news crew.
- The fence line was patrolled, ploughed, and raked freshly three times daily, and making our way across it would be difficult. Not impossible, but difficult.

Doc suggested that we might try to trap some rabbits, then release them to see how the guards reacted when the bunnies tripped the sensors. I rejected that plan out of hand because it would take too long to achieve any results worth a damn.

The obvious way to go would have been to capture one of the regular vans that made deliveries and impersonate the driver. But, as Wonder noted, since the greengrocer was Japanese, and we weren't, it would be hard to impersonate him at the gate. Could we sneak aboard his truck and make it through the gate, then slip away and hide?

Not really. He drove a vintage pickup, with the boxes of mesclun and other delicate greens stashed in the cab. The Pajar van was another possibility—but getting aboard might prove difficult, as it was driven by a staff driver. The other visitors were not regulars. There were no patterns. We were about to be goatfucked.

Hour 135. Wonder, pristinely laundered, played with the computer. We surfed the Internet, skimming through militia and wanna-be Usenet news groups. We scrolled past the usual conspiracy theories about Waco and Oklahoma City, complaints about the ATF, and love notes to G. Gordon Liddy. Then, buried in the Misc. hierarchy, Wonder came upon a news group we hadn't seen before, alt.politics.parker-lc.

I had Wonder key in. You see, I know something that you probably don't: John Parker was the Colonial militia commander in the Battle of Lexington—the very first engagement of the Revolutionary War. Guess what the date was, friends. It was the morning of April 19, 1775. That is precisely 218 years prior to the Waco fiasco, and 220 years before the Oklahoma City bombing. Lightbulb.

We scrolled through two dozen articles—boilerplate debates on Madison's *Federalist* papers, gun control, and crime. Wonder scratched his head, "WTF, Skipper? There are twenty other boards that have this kind of stuff on 'em."

But not with an April 19 peg. The boilerplate had to be chaff. "It's camouflage. Keep going."

There were 160 articles in the list. Number 93 was the one I'd been looking for.

> From: jparker@lc.com (John Parker)
> Subject: Arousal of Lincoln Militia
> Remember the gallant deeds of Sam Prescott and emulate them on his anniversary. The time is now. Freedom awaits.

Remember your high school American history, gentle reader? Sam Prescott was a twenty-three-year-old doctor who rode out on the night of April 18, 1775, to warn the patriots that the Brits were coming to capture them. Yeah—Paul Revere's the one who got all the credit for that midnight ride. But old Paul was actually captured by the Brits. It was Doc Prescott who got the minutemen —what our militias were called in those days—up and ready for the battles of Lexington and Concord. Hey—take a good look at those names, friends. Lexington and Concord. *L* and *C*. As in Lyman and Clyde. As in LC. As in LC Strawhouse. Sometimes I fucking amaze myself.

We scanned the rest of the news group. There were nineteen messages that took note of the jparker item. Wonder snared them on the hard disk and printed them out. I called Mugs and passed on the list of names and addresses. While I did that, Wonder went back into his Trojan Horse program, played with it for half an hour, then logged back onto Internet.

He was about to pull a Robert Roger—circle behind the bad guys so we could ambush 'em. The program would allow him to backtrack—discover the identity of anyone who added a message to the alt.politics.parker-lc. news group. Once we'd done that, I could pass the information on to Mugs and Grose—who'd shut the doors on the bad guys without alerting LC's network of snitches or pals.

Wonder, satisfied with his handiwork, then broke into the Department of Justice Intelink. He used it to move onto the big classified system itself, then cruised for half an hour or so, perusing top secret message traffic from half a dozen agencies. If anybody had the same theory as I did about the Oklahoma City/Waco/ Lexington and Concord anniversary, they sure weren't talking about it on Intelink. It was as quiet as Pearl Harbor at 0630 on December 7, 1941, out there.

There was something very wrong going on out there. I know that when you don't hear crickets, there are tangos in the bushes. The same thing goes for chatter. It was almost as if Intelink was on some kind of ERS—Enforced Radio Silence. I had Wonder scan again. There was nothing. Nothing about LC. Nothing about the arms activity. Nothing about the search for your's truly. All that sound of silence made me very nervous.

I checked in with Grose, using the SATCOM suitcase unit we'd brought, and brought him up to speed. It all made sense to him. For his part, he reported that he and "the lads" had already scooped up three boatloads of tango assholes—or "sea sphincters," as he piquantly described them. The detainees included five representatives of a Puerto Rican ultranationalist group, a quartet of white supremacists, and six very seasick Crips—drug-dealing urban refugees all the way from Chicago. My friends, this country ain't called the Great Melting Pot for nothing. He'd scuttled two of the three boats—saved one for emergencies.

I started to bring him up-to-date on the news from Mugs. BTDT, Grose growled. In fact, he'd already been in touch with one of Mugs's fax net buddies—a former UDT Frog (and retired Louisiana state trooper) named Boo, who was on his way to PP-22 with a big, borrowed shrimp trawler and a suitcase full of handcuffs.

It was good to see that the old Frogs had things under control. I wish this young one could report the same. But my condition was not as good as his.

- I was still wanted for murder.
- We had to deal with LC Strawhouse before he and his people went ballistic.
- And the Priest was somewhere in the middle of this muddle, but I had no clear picture of whose side he was on—other than his own. Was he a part of the fucking problem—or part of the goddamn solution?

I had no immediate resolution to any of those problems, which is what I said to Grose, adding that even after our forty-eight-hour surveillance, getting inside the compound without attracting attention was going to be tough.

I listened to Grose take a long pull on a can of Coors. "Listen, you asshole," he growled, "the problem is, you are not thinking like a fucking unconventional warrior but like one of those pretty-boy admirals currently running the show."

That kind of pissed me off. What was his point?

His point, he told me in the simple, declarative, well-seasoned sentences common to world-class master chiefs, was that when the situation got desperate, it was my job to make things happen. The rest would take care of itself. I, he said, was looking for some complex and intricate solution. Instead, why the fuck didn't I just keep it simple, stupid?

Such as?

"Put down the goddamn computer and do something concrete. Go fuck with their phones, you lard-ass shithead. Make their alarm system go ka-blooey. Then you hijack the repair truck when it shows up, and you get your butts inside."

Simple solutions have always made sense to me. So there was only one thing to say in response: "Aye, aye, Chief—will do."

* * *

We went back to Duck Foot's videotape and screened it again. This time we paid attention to the phone cables. They were thicker-than-normal ones, which meant he had six, eight, maybe even ten separate phone lines. Each line was capable of handling four in/out pairs, and an unknown number of separate wires for the security system. Those phone lines ran up the mountain to LC Strawhouse's compound from the main road, strung atop a series of towers he'd probably paid to have installed by the phone company. From the edge of the plateau, a queue of telephone poles ran to within fifty yards of the fence line. From there, the wires went underground to the hacienda, the town house complex, and security system jacks.

There was no use blowing a tower and bringing the line down, or messing with the telephone poles anywhere outside the compound. These days, the phone company can diagnose a line problem from the business office—all it takes is a finger or two on the computer. No—we'd have to blow the phones inside the hacienda so LC's people would call for the repair man. Oops—that's repair person in these days of genderless description, isn't it?

That was *bonne nouvelle* and *mauvaise nouvelle.* It was *bonne* because, knowing what I knew about LC Strawhouse, his phones would probably be state-of-the-art. And it is much easier to screw with phones filled with computer chips and transistors than it is to fuck with the old-fashioned, wire-coil, rotary dial, five-pound ebony black Bakelite Bells with which I grew up. You could repair those phones with chewing gum and baling wire. When these new ones break you just throw 'em away. The old rotary dial jobs could survive a direct lightning strike. The new phones cannot take a huge power surge. Hell—they can't even take a small power spike. All we had to do was send a blast of current up the line, and we'd blow every receiver in the place.

Easy, right? Well . . . not quite your everyday piece of cake, Tadpole. Blowing the line meant getting close to the terminal box, which is where the phone lines go from terranean to subterranean. That box was fifty yards from the electrified perimeter fence—and in clear view (although two hundred yards away) from a gatehouse. Which meant we'd somehow have to get up close to the fence line without attracting attention to ourselves. The operative phrase here, friends, is "attracting attention to ourselves." As previously noted, the guards at Rancho Mucho Macho were efficient assholes, and we'd have to be inventive. And we'd have to be inventive quickly. We were at Hour 131 already.

The first problem was creating a current surge. The surge had to be introduced into the lines after they'd come out of the junction box and were headed directly toward the house. That was because once they'd come down the pole and passed through the box, the phone company wouldn't be able to tell whether the problem was in the buried trunk lines, the wiring inside the hacienda, or within the phones themselves. They'd have to come out and investigate.

Here is a piece of trivia for you. Phone lines carry a six-to-seven-volt load.

You say you want to know what that means in English? It means that the 650-amp, twelve-volt battery in our van—the handiest piece of equipment we had to create a power surge—wasn't going to do the job. We could get a generator, but schlepping it up to the junction box, then starting it, then . . . well, you get the idea.

It was Wonder who came up with the most workable solution. The van's alternator surged at 60 amps. If we ran a line from the alternator, used pin probes, punctured the phone cables and spiked the lines, the surge from the alternator would fry every phone line our spikes were touching. That left the small problem of getting the van within proximity, running a few yards of cable, spiking the phone line, revving the engine and frying the phones, removing the cable, and exeunting, south (let's all repeat this mantra together, shall we), *without attracting attention to ourselves.*

But attention was exactly what we'd attract. There was no way to spike the line without using the van. And there was no way to use the van without attracting . . . *l'attention,* as the French say. Oh, sure, we could simply eliminate the guards at the gatehouse. But we weren't here to play—we were here to work.

We square-one'd over Tex-Mex and pitchers of Coors Light. I looked at the watch on my left wrist. One hundred and twenty five hours to go—just over five days until Armageddon.

Chapter 20

HOUR 124. THE DAMN SOLUTION HAD BEEN SITTING IN FRONT OF MY thrice-broken nose all the time—I just hadn't seen it. "It" was a suitcase that measured twenty-six inches wide, nineteen inches deep, and seven inches high. It weighed forty-eight-and-a-half pounds. It was the SATCOM transmitter-receiver we'd brought with us from PP-22.

You're asking what the hell am I talking about, right? Well, friends, it goes like this: Remember when I told you that newfangled phones are subject to power surges? You do? Good. Then you should also know that one of the most dynamic power surges one can produce is the pulsating, throbbing, undulating, oscillating signal flood that accompanies encrypted material through a phone line.

Have you ever faxed to, or tried to receive a fax from, a secure—that is, encryption-capable—fax machine, on a machine that is not built for secure message traffic? If you have, and you've seen your machine react, you know what I am talking about.

If you haven't, suffice it to say that the fax just plain goes crazy—all the goddamn lights and indicators and error messages go flashing on and off simultaneously like a bunch of goddamn Christmas lights. And that's when the material being sent is unencrypted. If you send encrypted material to an unencrypted station, then it's instant overload.

Well, we could do that here. All we needed to do (!) was attach the transmitter to the hacienda's phone lines and launch a long burst of encrypted high-speed message traffic into the compound. The result? As Grose would say, "Ka-blooey!"

When the modems, faxes, and phones blew, LC's people would call the repair man. We'd intercept the van and borrow it. Duck Foot would borrow the driver's uniform and ID badge, impersonate Señor Repair, and drive the van inside the complex, where he would "fix" the phones—adding a couple of goodies in the process to allow Wonder access.

Doc and I would secrete ourselves inside the van (doesn't that sound like the sort of fun the priests used to tell me would give me hairy palms?) and slip through the hacienda's security net. We'd sneak out during the service call and find cover.

As soon as the lines were up, Wonder and his faithful laptop computer, Big Byte, would do their own sneak and peeking. They'd break into the hacienda's system electronically and purloin its files. Then Wonder would leave a lovely and deadly computer virus behind. Once he'd siphoned off all the relevant information, he'd radio me, and Doc and I would go hunting. We'd find LC and take him down, then slip away without leaving any evidence behind. The odds Doc and I would face were, oh, twenty-five to thirty to one. But after all, we're SEALs, and those sorts of odds make the playing field just about even.

Besides, this scheme was so keep-it-simple-stupid it *had* to work.

I dispatched Wonder to find the local Radio Shack, where he arrived breathless six minutes before they closed for the evening. He bought three transistorized telephones (guinea pigs for us to blow up), every book of telephone junction-box schematics they had, a dozen alligator clips, two reels of telephone wire, two spools of shielded cable, two dozen pin probes, and a pair of one-to-twelve telephone signal splitters. Best of all, he pulled a hands-free telephone headset and a series of connectors from the bottom of the plastic bag. These, he transformed into an earpiece-and-lip mike for my radio with the help of a five-dollar Radio Shack soldering iron, a pair of needle-nose pliers, and a screw-hold tabletop vise. Bless the boy.

While Wonder assembled the components, Duck Foot charged the batteries for the transmitter and laptop, ran a weapons check, and studied the schematics books and wiring diagrams for the telephones. He'd have to be able to "talk" telephone, because he'd be playing the part of the phone repairman.

And me? I drove to Palm Desert, found a pay phone, punched the Priest's number into it, and entered the codes.

He came on the line quickly, his voice edgy and anxious. "Dick—"

I was very cool. "General . . ."

"Can you sit-rep me?"

Yes I could—after a fashion. But there were other things to discuss first, I explained. Like the bogus murder charge. I wanted it to disappear.

"I told you I couldn't do anything about that until you came up with hard evidence about the weapons smuggling," he said.

"Bullshit."

"What?" That rocked him back on his heels.

"I said bullshit. You already have all the fucking evidence about weapons smuggling you need. You know it and I know it, so cut the shit and let's deal."

He tried to bluster like generals do—full of outrage and indignation. I was having none of it.

"Look, you son of a bitch, I lost a man doing your dirty work. Now I have a fucking warehouse full of weapons, and a bunch of tangos, and if you'd like 'em, I'd be happy to make a deal. If not, there are half a dozen local police agencies who'd be more than willing to take receipt."

He didn't like the sound of that at all. "No locals, Dick—we have to keep this operation under wraps, and locals can't guarantee security."

That was a laugh. The fucking Federal system was a goddamn sieve, and he was complaining about local leaks.

"What about the murder charge?"

He sighed. "I can get the indictment quashed."

I needed better than that. "Quashed, smoshed. You make the whole fucking thing disappear or I'm gonna go public on this."

Silence. Then: "Okay—deal."

"When?"

"A couple of days."

"Fuck you."

"Goddammit, Dick—"

"Don't screw with me, General. I'm not in the mood for BOHICA right now. I want results."

Another pause on the line. "Okay, okay—I can get things fixed up in a couple of hours."

He was being too easy about it. Generals don't give in like that to four-stripers. So he was playing me. Was he tracing the call? Probably. But I didn't give a shit. In fact, I wanted him to know where I was—wanted him to know how serious I was about dealing with this fucking traitor.

I hung up on him.

Now, early on I'd made a command decision: the assault team would be two men only—Doc and me. Wonder had his own work to do. First, he'd be responsible for knocking the phone lines out. As soon as Duck Foot had fixed 'em, he'd tap into LC's computer files. Duck Foot would drive the phone company van Doc and I would use as our Trojan horse. He'd play with the phones, then make up some excuse about not having all the right parts, and split. Once he was clear, he'd pick up Wonder, drive back to the hacienda, pick up Doc and me, and we'd extract, leaving no signs of having come and gone.

LC would be, ah, neutralized. And Mugs would have the last of the information needed to set local cops all over the country loose on whatever tangos still needed taking down. In other words, by the time we completed our mission, God would be in His heaven, all would be right with the world—and a big Kodacolor rainbow would stretch from sea to shining sea. Right. Sure. *Absolument.*

To be perfectly honest with you, I wasn't ecstatic about this upcoming foray despite the KISSness of its scenario. But LC's death warrant had been signed. First of all, the son of a bitch was plotting treason, sedition, or whatever the fuck you want to call it. Second, he'd caused the death of one of the best warriors ever to draw breath. So we'd go balls to the wall. Either I'd be victorious, or I'd be dead.

To improve the odds, while I was playing with the Priest's titillations Doc Tremblay visited the local drugstore. There, he sweet-talked the pharmacist out of the specialized medical equipment we'd be taking with us to Rancho Mucho Macho.

Specialized medical equipment, you ask? Yeah, bub. I was planning to use a gimmick that was developed by my friends at Christians in Action in the late seventies. See, after the Church Committee hearings in 1975—you all remember the late and unlamented Senator Frank Church, Democrat of Idaho, the liberal's liberal, who made the lives of spies working against us so much easier by making it impossible for the CIA to do its job effectively—all rude and ungentlemanly action (such as assassination) was *verboten.* No more sniping at Castro, no cyanide in Markus Wolf's breakfast cereal, no snake venom jobs against double agents—even when they'd killed one of our own. You did things like that—and you went to jail.

But there were still a lot of bad guys out there who needed to be disposed of. So a few insiders at the CIA's DO, or Directorate of Operations, built themselves an organization. They used front companies and cutouts—a veritable maze within a maze within a maze. And they also developed a series of lethal goodies that killed but left no trace if they were used correctly. Then they sheep-dipped a select few guys like me to hop and pop and pull the op. Get in, slip a mickey to the target, and get out. No fingerprints. No trails. Nothing. We're talking about ops so fucking covert they never even talked about 'em at Langley—or anywhere else. But I know about them because I was one of the dipees. Between 1979 and 1985, I pulled off three assassination operations. The first was in Argentina, the second in Lebanon, and the third in El Salvador. Each of these hit-and-runs neutralized someone who had killed Americans and thought himself beyond our reach.

Now, let me tell you how we did it. We used chemical agents. And the most effective of them was Tabun, the very same nerve agent we'd discovered in the CWO kits. I talked to Doc and had him do some calculations. The dosage in the kits wasn't as powerful as I might have wanted, but it was certainly capable of doing what I needed it to do.

Doc pulled on a pair of tight-fitting rubber surgical gloves. Then, carefully, he used a sterile insulin syringe he'd bought, removed a quarter of a cubic centimeter of Tabun, and injected it into a soft gelatin cap. Then he enclosed the gel-cap inside a two-part, coated, nonsoluble plastic capsule that I could carry in my mouth.

My mouth? Absolutely, Tadpole. When you're searched, people may be perfectly willing to stick their fingers up your ass. But they seldom want to run them around inside your mouth. Mouths—Yeech.

Despite my objections, Doc built a second cap for himself. "Fuck you, sir, but since I'm going along, I get to kill somebody, too," he said.

Who was I to deny him his fun? I shrugged. "Be my guest."

Now, I know you're wondering what would happen if we

chomped our capsules by accident—like if we were stressed and the caps slipped? Then it would be doom on Doc and Dickie time. Except—as I knew from previous experience in the field—just prior to insertion, we'd inject ourselves with Atropine. That would make us impervious to the Tabun for four hours—enough to get us safely inside and wait for Wonder's message. And to factor Mr. Murphy in, Doc would bring two additional doses of anti-Tabun antidote, just in case Wonder ran into problems and we had to delay our nefarious activities inside. That gave us eight hours—a margin of safety hefty enough to keep even the omnipresent Señor Murphy out of my thick, Slovak nose hair.

Hour 113. Up betimes, as olde Sam Pepys used to write. I called Mugs on the cellular, told him we were a "go," and that the roll-ups should start right away. He rogered the message—there were two dozen local police departments primed and ready to move. The rest would follow as soon as he had the info from Wonder. "One thing you should know, Rotten Richard," he said. "Last night you told me the murder indictment was being lifted."

"Yeah?"

"Bullshit," he said. "I checked with the Detroit cops. You're still in the computer."

That told me everything I had to know about whose side the Priest was on—he was on his own side. "Thanks, Chief."

"No prob. Keep your head down."

"Will do."

I rang off. I gave Doc, Wonder, and Duck Foot a sit-rep.

Wonder's face wrinkled. "Gimme two hours," he said, and opened his laptop. I looked at my watch. I'd built a three-hour Murphy cushion into the schedule. I answered him with a raised thumb.

While Wonder worked, we checked our gear yet one more time and loaded the truck. In 135 minutes he looked up, a wide grin on his face.

"What's up?"

"Fucking LC Strawhouse, for one thing." He showed me what he'd done, then explained how it worked.

Let me put it in plain English for you. Wonder had just engaged in the latest form of unconventional warfare: cyberwar. He'd written a nasty little computer program called a one-time trap door. Trap doors surreptitiously work inside other programs and cause them, and their host computers, to crash. Disintegrate.

Dissolve. Fry. One-time trap doors are the byte-time version of the Tabun assassination capsule I'd be carrying. They act—then disappear into the cyber ether, leaving absolutely no trace.

Wonder had slipped it in LC's computer by using his Trojan Horse program. Through it, he'd managed to backtrack from the alt.politics.parker.lc Internet news group and key on the correspondent who called himself jparker@lc.com—LC Strawhouse. Then he worked his way inside LC's computer. He stole as many pertinent files as he thought prudent—no need to rouse any suspicions—and then he planted the trap door. It would activate when LC tried to access the Internet.

Now, you're probably skeptical. You ask how Wonder could accomplish all of that so easily. The answer is twofold. First, Wonder knows how to do this kind of shit. He did it in Iraq when we went there masquerading as a UN nuclear-weapons monitor. But there is a second, more basic point to be discussed here. It is that most people don't install any security protection on their personal computers at all. Remember when we broke into Grant Griffith's office in *Red Cell?* Remember what we found? That's right—all his incriminating files. With no security or encryption.

There's more, too. If you leave your PC turned on, and there's an internal modem attached, your PC can be cracked just like an egg—with one hand.

Our guerrilla cyberwarfare completed for the moment, we hauled balls for the hills. Wonder carried his improvised commo gear in a musette bag. We left the truck below the crest of the plateau and worked our way about a mile and a half on foot in the dark, moving single file along the shoulder of the road.

The compound lights were still on as we approached the fence line. Duck Foot and Doc dropped back. Wonder and I crept forward, moving as slowly and deliberately as possible from telephone pole to telephone pole while lugging the SATCOM suitcase, the laptop computer, and Wonder's bag of goodies. Suffice it to say that the trip was not a pleasant one. The suitcase was bulky—and it got heavier and heavier as we moved slowly, using the scrub brush and roadside rocks to help break up our silhouettes. Finally, after half an hour of humping, lumping, and bumping, we reached the pole from which the phone lines disappeared into the ground.

We crawled to it and lay on our sides, panting. Let me tell you, this is much easier to describe than it was to perform. Anyhow, just above ground level there was a gray plastic junction box. The phone cables, encased in a conduit, ran from the top of the pole down to this box. Working quickly, Wonder retrieved a Gerber Multi-Plier from the ballistic cloth sheath on his belt, flipped it open to reveal a Phillips head screwdriver, and unscrewed the box cover.

He cursed under his breath. "Gimme some light, will ya?"

I rolled over on my side, careful not to crush the laptop in its padded carrying case, turned on the red-lensed minilight I carried, and handed it over his shoulder. Wonder clamped it between his teeth like a stogy and went back to work. I could see that the outer cover of the junction box, which Wonder had unscrewed, revealed a second box within. It was sealed with the kind of screws that cannot be removed without leaving telltale signs.

He shook his head. "Dammit."

"What do you suggest?"

He shrugged, flipped out the pry blade on the Multi-Plier, and grinned. "What the fuck, Dickhead—I say we go for it."

That made sense. If we put the cover back neatly, maybe no one would notice. I gave him a thumbs-up, and he went to work.

He pried the cover off the inside junction box. Inside, the beam from the flashlight revealed ten pairs of wires. Wonder pulled the signal splitter from his bag. He'd rigged it with twelve pairs of probe pins attached to four-foot lengths of shielded cable. The splitter's backside had been wired to accommodate a telephone jumper cable, which would in turn attach to the transmit port of the SATCOM scrambler.

"Okay—I'll set the pins." Wonder chomped the light between his teeth and stretched out. He took the probe pins, pair by pair, and sank them into the eight lines. Then he crawled back to where I hunkered.

"Computer."

I unzipped the case and handed the laptop to him. He attached a serial cable to the connector, ran it to the SATCOM's serial port, and fastened it securely, then booted the laptop. Then he worked his way into the communications program.

The laptop data would move through the SATCOM, where it would scramble. Then, having picked up the right amount of energy, it would go down the line through the probe pins, into the hacienda's phone lines, and we'd have instant overload, resulting in fried phones. It was early enough now so that we'd be able to exfiltrate, and no one would notice anything awry until later—when they'd discover that their phones were phucked.

Wonder played with the keyboard. "Okay—heat up the scrambler—"

I opened the suitcase, turned on the main power switch, and set the key to TRANSMIT. "Roger-roger."

"Okay—now connect the splitter to the SATCOM's phone jack."

"With what?"

"With the fucking two-wire extension cord in the case."

I hadn't seen a two-wire cord. I checked the case. There was no fucking extension cord. I checked the case again. Still no cord. I went through every pocket and crevice of the laptop case, the SATCOM suitcase, and my pockets. Nada.

Wonder and I stared at the gap between splitter box and SATCOM transmitter for a few seconds of the sort of baleful, speechless agony that only Mr. Murphy can bring on.

I turned the SATCOM off. No need to waste battery power. "Okay—let's go to Plan B."

That intrigued Wonder, who hadn't, until now, known that we had a Plan B. So he asked the only proper technical question: "What the fuck?"

I replied, "Is there any way we can hotwire the SATCOM directly into the signal splitter?"

Wonder disengaged the cable from the laptop's serial port and examined it. "Maybe."

"Get to it." I took my light and played it across the diagrams on the suitcase's inside cover. Then I retrieved the flat antenna from its retainer, switched the power back on, and held the antenna out toward the southeastern horizon, where the diagram told me a WestCom satellite sat in orbit, twenty-two thousand miles up. I plugged the SATCOM headset into the board and played with the frequency dials.

My head was suddenly filled with signal traffic. Of course it was —I was eavesdropping on whatever was moving across the satellite. Now I refocused the antenna to the north. That was where I'd find the signals from No Such Agency's communications satellite, code-named RSQ-121. RSQ-121 relays some of the agency's most secure message traffic from a listening post eleven and a half miles southwest of Alice Springs in South Australia's wild outback that is known as Pine Gap. It is operated in conjunction with the Australian Defense Signals Directorate, and its encrypted signals are beamed to NSA headquarters at Fort Meade, Maryland, thirty miles from Washington.

I see you all out there. You're dubious. You're wondering how I know about all this shit. You think I'm making it up. Well, friends, just check your reference sources. You'll find an accurate although somewhat generalized description of the Pine Gap facility in James Bamford's seminal work on the National Security Agency, *The Puzzle Palace.* And you will find a reference to the RSQ-121 satellite buried deep within the Defense Department's fiscal year 1989 budget request, if you can still find a copy thereof. You have to look hard—but it is there, I promise. Besides—I've been to Pine Gap, and I've sent transmissions over RSQ-121. So there.

Now, the SATCOM receiver I had couldn't decipher the signals from Pine Gap. But it could receive them—which is all I'd need it to do to overload the hacienda's phone system.

Wonder labored on the cable. It took him about half an hour of sweat and ingenuity, but he finally made it work. He plugged his jury-rigged cable into the back of the SATCOM. I held the antenna steady. I listened. The welcome sound of electronic mishmash filled my headset. I gave Wonder a double thumbs-up and turned the switch to transfer the signals into the cable.

Wonder gauged his success with a meter he'd brought. It didn't take long—we figured that after fifteen seconds of massive message traffic the lines were totally fucked. Wonder removed the probe pins, and ran a line check.

"Issi-doombu," he said, telling me the line was dead in pidgin Zulu.

"Awuyelelemama, cockbreath," I answered playfully in the same pseudolanguage—you guys out there can make up your own translation to *that.*

Hour 109. They must have used one of their cellular phones to call out. Shit, somehow, we'd overlooked the fact that they'd probably have cellulars. Mr. Murphy, who is a fucking scene stealer, will always find a way to make an appearance—because at 0850 we saw a Southwestern Bell van turn off Varner Road and begin the climb toward the hacienda gate. We had the road blocked with our own truck about halfway up. The hood was raised, and Doc was leaning over the fender, working away on the motor.

The van eased to a halt ten yards from the truck. I watched as the driver leaned out and asked, "What's the trouble? Can I help?"

I am a highly trained individual. I have a master's degree. And I could see that Duck Foot was gonna have a problem impersonating this phone company employee. The driver, you see, was female. An EEO hire, no doubt.

Well, I have my own Equal Employment Opportunity theory: I treat everyone alike—just like shit. So I reached in and pulled said repair person out of the vehicle, backed her up against the van, and explained the situation in words of one syllable or less.

"That's kidnaping," she said.

So, nu?

We taped her wrists and ankles, rigged a comfortable gag that would still keep her quiet, and stashed her in our truck after we'd relieved her of her hard hat, her phone-repair belt, her ID badge, and her official issue size-large shirt. The name—embroidered thereupon—was Sean. Well, Duck Foot could pass for a Sean if he had to.

"You know your hair is longer than hers?" I asked.

"So's my mustache." He gave me the finger. He has no respect for his elders.

I glanced at the repair order that sat on the front seat of the van. They'd complained that five phones had gone dead, and two fax machines and a modem line weren't working. Sounded like a job well done to me.

Doc punched me full of Atropine, then did the same to himself. I checked my watch. 1012. We'd need a second helping of antidote just after 1400. I was hoping it wouldn't be necessary. He inserted the two backup doses—labels removed and switched—in a pair of morphine Syrette carriers. "Camouflage," he explained.

The Syrettes, safely packed, were stored in the belt-pack first aid kit Doc always carries. Then he handed me my Tabun capsule. I took it gingerly and stuck it upside the left part of my cheek the same way you'd tuck snuff or chewing tobacco.

Except this was one goddamn lethal chaw.

Doc and I clambered inside the phone company van and moved piles of stuff around until we'd created a pair of burrows into which we and our equipment could crawl. Duck Foot and Wonder covered us with miscellaneous supplies, cable reels, and other crap. "Careful with that shit—" I didn't want them piling stuff on so it would collapse noisily when we made our exit.

Hour 107.5. Up the hill. Duck Foot stopped at the pole where we'd been, got out, and once-covered the box. "It's all cool," he said as he threw the van into gear. He gave us a running commentary as he drove, and a final warning not to sneeze or cough when he was thirty yards from the gate. I hadn't thought about doing either until he brought it up.

The van stopped.

"Howdy." That was Duck Foot's voice. "You fellas called about your phones being down?"

"Yup."

"Well, just tell me where to go—I checked the junction box on the way up here, and the lines are good right up to there, so it's gotta be somewhere between the box and the house."

"Right," said a voice. "Come on in—but we gotta check the van."

"No problem."

The van moved about three yards. Then I heard Duck Foot's voice again. "What's the mirror for?"

"Makes it a lot easier to look underneath."

"Cool." Duck Foot sounded impressed. The back doors opened. "Want to look inside?" He paused. "Sorry about the mess. Someday I'm gonna clean this sucker out."

A pause, and minor scraping. The sound of doors slamming. The van rocked slightly as Duck Foot climbed aboard. "Thanks, guys."

"No prob—that's what we get paid for."

"Okay—which way to the house?"

"Follow the road straight about a half mile. At the fork go left, it'll be another quarter mile or so. Then swing past the driveway left again, and you'll be right at the service entrance. We'll phone ahead and somebody'll meet you there."

"Okay."

Another pause. The engine turned over and the van started to accelerate slowly. Duck Foot stage-whispered, "We're in."

He was right, too. We *were* in—in deep shit.

Chapter 21

I COULD MAKE OUT SHARDS OF VARIEGATED, COLORED LIGHT AS DUCK Foot, bantering easily with the security guard, threw open the phone company van's battered twin rear doors. There was ambient scratching and rasping as he poked around to remove his equipment and his phone belt. He even bitched loud and long that he could never find anything in this goddamn van after the relief night man drove it. Then he eased the doors closed, his voice trailed off into the distance, and the darkness returned.

I waited under my mound of cardboard, Masonite, canvas, and plastic-foam camouflage. Yes, it was uncomfortable, hunkering there, bent and twisted almost in two, frozen in an unnatural position with all the joints in my arms and legs held in weird positions. Yes, it was difficult to control my breathing so that it was imperceptible. Yes, I was sweaty—the morning sun was beating down on the van, and it was rapidly getting real hot in there. And just to make things interesting, a huge, fat brown spider had lowered itself from one of the van's roof struts, eyed me malevolently in the half light, then—taking advantage of the darkness when it came again—dropped another five inches, slipped under my collar, and established itself in the hollow between my neck and my shoulder.

But uncomfortable is a fact of life when you are a SEAL. It starts at BUD/S—Basic Underwater Demolition/SEAL training. You train so hard, and under such inhumane conditions, that from then on, nothing bothers you.

Cold? You're impervious. Heat? WTF. Creepie-crawlies, snakes, and other nasties? What's your point? *My* point, gentle reader, is that for a SEAL, just arriving on scene for his mission is a life-threatening experience. HALO parachuting. Dropping off a MK-V Special Operations Craft at thirty knots into four-foot seas. Emerging from a DDS—that's a Dry Dock Shelter like the one we used in *Red Cell,* remember? It's a clamshell apparatus that sticks out like a sore deck atop those retrofitted Boomer submarines. Anyway, think about emerging out of one of those with your crix (that's what we call the current Combat Rubber Raiding Craft) at a depth of sixty feet, popping to the surface without infusing your system with nitrogen, then paddling six miles to shore through hostile water. The actual shoot-and-loot becomes a form of release, because your sonofabitching SEAL is just happy he's survived the infiltration.

Likewise, you learn to lie (or crouch, or sit, or hunker) motionless for hours—sometimes even days—when you are waiting in ambush, or observing things in the same way Stevie Wonder used to do on his lonely patrols in Vietnam.

Something I have always taught my SEAL pups is that, no matter how well trained you are, there's probably someone out there just as well trained, and just as devoted to his cause as you are to yours, who would like to kill you. So you must be even better than he—and that calls for discipline. Discipline is the difference between life and death on a battlefield. I'm not talking about the kind of Salute It Because It's Got Stars on Its Collar discipline here. I'm talking about other kinds. There is fire-control discipline—knowing where to shoot, and how to control your automatic weapons bursts. There is vision discipline—keeping yourself from tunneling and missing a threat.

The discipline I'm talking about here, is body discipline. It enables you to lie in a fetid shithole of a canal waiting for your enemy *until he shows up. Sans* eating—no munchie-munchie because your enemy will smell food coming through your pores. *Sans* talking, or smoking, or just about anything else. You piss and shit on yourself—the water's so dirty no one can tell the difference. You're devoured by ants and other insects. And I'm not talking about a 0500 arrival and an 0600 ambush either. I'm talking about getting to your site one, two, even three days early if necessary, so that you, not your enemy, holds the advantage—just as General Sam taught his Special Forces troops.

Those, friends, are the sorts of disciplines I preach. But in the end, they all come down to two important words in the Warrior's Code: mental discipline. You *think*, therefore you win.

And so the fact that I was cramped, sore, and had a large, itchy spider bite welt on my neck was really unimportant. The significant thing was that, straining as hard as I could to listen for unfriendlies out there, I couldn't hear a fucking thing.

It had been nine minutes since Duck Foot left—I'd been counting seconds—and it was time to move. First, however, I mashed the fucking spider. Then, slowly and deliberately, I eased the boxes and cartons aside and emerged, a joint at a time, from my burrow, careful not to make a whit of noise. I'd made it about halfway when I heard voices approaching. To be precise, I picked out Duck Foot's voice. He was speaking loudly and distinctly—a quick-thinking SEAL early-warning system in action. I muttered, "Shit" and went scrambling back toward my lair, trying to be fucking stealth itself as I replaced the cartons, boards, tarp, insulation, and reels.

I was almost there when the van door was opened. My head and torso were covered. My legs were semiconcealed. But my size eleven, double-E black nylon running shoe was out in plain sight for all to see.

Luckily for me, Duck Foot saw it first. He never stopped his monologue as he rooted around noisily, tossing miscellaneous ratshits, batshits, and widgets thither and yon—*yon* being the twenty-pound reel of four-line, shielded cable he dropped over my ankle and directly on my big toe, the better to disguise it.

Shit, that smarted. The few minutes after he'd closed the doors and gone off I spent designing Duck Foot's damn denouement. Trust me—the boy was gonna suffer.

Another six minutes passed. I heard vehicles moving in the distance—two of them coming up the drive from the sound of it. Indistinct voices in the distance. I counted off another 180 seconds. Then it was time to move. This time, however, I let Doc go first.

106.5 hours—1048 on the big-watch-little-pecker Timex on my left wrist. I poked my nose between the seats and peered out the windshield. Duck Foot had parked the van next to what must have been the service entrance. There was a small loading dock that led to double gray steel doors. Next to the double doors was a single door. The house itself was built of stone. Manicured bushes bordered the loading dock, and on the far side, a lush, green lawn rolled toward the east.

I peeked upward. A lone television camera was mounted at a forty-five-degree angle in the elbow of the wall, so it could take in the loading dock and single doorway in one shot. Duck Foot—bless him—had parked the van so that, if we left via the rear door of the van, we'd be out of range.

Doc and I loaded up then moved quickly away from the van, working our way to our right on hands and knees, using the low clumps of bushes to conceal ourselves. I gave Doc a silent signal to wait while I took point. Carefully, I edged around the periphery of the house to the far corner, and peered through a minioasis of mature date palms. From there, I could see the main entrance and circular driveway. A Lincoln Town Car sat unattended. Under the stone portico, a pair of cameras looked lazily left and right, covering a 180-degree angle.

So far, so good. I was unobserved. But all of this sneaking and peeking wasn't getting me inside—which is where I wanted us to be. I reversed course and cut back through the trees. At the side of the house were three windows. I ducked under them and crawled back the way I'd come. Doc silently asked if we had a possible route. I shook my head and mouthed, "Negatory."

So we worked our way around the rear, wriggled under the rear of the phone truck, and edged behind the loading dock. At the far side, behind a low bush, was a single, narrow casement window. It was partially open. I snuck a look inside. It was a bathroom. And guess what: the lights were on but no one was home.

I took the ATAC folder from my pocket, flipped it open, and pried the screen loose. I caught it as it fell and handed it to Doc. Then I squeezed my arm through the window and cranked until it opened, sesame. I pulled myself up and through, slid face first down the wall, over the sink, and onto the tile floor. I stood up, took the screen from Doc, and then helped him clamber inside. Then we replaced the screen and closed the window.

Doc ran a quick inventory while I stood guard. Then we reversed roles. I adjusted the telephone headset over the top of my head until it sat squarely on my left ear. Then I adjusted the wire lip mike, plugged the jury-rigged apparatus into the radio's send/receive jack, and switched the damn thing on. I tsk-tsked twice, and whispered, "Yo—"

In my ear, I heard Wonder's voice. "Read you five by five." I nodded toward Doc and gave him a vigorous middle-fingered salute—we were on-line. He threw me a raised thumb, then dropped the ready stance and adjusted his own gear.

Three minutes later we were ready to roll. The question, of course, was where we'd be rolling.

I cracked the bathroom door. We were in a long corridor—part of the back of the house, where the servants and other minions worked. I nodded once and out we went. Sneaked to the left. Skulked past the kitchen. Slinked around the butler's pantry, and slipped through a swinging door.

We crept into the darkened dining room. It was impressive, even in the dim light. The table was a triple pedestal that was set atop a huge, antique silk Qum. Atop its polished surface, three silver candelabras that looked almost a yard tall stood silent sentry duty. Around the table, two dozen antique Chippendale chairs, covered in tapestry, sat in perfect order. To our right as we came through the door hung a thick, ornate gilt frame containing a mirror. The whole package must have run eight feet by ten feet. On the opposing wall was a huge Gauguin oil depicting two Tahitian women dressed in intricately patterned sarongs. They were carrying breadfruit, and they'd been caught walking between a perfect beach and half a dozen rustic South Pacific hootches. Above the humongous sideboard, a wide Canaletto from the artist's London period depicted the Canal and beyond it, Whitehall.

A soaring archway to my right opened on a marble-floored hallway. Beyond it, I could see part of what had to be the living room. Moving quietly, we patrolled across the dining room as warily as if it were mined, cutting between the sideboard and the port side of the table.

Voices from the right. I looked around for a place to hide. Doc had already found one—under the table. I followed him and lay flat, wrapped around a pedestal and the claw-and-ball table legs.

I knew one of those voices—it was LC Strawhouse's nasal twang. The other was female. From the sound of the conversation, it was Mrs. Lyman Clyde, and she was on her way to Rodeo Drive for a day of shopping, via the Pajar private jet.

They came into view. He was in well-worn jeans, faded denim shirt, and prole cowboy boots. She was a demure, perfectly coiffed blonde woman in her midsixties. She wore Chanel. I could smell her perfume from where I lay. The pair of them walked hand in hand, their arms swinging like sitcom lovers or newlyweds.

They stopped almost directly in front of us and put on quite a show. "Don't worry, kitten," LC drawled, taking both her paws in one of his long, bony hands and patting them delicately with the other. "I got myself a full day's work right here—that's *f-u-l-l* day. Won't even get the chance to miss ya none—unless you're not here come dinnertime. Then I'd be all lonely and bereft."

Lonely and bereft? C'mon, LC, give us all a break. He dropped her hands and kissed her on the forehead. She giggled, and they moved on, sailing starboard to port. As their voices faded I heard LC's wife laugh again.

Well, that conversation told me he'd be right where I wanted him. Moreover, from their direction, I now knew the front door was to my left, and the family quarters to my right. I turned to look at Doc's face. He was receiving the same messages as me.

We remained motionless for several more minutes, until LC strode past us again, heading back toward the family quarters. We could hear his boot heels toc-toc-toc in a purposeful diminuendo on the marble parquet.

I turned to Doc and signed that it was probably okay to move. His hands suggested that we wait a couple of minutes more—just to play it safe. I tossed him a thumbs-up. Prudence was indeed, dictated.

Now as we lie here, you are probably wondering why the Strawhouses hadn't seen us. The answer is that they weren't looking. Normally, people aren't alert inside their own homes—especially if they're surrounded by TV cameras, electrified fences, and huge security forces. Problem is, all those things are outward looking—and once you manage to get inside, it's all wide open.

"Yo—" Wonder's voice in my brain caused me to start. I flinched, and hit my head on the tabletop. Doc gave me a dirty look.

I dropped back on the rug in a defensive posture and waited for the enemy to arrive. When it became clear that no one had heard me except for Doc, I responded—quietly—to let Wonder know I was listening.

"Sit-rep," he said. "Mugs is in business—lots of tangos neutralized." A pause. "Hey—the phone van's on its way out," he reported. "I can see it coming through the gate, rolling this way."

"Copy that." At least a few things were going right. I rolled over to tell Doc in sign language that Mugs was working and Duck Foot was clear. In doing so, I wrapped the line from the earpiece around my elbow, and pulled the soldered connection apart. Oh, the jack itself was still firmly in place, but I'd snapped the fucking wire neatly. If I'd brought some electrical tape I might have been able to fix the fucking thing. But I had no electrical tape—or anything else. I stared at the popped copper wires in disbelief.

Doc did, too. *"Szeb,"* he mouthed, calling me a dick (but certainly not a Richard) in Arabic. *"Enta mak foul mok."* You have fartbeans for brains.

I tossed him a dirty look for stating the scatologically obvious and tried to adjust to the situation. Oh, I could still communicate with Wonder. All I had to do was yank the jack out, which would activate the radio's internal mike and speaker, making it into a walkie-talkie. But if I did that, the entire goddamn compound would be able to listen in on our conversations.

Okay, so Mr. Murphy was playing doom on Dickie. But WTF—I'm an optimist, so I chose to think of this development as enforced radio silence.

I pulled the headset and lip mike off and stuffed them into a pocket, turned the radio off, and stuffed it, too. Well, at least one thing had gone right lately—Duck Foot was clear. Now it was up to Doc and me. I windmilled my index finger in the old cavalry-charge sign. Time to move.

The house was much more impressive on the inside than it was on the outside, I had to give LC that much. He must have had fifty million dollars' worth of Impressionist art on the walls. I snuck a look inside the living room as we passed by. A five-by-five Renoir canvas of children at play in a garden hung above the stone mantel. It was flanked by Monets and Manets. We worked our way down the hallway. On our right was a series of Degas pastels that chronicled life in a nineteenth-century ballet studio. On our left, a pair of Van Gogh oils depicted the harvesting of olives somewhere in Provence.

I looked back at Doc and wondered if he'd sensed the same thing as I had—which is, that despite the huge amount of space, there weren't a whole lot of rooms in this place. The kitchen wing was large—with storage space, pantries, and prep areas that made old man Gussy's luncheonette back in New Brunswick seem small. And what I'd seen of the living room told me he had more square footage in that one area than I had in three floors at Rogue Manor.

But judging from the layout, we were inside a two, maybe three-bedroom house at most.

We worked our way carefully through the living room and passed along a short corridor. There was a doorway. I put my ear to it and heard nothing. I peered underneath and saw only darkness. I eased the door open and discovered a powder room.

We backtracked and worked our way to the main hall. At the end of the passageway were two doors, one at each side. To the right was an antique door of heavy, ornately carved distressed wood, more than eight feet in height. It was heavy and old enough to remind me of the front doors of Notre Dame in Paris. To the left was a padded, leather-covered door.

I stuck my chin to starboard. Doc nodded in agreement. He had his pistol drawn and ready in his right hand. His left, he rested on my shoulder. I slipped my hand onto the ornate door handle. Doc's hand squeezed my shoulder, telling me that he was set.

Slowly and evenly, I turned the handle until it stopped. Then I cracked the door open. There was no reaction from inside. I drew my pistol, then pushed the door another six inches. Nothing. Now I was able to see inside. We'd come upon the hacienda's master bedroom suite.

I edged inside, Doc at my shoulder. We followed textbook procedure for a two-man room clearance. I moved left, my back roughly a foot from the wall, my pistol sweeping from the wall across a hundred degrees. Doc went right, mirroring my movements. His field of fire intersected my own over the huge canopy bed.

I moved along the wall, working my way around the dresser and silent butler, searching for threats. He went over the settee. We met at the bed. I peered underneath. Nothing. The room was perfect—nothing out of place. I checked the top of the inlaid dresser. Two silver jewelry boxes held cuff links, collar stays, and other miscellaneous items. Doc slid open the drawers on the pair of Empire-style night tables. He wriggled his index finger in my direction and I went over to Mrs. Strawhouse's side of the bed. Doc pointed at the night-sighted Glock 19 in the drawer. Not bad. I picked it up, dropped the magazine, and racked the slide back. A single round of Winchester Black Talon fell from the chamber. I sharpened my left index finger on my right, making the old public-school sign for naughty-naughty, then emptied the magazine and pocketed the shells.

I checked LC's side. His drawer was empty—not so much as a

box of Kleenex. We searched the big, well-designed his and hers walk-in closets. We examined the pair of master baths. The masculine one had a huge Japanese-style soaking tub, double stall shower, heated mirrors, electric towel racks, sauna, and steam room. The other featured a Jacuzzi. I looked at Doc. He shrugged and hooked his thumb back toward the doorway.

1149. Silently, we retreated back the way we'd come. I pulled the big door closed. Then we turned our attention to the opposite doorway.

If the bedroom door had been taken from a cathedral, then this one looked as if it had been removed from a London club room. It was coated in plush, worn brown leather, studded with dimpled brass tacks that formed LC's sheaf-of-straw design. There was a big, mirror-polished brass handle that was straight out of Gilbert and Sullivan.

We assumed the stack position. Doc squeezed my shoulder. Pistol at the ready, I pushed down on the elongated lever. The door eased open—it was built to such close tolerances that you couldn't see any light between the stile and the jamb—dangerous because you can't see the shadow of anybody hiding behind it.

Well, what's life without challenge? As it swung wide I stepped up so I could "cut the pie—" which is to say work my way inside and move left, just as I'd done in the bedroom.

"Hey, c'mon in, fellas," LC Strawhouse drawled. "It's like we been waitin' on y'all forever. Just finished brewin' a fresh pot o' Java, too. So pull up a chair and let's chaw the fat some."

Chapter 22

YOU HAD TO HAND IT TO HIM—HE WAS SMOOTH. AS I SLID THROUGH the doorway, the muzzle of a small pistol had been jammed roughly, tightly, into my right ear, its front sight breaking skin. From the way it felt I knew it was probably a .22 or .25-caliber pocket gun with a narrow blade front sight—either a Beretta, a Walther, or maybe a Budischowsky. I also knew it would be cocked, and the trigger would be staged—that is, it would need only a very slight amount of finger pressure to fire it.

The small-caliber pistol in the ear is an OSS technique that dates from World War II—and it works, because it's so KISS-simple. See, there's no way to dislodge that pistol without getting shot first. Forget all the Rambo-jambo judo-Ninja-karate bullshit you see in movies. Believe me, when a pistol's jammed into your concha just right, right between the intertragic notch, the tragus, and the antitragus—that's the $150 way of saying right up your fucking ear—the barrel is held firmly in place.

Go ahead: try it. Plug your own index finger into your ear tightly. C'mon, c'mon—do it. Okay. Now, try to wiggle your finger. See? It doesn't wiggle very easily. Well, when the muzzle of a pistol's as tightly jammed into an ear canal as your finger just was in yours, more than 90 percent of the people it's done to simply can't react fast enough to knock it aside before the trigger gets pulled. Result? As Wonder might say, *"Issi-doombu."*

On the one hand, I am not part of that 90-plus percent. On the other hand, this was not the time to demonstrate the playful yet lethal technique I have developed to counteract it. Besides, when Sun Tzu wrote, "Sow confusion: when well armed, appear disarmed," in *The Art of War,* he made good sense.

So, I looked across the room at LC. "Win some, lose some," I lied, removing my finger from the triggerguard of my own Beretta and raising it so that its muzzle pointed at the ceiling.

A voice from behind me said, "You got that right." The door shut behind us. Dawg Dawkins leaned on it. Then he reached around the man holding the pistol to my ear, took the gun out of my hand, plucked Doc's weapon, and stuffed both of them in his waistband. Then he ran his hands rapidly over us to make sure we weren't carrying any other weapons. He retrieved the Black Talon shells from my pocket and dropped them in his own. Then, satisfied, he stepped away.

Dawg placed our pistols on the thick pad in front of LC Strawhouse, who opened the bottom drawer of his nicely inlaid wood desk and deposited them inside. The pistol was removed from my ear, and the blue-blazered BAW who'd held it there retreated, standing silent sentry duty against the wall.

LC Strawhouse beamed across the room at me. I'd seen that smoldering look, that wild-eyed maniacal glow before—on Grant Griffith's face, and Call Me Ishmael, Lord Brookfield's, too. It was the smile of self-proclaimed visionaries—and sociopathic killers. He said, "Have a seat, fellas."

When we didn't do anything, he looked back at us, somewhat annoyed. "I said to park it."

Actually, I hadn't thought he was being serious. "Sure." I took the corner of the tapestry couch against the wall. Doc dropped into a nicely worn green leather wing chair off to the side.

"Think nothin' of it," said LC Strawhouse, to no one in particular. He looked us all over as if we were kids in a homeroom class. "Now, gents," he said, "we can get down to bidness."

There was something about the way he said it that just pissed me off. "Fuck you, LC."

Dawg growled, "None of that," and moved in my direction.

LC waved him off. He looked at me. "We gotta talk, Dick—you don't understand the game plan."

I didn't give a shit about LC's game plan, and I'd just started to tell him that in piquant language when I was interrupted by the insistent tone of the phone on his desk. That meant they'd fixed the lines somehow.

He punched a button and plucked up the receiver. "Yes?" He paused. "Sure, sure—let him in."

Strawhouse looked at me. "Friend of yours at the front gate," he said. "Let's wait till he gets here—no need to repeat myself."

He? Who he? We sat in silence for three minutes, until the question was answered and Major General Stonewall Jackson Harrington was shown into the office by a BAW. The fact that he was here didn't exactly surprise me, although it made me goddamn mad.

I saluted him with my middle finger. He chose to ignore it, turned his back on me, and took a seat in the armchair that faced LC's ornate desk.

LC waved the BAWs out of the room. Then he turned to the Priest and said, "Stonewall, we're about to have ourselves a nasty situation here."

"Nothing that can't be remedied," the Priest said, obliquely.

"Are you sure?"

"Trust me."

The billionaire paused momentarily. "What did they say in Washington?" he finally asked.

The Priest examined the nails on his left hand, then looked across the desk. "They said that if you hold up your side of the bargain, you're not to worry. Everything's been taken care of."

"I don't have any problem with that," LC Strawhouse said. "Deal." He reached his long arm clear across his desk. The Priest took his hand. They shook up-and-down once. It made me sick to watch.

"Good." The Priest's head also shook once in assent. Then he stood and turned toward me. "Dick," he said, solemnly, "you're off the case. You've done good work—and we all appreciate it. But now we in charge have to deal with the situation—and we have to do it politically, if you catch my drift."

Drift, shmift. I don't know about you, friends, but I was sick and tired of all this fucking obliqueness and evasive talk and political insinuation.

I knew why I was here, and I knew what had to be done. I was here to take an Old Testament revenge for the death of one of my men. I was here because there was a madman loose—and he had to be stopped.

I looked at S. J. Harrington, major general, and saw him for what he was: at best, a political opportunist; at worst, a traitor. Oh, I was here because the Priest and those running him—Gunny Barrett and the president were the ones who came to mind right now, but maybe there were others, too—had cut me loose not so long ago to do what I do best: hunt men. Yes, they'd told me they wanted the weapons hemorrhage stopped. Well, I'd found it for them—and staunched it, too.

But I realized now that these politicians and paper warriors had a second, hidden agenda, as well: they'd wanted LC flushed out. But more important, they wanted him politically neutralized. Gunny Barrett's handwritten, secret code-word note to the Priest had been oblique, too. And only now did I fully understand its significance.

"Read enclosed *pages,"* it had said. And what had the Priest shown me? He had shown me *one page.* The FBI fax about hijacked weapons. Not the second, or third, or fourth, or however many pages—the ones about removing LC Strawhouse from the political arena without leaving any telltale fingerprints.

Well, they'd picked the right man—and the wrong one—when they chose me. I am not a political animal. I am a carnivore. I am a warrior. And I'd recently lost one of the best warriors ever to draw breath. Cherry Enders was dead because political opportunists like the Priest and LC Strawhouse were playing chess games, with real people as the pawns.

That's the way it all too often is, friends. Every time some fucking politician in Washington gets a wild idea up his ass, some young SEAL pup, Marine grunt, or Army sergeant gets wasted in a godforsaken place like Beirut or Mogadishu. The politicians sent troops to Lebanon as peacekeepers—but tied their hands with moronic, politically correct rules of engagement that got our men killed. In Somalia, diplomats kept the shoot-and-looters from doing their jobs—and guess who died. They habitually use brave young men as pawns. Use them with reckless disregard. I'd already lost one man in their game—and that was one too many.

I saw what had happened: LC had felt the heat of the chase, so he'd cut a deal in Washington. Maybe he'd promised he wouldn't run for president. Maybe he'd told the Priest he'd turn over his list of tangos to the Feds. Frankly, I didn't care, because things had gone way beyond politics, so far as I was concerned.

The Priest looked at me smugly. He thought he'd won. He thought the game was done. Maybe it was—for him.

But my hunting season was far from over. I walked past the Priest to the desk and looked down at LC. "You are a piece of shit," I said. "You are a traitor. You deserve to die."

The Priest tried to come between us. I swatted him away. LC pushed his chair back, swiveled, and turned toward the big computer screen that was sitting, its screen saver making lines of toy soldiers march from left to right, on his antique French walnut credenza. "Traitor? We'll see who's a traitor. You watch—see what I can do. Learn how many people out there support the same things I do. Know what kind of an army I can summon up."

"Now, LC—" The Priest was getting real agitated now. "That's not part of any understanding."

"I don't give a shit about that, Stonewall. He has to see what I can do—what I could have done." LC slid his hand onto the mouse. The screen saver immediately disappeared, replaced by his Windows program screen. LC looked up at me, the crazy grin still on his face.

He double-clicked on his Internet icon.

And I looked on in horror as the screen filled with a golden image of the SEAL Budweiser, followed by a hand giving him the finger, followed by the words FUCK YOU, LC.

Followed by blackness.

The billionaire double-clicked two, three, four times. Nothing happened. He whacked the mouse on the desk surface and tried again. Nothing. He smashed the case with a bony fist and got no result. He tried the master switch to reboot. The fucking computer wouldn't boot.

Of course not: Wonder's one-time trap door had fried the fucking thing—and everything inside it.

LC looked up, his face livid and panicked. "What . . . how . . ." he blustered. I answered him with silence.

I turned to the Priest, who'd gone white, too. "I don't know what the fuck you and the boys back in Washington planned," I said, even though I actually had a pretty good idea about what was going on, "but don't worry—there's a bunch of domestic tangos being swept up right now by local cops, all across the country."

The Priest was enraged. "I told you—"

I knew damn well what he'd told me. And if you think I'd ever trust him, I have some beachfront property in Arizona to sell you.

I picked up movement at my back—LC's hand crept across the desk, toward the intercom phone. I half-turned and slammed my fist atop it. I heard bones break.

He screamed.

Dawg saw the look in my eyes. He reached inside his suitcoat and moved to come between us. Doc cut him off. Dropped him right where he stood with a single, devastating blow. That was good—because I didn't want to waste any energy on Dawg ever again.

One down, one to go.

LC Strawhouse's face took on a real panicked expression. Cradling his hand he rose from his chair and backed away from me, but I stayed with him. I took the front of his shirt in my hands.

I got close enough so that he could hear me loud and clear. "Remember Detroit?"

"Detroit?"

"Your penthouse. I told you I'd hunt you down—I said your head was gonna look great on my wall."

His eyes went wide. I never let go of his shirt.

I looked at Doc. "What time is it, Master Chief?"

"Thirteen sixteen, Skipper."

I had an hour left. Plenty of time. Good safety margin. I cracked the Tabun capsule between my teeth, brought LC Strawhouse nose to nose with me, and stage-whispered, "I have your computer files. I have your lists. I have your army of wanna-bes—and now I have you." I watched his eyes widen. I said, "It's time for you to die, LC," exhaling as wetly as I could, directly into his face.

I let loose of him. He stared at me goggle-eyed, his mouth moving incomprehensibly. Then he sucked in a single breath, clutched his chest with his good hand—and dropped like a stone.

Hey, that fucking Tabun *works.*

"Whoa—" I swallowed the capsule and grabbed at LC's body as it sagged to the floor. "The motherfucker's having a heart attack!"

"You start chest massage—let me breathe into him." Master Chief Hospitalman Doc Tremblay knocked me aside and began mouth-to-mouth right away.

I knew what he was doing. I thought, Right on, Doc—nothing like a double dose, just to make sure.

We dutifully CPR'd LC Strawhouse's limp-as-an-NIS-agent's-dick body for fifteen minutes. But he didn't respond.

Gee, I wonder why.

Finally, I'd had enough of the charade. I stood up. I looked at the Priest. "You can clean this mess up, sir," I said, careful to spell it with a *c* and a *u*. Yeah, knowing him, he probably had the assets to do it parked somewhere close by.

I wrote thirteen words and a date on a sheet of paper and handed it to him. "But first, you can sign this."

It was a short message but a good one. It went: *"I resign from the U.S. Army effective immediately. Major General Stonewall Jackson Harrington."*

He protested. He objected. He remonstrated. He inveighed. But he signed.

He signed because he knew that I had a pretty good idea what they'd been planning—an endgame that was the most fucking cynical and dirty thing I'd ever come across.

You don't get it? Let me postulate, gentle reader. It was my opinion that the Priest and his politician handlers had planned to let the tangos have at it—to allow a brief but violent wave of domestic terrorism, then crack down, hard, on the perpetrators. It was my opinion that LC Strawhouse was going to turn over his lists and files—the very ones Wonder had purloined from LC's now-defunct computer—to the Priest.

I see you all out there waving your hands like kids in a classroom. You are asking, Why would anybody let tangos kill people, when they could be stopped beforehand? It does kind of boggle the mind, doesn't it, gentle readers?

Well, even though I had nothing I could take to court, I accepted that they'd do it because some misguided twentysomething confidential assistant sphincter to an ill-advised, ambitious deputy assistant asshole in the White House had probably figured if the fucking president's ratings had jumped thirty points after Oklahoma City, they'd jump fifty points after half-a-dozen or so similar incidents. And this was an election year.

I fixed the Priest in my sights. So far as I was concerned, anybody who'd sign on to a gambit like that was a disgrace to the uniform. Stonewall Jackson Harrington had stopped serving his country when he became a political errand boy.

There is a long stretch between civilian control of the military—which is a good idea, friends—and political manipulation of the military. By turning politician he'd betrayed the military brotherhood, and all the brave warriors who have died to defend our nation. I would have killed him on the spot—except I wanted to use him to take a message back to the assholes who had used him as their errand boy. I wanted them to know *I* had LC's files, *I* had the paperwork from the oil rig, and I knew that hundreds of tangos were being scooped up right this very minute, thanks to Mugs, to Grose, and two dozen or so local police agencies all across the country.

I walked over to the copier in the corner and ran half a dozen prints of the Priest's resignation. "You have forty-eight hours," I said, giving him a copy. "I expect to read about a huge fucking bunch of resignations in Washington in the papers. If I don't, I'll come after you—and all the people who sent you here."

I paused long enough to look at LC's corpse. "Just the same way I came after him." I paused for effect. "Got it, *sir?*"

The Priest nodded dumbly. Yeah—he got it. Except, I could see that he didn't quite get it. He had absolutely no idea how *what* had just happened to LC Strawhouse, had, in fact, happened to LC Strawhouse. Except that he was stone dead, and that I'd killed him without leaving any trace.

Well that was just fine with me. Because the truth of the billionaire's fate was exactly the same as the fucking sign on the door to the Priest's own soon-to-be-vacated suite back at DIA.

It was Nobody's Damn Business But Mine.

Glossary

ADAM: Alpha Detachment Armed Militia. Underground tango group bent on violence.
Admirals' Gestapo: what the secretary of defense's office calls the Naval Investigative Services Command. See SHIT-FOR-BRAINS.
AK-47: 7.63 X 39 Kalashnikov automatic rifle. The most common assault weapon in the world.
ATF: antiterrorist task force, or ambiguous (amphibious) task force.
Atropine: antidote for biological warfare nerve agents such as Sarin or Tabun.
AVCNO: Assistant Vice Chief of Naval Operations

BAW: Big Asshole Windbag.
BDUs: Battle Dress Uniforms. Now that's an oxymoron if I ever heard one.
BIQ: Bitch-in-Question.
BLU-43B: antipersonnel mine currently in use by U.S. forces.
BOHICA: Bend Over—Here It Comes Again!
Boomer: nuclear-powered missile submarine.
BTDT: Been There, Done That.
BUPERS: Naval BUreau of PERSonnel.

C-130: Lockheed's ubiquitous Hercules.
C-4: plastic explosive. You can mold it like clay. You can even use it to light your fires. Just don't stamp on it.

C²CO: Can't Cunt Commanding Officer. Too many of these in Navy SpecWar today. They won't support their men or take chances because they're afraid it'll ruin their chances for promotion.
CALOW: Coastal And Limited-Objective Warfare. Very fashionable acronym at the Pentagon in these days of increased low-intensity conflict.
cannon fodder: See FNG.
charlie-foxtrot: polite radio talk for CF, or clusterfuck.
Christians in Action: SpecWar slang for the Central Intelligence Agency.
CINC: Commander IN Chief
CINCLANT: Commander IN Chief, AtLANtic.
CINCLANTFLT: Commander IN Chief, AtLANtic FLeeT.
CINCUSNAVEUR: Commander IN Chief, U.S. Naval forces, EURope
clusterfuck: see FUBAR
CNO: Chief of Naval Operations.
cockbreath: SEAL term of endearment used for those who only pay lip service.
CONUS: CONtinental United States.
CQB: Close-Quarters Battle—e.g. killing that's up close and personal.
CQC6: Ernest Emerson's titanium-framed Close Quarters Combat folding knife.
crackers: CRiminal hACKERS—cyperpunk tangos.
CRRC: Combat Rubber Raiding Craft. Latest generation of SEAL inflatable small boats.
CT: CounterTerrorism.

detasheet: olive-drab, ten-by-twenty-inch flexible PETN-based plastic explosive used as a cutting or breaching charge.
DEVGRP: Naval Special Warfare DEVelopment GRouP. Current designation for SEAL Team Six.
DIA: Defense Intelligence Agency. Spook heaven based in Arlington, Virginia.
Dickhead: Stevie Wonder's nickname for Marcinko.
DIPSEC: DIPlomatic SECurity.
dipshit: can't cunt pencil-dicked asshole.
dirtbag: the look Marcinko favors for his Team guys.

Do-ma-nhieu (Vietnamese): Go fuck yourself. See DOOM ON YOU.
doom on you: American version of Vietnamese for go fuck yourself.
DSD: Defense Signals Directorate. Australia's SIGINT agency.
dweeb: no-load shit-for-brains geeky asshole, usually shackled to a computer.

EEI: Essential Element of Information. The info-nuggets on which a mission is planned and executed.
EEO: Equal Employment Opportunity. (Marcinko always treats 'em all alike—just like shit.)
ELINT: ELectronic INTelligence.
EOD: Explosive Ordnance Disposal.

flashbang: disorientation device used by hostage rescue teams.
FNG: Fucking New Guy. See CANNON FODDER.
four-striper: Captain. All too often, a C²CO.
frags: fragmentation grenades
FUBAR: Fucked Up Beyond All Repair

GFC: Ground Force Commander.
goatfuck: what the Navy likes to do to Marcinko. See FUBAR
GSG-9: Grenzchutzgruppe-9. Top German CT unit.

HAHO: High-Altitude High-Opening parachute jump.
HALO: High Altitude, Low-Opening parachute jump.
HK: ultrareliable pistol, assault rifle, or submachine gun made by Heckler & Koch, a German firm. SEALs use H&K MP5-Ks submachine guns in various configurations, as well as H&K 93 assault rifles, and P7M8 9mm, and USP 9mm, .40 or .45-caliber pistols.
HUMINT: HUMan INTelligence.
humongous: Marcinko Dick.

IBS: Inflatable Boat, Small—the basic unit of SEAL transportation.
IED: Improvised Explosive Device.
Issi-doombu: Pidgin Zulu for dead.

Japs: bad guys.
Jarheads: Marines. The Corps. Formally, USMC, or, Uncle Sam's Misguided Children.
JSOC: Joint Special Operations Command.

KATN: Kick Ass and Take Names. Marcinko avocation.
KISS: Keep It Simple, Stupid. Marcinko's basic premise for special operations.

LANTFLT: AtLANTic FLeeT.

M-16: Basic U.S. .223-caliber weapon, used by the armed forces.
MagSafe: lethal frangible ammunition that does not penetrate the human body. Favored by some SWAT units for CQB.
Mark-O Mod-I: basic unit.
MILCRAFT: Pentagonese for MILitary airCRAFT.
MK V SOC: Mark V Special Operations Craft. The latest SEAL delivery vehicle. It is eighty-one feet long, cruises 550 nautical miles, and fits aboard a C-5 aircraft. It takes a five-man and can hold a SEAL Platoon, four CRRC craft, and six outboard motors.

NAVAIR: NAVy AIR Command.
NAVSEA: NAVy SEA Command.
NAVSPECWARGRU: NAVal SPECial WARfare GRoUp.
Navyspeak: redundant, bureaucratic naval nomenclature, either in written nonoral, or nonwritten oral modes, indecipherable by nonmilitary (conventional) or military (unconventional) individuals during normal interfacing configuration conformations.
NEXIS: private database.
NIS: Naval Investigative Service command, also known as the Admirals' Gestapo. See SHIT-FOR-BRAINS.
NMN: No Middle Name.
NOC: Non-Official Cover. Spook talk for covert operator, usually from Christians in Action.
NRO: National Reconnaissance Office. Established August 25, 1960, to administer and coordinate satellite development and operations for U.S. intelligence community. Very spooky place.
NSA: National Security Agency, known within the SpecWar community as No Such Agency.

NSCT: Naval Security Coordination Team (Navyspeak name for Red Cell).
NSD: National Security Directive.

OBE: Overtaken By Events—usually because of the bureaucracy.
OOD: Officer Of the Deck (he who drives the big gray monster).
OP-06: deputy CNO for operations, plans, and policy.
OP-06B: assistant deputy CNO for operations, plans, and policy.
OP-06D: cover organization for Red Cell/NSCT.
OP-06-04: CNO's SpecWar briefing officer.
OPSEC: OPerational SECurity

P-3: Orion sub-hunting and electronic-warfare prop-driven aircraft.
PDFL: Pretty Dangerous Fucking Location.
PDMP: Pretty Dangerous Motherfucking People.
PIQ: Platform In Question.
POC: Point of Contact.
PT: physical training.
PUS(NUT): Paranoid Ugly Shithead (Nefariously Unforgivable Tango).

retarded: Frog slang for retired.
RSQ-121: secret code-word program No Such Agency satellite.

S^2: Shut the fuck up and sit the fuck down.
SAC: Special Agent in Charge. FBI's local office top-gun (all too often a pussy-ass paper-cruncher).
SATCOM: SATellite COMmunications.
SCIF: Special Classified Intelligence Facility. A bug-proof room.
SDV: Swimmer Delivery Vehicle. Wet sub.
SEAL: SEa-Air-Land Navy SpecWarrior. A hop-and-popping shoot-and-looter hairy-assed Frogman who gives a shit. The acronym stands for Sleep, Eat, And Live it up.
Semtex: Czecho C-4 plastique explosive. Used for canceling Czechs.
SERE: Survival, Evasion, Resistance, and Escape school.

SH-3: versatile Sikorsky chopper. Used in ASW missions and also as a Spec Ops platform.
Shit-for-Brains: any no-load, pus-nutted, pencil-dicked asshole from NIS.
SIGINT: SIGnals INTelligence.
633HB: lightweight 9mm submachine gun.
SLUDJ: Top Secret NIS witch hunters. Acronym stands for Sensitive Legal (Upper Deck) Jurisdiction.
SMG: submachine gun
SNAFU: Situation Normal—All Fucked Up.
SOAUS: Special Operations Association of the United States. Trade group for SpecWarriors and SpecWar wannabes.
SOCOM: Special Operations COMmand, located at MacDill AFB, Tampa, Florida.
SOF: Special Operations Force.
SOS: SAC Of Shit.
SpecWarrior: One who gives a fuck.
SSN: nuclear sub, commonly known as sewer pipe.
STABs: SEAL Tactical Assault Boats.
SUC: Marcinkospeak for Smart, Unpredictable, and Cunning.
SWAT: Special Weapons and Tactics police teams. All too often they do not train enough and become SQUAT teams.
Syrette: self-injection dose, usually of morphine.

Tabun: deadly and untraceable nerve agent.
TACBE: TACtical BEAcon. Homing device.
TAD: Temporary Additional Duty (SEALs refer to it as Traveling Around Drunk).
TARFU: Things Are Really Fucked Up.
TECHINT: TECHnical INTelligence.
THREATCON: THREAT CONdition.
tiger stripes: The only stripes that SEALs will wear.
TIQ: Tango-In-Question
TTS: Marcinko slang for Tap 'em, Tie 'em, and Stash 'em.

UGS: Unmanned Ground Sensors. Useful in setting off Claymore mines and other booby traps.
UNODIR: UNless Otherwise DIRected. That's how Marcinko operates when he's surrounded by can't cunts.

VDL: Versatile, Dangerous, and Lethal.

wanna-bes: the sort of folks you meet at *Soldier of Fortune* conventions.
weenies: pussy-ass can't cunts and no-loads.
WTF: what the fuck.

Zulu: Greenwich Mean Time (GMT) designator used in formal military communications.
Zulu-5-Oscar: escape and evasion exercises in which Frogmen try to plant dummy limpet mines on Navy vessels while the vessels' crews try to catch them in *bombus interruptus.*

INDEX

INDEX

All entries preceded by an asterisk (*) are pseudonyms.